MW01514557

In The Course
Of
Three Hours

C. J. Rysen

ISBN 978-1-63525-148-7 (Paperback)
ISBN 978-1-63525-149-4 (Digital)

Copyright © 2017 by C. J. Rysen
All rights reserved. No part of this publication may be reproduced, distributed, or transmitted in any form or by any means, including photocopying, recording, or other electronic or mechanical methods without the prior written permission of the publisher. For permission requests, solicit the publisher via the address below.

Christian Faith Publishing, Inc.
296 Chestnut Street
Meadville, PA 16335
www.christianfaithpublishing.com

Printed in the United States of America

Acknowledgements

This book was made possible not solely by my efforts, but also from others who provided me with inspiration and input along the way.

First, my wife who at first couldn't understand why I stayed up all night many nights working on it, but who later took an increasing interest, stood by me, and provided me with some valuable ideas. Second, our pastor who through his sermons provided me with ideas and further inspiration. It was uncanny that although I know his sermons were not intended just for me, they always seemed to deliver a special message that was meant to be worked into the book somewhere. Third, my two children who read the original versions of the book and provided me with further input. Fourth, certain members of my wife's family who also read the initial outline and first versions of the story and who provided me with some additional feedback. Fifth, two "born again" friends and acquaintances who took an interest in the project and who provided me with some additional thoughts from a Christian and Biblical viewpoint.

And lastly, what started the endeavor in the first place were visions that essentially came out of the clear blue sky above that compelled this writing. I do believe He was and continues to be most inspirational to me and deserves the utmost gratitude and to Whom I am forever indebted.

I extend my sincere appreciation to all who contributed in one form or another and made this book possible.

C. J. Rysen

Part I

Part I

Chapter 1

My name is Michael. My middle name is Alexander. When I was in school in my earlier years, people started calling me Alex. I think it was because in school, there were other boys named Michael, and the teacher started calling me Alex to differentiate me from the others. The name stuck, so I have kept that nickname, and that's what I go by now. I'm also known as Grandpa.

I'm a descendant of a Middle Eastern family who I believe once lived in Egypt. My father and mother immigrated to the United States after I was born back in the late 1940s. Although I have a Middle Eastern heritage, I don't really look it; and although I have somewhat of a bronze tone to my skin, I am very much Caucasian. I have always listed my ethnic background as *white* whenever I was required to provide this information on various forms throughout my life. Although my father was fluent in several languages, I was raised speaking in English.

When I was about five years old or a little older both of my parents died. I don't know much about their deaths except that they had something to do with a house fire. I remember somebody said they were unconscious when they were brought to the hospital, and my father's eyes became glassy right before he died about three days later. Because I had no other family, I was put up for adoption following their deaths.

After spending several months in foster homes, I was eventually adopted by a couple who lived in the Midwest. They raised me just like any other normal American child. My adoptive parents died several years ago, both from natural causes.

Both my biological father's last name and my original last name was a word I couldn't pronounce or even spell. It was of a Middle Eastern dialect, but I have no idea what it was. I remember laughing when I would hear him or my mother or someone else pronounce it. He told me that our ancestry name was meaningful and that I should always cherish it, but that I wouldn't understand why until later in life after I have grown up and have children of my own.

Because my father named me after him, I would like to research it to find out if there is any official record of my parents or other information about the name; however, I can no longer remember it. I suppose I could find it through my adoptive parents' records if I made the effort. After I was adopted, my name was changed to Michael Alexander Fisheramen, and I have gone by Alex ever since I started going to school.

I thought that this was an interesting name. My adoptive father told me that to pronounce my last name correctly, the accent is on the *er*. I remember asking him right after I was adopted how I got a name like that. He told me that it was a secret and that it was my destiny. I figured what he meant was that I was fortunate to have been adopted by him and my mother. My adoptive parents were loving people and brought me up to be obedient, loving, and respectful. I miss both my biological and adoptive parents, and I think about them often.

In the meantime, I was most happy to have had my name changed, and I have gone by simply Alex Fisheramen ever since. I could just imagine all the other kids making fun of me during my childhood years if the teacher would try to pronounce the name given to me by my biological parents. So, I have been quite happy that others are not aware of my ancestral name. What kind of name was that anyway? I couldn't even spell it much less pronounce it. I always liked being called Alex or Alex Fisheramen better, not only when I was a child but even now as an adult.

From what I can remember, my biological father was somewhat of a mysterious man, but in a good way. I remember that he was a devout Christian and had been a deacon and elder of the church. I have been told that he was very wise, that he may have had healing powers, that he was a prophet of sorts, and that he could make the hardest of all sinners admit to their sins and repent.

But what was most profound, I was told, is that he could convert the most hard-core atheists and agnostics to Christianity. Apparently, he could identify anyone out of the clear blue sky who did not believe in Jesus, and he never failed to transform them into a Christian. He also could do other things that were equally amazing that other people just couldn't do. I don't know if all this was merely hearsay or whether there was really something to it. I was too young to really understand and couldn't verify anything. But I was told he became well-known for these abilities.

My biological father always had me sit on his lap and got a kick out of playing tricks on me and telling me puzzles, riddles, or other brainteasers that made me think. He was a large, burly man with a dark tan. He had a lot of whiskers and talked with a deep gruff voice with a very heavy accent. I remember that being only five years old or so, I used to think the reason for these sessions was that he enjoyed it, and a lot of the tricks were some sort of magic or hocus-pocus just to entertain me.

Although it was all amusing at the time, I didn't pay much attention to the questions that he would ask me. I was just too young to understand, and there were other things that I would rather do that I could relate to much easier.

His stories, riddles, and puzzles were always strange. It was as if they had hidden meanings or were symbolic in some ways. They all required a lot of thought to figure out. I was just too young to understand them much then, but I listened to them anyway. Some were like parables similar to those found in the New Testament. Some were conundrums that had some mysterious meaning that I couldn't understand then. They all were designed to make me think. I didn't want to do such serious thinking at that age.

He would tell me that I would need to be able to figure out puzzles and especially the puzzle of life when I grew older. I remember that he always told me that I need to think outside of the box. At the time, I had no idea what he meant by that. After hearing him tell me this many times, I finally got fed up one time and told him I'm not in a box and therefore I'm already thinking outside of it.

In that instance, he looked at me with an amazed look on his face and told me I have a good future ahead of me. But then he would say that for me to know that I wasn't in a box, I would need to know what the box looked like. He asked me to describe it. I answered "I don't know because I'm not in a box and there isn't any box." He then asked me how I knew I wasn't in a box if I couldn't describe it. He then asked me if I was absolutely sure about that.

But he asked it in such a way that I had this strange feeling that he could really see the box and he could see that I was in the box, even though I couldn't. He knew that I was definitely in a box. But as far as I knew, I wasn't. Deep down inside, I knew he was right, but I didn't understand why. That was an unsettling feeling, and I never quite knew what he was talking about.

However, I remember another time when I made my father proud when he told me to think outside the box. One Easter Sunday we had an Easter egg hunt, and he told me that I needed to find three invisible Easter eggs before I could look for the other eggs that had candy or coins inside them. He thought that I would get upset and perhaps cry because I would not be able to find any eggs that were invisible.

But after giving it a little thought, I ran around the outside of the house and returned with my basket and told him I found all of the invisible eggs. He asked me how I found them and to show him the eggs. I showed him the empty basket and pointed to it and said "They're invisible." I'll never forget the expression and smile on his face.

I found these puzzles and riddles fascinating, and I really did enjoy them, but at the same time, many of them made absolutely no sense to me at all. Actually, some of them still don't. However, for some reason I'm still mindful of the puzzle of life that he repeatedly told me about that he emphasized was so important. He told me that I would need to think outside the box to solve it when the time came.

He insisted one day I would need to solve it when I was older, but all he could do when I was a child was to give me hints that I didn't understand at the time. Now, I have long forgotten them. I'm always regretfully waiting for that day to come, but to date, it hasn't. I hope if and when it does, the hints will come back to me so I'll know what to do to solve it.

Interestingly, my adoptive father and mother reminded me a lot of my biological father and mother. My adoptive father also liked to tell stories, puzzles, and riddles similar to those told by my biological father. He instilled in me that I would need to think to figure things out on my own, and for some reason he also told me that I need to think outside of the box. I wondered why this was so important.

In many of his stories, my biological father somehow instilled in me, quite profoundly as a matter of fact, that he would always guide and protect me and be with me throughout my entire life. Someday I would know more about him and what he meant by that. He told me that when I am older, I would experience great things, that I had a purpose in life, and that I would be a great man. He told me that when I was grown, I would have my own family and my own son who would also be a great man.

I didn't think much of this because I was only a child at that time. I couldn't even begin to try to comprehend the thought of having children of my own one day. What he said made no sense to me whatsoever, and it still doesn't.

I figured that every father or grandfather tells the exact the same thing to his children. That is, if they try their very best they can do anything and be great. Every child is told that. Therefore, I figured that there was really nothing special about any of this.

A lot of his stories were religious in nature. Because he was such a devout Christian he was always talking about the Bible, Jesus, heaven, hell, Satan, the devil, sin, and the like. I especially remember him telling me stories about Jesus and his disciples. I recall once asking him if Jesus had any brothers or sisters. But when I asked him that, he looked into my eyes in such a way I got this feeling that perhaps I shouldn't have asked that question or he thought I knew something that I didn't. After some hesitation, he told me that He did, but he continued to stare at me as if he was surprised I would ask him that.

But the only sibling of His I can remember he talked about is James. I don't know why, but ever since then, I've always wondered about that conversation with my father. That was a most unsettling experience.

Now that I think about it, many of his stories were like sermons. In one story that he told multiple of times, he told me that in order to enter heaven, one must be completely free of sin—which is impossible—or believe that Jesus is our Savior and that he died for our sins and to have faith in Him. We also must repent our sins. Or perhaps it would be God's decision if we must pay the price to enter heaven.

He never told me how God would make that decision or what the price was if God decided that we had to pay it. Being only five years old, I figured that it cost some money, but I didn't know how much.

I didn't like it when he talked about such things as this because it made me very uneasy. I remember one time sitting on his lap, and as soon as he would finish talking about sin and hell, I would develop a bad feeling about already being in trouble because I knew I had already sinned.

I remember one time being a bad boy just right before I climbed up onto his lap. He had asked me to rinse out my ice cream bowl, but I didn't do so. I knew that was a bad thing and assumed that I had sinned as soon as he talked about it.

But I remember that my mother would smile at me and simply say something about me forgetting and that she would wash out the bowl for me. So I had always figured that I was pretty much good to go, despite the fact that I had sinned by not rinsing out my bowl and despite what my father said.

I remember asking him about angels. He said there are many different types of angels and that each does different things and delivers various messages to souls on Earth, but only if it was the will of God. I asked him if I would ever see an angel. He told me that when I die, I might see an angel who would accompany me to see

God on judgment day, a day to determine whether I would go to hell or to heaven.

He would then stare into my eyes and ask me again if I had been a good boy or a bad boy.

Well, there's that word *hell* again. It gave me the jitters to hear him talk about it. After hearing my father mention the words *hell* and *sin* again and then ask me once again if I had been a good boy or a bad boy, I would again think about my failure to rinse out the ice cream bowl. Then I would get the bad feeling all over again that I was doomed.

But when I would look up at my mother, she simply would smile at me, and her comforting look always washed away any bad thoughts that I would get about my future in the afterlife.

This all sounds interesting now, but again at that time, why would a five-year-old child even think about or remember these stories two minutes after hearing about them when there was other fun stuff to do?

His stories were very profound at the time, but I would soon lose interest as I would rather have fun with my toys or go outside to play. But somehow, bits and pieces of these stories remained in the back of my mind throughout my childhood and during my life as I grew older. Especially what he said about the puzzle of life that I would need to solve someday.

When I think about it, although he told me so, I still don't know how he could ever guide me and be with me during my life. He died a long time ago. So it could no longer be possible that he could do this because he's no longer alive. Perhaps what he meant was that I would remember his stories about trying to live a good life and not to sin and this is how he would be with me and guide me after he died.

But then again, I still don't understand what my purpose in life would be or how I would be a great man. I figured that he told me his stories to inspire me and to amuse a five-year-old child. Again, every child is told that if he or she tries their hardest, they can do anything.

What could my father do now in my life to help me after he is no longer here? I have done well for myself, and I have not needed him anyway. How can I be a great man or have a special purpose? I'm just your average person and have no desire to be anyone other than who I already am. There is nothing special about me. I suppose I can try and remember that he told me to live a good life and keep him in my thoughts. I think that's probably what he meant.

I remember that he told me I would eventually have a son who would also be a great person. But, how can he tell me that my son will be great for crying out loud? I can't get my son to do much of anything. He's lazy, doesn't work, and has gotten into some serious trouble several times during his life. Despite doing everything we could to try to raise him to be a Christian in his upbringing, now that he's a young adult he has no interest in religion at all. He also needs to learn responsibility, and still has a lot of growing up to do. He is pretty much a hard core atheist and is proud of his conviction.

On the other hand, Andrew loves his children and would do anything for them. But, despite his love for his family, his maturity still leaves a lot to be desired, and I don't see how he can be great at anything except for his love for his kids.

So, I figured that a lot of the stories that my father told me were simply to impress upon me at an early age that I needed to be a good boy, that I should always try my hardest, that my father had good intentions for me and my children, and that I should try to remember all of this.

I also remember that when I was about five years old, I had a sister. She was a little older than I was, perhaps by a year or two. My father would also have her sit on his lap and he would tell her similar stories, riddles, and puzzles. But those were separate sessions. For some reason, she was not allowed to be present when he would tell them to me, and I was not allowed to be present when he told them to her.

All I knew is that he also discussed some sort of puzzle of life with her as well that she would need to solve someday, but I have no idea what that was about. I had an idea that it might affect me for some unknown reason, but I had no idea how. When she had her sessions with him, my father always required that she hold a bouquet of orange blossoms. She never failed to take these with her.

14

When my parents died and I was put up for adoption, my sister also was put up for adoption. She lived in different foster homes for a while and was eventually adopted by a different family than I was. I think I recall my biological mother once saying that she was adopted by her and my father, but I know nothing more about that. I suppose that may or may not be the case, but either way, I didn't care then.

Since we were adopted by different families, we eventually lost track of each other. I have neither seen nor talked with my sister since I was a young child. That was about sixty years ago. Perhaps I could do some research to try to find her someday. I have thought about doing that from time to time but never did follow up. I have always been too busy doing things with my own family. But even if I tried, I'd probably never find her. She could be anywhere in the world and I wouldn't have a clue where. However, I do wonder what she's like these days and if she ever thinks about me.

Now, she's an older woman, a little older than me. I can just picture her being a deserving Christian somewhere, very active in the church doing the work of God. Or perhaps she may even be a nun someplace. As a young child, she could do no wrong and was always volunteering to do everything for others. It wouldn't surprise me if she was free of sin or came very close to it. She was always the angel of the family back then.

The last thing I remember about my childhood and my biological father was that he told me he wanted me to have two artifacts passed down from his father that had been in the family for many years. He said that I would inherit a special handwoven blanket that was as pure and white as newly fallen snow and that it had been preserved for many years.

He said the blanket goes back many generations and has a Middle Eastern origin. He said it was a very special treasure that has always been in the family and must always remain in the family for future generations.

I asked him who owned it back then. He told me it was woven for a distant relative who was in our family many generations ago. When I asked him how old it was, he asked me to guess. I said a hundred years. He said it's much older than that. I said a thousand years, but being only five years old, that seemed like forever. He then simply gave me the most comforting smile, a smile I'll never forget.

He told me that when he died, I would inherit this blanket and I should always treasure it as a most precious heirloom. I am to take special care of it because it is supposed to be very important. He almost made it sound mystical or that it had some magical qualities of some sort. At that time, being a small child, I just figured that it was more of his magical nonsense that my father liked to play with me. But I do remember that the blanket was and still is a mysterious artifact that could be invaluable and that I should always make sure it is safe.

He never talked about the second item but he sort of made it sound like it had something to do with the blanket. He implied that it was also mystical in some sense and perhaps invaluable as well, but he never talked about it. I didn't really have an interest at that time and thought it was just another old heirloom I would inherit when I got older. At that time, I sort of assumed it was all a game he was playing with me, probably because I was a vulnerable and naive five-year-old who didn't know any better.

I'm now in my mid-sixties and have been married for over forty years to a most wonderful wife, mother, and grandmother named Sonja. Sonja is also known as Grandma. Like me, she is of Middle Eastern lineage and spent her later childhood in Turkey. We met at a foreign exchange program when I attended college, and she moved to the United States permanently when we got married.

When I first met her, I fell in love with her at first sight. It was like I had already known her for years and we immediately bonded. The chemistry between the two of us oozed with love and devotion, and still does today. She never talked much about her childhood, and I don't know much about it. Perhaps she doesn't want me to know about it or she simply doesn't remember much of it. Her childhood background has been a mystery, but for some reason, it doesn't bother me that I don't know much about it. In fact, something in the back of my mind tells me that I don't want to know.

She's a fantastic cook and loves to create dishes, especially desserts, using orange blossoms, essential oils, and orange blossom water. She always has the bouquets of the flowers and jars arranged on the kitchen counter and is always experimenting with them. I have always wondered where she got the idea of using these blossoms, but she won't reveal her secrets.

I suspect this may go back to her childhood days or when she lived near the Mediterranean before we got married. Her obsession with orange blossoms brings back memories of my sister when she would carry a bouquet of the flowers with her to her sessions with our father. I find the facts that both have an obsession with orange blossoms and both were born in the same part of the world about the same time to be a most interesting coincidence, but for some reason, I find it comforting. I suppose it's because I miss my sister after all of these years and because Sonja reminds me so much of her. The blossoms are hard to find where we live, but Sonja has her sources.

We are both US citizens and are both very much American. We are both college graduates and live an upper-middle class lifestyle in a typical suburb of a major Midwestern city. We have both been retired for several years after having long and successful careers.

We have two children, Andrew and Julie, who are both in their mid-thirties. Like me, Andrew goes by his middle name. His given first name is actually Thomas; however, he doesn't like it when people call him Thomas, Tom, or Andy and prefers what he thinks is the more mature-sounding name of Andrew.

They both have families of their own, and live in typical suburban neighborhoods not too far away from where we live. Andrew and his wife, Alana, have three children: Matthew, who is six years old is in first grade; Daniel, who is about five years old is in kindergarten; Hannah is about two years old.

Andrew has always been somewhat of a slacker, is lazy by nature, and took a wrong turn when he was in college. He has been, and to some extent still can be, a loose cannon at times. Although Sonja and I tried our best to raise him to be a Christian and took him to Sunday school or church each week, he decided to follow a different path when he moved out of the house and went to college.

He got caught up in the usual peer pressure and negative influence of some immoral company. He was mixed up with some gangs for a while and was in trouble more than once. After dropping out of college, he finally went back and barely graduated after an extended stay.

I don't even want to think about what sort of sins he committed during his younger days. He had lived a relatively debauched life. He has been mostly unemployed but now works odd jobs when he wants and when he can find the work. His family generally relies on the income of his wife, Alana, who is a registered nurse.

Although Andrew doesn't do much and never volunteers for anything, family life is important to him. He actually relishes the position of being the homemaker and staying home with his kids while Alana works. Although he has straightened out his life somewhat, especially at home, he still has a very long way to go. His insistence on not being a Christian and not adopting any religious values is heartbreaking. I tried to give him a new Bible on two occasions. The first time he said he "somehow" lost it within a week. The second time he refused to accept it and wouldn't take it.

He and Alana have stayed together despite the fact that he has, for the most part, lived an immoral life and still has not completely turned his life around, primarily because he is a good father to his children. He loves his children and would do anything for them. They mean everything to him. He would rather sit around and play with them than do anything else.

On Sunday mornings while we're all at church, he's always at home recovering from his weekly Saturday night drinking bout with his buddies. These are the same guys that steered him into trouble when he was younger. Every Saturday night is escape night for him, as he dedicates that night to playing poker, going to night clubs, drinking, and doing who knows what else with these same buddies of his.

Every Sunday morning, he dedicates to recovering from the night before while Alana and the kids are at church. He has no interest in going to church and has no interest in Christianity whatsoever. The rest of the week, he generally stays home; and for all practical purposes, he does nothing except play with his kids and do some housework now and then.

Julie, on the other hand, is a very successful corporate executive; and her husband, Garrett, is a very successful chief financial officer of an investment firm. They also have three children: Elizabeth, who goes by Lizzy, is about four and a half years of age. Michael who everybody calls Mikey is about three years old. Emily, who was born prematurely, is now about nine months old.

All our six grandchildren are for the most part typical grandkids in every way. Matthew and Daniel are out of school for the summer and do things like Little League baseball, soccer, and summer camp. The children of Julie and Garrett attend Mother's Day Out, a Christian day-care program three times a week. The other two days of the week they are watched by their grandmothers while their parents work.

The only unusual thing about our grandchildren is that Lizzy still doesn't talk much yet. She should have started talking over two years ago, but for some reason, she either refuses to or just can't. Her younger brother Mikey converses much more than she does. And he is about a year and a half younger.

Julie and Garrett have had her tested for many things including hearing, autism, aphasia, physical dysfunctions, neurological disorders, and abnormal psychological development that could impair her ability to talk. But all tests have turned out normal.

She is extremely smart and inquisitive for her age and understands just about everything told to her. She listens intently when others speak. She is absolutely fascinated by books and words and loves to try to read even though she can't yet. She knows her alphabet and loves to point out words in books and wants to know what they mean. There is no stopping her willingness to try to learn.

She has a remarkable ability to think and observe beyond the norm, but for whatever reason, she simply can't put words together in verbal or written form. The doctors think she might suffer from dyslexia, but she is not quite old enough yet to be effectively tested for this.

They have said that if she's dyslexic, it's possible that might have something to do with her inability to put words together in conversation and her inability to speak. She does have an expanding vocabulary but will speak only one or two words at a time, but that's about it.

The doctors say that she simply appears to be a "very late bloomer" and that we shouldn't worry. But it's hard not to be at least a little concerned about her, because she will be going to school soon. The older she gets, the more we're all afraid it will affect her developmental skills. Julie and Garrett are considering putting her in a special education program but, to date, have held off doing so.

For now, the doctors say not to push her or punish her for not talking, and not make a big deal about it, just let nature takes its course. Oh well, time will tell.

Sonja and I are very fortunate to live within only a few miles of our children and grandchildren, and we can see them often. We are a very close-knit family and have numerous opportunities to be with them. We love our grandchildren dearly and probably spoil them like most grandparents do. Our family room is crammed with toys all lined up around the walls, and it's converted into a romper room whenever they come over.

We're always anxious and excited to see them. Sonja volunteers to babysit whenever needed, and she would be a basket case if she didn't get her grandkid and baby fix at least once or twice a week.

We try to teach our children and grandchildren to be Christians and to teach them the values of life. Everybody in our entire family, except for Andrew, is a member of the same church; and we all, except for Andrew, attend on a regular basis.

He is reluctant, refuses to accept Jesus as his savior, and always avoids the subject. We feel he was influenced by the wrong people during and after college.

I still try to instill Christian values in him, and I bring it up as often as I dare. But it's a balancing act. I have become increasingly reluctant to address the topic with him. I certainly don't want to jeopardize the otherwise good relationship that we have as father and son or the relationship that I have with his kids. Nevertheless, it breaks my heart that he has no interest whatsoever in being a Christian.

It's ironic that Andrew prefers that name because he thinks it's more mature-sounding. He still has a way to go before he can be considered mature. I still think Thomas is a more appropriate name for him, especially considering the circumstances and for religious reasons, but I'm not going to argue with him.

Maybe one day something will happen and he'll change his ways, but for now, I'm not optimistic. It seems like his atheist beliefs are so ingrained within him, there is no way he would ever believe otherwise. I often wonder, if my father was alive whether he could convert him to be a Christian. Since it was said he could convert anybody and always did, I'd like to see him try. But he's long gone. Now it's up to me, but I don't see how I can ever do it. I sure wish he was still alive and here. But he's not.

Chapter 2

It's been a long day. Sonja and I have spent all morning, afternoon, and evening cleaning house, doing yard work, and preparing for tomorrow's Fourth of July BBQ and annual neighborhood block party and fireworks display. Andrew, Alana, Julie, Garrett, and our grandchildren will come over later in the afternoon after church, and we will all join our neighbors in the festivities. This has become an annual tradition, and everybody looks forward to it.

Sonja and I have finished dinner and are spending a few hours watching TV together on our big screen downstairs. We are watching the developing news about more persecutions by the radical Islamic extremists and speculation they may be planning something very big in the United States in the near future.

As we settle into our couch, Sonja asks me, "Alex, have you seen that strange old white van lately? You know, it seems to be around more and more. It's actually getting to be quite frequent."

"As a matter of fact, yes. It was parked across the street when I went to the store earlier today, and it actually followed me there. On the way back home, it showed up again and followed me home. It's almost like someone's been stalking us."

"I know what you mean, Alex. I'm getting very nervous about it. Do you think that we should call the police?"

"Did you see who was driving it?"

"No, not really. I haven't been able to get a good look at him, but he looks like somebody from the Middle East, like an Arab. He was wearing something like a turban, but I didn't get a good look at his face. It looked like he was trying to hide it."

"Well, I suppose if it continues, we should think about calling the police, but for now, perhaps we should just watch him and leave things alone."

We sort of passed it off as us being paranoid over nothing. But I knew that it's most unusual to see somebody like him in our neighborhood. For now, he isn't doing any harm, but his constant presence sure is disturbing.

After watching some of our favorite outdoor reality shows together, we turn the channel to the news and learn from a special report that Homeland Security has raised the national security level. The Islamic terrorists have directly threatened the United States and have announced that they will soon declare specific actions that they will take. They've hinted that it will involve massive destruction across the country. A video shows Islamic Jihadists chanting, "Death to America, death to America," over and over.

The news reporter states that the government has credible evidence of these threats and that they're taking them very seriously. We change channels, and every major network has interrupted their programming to report these developments.

As soon as the news ends, the telephone rings. I answer it, and the person on the other end asks for me and then attempts to say something but then hangs up or is disconnected.

"Sonja, this is about the third or fourth time this past week this person has called. And every time, it's the same. The caller appears to be very serious about something, and I wonder who this may be."

"I don't know. It's about as mysterious as the white van that showed up lately."

After a little while, Sonja begins to nod off. "Alex, it's been a long hard day. I'm getting tired, and I'm ready to go to bed. Do you mind if I turn in?"

I hesitate and then respond, "No, not at all. I may stay up for a bit, if that's okay."

As she heads upstairs, she asks, "Do you think we'll see our children at church in the morning since it's Independence Day?"

I nod affirmatively, but don't need to answer because we both know that although we may see Julie and Garrett and their children there, and probably Alana and her children as well, there's no chance that Andrew would be there.

Again, the thought that Andrew rejects even the opportunity to go to church or to try to believe hurts me deep inside.

I know as a Christian, I have the obligation to spread the Word of God and Jesus, and I feel that I must try my best to convince him to go to church and believe. But in addition, he's our son, and we committed to raising him as a Christian when we had him baptized. However, I'm nearly at my wits' end and am getting more and more hesitant to bring the subject up with him. It's becoming useless to do so, and I am tempted to simply give up.

As each passing day goes by, I get more uncomfortable in even raising the subject with him because of his profound reluctance and my desire not to start any arguments between us.

As Sonja turns out the lights and retreats upstairs, I decide to surf the channels to see if there are any interesting documentaries on in which I may have interest. I enjoy watching programs on controversial subjects involving explorations into the unknown or analysis of disputable issues in which she is not always interested. These may entail political, religious, metaphysical, paranormal, and other topics that solicit debate. I also enjoy watching documentaries that provide historical information about biblical times and that delve into the facts and controversies within it.

For example, according to the Scriptures, God created Earth and the heavens and all that is in it including man. This is clear and indisputable. Furthermore, pursuant to the common interpretation of Genesis and the genealogy found in the Old Testament, if the words are taken literally in their ordinary meaning, God's creation occurred only a little over six thousand years ago. However, scientific evidence overwhelmingly supports and all but proves that the universe and Earth have existed for billions of years and life results from billions of years of evolution after a "big bang," not from suddenly being created only about six thousand years ago.

Can the Bible be wrong? Do we dare challenge that the words of the Gospel are not true? If we do not believe in creationism as stated in the Gospel and instead believe in the evolutionary principle overwhelmingly supported by science, then are we defying the Word of God? Do we really want to do that? So, which is right? They can't both be correct. Or can they? Maybe they can. But how can this be possible?

These programs explore such questions, the unknown, and attempt to explain the possibilities, or even attempt to prove the truth or analyze how something normally thought to be unrealistic may be possible. I enjoy watching these programs and find them fascinating.

Although I don't necessarily believe in some of the more radical theories presented regarding the most controversial topics, I find a lot of the information intriguing. I have come to think that perhaps some of the things in which others don't believe just might actually be possible. Not that I actually believe in them myself. I'm really not sure. Perhaps this is what my father meant by thinking outside the box. It has not been proven to be possible, but it also has not been proven to be impossible either.

This conforms to the ghost in the closet theory. For example, how can you prove without any shadow of a doubt whatsoever that there is not one in your closet? You can't. Therefore there is at least a possibility (without any regard to the degree of probability, which in such theory is not relevant) that a ghost just might be in there. In other words, it's possible that it exists because it cannot be scientifically or otherwise proven that it doesn't.

Therefore, for example, just maybe Sasquatch exists in our deepest forests, or UFOs exist in our skies, or ancient alien history is fact, or mermaid creatures or the Kraken exist in our oceans. Nobody has proven that they don't exist. So therefore maybe it's possible that they do.

Until it can be proven that they don't exist, then the possibility remains that perhaps they just might be real. Although one may be tempted to apply the probability factor, that doesn't come into play when merely addressing whether it's possible. Furthermore, that would be subjective.

At one time many years ago, everyone laughed and thought it impossible when it was said that the giant panda bear, the lowland gorilla, and the giant squid really existed, but these were eventually proven to be real. A long time ago, people thought the Earth was flat. People were arrested for claiming the Earth was round. If you lived just a few hundred years ago and somebody told you that it would be possible to talk to each other thousands of miles apart by using little boxes you could hold in the palm of your hand, that would also serve as a full encyclopedia that has an immediate answer for everything, or that you could watch things happen in real time on the other side of the Earth by looking at a piece of glass, you would think they were crazy. Well, not anymore.

People would have thought you were out of your mind if you said these things were possible. Likewise, something thought to be absolutely ridiculous and impossible today will be proven real tomorrow.

So, what's in store for the future? Probably absolutely incredible things will be discovered that are deemed totally inconceivable, impossible, and beyond belief today. Looking at it in this perspective, perhaps anything is possible.

So why would this be any different when it comes to big foot or aliens or mermaid creatures or the Kraken or other such things? Maybe they do exist. It has not been proven that they don't.

I suppose the same can be said for Jesus Christ and God. The possibility of His existence is not inconceivable. It has not been scientifically proven that God exists. But the opposite positively holds true as well. It has not been scientifically proven that God does not exist either. But I believe He does.

Tonight, I'm going to watch the first of a two-part series documentary about the theory of multiverse including parallel universes and other dimensions.

As usual, I'm captivated by the documentary and hate it when the commercials come on and I have to wait for the program to resume. Often I'll record these programs and then fast forward through the commercials, but this program is coming on now, and I want to watch it. I'm not that tired yet.

As usual, this is going to be a very fast two hours. After a short commercial, the documentary begins. The host commentator opens the show by saying, "Many leading scientists, physicists, theologians, and others throughout the world believe in the existence of multiverse. Although this theory has been kicked around in science and theological circles for many years, recently there has been a renewed attention and focus regarding the possibility.

> Multiverse is the hypothetical set of infinite or finite possible universes including the universe we consistently experience that together comprise everything that exists: the entirety of space, time, matter, and energy.

"In this program we will explore whether there are other universes other than the one in which we live, as well as the possibility of the existence of parallel universes or other dimensions.

"A parallel universe may include a world just like ours wherein everything about it is identical to our Earth, with the same places and the same people that look and behave identical to us. They are essentially clones of us, possibly living in the same houses as us, possibly wearing the same clothes as us, and perhaps doing the same things as us. They may live the same exact lives of us. One could not tell the difference between us.

"But there may or may not be an important difference. Certain events in their, or should I say our, lives may take a twist and may be diverse. Therefore not all events may be equal, but everything else is the same.

"Now, just how can this be? What do the religions of the world say about this? What does the Holy Bible say about this? What does science say about this? Most people have never given any thought to the possible existence of other universes much less parallel universes, and naturally, most who have thought about it don't believe they exist. Most people think this is pure nonsense.

"But the scientists, physicists, and now even leading theologians throughout the world, are again in the process of researching and studying the possibility of this phenomenon and are attempting to prove this theory. Stay tuned. In part 1 tonight, we will explore these questions and talk with the experts who will try to decipher this for us. The possibility will be explained using scientific studies in the various theories of cosmology and will also explore how the religions of the world have addressed it.

"In part 2 next week, they will provide scientific facts including indisputable evidence as well as theological conclusions that they claim will reveal an incontrovertible answer. Does multiverse, including perhaps parallel universes and other such dimensions, really exist or not? This question has to rank among the most fascinating and astounding questions ever raised in all of time."

Now, I think how in the world could they arrive at an incontrovertible answer to this question? I think that has to be entirely impossible. There's no way they can prove or disprove it. Nevertheless, this is going to be a very interesting program, and I sink down in the couch in a position that any chiropractor would loathe. I settle in to take in the words of every interview with every scientist, physicist, theologian, and soak in every piece of information presented throughout the two-hour show.

This is all indeed very controversial, and I must admit to that. These documentaries simply provide information about such controversial topics for evaluation purposes so that the viewers watching can come to their own conclusions. I know that this is all very contentious.

I realize that most people consider such things as totally bogus and these programs are nothing more than entertainment. There is no bigfoot living in our deepest forests. There are no aliens who have visited Earth. There are no mermaid-like creatures living in our oceans. Stories that the Kraken still exists today are entirely preposterous. And it's entirely unreasonable to think that another universe or a society that's a clone of ours exists elsewhere. How can any of that be possible? Just how can it? It doesn't make any sense at all that it could.

But I am still intrigued by the possibilities because it has not been proven that such things cannot exist either. After all, these are very famous scientists and physicists and well-known theologians that are being interviewed. And some of what they say appear to be rather persuasive and compelling. For now, I'm inclined to think that this is all ludicrous and total nonsense. But who knows for absolutely sure? I want to at least hear what they have to say.

I am most interested in the theory from a Christian perspective. The documentary explores both points of view. It can be inferred from the Bible that Earth is the only place in our universe where intelligent life exists. It addresses mankind and sin in such a way that suggests we are alone in our universe. According to the book of Genesis, God created Earth *before* He created the rest of the universe, not at the same time or after it. It is unique. Earth holds center stage in God's Creation. It is implicit in the Scriptures: What He created in our universe with intelligence other than angels only exists on Earth.

The Bible suggests that the fate of the universe is dependent on God's timetable and plan for mankind and the Earth. It states one day, our Earth will be destroyed and He will create a new heaven and Earth. The weight of sin following Adam's fall is upon all of God's creation. If the universe will also be destroyed along with Earth, why would God create other intelligent life in our universe, not mention it in the Scriptures, but then have their lives depend on the failures and sins of mankind on Earth? That is simply not reasonable and would be totally unjustified and inequitable. Why would God do that?

Therefore this would explain why other intelligent life in our universe would not exist. God created man in His own image and through Him Jesus Christ came to Earth for our salvation. He will return to Earth, and that is that. Our Earth and mankind are so finely tuned there is no other intelligent life elsewhere in our universe.

However, this reasoning is implicit, and in many respects the Bible focuses on only our universe, and it is not definitively revealed to us whether or not He has created anything outside of it or whether other intelligent life exists anywhere else. The Bible contains several passages that suggest that other worlds may exist, but this is open to interpretation. The Scriptures focus on Earth as it exists in our universe and do not explicitly confirm or deny the existence of other universes or intelligent life elsewhere. Although it is not revealed to us whether or not God also created other universes in other realms, do these facts preclude the possibility that He could have created or could create other universes and worlds within them, outside of ours, which may be outside of what is written in the Gospel?

From a scientific point of view, the documentary discusses the possibility by addressing such things as quantum physics or quantum mechanics, the string theory, multiverse hypotheses, and other mathematical concepts that are way beyond my understanding. But some theories appear reasonable and simple to understand. For example, many scientists say our universe alone has no end and is expanding. In the process, new galaxies and planets continue to form. So, based on this, regardless whether or not they may be eternal, there are no boundaries or limits to their creation at least at this time. To put it simply, this means that currently the possibilities of existences are infinite.

Therefore it's possible that another world like ours exists because there is no limit to the possibility of existences. As long as there is a continuing creation of new galaxies and planets, mathematically, it is very much possible.

Scientists estimate that there are tens of billions of Earth-like planets in the Milky Way Galaxy alone. And scientists believe that there are hundreds of billions of galaxies in the universe. When you multiply these figures and do the math, the result is of astronomical proportions. To put it into perspective, this would be more than the number of dots the size of a period at the end of a sentence touching each other in a string from the Earth to the moon and back multiples of times. How can there be that many planets similar to ours in our universe without a single one of them harboring intelligent life?

But the possibility of other intelligent life in our universe in this perspective violates what is implied in the Scriptures. However, this contemplates only our universe. But what if there are other and potentially infinite universes besides ours, say in other realms or dimensions, on which the Gospel appears to be silent? The immensity of this concept is absolutely incomprehensible.

On the other hand, even if another world like ours exists, the variables of life and life events are virtually endless as well. So based on this, one would think there's no way a parallel world could exist in this regard. There are just too many variables to allow it to happen. The evolvement of history consists of variables that are absolutely immeasurable. Considering that events and people each have a cause-and-effect relationship with each other, whether happenings are random or otherwise, taking into account the unlimited variables in this regard, how could this be possible? In such case, how does one reconcile the effect of events on the existence of people, especially throughout all of history? It seems literally impossible for it to exist, unless perhaps a Governing Force creates and controls everything about it. But could that be possible?

Otherwise, what are the odds that the placement of every atom or cell and each and every single action and event would be identical, exactly the same, to produce an exact clone of the history of people in and of our world as it is? And this doesn't even address the immeasurable odds that a similar planet, in our universe or another, could even be so finely tuned as ours to be capable of sustaining intelligent life exactly like ours in the first place. The odds of that alone are so enormous they're off the charts.

However, if there are an infinite number of possibilities of existence, in our universe and in others, it cannot be proven to be impossible. The documentary explores the theory from every perspective, both pro and con, and attempts to compare and reconcile the facts and hypotheses of science with what is written and perceived to be the Word of God, but also considers what is not revealed to us in the Gospel as well.

Two hours later part 1 of the documentary concludes, and despite how improbable the theory appears to be, I look forward to part 2 to air next week to see the conclusion. I turn down the volume on the TV, close my eyes for a minute, and contemplate this premise further. I begin to wonder about the theory from a religious and philosophical perspective. Soon, I'm in deep thought and asking myself some questions.

I just do not see how it can be possible. How can it be justified?

Then I happen to think who or what created God to begin with? Where did He come from? But it is said, He always has been and always will be. If events and subsequent events occur in a linear time frame, if He was never created and if He has always existed forever going backward, then why would it make any sense that He would wait all that time to create Earth and the heavens of only our universe until only about six thousand years ago? What did He do for eons of eternity going backward before that? Certainly He didn't twiddle his thumbs and be alone by Himself and do nothing that entire time. That would be totally illogical. Why would it make any sense whatsoever for Him to wait so long to create anything? Although God is self-existent and does not need anything else, it just doesn't seem reasonable that He would want to be alone with nothing else.

So, perhaps instead is it reasonable that He has been creating multiple universes forever going backward and perhaps may continue to do so forever going forward? If He has existed forever going backward in time, then perhaps it is reasonable that universes have also. And if a universe eventually collapses, expires, or is destroyed, perhaps another one is formed. In other words, *if* God has always existed and was never created, then isn't it also reasonable that perhaps He has created multiple universes in a continuing process without a beginning too? That would be absolutely consistent in theory and seem more logical. Otherwise, God would have existed all by Himself with nothing else. Why would He do that?

However, it is also said that God exists outside of our time, say when time stands still. Linear time is not created for a universe until the universe is created. So if this is the case, then does it not appear that He would be eternally omniscient of what happens before it does? And if so, why would he create only a single universe that is supposed to expire or be destroyed some day? Regardless, does this mean that He categorically created or will only create one universe during His entire existence even though He exists outside of time?

It seems reasonable that He would have created more than one universe, especially if all matter in a universe eventually expires and collapses and thus is not eternal, as many scientists claim and many say the Bible implies that our universe will eventually be destroyed one day. Otherwise, God would have existed by Himself with nothing else regardless whether He exists outside of our time. And although

He would not need anything else, this just does not seem to be logical that He would want to self-exist with nothing else. Therefore is it not reasonable that He may have created more than one universe?

Per the first chapter of Genesis, it is stated that God created light and separated light from dark, calling them day and night, and there was evening and morning, the first day. Then God created the sky, the firmament of the heavens, and there was evening and morning the second day. Then God created the Earth, and there was evening and morning on the third day. On the next day, God set the lights in the sky to give light upon the Earth. He created the sun, the moon, and the stars in the expanse of sky to serve as signs to mark the seasons, days, and years, the fourth day.

Now, I understand that light and other words may be symbolic and also subject to the disparities of translation and interpretation. However, if light, and especially day and night, and evening and morning are interpreted in their ordinary literary meaning, then how can that be that He created light, day and night, evening and morning, and then Earth before He created the sun and the moon and what appears to be everything else in the universe? Assuming the text is the Word of God in a translation in the ordinary literal sense, wouldn't at least the sun and perhaps the moon need to exist before there can be light, day and night, and evening and morning?

However, given some thought, the same question also applies if taken figuratively as well. At any rate, creation in that chronological order seems logically impossible.

But if day and night and evening and morning can exist before the creation of the sun, then how could that be possible? Did He perhaps create a new Earth in some sort of alternative universe cloned from another that had existed for billions of years—one that had dinosaur bones and much other evidence of its prehistoric age? Is that possible? If He did, then perhaps that specific order of creation may not be relevant for that to happen, because God had already identified with day and night and evening and morning in another universe before He created it in our universe. So, on this basis perhaps it is possible.

So, hypothetically, based on the assumption that He may have created Earth and our universe only about six thousand years ago by cloning another as it existed billions of years after He created it and by doing so, He also created the appearance of evolutionary fact in the process; is that fact perhaps a test to determine if mankind would believe in creation per the Word of God instead of the scientific evolutionary principle that is so manifest before it?

Would all this be a logical explanation and legitimate reasoning for the appearance or illusion of evolution and how it came to be considering the Bible states Earth and our universe was created by God only a short time ago? If this is the case, the principle of creation by God would still hold true, and the overwhelming scientific evidence of evolution would be justified as well. In other words, both theories would hold merit. I wonder whether others think this is a reasonable hypothesis, and if not, why? Has it been proven to be impossible? How else can it be explained that overwhelming evidence of billions of years of evolution exists, when if interpreted literally, the Bible specifically states that God created Earth and life and apparently only a short time ago?

So, I wonder, based on this, because it took God six days to create everything, and if He did this only about six thousand years ago, as the literal interpretation of the Old Testament suggests, then this implies He does exist in a linear time frame instead of outside of time. In other words, how can He exist outside of time but take six days to create everything, as stated in the book of Genesis? And if this is the case and if He does exist in a linear timeframe, then the hypothesis that He has been creating multiple universes forever is all the more reasonable. Otherwise, God would have existed by Himself with nothing else. And although He could, why would He?

And, based on the fact that He created the Earth before He created the stars and other heavenly bodies including the sun and the moon, then how could Earth and the Universe have resulted from a "big bang"?

However, per the Scriptures, with God a thousand years is like a day and a day is like a thousand years. That suggests that time is not the same in our universe as it is with God and in heaven. So likewise under the same premise, is it then not inconceivable that He could create more than one universe in a different time or outside of time?

However, to put things more simply, on the other hand, if our finely tuned Earth holds the only existence of intelligent life, why would we be so unique that God would create an immeasurable and perhaps endless and infinite universe but intelligent life on only one planet, regardless if the universe is eternal? If that's the case, then what is the purpose of the creation and existence of the perhaps infinite everything else out there in our universe, of which we will never know? But if Earth is so unique that there is no other existence of intelligent life in our universe as implied in the Scriptures, then does this mean there cannot be another universe in another realm of which we have no knowledge?

But once God created man and there became angels and souls in heaven, He would never again be by Himself. This would certainly appear to hold true after the ultimate Rapture per the Scriptures. Therefore, although this may possibly justify why future or coexisting universes might not exist, would it necessarily preclude their creation? But what about before the creation of man and Earth? This does not justify why prior or coexisting universes may not have existed either. In other words, regardless of the time factor, would the events prescribed in the Scriptures preclude His creation of another universe outside of what has been written?

I don't think the Gospel definitively states multiverse does not exist or is not possible. And if such is the case and if the multiverse hypothesis is fact, maybe the theory advanced in the documentary is plausible. It would increase the possibility by an immeasurable amount.

But it just seems so unlikely.

The concepts of time, space, energy, and matter from a physics or other scientific viewpoint are way beyond my understanding. I'm no physicist and I don't have a desire to try to try to understand it all from that perspective. I'm not that smart. I just want a simple explanation and want to know if it's possible. But as far as I know, again, it's not been proven to be impossible.

As I think about these things, I'm absolutely fascinated; however I laugh at myself for even giving any thought about this. The theory is so complex to understand, both scientifically and theologically. It's ludicrous to even think for a minute that it could be possible. Why do I even watch these programs? They sure do a good job in providing entertainment to the gullible I suppose. But I'm not gullible. I merely want to listen to what they say and evaluate the possibilities. There are absolutely countless questions that deserve to be explored.

Wow, this is pretty heavy stuff. Really heavy stuff. But it's so questionable. I can understand why many people think it's ridiculous to even think about it. But this is why I like watching programs such as this. It allows me think about the possibilities because they have not been proven to be impossible.

It's now after midnight, and I realize that I'm getting tired and that it's time for me to retire and get a good-night's sleep. I quickly turn back to the network news station, turn up the volume, and now learn more what the radical Islamic terrorists have stated about their plans against the United States. Every time I watch the news, these developments escalate and get worse. I'll have to watch this and catch up on the latest developments first thing in the morning. The thought that our country may be under imminent attack by terrorists in a very big way is more than worrisome.

It's going to be a long day tomorrow. Actually, a much longer day than I currently anticipate, but I would find out about this later. I turn off the TV and the lights and take a few minutes to open the downstairs walk-out door and let Crackerjack outside before I head to bed. Crackerjack (sometimes called C.J.) is Julie's golden retriever who we are dog-sitting for the night.

I let him outside for a few minutes so that he can do his thing, and while waiting for him, I can't help myself from stepping outside on our patio to gaze up into the stars and briefly wonder a little more about everything that I just saw and heard over the last few hours. It's dark and crystal clear without a cloud in the sky. There is a new moon, and the stars are very bright tonight. I quickly become absorbed by the deafening sound of the chorus of chirping crickets, and the buzzing of the katydids and cicadas in the woods. Soon I find myself in very deep thought briefly again as I gaze up into the star filled sky.

I suppose when you think about it, heaven and hell are actually different dimensions than ours, so if they can exist, then I suppose anything is possible regarding the existence of other worlds, say in other universes or in other realms or dimensions. There are supposedly more than a billion trillion planets similar to ours in our universe alone, and their numbers may still be increasing. It seems improbable that other intelligent life cannot exist, but that is not what the Scriptures imply.

But this only contemplates the dimension of our universe as we know it. What if there are others of which we are not aware, where it could be possible? What about the multiverse hypothesis? The Scriptures appear to be silent regarding this. From what I understand, they neither definitively confirm nor deny the possibility.

Then I wonder—okay, let's assume other universes do not exist. If that's the case, then can God create another universe if and when He wants to, by design, for a God-known purpose? Is there any possibility that perhaps it could be God's will and what if it's inherent in His overall creation of everything, both known and unknown to us? Is it possible that it could be part of His master plan with a purpose and we simply have no idea?

Perhaps is it possible that what God may have created or could still create, including what may be outside of what we know, outside of our universe considering its size by itself is unfathomable, is of such immense magnitude that it's entirely incomprehensible to us? I suppose that the power of God is so absolutely immeasurable He can do anything He wants, and we will never know.

In this regard, it appears that the creation or existence of another universe or world like ours in it could be possible, but as long as it doesn't violate the Scriptures and especially if it doesn't add to or subtract from the prophecies, and especially those written in the book of Revelation. The Word of God is what it is. It cannot be breached. However, if the Word of God including the prophecies of Revelation is not infringed upon by such theory, and if the Bible doesn't address it one way of the other, then I'd be interested in knowing how it cannot be possible.

When the vast cosmos and the infinite of the unknown are considered as well as all the things that were ruled a virtual impossibility many years ago but now have been proven to be real, then imagine the prodigious and incredibly inconceivable things thought to be impossible now that actually may be real, regardless whether or not they are proven to exist tomorrow. Thinking about it in this context, I suppose one should not discount the possibility. After all, the book of Revelation does say something about God creating a new Earth and a new heaven at the end of time and the beginning of another. That is a stated certainty.

One definitely needs to think outside of the box to comprehend the possibilities.

I very much look forward to part 2 in several days. I certainly don't want to miss it.

My thoughts then bounce back and forth between the documentary and the more real frightening earthly news about the Islamic terrorists and their threats against the United States. After a few minutes of being lost in deep thought and gazing up at the stars, I'm startled by a wagging tail brushing against my leg. Crackerjack is at the door wanting in. We come in from outside, head upstairs, and in a few minutes I'm in bed and sound asleep.

Chapter 3

It's early to midmorning, and I wake up to the rays of sunshine through the window dancing across my face. As I contemplate getting up, I remember that today is both Sunday and Independence Day, and both Sonja and I have a lot to do. As I roll over in bed, my eyes fall upon Sonja's as she also wakes up. "Happy Fourth!" I whisper to her.

She smiles. "Happy Fourth to you too. But more importantly, Happy birthday to you, Alex. I hope it will be a very special day for you today."

"Thank you. I hope so too," I reply. Little did I know just how extraordinary my birthday would be today. But I would find out about this later.

It's going to be a very busy day and a very hot day. The sun is shining brightly and there's barely a cloud in the sky. The temperature outside is already approaching ninety degrees, and it's not even midmorning yet.

As I get out of bed to walk to the bathroom, I look out of the window. There sits the old white van up the street again. Nobody in our neighborhood owns such a van or has visitors with such a van. Why is it always there?

There's someone in the van who looks like the same person Sonja and I have seen before. I wonder where he lives. Why is he always in the van? Does he sleep there too? Why does he appear to be following us whenever we go someplace? What's he hiding? Does he want something from us? But my need to go the bathroom after being in bed for about eight hours precedes my disposition to worry about the van anymore, and I scamper into the bathroom before Sonja does.

While eating breakfast I turn on the TV, and as expected the news again is addressing the Islamic terrorists and their threats against the United States. The news indicates that the matter is getting worse, but instead of listening to any more of this, I decide to finish eating breakfast quickly because I want to go for a walk before getting ready to go to church. I'm interested in the old white van that is still parked up the street.

As I get ready to go, the phone rings and Sonja answers it. She listens for a minute and says nothing and then hangs up.

"Who was it?" I ask.

Sonja looks at me with a blank stare. "I have no idea. That was the strangest call I've ever gotten. It appears to be the same person who has called before. The voice sounded like a woman's, and she sounded afraid to talk as if she was in some sort of trouble. Or maybe she was trying to get up enough courage to say something."

"What did she say?"

"Alex, she was asking if you lived here. She said that she needed to talk with you and that she had something very important to tell you. But then her voice started quivering, and she hung up. Or maybe we got disconnected. I don't know."

"Did you recognize her voice? Was it Julie or Alana or anybody we know?"

"No. Nobody we know. She had some sort of accent. I assume it's the same person who called before and hung up without saying anything."

I find this very odd and try to think who this woman may be. For an instant I wonder if these calls are related to the white van that we have seen lately, because they started happening about the same time. But I soon forget about the call as I have more important things on my mind.

I want to learn more about this strange van that has been parked just up the street and its driver. I call for Crackerjack to take him for a walk, and he and I head up the street where the old van is parked.

We live at the end of a cul-de-sac and there is only one way in and one way out. Our street is very quiet with little traffic except for the residents who live there. As I approach, I can see the driver in the van. He is as Sonja described him. But I can't get a good look at his face through the window.

Although I can't see his face, he doesn't appear to be pleasant looking at all. Suddenly, I think of the news lately and thoughts of the Islamic terrorists shown on TV race through my head.

As I approach closer and can see a little better through the windshield, it appears that the van is equipped with all sorts of computers, monitors, wires, antennas, and other electronics in the back, but it is hard to see. On the side of the van there's some lettering that reads MHI Inc. followed by a logo that resembles a bird of some type. It appears to be an eagle, but I'm not sure. Underneath are some words that appear to be an Arabic name of some sort in small letters. Underneath that is a phone number that has partially faded away.

I think to myself, "Wow, this is just like the CIA or FBI or some sort of other secret undercover operative that one sees in the movies. But why is this guy dressed like an Arab? And more importantly, is he a terrorist? Why is he here? Why has he been following me around?"

As I get closer, I act like I am simply taking my dog for a walk and appear nonchalant; but the closer I get, the more apprehensive I become. Within seconds, I actually find myself quite scared and wish I hadn't walked up the same side of the street as the van. I think that I really do need to report him to the police. I wonder what I should do. Maybe I should simply turn around now and go back home.

The occupant, who appeared to be attending to the electronic equipment in the back of his van, turns around and sees me as I approach. I get another quick glimpse of him but still can't see his face, and I'm instantly terrified. There is some sort of mystic appearance about him, but he clearly doesn't want me to see him.

Suddenly, I hear a vehicle approach and see a police car turning down our street. It turns out to be a routine police patrol as he is driving very slowly. I think, "Thank God. He could not have come at a better time."

As soon as I spot the patrol car, so does the Arab. He jumps into the driver's seat, starts the engine, turns around, and speeds off. He drives right past the patrol car going in the opposite direction, accelerating all of the way as he passes the patrol car going up the street.

I watch all this unfold and assume the policeman will turn around and chase the van. But instead, the police car continues to slowly make its way toward the bottom of the hill. I wave down the patrol car, and it stops in the middle of the street. The police officer rolls down his window and I tell him all about the old van that has been parked on our street and explain that it has been following us when we leave the house. I tell him what I think I saw inside the back of the van and ask him what his opinion is since he had a good look at it when he came down the street.

The officer looks at me with a confused look on his face. "Have you been drinking?"

"What? No, it's Sunday morning and I'm just walking my dog. I'll be going to church in the next hour. Why do you ask?"

He appears to be totally oblivious about the van. "What did you tell me you saw?"

I repeat my story and continue. "The van just sped off and went right by you."

He looks at me with a blank stare.

"The van just passed by you going at a high rate of speed."

He looks at me dumbfounded and again he says nothing.

"Didn't you see it? How could you have missed it?"

By now the officer is getting agitated. He adjusts his big aviator-style sunglasses that rest on his forehead and adamantly states, "Look, buddy, you didn't see any van. There was no van. I don't know what you've been drinking or smoking, but there was no van here. You didn't see anything, understand?"

He then proceeds to accuse me of seeing things that don't exist and in a very disgusted manner tells me to go home and go to church like I said I was going to do. I'm flabbergasted. In the meantime, Crackerjack is looking up the street where the van disappeared. His tail is doing a slow wag, and he looks at the patrol car and starts to whimper. He then looks up at the police officer, and his whimper changes to a soft growl. After the police officer finishes lecturing me, Crackerjack then barks.

Crackerjack never barks, and I'm surprised. I've read that dogs have extrasensory abilities that people don't have, and for a fleeting instant I wonder if Crackerjack knows something. Does he not like the Arab, or does he not like the police officer? But soon I figure that he's behaving just like a normal dog and doesn't like either one of them, or perhaps the officer in uniform, or perhaps he senses his negative personality toward me.

I politely thank the police officer for his time and say some calming words to Crackerjack. We return to the house so that I can get ready to go to church. The police officer resumes his slow drive down the street, turns around, and disappears back up the street.

As I enter the house, I tell Sonja what had just happened, and she just looks at me totally perplexed.

"I don't know what to say, Alex. I was watching you out the window because I was afraid for you walking towards the van. I saw everything. I know I saw it, and I know you saw it. I can't believe the officer in the police car didn't see it. I'm speechless."

As we get dressed for church, we discuss it a little more and wonder if we should report the incident to the police station. But we decide not to. Surely the police officer will defend his story, and then we'll have everyone at the police station and who knows who else wondering about our mental capacities. We decide to just let the incident drop for the time being and see if anything else develops. We then finish getting dressed and head on to church.

As usual, everybody is at church, except for Andrew. The service is very nice, but the sermon is somewhat intense. This is the second Sunday in a row that our pastor, Reverend Gabriel, delivers a sermon that is a lot more powerful than usual. Normally, his sermons preach the Gospel and are teachings and interpretations of the Bible. His sermons are usually very good, informative, and thought provoking.

However, for some strange reason, his sermons the past two Sundays have gotten away from the norm as if he intends to deliver a special message perhaps with a motive known only to him. To say these last two sermons are a digression from the traditional preaching of Christianity is an understatement. His last two sermons are more abstract in nature and appear to be designed on purpose to make the congregation uneasy and uncomfortable. Maybe it is for good reason. But why? These two sermons certainly are not the type of what he usually preaches.

Last Sunday, he started off the sermon by reciting for a good solid minute, "Waiting to die. Waiting. To die waiting. To die. Waiting to die. Waiting. To die waiting. To die. Waiting to die. Waiting. To die waiting…"

He then went on to preach "Are you waiting to die, or are you going to die waiting?" In his sermon, he spent about twenty minutes scaring the congregation into thinking that they could keel over in the next few minutes and that their death is imminent. He asked them if they are really prepared spiritually to die right that instant.

He preached that the longer you wait to prepare yourself spiritually, then the less time you will have before you die to enhance your faith and to accomplish God's purpose in your life. Are you willing to take up your cross and follow Jesus to achieve what He wants before you die? Will you have enough time or are you going to run out of time and it will be too late?

In other words, have you considered the balance of time issue? Are you gambling with your time? Just how deep is your faith? Have you let Jesus not only be your Savior but also your Lord, and have you truly followed Him? Or are you going to rely on a "Get out of jail free" card at the last minute of your life and hope it will be sufficient to save you? It may not. Are you really willing to risk that? Because if you have not adequately prepared when the time comes, which could be anytime, at any minute, at any second for that matter, only you will be responsible for what will happen to you in your eternal afterlife. The entire congregation was most uncomfortable after that sermon.

Today, his sermon addresses the subject of what would you be willing to do to enter heaven. Would you be willing to go to hell first and suffer beyond comprehension for a period of time to have a guaranteed eternal life in heaven, or would you take the risk of judgment day to possibly go straight to heaven without having to suffer in hell first, but risk spending eternity in hell if you choose wrong?

Now, I think this question is pretty intense but reason that it's a fair query. I figure what he's trying to do is to ask everyone how comfortable they are with the way they've lived, their level of faith, and whether they truly believe they have followed Jesus. In other words, just how sincere and sure are we? Or are we willing to gamble to avoid suffering in hell for a bit? But as intense as this question is, I'm really surprised and shocked when he asks the next question, which turns out to be the kicker.

Reverend Gabriel then addresses the question whether if given the opportunity, would you be willing to pay the price and go to hell and suffer in torment and torture beyond comprehension so that everybody else could go to heaven? Would you sacrifice yourself for everybody else? Or would you be selfish?

After asking this question, Reverend Gabriel then stops, looks out over the congregation, and appears to gaze into the eyes of every member, one by one. He then raises his hand and shakes his finger at us and asks "Would *you* do this if you had the chance?"

With his powerful voice shaking the rafters, I see that he has some people extremely uneasy and a few trembling in the pews.

Now I ask myself, "What kind of question is this? This has to be the mother of all questions that any pastor or minister can ask any congregation. How can he expect us to repeat what Jesus did? No one would be asked to do what Jesus did for us. But I think I realize what Reverend Gabriel is doing. Based on one premise that Jesus may have descended into hell to suffer for us before He ascended into heaven, perhaps Reverend Gabriel wants us to truly understand what Jesus felt at the time of His crucifixion and why he died for us. And he wants us to realize that we must sacrifice in some ways on Earth and contemplate what we are willing to do to accomplish God's purpose.

In other words, in order to enter heaven, we need to develop a *personal* relationship with God through Jesus Christ. We must truly understand and feel His sacrifice for us. But why would he preach this in such a way and ask this question to get that point across to us? What if some people were to misunderstand this?

This certainly has an effect on me, and I just wonder what each member of the congregation is thinking and what their level of emotion is to his question. I certainly don't want to ever have to answer the question, and hope I will never be asked this when I die. I try to forget that he even asked the question in the first place.

After the sermon, the service continues with song and prayer. Then right before the benediction, as he occasionally does, Reverend Gabriel holds up his copy of the Holy Bible, which has a very bright white cover. He proclaims, "This is my blanket. It covers me with the Word of God and it secures me. I hold it dear to my heart. You should keep your blanket close to your heart too."

We like Reverend Gabriel very much, but I'm somewhat surprised and disappointed that he delivered such a sermon and asked this question, especially on Independence Day. I think he could have chosen a more appropriate topic for today. But I suppose that he had his reasons for doing so.

Oh well, I didn't want to let this affect what is otherwise supposed to be a joyous holiday and try to forget what he said and forget the question he asked so that I can enjoy the rest of the day.

Upon leaving the church, the family gets together briefly to set a time to come to our house later in the day for the BBQ and Fourth of July celebration. Then everyone departs his or her own way until later. As we drove home, in my rearview mirror I see the old white van following us again and mention it to Sonja.

As we turn to enter our subdivision, what appears to be the same patrol car comes from the other direction, and the old van stops and parks at the top of the street. I figure that's good as he has parked farther away this time. I suppose that even though the police officer was not helpful and that he was actually offensive to me earlier, perhaps he is helping distract the Arab from coming around by his increased patrols. So, maybe everything is okay despite my concerns.

In other words, maybe the police officer really is aware of something about the old van and doesn't want me to know. Just maybe he has increased his routine patrols to keep an eye on things and to protect us. However, within seconds of us coming in the house, the police officer pulls into our driveway, parks, and is soon at our front door. We are quite surprised.

Chapter 4

I answer the door and he asks if he can come in. Sonja and I are quite uneasy about the situation but figure we need to confront what's going on with him and the Arab. We invite him in.

The police officer introduces himself as Officer Asad Namirha Mustafa and throws himself down on the sofa. He's a heavyset man with a dark complexion but appears fit and healthy. Although its morning, his face sports a dark five o'clock shadow, and his intimidating look immediately changes to a friendly disposition as he apologizes for his behavior earlier in the morning.

"I need to tell you I'm so sorry for doubting you and reprimanding you earlier this morning. I should not have acted that way and hope you will forgive me. I've actually been aware of the van and the driver but couldn't let you know that at the time."

He doesn't tell us why and we're afraid to ask. He again apologizes for how he acted.

"I've actually talked to the driver of the van and investigated him a little. I can reveal to you that the driver's name is Misa Hajiba Ihcalam and that he works in the private security and investigative service business."

Remembering what I saw on the side of the van and in the back of the van, this makes sense. But how strange this is that both the police officer and the driver of the mysterious van appear to be of Middle Eastern descent. Although Sonja and I were also born in the Middle East, this is most unusual and especially in our neighborhood. I can't help to not think about this and wonder if this is a coincidence.

The officer continues, "Although the driver of the van does appear to be somewhat suspicious, he's done nothing wrong, so there's nothing that the police can do. I can't arrest him. He hasn't violated anything. I suggest you ignore him and let me keep a watch on him for you."

"Any idea why he's following us around?"

"No, I have no idea at all. Perhaps he's doing some private investigative work, but unless you've done something wrong yourself, I wouldn't worry about it."

This sounds fair and reasonable; however, the fact that he's advising us to ignore the Arab sounds odd, as if he doesn't want us to acknowledge that he even exists. He then tells us that if we should have any questions to let him know. He reiterates that he would keep an eye on the Arab for us and that it's his duty to protect us.

After this short meeting, in which he appears to be a little abrasive notwithstanding his apology, he seems friendly enough and helpful. I ask him about the origin of his name, and he laughs.

"Well, I was born in Eastern Turkey, but my family moved around somewhat. We lived for a while on the coast of the Eastern Mediterranean in several countries, and moved here later when I was an older child. I'm proud that I've been an American citizen for many years and long before I graduated from the police academy."

"How do you like being a police officer?"

"It's okay. I enjoy looking out for people and take my responsibility seriously. The only thing I hate about it is the appearance protocols the force imposes. I have such fast-growing thick whiskers. I need to shave three times a day to meet their clean-shaven rules when I'm on duty. I wish I could just let the beard grow."

I look at him closely and immediately think of my father when I was a little boy. I can't believe the resemblance. It's remarkable.

We share our similar heritage and background with him and he immediately becomes very friendly with us since our original ancestry was somewhat similar being from the Middle East. Because of this common trait and having roots in the same region of the world, he thinks we have some sort of bond between us.

Before leaving, he notices that there is a large bouquet of orange blossoms and some sealed jars on the counter behind Sonja. "Are you perhaps going to make some orange blossom water or essential oil? Or do you plan to use the oil for some sort of magic?" he jokingly laughs.

"Why yes," Sonja answers. "I use it as an ingredient to cook special dishes, especially my desserts. These blossoms are hard to come by where we live, you know."

She's somewhat surprised that he would know this and mulls over his comment. But then on second thought, considering that he has a Mediterranean background, it should not be surprising that he's aware of the cooking value that orange blossoms have. But she is not at all prepared to or has any desire whatsoever to discuss any magical properties that the blossoms may or may not have.

"I have some dynamite Mediterranean recipes using orange blossoms to make some fantastic desserts. Perhaps I can share these with you sometime," he adds with excitement.

Sonja nods in acceptance. She would really enjoy that, and that leaves her with some comfort that perhaps he's okay after all.

As he is leaving and walking out the front door, again apologizing for his earlier behavior, I see his eyes scanning everything inside of our house. "Typical policeman behavior," I think. After all, he did spot the orange blossoms and the jars. Crackerjack is lying near the front door stretched out on a vent, and I can see his eyes intently watching the police officer and every move he makes. I again hear a whimper. I mention to him that the dog apparently doesn't like people in uniform, and he understands.

The officer turns around and in a very friendly manner says, "By the way, some people call me Musty, but when I'm on duty, I usually go by Officer Mustafa. You can call me Musty or Officer Musty for short if you like."

We thank him very much for his visit and for telling us that he'll increase his patrols and keep a watchful eye out for us.

After he leaves, Sonja and I briefly discuss his visit. As a result of the earlier incident, there still appears to be some room for him to gain our trust; however, he was friendly and helpful. We acknowledge that he's a little rough around the edges and has somewhat of a harsh demeanor; however, we decide to ignore this on the basis that it's his ultimate objective to help us. Therefore we shouldn't have any reason to feel otherwise. Also, Sonja is a little excited about perhaps getting some new dessert recipes using orange blossoms.

We then go into our bedroom and as we are changing out of our church clothes to more comfortable apparel we turn the TV back on. Sure enough, there's more news about the terrorists' activities.

The news reporter announces that the terrorists have escalated their threats and that the government has credible evidence that terrorists are already in the United States and are in the midst of planning something big. However, the specific nature of the threats has not yet been revealed. There is a wide scale attempt to locate the whereabouts of certain known terrorists all across America.

The US government has reliable evidence that the threats against the United States are very real and that the terrorists are extremely dangerous and could be anywhere. The news goes on to say that it is expected that the terrorists' specific plans should be known very soon. There is speculation they are planning something very big across the country. People of authority are instructing the general public about the concern and are warning people to be extra vigilant and to report any suspicious behavior or activity.

My thoughts immediately turn toward the Arab in the van. But then I am somewhat comforted to know that Office Musty is aware of him and now is watching him for us. So my thoughts quickly return to the news as it continues.

The news reporter then states, in addition, certain flights from certain airports have been grounded due to additional threats from the terrorists, and there is speculation that all flights will soon be canceled across America, perhaps within the next few hours. Moreover, some airports are reported being closed. A national address from the president of the United States is expected to be made later this morning.

I suddenly realize that apparently, this is no longer a simple passing news story but is rapidly becoming a major event that everybody should monitor very closely. Sonja and I share our concern about what's developing throughout America, and we are not at all optimistic based on what we've heard.

As Sonja prepares a light lunch, I check the weather forecast. I see that although it's sunny and extremely hot, there's a wave of thunderstorms that's predicted to be here in a few hours. So after checking with Sonja, I decide that it's best to BBQ the meat in advance and hold it in the oven rather than wait for everybody to come to start the BBQ later. The storms are predicted to pass through before evening though, so the fireworks display should still be good to go later when it gets dark.

After standing over the fire from the BBQ pit for over an hour, I finally finish and go back inside where it's cool. I bring the cooked meat to Sonja, and she wraps it in foil and puts it in the oven. She then returns to preparing the other food for the dinner.

The air conditioner is on full blast and it feels good. I sit down for a moment to contemplate what I'll do next. So far today, I have gone for a walk, had the encounter with the van and the police car, went to church and heard the mother of all sermons, had the unannounced visit from Officer Musty, and now am worrying about the terrorists after having finished laboring over a hot BBQ pit in ninety-five-plus-degree temperature.

The day is only half over, and it's been very busy already. I turn on the news, and again, it addresses the terrorists and their threats to the United States. I continue to watch the news, changing channels every few minutes.

Now there is some speculation that the terrorists have nuclear bomb capability and the means to successfully deliver them to or possibly plant them in the United States. The news goes on to say that although there is some isolated concern in some areas of the country, most Americans are not taking the threat seriously at this time.

In thinking about what's going on in the world and the fact that the news is becoming increasingly distressing, for some reason I happen to think of my biological father. Suddenly, I get the urge to look through the things that I inherited from him after he died. This is all stored away in a large metal chest in our attic. I'm curious to see what's in the chest. I haven't looked at it since I received it many years ago, and I have forgotten what all is in there.

I've often thought about going up to the attic to look in it but never did follow up. It's been so long ago I can't remember the last time I saw it, and for some reason I get curious and decide that now is as good as time as any to get it and open it. I have plenty of time before everybody arrives later in the afternoon.

So, I go up into the attic, and after negotiating my way around all sorts of things stored up there, I eventually find a very heavy metal chest buried underneath a bunch of other cardboard boxes. All the boxes are dusty, and there are cobwebs everywhere. I see some spiders scurry away here and there. I think, "Great, another job for me to do sometime." The attic is extremely hot. It's like an oven, and there's no air circulation whatsoever. As a result, I begin to sweat profusely again.

I'm not sure if this is what I'm looking for, but I think it is. There's something unusual about the chest, and my curiosity increases. When I try to lift it, I'm surprised how heavy it is. I try to wipe it off a little, and after struggling with the weight of the chest and difficulty in getting it down the steps, I'm finally able to bring it downstairs.

I wipe away the remaining dust and cobwebs and drag it into the room. I sit it on the floor in front of me, sit back down on the couch, take a few deep breaths, and try to open it up. Sweat is running into my eyes, and I can hardly see. There's a lock on the handle in front of the chest, but for some strange reason, when I gently pull on it, it comes undone almost by itself. "Wow," I say to myself. "How did that happen?" I open it up to see what's inside. By now, I am sweating even more profusely after struggling with the chest in the hot attic and bringing it down the steps. As hot as it was, it is like hell up in the attic.

Inside the chest are various small antique items, some old books, and some photos. It appears that some of these are from the Middle East and my childhood. After rummaging through the chest some more, I find something wrapped in a small white sheet. I unwrap it and find a shirt that my father had me wear when he would tell me stories and puzzles when I was about five years old. It's exactly how I remembered it except it's a lot smaller than what I expected. I then remember that my father always wore a similar shirt.

I take a minute to think back to when I was five years old and the times I would wear the shirt. I remember my father telling me stories, riddles, and puzzles then. I take a minute to stare at the shirt. There are three lines on it and some faded symbols or lettering on the middle line that I can't read. I take a minute to reminisce, and when I hold the shirt and look at it for some reason, I remember that my father told me he would always be with me. I can feel his presence in the shirt and remember sitting on his lap. I take another minute to reminisce some more and then lay the shirt down gently and wonder again what the faded symbols or lettering on the second line says. I wish I could read them, but I can't. Then I see what else is in the chest.

In the bottom of the chest, there is something else wrapped up in another white sheet; this one much larger. As I start to unwrap it, I get a strange feeling that perhaps I shouldn't be doing this. But as I hesitate for some reason, it welcomes me and I get the sense that it's calling me to open it. How strange this feeling is. My curiosity wins. I'm afraid a giant spider or something is going to jump out at me, but I slowly unwrap it anyway. There's no telling how long it's been wrapped up like this.

Folded up into a large triangle as if it were brand new is the handwoven white blanket that my father said has been passed down in the family for many generations. Now it's mine, and it's my responsibility to keep this heirloom safe and pass it down to the next generation. That would be Andrew. But I know that he's not yet responsible enough to have it. For now, it's mine to keep and treasure. I remember my father telling me that it was first owned by a distant relative well over a thousand of years ago.

I sense that it has a mysterious or magical quality about it as well. I remember my father telling me that someday I'd find out more about the blanket, and my son, Andrew would also learn about it, but not until my father decided the time was right. But how could my father decide when the time is right now that he passed away about sixty years ago? Now that he's gone, will I ever find out? And how would Andrew ever find out about it when I don't know about it and my father is no longer here to explain it to him either? What a mystery this is. Although I'm extremely hot and still sweating, when I touch it and think about these things, I feel shivers run down my spine.

Thoughts of the puzzle of life that my father told me about when I was a little boy pop into my head. I wonder for an instant when the puzzle will present itself and when I'll need to solve it and whether the puzzle has anything to do with the blanket or shirt. But these thoughts quickly fade away.

I remember that my father said this blanket was very special, but he never did say why or how it is so extraordinary. If it has any mystical qualities, I have no idea what they may be. I unfold the blanket to admire it, and there inside the blanket is a Bible with a shiny white cover. I look at it and think, "This looks exactly like the same Bible with the white cover that our Reverend Gabriel holds up at the end of the service sometimes." I want to open it and perhaps read a few verses, but for some reason, the cover won't open. The Bible appears to be locked shut. I figure perhaps because it's so old and the pages may be stuck together. However, they're not, and the Bible looks brand new.

I mention this to Sonja. She responds, "Well, that's a shame. The Bible looks like it's in perfect condition and perhaps never been used. The one you always read is so old, it's coming apart. The binding is taped together and otherwise it's falling apart at the seams, and some of the pages are torn. You could certainly use a new one."

"I know. I sure would like to get a new one. But this is so strange. When I hold this Bible and look at my old one and think about getting a new one, I get the feeling I am supposed to wait and not get a new one right away. Why is that?"

"I have no idea."

But rather than struggle with the Bible any more, I realize that I'm too hot and tired anyway and abandon any more thoughts to try to open it.

The phone rings and Sonja answers it. It's the same woman who had called earlier. This time, Sonja puts her on the speaker and

I can hear her voice. What she says is almost identical to the phone call from before. The voice says that she needs to talk with me to let me know about something extremely important, but then her voice starts shaking as if she is sobbing, and then she hangs up or the call is disconnected. She sounds extremely serious.

I don't recognize her voice but notice she does have an accent. For some reason, I get an eerie feeling about this person, but what for or who it may be, I don't know.

Sonja asks, "Alex, don't you think we should call the police and report these calls?"

I take several seconds to answer. "Maybe we should, but I'm inclined to wait to see if she attempts to contact me again. I'd like to talk with her if I can."

Chapter 5

I carefully fold the shirt, wrap it back up, and put it back in the chest. I then become aware that I'm actually very tired. I decide to take a short nap before everybody comes over for the BBQ later in the afternoon and the block party and fireworks display in the evening.

I lie down lengthwise on the couch and prop my head up on the sofa pillow. My body temperature finally feels like it's coming back down to normal, but my body still glistens with perspiration. As a result from coming into the air-conditioned room after sweating up in the attic and wrestling with the heavy metal chest, I realize that now I'm a little chilly.

I fold the blanket back into a large triangle as it was and drape it over my chest with one corner resting on my neck, rest the Bible on top of the blanket, and close my eyes to take a short nap. In the meantime, Sonja is busy arranging her orange blossom flowers and jars, stops for a minute and temporarily lays a small bouquet of orange blossoms on top of the Bible as she stands behind the couch.

As I lie on the couch, I close my eyes and begin to doze off. As I do, visions of my biological father come to mind when I was a little boy, and soon I become lost in thoughts that start to race through my mind.

My father was such a mysterious man. He was such a devout Christian, but there was always something about him I didn't understand. Especially how he could convert every atheist he met to

Christianity. Just how did he do this? I wonder if he could convert Andrew if he was still alive.

I remember when he would tell me his stories, riddles, and puzzles, he always had me sit on his lap. But now I remember when I listened to him, he would wear a special shirt that had three lines on it similar to mine. There were some small strange symbols on the top line, but I have no idea what they meant. I assume they were some sort of hieroglyphics that only he knew. It looked something like this:

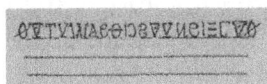

When he told me his stories, riddles, and puzzles he always wanted me to wear a similar shirt. It was the same shirt I found in the chest. On my shirt there were also three lines, with some symbols on the middle line. I couldn't read them on my shirt because they sort of blended in with the background and were faded. I suppose that if they were also some sort of hieroglyphics, I wouldn't be able to understand them anyway. When I asked him what they meant on either shirt, he told me I would find out one day, but that he could not tell me at the time.

But it really didn't matter then because on my shirt the symbols were so faded that neither I nor anybody else could read them anyway.

When I outgrew the shirt, it got stuffed away in a box for safekeeping. My father told me that I should always keep this shirt to remember him by and there will be a day when I will need to look at it after I was grown. I asked him why I would need to look at it then. He simply told me I would eventually find out, but he couldn't tell me anything more about it. But now that I've looked at it, I still don't know.

I never knew why he wanted me to wear this shirt or why he wore his shirt when I would sit on his lap to listen to him, but it made him feel good that I wore it. So I agreed to wear it because I knew it made him happy. He told me that one day when I am grown that I would know the meaning of all of this. I suppose I would find out when I found the occasion to look at it then. Maybe I'll need to look at it again sometime.

I remember he said that one day, Earth would have something that a lot of people would think is an Apocalypse. But I also recall he said that in order for God to defeat Satan, God would need help from special angels.

I remember asking him how God made the angels. He said that some angels came from souls on Earth, those who were the purist, who had the most profound belief and who had the strongest faith in Jesus Christ. But he went on to say that some angels resulted from souls chosen by God who had to pay the price. These sometimes become special angels. Again, I had no idea what he was talking about. I would ask, "What price? How much does it cost?" He never answered me.

Now that I'm older, I wonder how strange these comments were. How can there be special angels? Why do they need to pay a price? I don't think the Bible says anything about this. Then I wonder if perhaps my father may be wrong about this or if this is another one of his riddles of some sort.

Then I think of my sister. I have not seen her or heard from her in about sixty years. I remember the sessions we both had with our father when we'd sit on his lap and listen to him when we were children. I don't know if he wore his special shirt with her or if she had a shirt like mine. I do remember that before she would go into his study for her sessions, she would always take with her a bouquet of orange blossoms that she picked from the orange grove. I had no idea why she always took these flowers with her. She always held them up and showed them to me before she closed the door after entering the study in an effort to tease me. "See how pretty these are? See how pretty I am."

I remember my father sensed I was jealous when she always carried her bouquet of orange blossoms with her when she had her sessions with him. I knew that he always wanted her to hold the flowers during her sessions. Maybe the orange blossoms were symbolic to her like the shirt was to me. I couldn't figure out what my shirt said and I have no idea what her flowers meant. Apparently it meant something because he wanted her to hold them. But I didn't like it that I didn't understand the meaning of any of this.

He told me that I shouldn't let that bother me and that I shouldn't be jealous of her holding the flowers. But he told me that if I ever saw her hold the bouquet of orange blossoms upside down, then it was okay for me to be concerned because that would mean something was very wrong. He emphatically told me I should never ever forget that. I should always remember to look to make sure she was holding the bouquet of orange blossom flowers right-side up. Always. If I ever saw her hold them upside down, then I should understand that something is not what it appears to be and then I should have reason to be very concerned.

Now, I have no idea why he would say something like that, and I thought it was just another one of his riddles. Because that was such a strange comment and because he was so incredibly insistent that I should always remember that for the rest of my life, the memory has stuck in the back of my mind.

I don't know what he told my sister during her sessions when she sat on his lap. He never told me and she was forbidden to tell me. All I know is that he told her stories, riddles, and puzzles, including her own puzzle of life to solve someday, but they were not the same as what he told me. He had a different message for her, but I have no idea what it was.

I remember asking him if I would ever learn what her puzzle of life was that he told her. He told me each of our puzzles would be the test of our lives. He also told me that her puzzle of life was different than mine, but in order for each of us to solve our own puzzle of life, we would both need to recognize the solution of the other's first.

Well, that seems impossible. How could I do that? I asked him how we could do that if we didn't know anything about it. He told me that one day after I am grown and had my own family a time would come to solve it, and I would need to figure it out. He told me that we both would have a great responsibility to solve our puzzles, but that I would be able to do it if I thought outside the box. "Wow," I thought, "how could I recognize the solution to her puzzle first to solve mine if I didn't even know what her puzzle was? And how could she recognize mine as well?"

I remember asking him why we would both have such a great responsibility to solve these puzzles of life when the time came and why we would need to recognize the solution to the other's puzzle first before we could solve our own puzzle. He emphatically said, "Your life and the lives of others will depend on it. It will be a huge responsibility. And, if you both don't solve your puzzles and pass the test, then you both would fail." So, if one of us fails, we both would. And the way I understand it, not only would we die, so would many others! Now I don't know whether to look forward to that day or not.

I also keep thinking about these puzzles of life and this great responsibility we both will have to solve them and wonder whether she has forgotten about what our father said to us about it. I hope she hasn't. It seems like we will need to somehow depend on each other to solve these puzzles when the time comes. But how can we do that now that we have lost track of each other for sixty years? And how will I ever know if she's ever holding a bouquet of orange blossoms upside down? I'll probably never see her or talk with again. I have absolutely no idea where she is. She could be anywhere in the world.

If there really is such a thing as a special angel, from what I remember of her, perhaps she could be one.

As tired as I am, my thoughts of when I was a little boy, my father, and my sister become intermingled with those of the day's events and those yet to come as I doze off further. In the process, I fall fast asleep and soon I'm out like a light. Little did I know that later I'd learn this isn't just an ordinary nap. In fact, I would find out later just how extraordinary this nap would be.

Chapter 6

It's late afternoon and the storms have come and gone. They didn't amount to much, but there was a lot of rain in a very short period. Now the sun has returned and everything is drying up very fast. It's very hot and humid. In fact, with the rain-soaked air, it's so muggy that just stepping outside for a few seconds brings on the sweat like a water faucet was turned on over my forehead. I'm returning from our bedroom after putting everything away, taking a quick shower, and changing my clothes.

Sonja, who's still in the kitchen, calls out, "Alex, Julie, Garrett, and the kids have arrived."

Lizzy and Mikey are running up to the front door, and we can hear them calling out "Grandma, Grandpa, Grandma, Grandpa!" What a delight it is to have them come over.

"Happy birthday!" they all sing together.

I am honored by their thoughtfulness and casually make a remark about it being our country's birthday, but they all continue to sing to me, which has me blushing after a while.

It doesn't take them long to find the toys lined up all along the wall, and within minutes, they're scattered everywhere. Romper room now is officially open for business. Julie and Garrett then follow behind, also wishing me a happy birthday. Julie is carrying Emily and a diaper bag containing all the necessary baby accessories, and Garrett is loaded down carrying several other bags.

One bag is full of more food for dinner. Another has some sparklers and other fireworks to light up later. Another bag contains two patterned sheets from one of the kids' beds and some socks that have some stains that Julie wants Sonja to help her get out.

Crackerjack bounds in with a tennis ball in his mouth, wagging his tail furiously. Surely, with all these people around, somebody will want to pet him or throw the ball for him to fetch.

He sure would not make a good watchdog. If a burglar entered the house in the middle of the night, instead of barking, he'd roll over on his back and expect to have his belly rubbed. He never barks or growls unless it's for something way out of the ordinary. That would have to be an extraordinary event though. Typical things that would prompt other dogs to bark with impulse are mere amusement to him. Typical golden retriever behavior, I muse.

They are no sooner in the house when the discussion immediately turns toward the news about the terrorists. Garrett looks at me and says, "Every time we turn on the news, it's worse. The developments are happening so fast it's hard to keep up."

I acknowledge the same thing. I have the baseball game on TV, but it's constantly being interrupted by the news. While we're watching the game, it's interrupted again by a special news bulletin. The news now announces that all airports have been closed throughout the entire country, resulting in all flights being immediately canceled. Many countries in Western Europe are following suit.

The news continues and states that the government is considering canceling all major sporting events and any other events where masses of people congregate beginning the next day. They fear the possibility of a wide-scale terrorist attack at such venues based on what the terrorists have threatened. It's then reported that the government is investigating threats that the terrorists will detonate nuclear bombs within the United States. They indicate they have credible evidence that this is very possible; however, they make it very clear that it's only a possibility and that nothing definitive has been verified.

The news then briefly addresses the question of how the terrorists would acquire the materials and knowledge to build a nuclear bomb in our country and why our government intelligence was not aware of this until now. But these questions go unanswered. At this point, much of this is merely speculation.

We then find out that the president and other world leaders have been trying to negotiate a peace settlement, but to no avail. The news reporter states that the terrorist leaders are ruthless, will not listen to anybody, and that they've made their threats very clear. In fact, the terrorists have officially declared that it is their mission to destroy America. They are absolutely adamant that it *will* happen and that there is nothing anybody can do to prevent it. Chants of "Death to America" can be heard.

The terrorists cannot be found. Their communication is always one sided. And they are merciless.

The news results in a trickle of tears that run down Julie's cheeks. "I can't believe this is really happening. Dad, tell me that this is not all for real, right?"

I softly say, "I wish I could, but I can't."

Garrett and Sonja try to comfort her and tell her that nothing has happened (yet), and that all we can do is live our lives as normally as possible and see if anything happens. Sonja takes her hand. "There's nothing that we can do to prevent any of this, and perhaps it will all just pass."

There's a knock on the door, and it's Andrew, Alana, Daniel, Matthew, and Hannah. They've arrived, and now everybody is here. Hannah makes a beeline to the toys where the other kids are already playing. Daniel and Matthew lag behind being a little shy for some reason. Almost in unison they ask, "When will the fireworks begin?"

Alana tells them, "That won't be until it gets dark and that we haven't even had dinner yet." They then join the other kids to play.

Alana wishes me a sincere happy birthday and then strikes up a conversation with Julie about her new house. Alana wants to know all about it, and Julie explains what it's like and pulls out some photos.

Andrew interrupts her and sarcastically says, "I hear it's a mansion, almost like a castle."

"Yeah, it's a large house, which means that there's that much more to clean. We're not so sure bigger is better. But it's really not as big as you think. It's not even anywhere as big as Dad's house."

"My house isn't that big," I retort, but in a friendly way.

"Oh yes, it is. It takes me a half a day to walk from one end of it to the other," Andrew adamantly exclaims.

Alana stares at Andrew and then glances at the rest of us. "Let me apologize for Andrew. He needs to learn not to be so jealous and to just keep his comments to himself. Have you heard the news about the terrorists? What do you think?"

Andrew makes another sarcastic remark. "Of course they know all about it. Who hasn't?"

Julie then asks Andrew, "Are you aware the government may cancel all major sporting events beginning tomorrow?"

"No, they wouldn't do that. One of my buddies has an extra ticket and asked me to go to the game tomorrow night. I'll be pissed if it's called off."

Alana again stares at Andrew. "You never said anything about going to the game tomorrow."

"Well, now you know."

Alana continues to stare at Andrew with a look that would freeze a cat.

Everybody heads outside except for Sonja and Julie. Julie shows Sonja the stains in the kids' sheets and socks that she thinks are from some markers the kids were using. Sonja treats the sheets and tells Julie she can soak them in a solution in the sink in the unfinished basement area downstairs. Sonja can't help from commenting on the unusual pattern on the sheets and tells Julie how much she likes them. Julie runs downstairs to soak everything in the sink and then soon returns.

Late afternoon is turning into evening, and a summer breeze has picked up somewhat. Some clouds have rolled back in, obscuring the setting sun; the temperature has dropped a little, and it's a little more comfortable. The kids are running around the house—some playing on the swings set up under the deck, and some playing with the hose and getting water everywhere. Garrett, Andrew, and I go out the front door to inspect the setup for the fireworks display and to greet some of the neighbors who are starting to assemble.

The fireworks are being coordinated by one of the neighbors, but it seems like all the men will have something to do with it. The middle of the cul-de-sac is where the action will take place.

Garrett comments on the old white van that's parked up the street. "Julie told me about it after she talked with Sonja earlier on the phone. What's going on?"

Andrew chimes in "What are you talking about?"

I explain, "The van has been following Sonja and me around lately, and it's been parking either across the street or up the street. It's always there. It appears suspicious, but so far, it hasn't really caused any problems. It's just a little nerve-wracking because we don't know anything about it."

Both are intrigued by this, and Garrett comments, "You know, the news on TV advised people to report any unusual activity or suspicious behavior because of the terrorist threats. Do you think you should do that?"

"Well, I've actually already done that. We talked with an Officer Musty earlier, and he's aware of it. Everything should be okay."

Garrett adds, "When we passed it coming down the street, I saw what looked like an Arab sitting in the driver's seat."

Andrew, surprised, asks, "An Arab?"

"That's what Julie indicated that Sonja said too."

Andrew asks again, "An Arab?"

Garrett more emphatically states, "Yes, a man dressed like an Arab. He had a turban wrapped around his head. Didn't you see him? I saw him when we drove by his van coming down the street here."

Andrew pauses for a few seconds. "An Arab...hmmm." He starts laughing and jokingly exclaims, "Yeah, I know about that Arab and what he's up to. He's a terrorist and has a bomb in his van just for us. He's here to blow us all up."

Andrew's the only one laughing though. At that time, Alana comes out and overhears what Andrew said. She adamantly declares, "Andrew, that's not funny! You should be ashamed of yourself. If Julie or any of the kids heard you talk like that, it would upset them even more. You need to apologize."

Andrew reluctantly apologizes but continues to snicker silently as if he thought that was the best joke ever.

By now, Sonja and Julie are inside preparing the buffet for dinner. The rest of us are outside in the front yard greeting some of the neighbors and friends who are starting to congregate. People are setting up lawn chairs and putting blankets on the lawns, and coolers begin to show up here and there.

Then, as if on cue, a police car comes cruising down the street. When it does, the white van turns around and leaves, but shortly returns and parks in the same spot. After stopping briefly several times in front of some other houses up the street, the police car approaches very slowly and parks in front of the house. Out steps Officer Musty.

"Hi, everybody," he says.

Everyone fears he's going to cancel the neighborhood fireworks display because the cul-de-sac is located within the outer shell of the city limits where setting off fireworks in a residential neighborhood is illegal. But instead, he's very friendly and starts up a welcoming conversation with everybody. He's rapidly making friends with everyone.

He then announces, "If you're wondering whether I am going to tell you that you can't set off fireworks tonight, you don't need to worry. I'm not going to do that. But don't tell anyone that I'm letting you do this. Mr. Fisheramen here is a good friend of mine, and I'll take care of things. In fact, I just might join you for a while, if you don't mind."

Everyone accepts him and graciously welcomes him as he chitchats his way through what now has grown to be a large crowd of neighbors and other guests mingling about. I, on the other hand, find it a little disturbing that suddenly Officer Musty is telling everybody he's a good friend of mine. That sure happened in a hurry. I only met him earlier this morning. But I pass it off as a trait of Musty's personality. I'm actually glad that Officer Musty is here because he's watching the Arab for us.

Officer Musty then approaches me and informs me that he noticed that the Arab is back sitting in his van at the top of the street. Apparently, the Arab is watching the block party from his van. He then comments, "Now don't you worry about a thing, Mr. Fisheramen. I'm here, so nothing will happen. You all enjoy yourselves this evening." Officer Musty then retreats to his police car for a few minutes and then returns to join the party.

Andrew, Garrett, Alana, and the kids go back in the house for dinner, but Andrew shortly returns outside to gather some toys left out in the yard by the kids. The dinner is a typical Fourth of July BBQ. Right before dinner is served, the family gets together and says grace. Everyone is present for the prayer except for Andrew.

Dinner is buffet style, and shortly after grace is said, everybody has filled their plates and is finding a place to eat. Some are eating out on the deck and some are eating at the kitchen table. Dinner consists of pork steaks, chicken, grilled hot dogs for the kids, corn on the cob, potato salad, coleslaw, and an assortment of casseroles and other dishes. For dessert, there's a variety of pies. A typical summer holiday BBQ. Everybody is stuffed in short order.

No matter where anyone eats, all conversation bounces back and forth between the terrorist threats, the Arab in the van, and the upcoming fireworks display. After dinner, the women clean up, and everybody else goes back outside. People are already claiming their spots in lawn chairs and on blankets laid out on the grass. The men are starting to separate and organize the assortment of fireworks that each proudly bought earlier in the day.

The kids are playing with other kids in the neighborhood, and some are playing with the hose again, still getting water everywhere. The kids are having a good time when Julie and Alana call them back inside so that they can wash up and get ready for the fireworks. They turn the hose off at the nozzle and leave the hose uncoiled by the front door. The kids drop everything to come inside.

They know that if they don't obey right away, they'd be sent to the corner for time-out, and tonight they don't want to risk that. PJs are put on some of the younger ones to facilitate things later.

The sun is setting and the evening sky is slowly turning from broken clouds to waves of gray, and more shadows appear as the light starts to fade.

Everybody is back in the house except for me. I'm out in the front yard talking to the neighbors. Officer Musty approaches and asks, "Well, what are the plans?"

"Well, I'm headed back in the house. My entire family will be inside together for a short while for a short family get-together and then we'll all come out to watch the fireworks. Actually, this will be the first time that all of us will have been together for some time. It seems like somebody is busy with work, kids, or other activities, and it's difficult for everybody to get together at the same time. Even Andrew will be inside with everybody. But we won't be inside long. The kids can't wait."

"Well, that's great. You go ahead and go inside and do what you need to do. I'll be around. No need to worry about anything."

Officer Musty then returns to his police car instead of rejoining the neighbors. It appears that he's watching the van up the street parked about a half dozen houses away.

I go back into the house and in the living room find Lizzy and Mikey playing and Emily asleep in her pumpkin seat. "Where is everybody else?"

Mikey says, "Downstairs. We're playing hide and seek."

I then go down to the lower level and find that Sonja, Andrew, Garrett, Julie, and Alana have briefly and unexpectedly stepped outside onto the backyard patio, so I go out to join them. I'm in the house for less than a minute. The backyard patio is obscured by bushes and trees, and nobody in the cul-de-sac can see us. Everybody out front assumes the entire family is in the house.

As soon as I walk outside the lower-level door and join them outside on the back patio, everyone is rocked and blown over by a massive explosion! The house shakes with incredible violence as if a commercial airliner fell out of the sky and hit the house. Then there's another explosion within a second or two later. Soon, everybody realizes that the explosions came from within the house and instantly realize the house is on fire.

Chapter 7

There are flames coming from some of the windows that face out to the backyard. As a result of the blast, everyone is knocked to the ground and is dazed and confused but appear unhurt. After gathering their composure and everyone comes to their senses as to what just happened, they frantically get up and instinctively run around the side of the house to the front yard to avoid the fire and burning debris which is starting to fall. They stumble but finally make their way to the front yard.

Within a minute, they make their way to the front yard and street, and they're frightened by the flames and smoke coming from both ends of the front of the house. They can see flames coming from some of the windows in the front of the house as well.

They along with the neighbors move farther up the street to get out of the way. Smoke now billows everywhere. Sirens can already be heard as at least one of the neighbors immediately called 911.

Everything is happening so fast, nobody can think straight. Then almost simultaneously, Julie and Alana hysterically cry out, "Where are the kids?"

Garrett screams "My God, they're still in the house!"

Everybody becomes hysterical. What happened? What caused the explosion? We need to get the kids!

The police arrive immediately and promptly set up a barricade and instruct everybody to retreat behind it, ushering everyone including all the neighbors up the street even farther away from the house. Alana and Julie are frantic and are crying out to the police, "Our kids are still in the house! Our kids are still in the house!"

One of the police officers calmly says, "We're not equipped to go in the house. You'll need to wait for the fire department. They should be here real soon."

That upsets Alana and Julie, who continue to scream at them. Some of the men move the cars parked nearby up the street, and the van parked up the street backs up farther toward the top of the street. By now the fire is rapidly spreading, and I shout out, "We can't wait for the fire department. Somebody needs to go in the house now! The kids are still in there!"

The police officer yells back at me, "The house is an inferno. Nobody can go in there right now. The fire department is on its way."

Both Garrett and I try to break through the barricade to get to the house but are restrained by the police. Garrett screams at them, "We can go in through the front door and at least look! The fire hasn't reached there yet!"

It's a very large atrium ranch house with five very large bedrooms, four and a half bathrooms, a massive great room, a large dining room, a country kitchen, a breakfast area, a lounge area, a study, a closed-in porch sunroom, and a large laundry room off the garage. One of the bedrooms has been converted into a home office. There are walk-in closets throughout the house. At one end of the house is an oversized three-car garage. There's a large wrap-around deck on the back corner of the house off the breakfast room that connects to the sunroom and a second deck off the master bedroom. The house is the length of at least two normal ranch houses on a one-acre lot.

The lower level is partially finished with a large entertainment area, a bar, another bedroom, a bathroom, and a large mudroom. There is a second walkout door that leads to a large patio that runs about half the length of the house. There's a sink and a rough-in for additional plumbing in the corner of the unfinished area. The unfinished basement area, in addition to the attic, is used for storage.

Both ends of the house including the garage are engulfed in flames. Flames are shooting from all the windows, and flames can be seen everywhere except for in the middle of the house by the front door. The garage end of the house is the worst hit, and another smaller explosion results in a garage exterior wall partially collapsing. The roof is also burning at both ends of the house. It appears that the entire perimeter of the house is engulfed in flames except for the front entryway and porch.

There's so much smoke, it's hard to see anything. The waves of intense heat and some flying debris from the side of the house drives everybody even farther away. The police are ushering everybody farther away up the street and move the barricade farther back.

The family continues to plead to the police, however are repeatedly told only the fire department is equipped to enter the house and they should wait for them. They're also told again that the fire department is on their way and will be arriving very soon.

Soon there are a few isolated fires on the roofs of both neighbors' houses, the result of falling debris from the explosions. In the meantime, Garrett and I continue to try to get through the barricade to approach the house to try to get the kids, but are now being physically restrained by the police.

Suddenly, Daniel and Matthew are seen running from the other side of the house in the neighbor's yard through the blowing smoke. One is struggling to carry Hannah. They are coughing and stumbling as they escape the fire and smoke. Then Garrett and I finally break through the barricade set up by the police and run up to them. We pick them up, and after making sure they're okay, they run to where everybody else is. Everybody asks them, "Where's Lizzy, Mikey, and Emily?"

Daniel cries out, "They're still in the house!"

Matthew adds, "Crackerjack is still in the house too!"

"Couldn't they get out with you?" shouts Julie.

Daniel blurts out, "No, we were downstairs! We couldn't get the door open but finally did and ran out. I think Lizzy and Mikey were upstairs on the main floor. They were going to hide from us."

Matthew adds, "I think Emily was asleep in her punkin' seat in the great room, but I'm not sure."

By now, Julie and Garrett are absolutely hysterical. A fireball explodes from the roof, and a corner of the house partially collapses.

The police usher both of us back behind the barricade. Everyone continues to yell at the police and plead to let somebody go in the house to try to rescue the kids. Julie drops to her knees crying. Her face is wet with tears. Garrett is practically fighting with the police and nearly breaks through the barricade again, but the police continue to restrain him.

My continued pleadings with the police are of no avail. The policeman looks straight at me and adamantly states, "There is no way anyone can enter the house until the fire is under control first, and that if anybody enters the house it will be the firefighters. Only they are equipped to enter a house with flames like this. If we let you go in there, we would be held responsible. It would be pure suicide without the necessary equipment."

I again start to push my way past the barricade, but am restrained and ordered to go back. I cry out at the top of my lungs "Doesn't anyone have any faith? How can you let those children die in there? In another minute or two it will be too late, and nobody will be able to get in there! We can't wait for the fire department!"

Garrett again yells out again to the police, "I told you, the front door is not yet on fire, we can at least look in there!"

Out of nowhere, Officer Musty shows up, and the other policemen move out of the way and retreat down the line to control the rest of the crowd as they're getting out of hand. One of the officers physically restrains Garrett and pushes him farther away. Officer Musty looks at me. "I thought you were in the house with all of your family. How did you and the others get out so fast?"

I look at him and wonder why he would ask such a question under the circumstances. "What about the kids?"

Office Musty then says softly, "If you want to go in the house to try to save the kids, that's okay with me. I'll help you get past the barricade. Just don't let any of the other policemen know I'm letting you do this. But I think it's too late…nobody's alive in there, and it would be suicide for you to even try it. But if you want to kill yourself trying, it's okay with me." He then points to an opening that he made in the barricade and whispers, "Go… go now…Hurry."

"Thank you, thank you." I look up to the sky. "We can do this."

Officer Musty exclaims, "Who's 'we'? I'm not going in with you."

"We have to at least try." Without even thinking twice about it or taking the time to evaluate anything, I bolt through the barricade opening that Officer Musty made and run straight toward the front door of the house. It now has been only just a few minutes since the explosion, but the fire is spreading rapidly.

Although I'm not aware of it, a few minutes after I enter the house through the front door, the fire department arrives and there's a flurry of activity. They immediately begin working with their equipment, dragging their big hoses across the lawn, and hooking them up. Julie screams at them repeatedly, "My kids and my father are still in the house! My kids and my dad are still in the house!"

In less than a minute or so, as the fire department rushes to work with their equipment and prepares to try to enter the house, the front porch and door erupt in flames, and part of the roof caves in at the end of the house.

Now there are flames at every door and window, front and back. Every entrance to and every exit from the house, including the front entry, is engulfed in flames, and there is no way in and there is no way out. There is no way that the fire department can enter the house anywhere. But at least I made it inside.

Chapter 8

I didn't want to even think about whether or not to try to go in the house. Even though I tried to break through the barricade, if I thought about it, perhaps I wouldn't have done it. But I made the decision on total impulse and instinct.

As I run across the yard and into our front yard, I pick up a large blanket on the way, one that the kids had put down to lie on for the fireworks display later. As I'm running, I drape it over my head, holding it up over me with the ends dragging on the ground around me. I figure even if it doesn't protect me, perhaps it may be useful if I should find the kids. Maybe I'll need it to drag them out on the blanket if they can't walk or if I can't carry them. That is, if I can find them and if they're okay.

As I approach the front porch, the heat suddenly becomes oppressive and almost unbearable. Smoke billows everywhere. As I'm running, I start praying like I never have before. "Sweet Jesus, please be with me and help me. I believe in you, and I have faith in you. We can do this."

I see the hose on the porch that the kids left and pick it up at the nozzle and turn it on. It works. Water is shooting out. "Wow! I can't believe this." I turn it on full blast and start soaking myself and the blanket that I'm holding up over me. I briefly turn around and look at the crowd, and I see Julie, Alana, and Sonja looking at me in horror. I see Garrett farther away being held by a policeman. I don't see Andrew anywhere.

I turn around, say another quick prayer, and open the front door. There are some small flames on the floor inside the door, but they're small enough that I can hit them with the hose and quickly step over them. I lift up the blanket higher so I can see as I enter the foyer and quickly survey the inside of the house. I find that part of the great room, the main hallway, and the office are in relatively good shape. The far corner of the great room was hit by the blast, and bits and pieces of burning debris flew here and there, but most of the great room is still intact.

The blasts from the explosions apparently came from the lower level and the ends of the house, and the center of the house survived the blasts. The small flames and debris just inside the front door seemed to have come from some flying debris from the corner of the great room.

The fire apparently looked worse from outside as the center of the house is relatively still free from flames, but I can see that the fire is spreading rapidly and will engulf the great room and front entry way within only a few minutes at the most.

With the exception of the foyer and front entryway, the entire perimeter of the house is engulfed in flames. The fire has not yet spread to the center and part of one side of the house, but I know it won't take long before the fire spreads to these rooms. If I'm going to find the kids, they will have to be in one of only these rooms, either the great room, the hallway, the office, or two closets. The rest of the house is either on fire or I can't reach them because of the destruction. I need to act fast.

I quickly think perhaps it's a good thing that our house is so large. If it were smaller, the explosions would have completely destroyed the entire house immediately. But because it's so large, just maybe they survived if they were in the center of the house at the time of the blasts.

As I enter the great room, I sense that the floor is unstable and realize that there's a possibility it could collapse any minute. I quickly look around while holding the blanket over me with one hand and dragging the hose behind me as I proceed into the great room. Surprisingly, there's not much smoke in the great room...yet.

I know my time is limited before the fire spreads to the middle of the house. I know the walls are being consumed by the fire from the other side and know they will collapse within the next minute or two. I will need to look around and get out of the house as fast as I can. The heat is already oppressive, but I can manage it for now. I can see and hear the fire spreading rapidly from both ends of the house to where I am.

As I quickly negotiate my way through the great room it becomes difficult to look ahead lifting the blanket out so I can try to see where to go and hold the hose over my head at the same time. I then remember I happen to have a pocketknife in my pocket.

I quickly pull it out and cut a slit in the middle of the blanket. I put it over me so that I can put my head through the slit. The blanket now rests around my neck on my shoulders. Although my head now is exposed, I can see and move around much better. Holding the hose over me, I feel the water soaking my head and face as well as soaking the blanket. The cool water feels good, and so far it's working to keep me cool, and I also hope that the wet blanket will keep any stray flames from burning me.

I start calling out to the kids. There's no answer. I make my way through the great room, quickly scanning every corner of the room that is still intact, and the kids are nowhere to be found. The far corner has been demolished. I quickly conclude they're not in here and proceed down the hallway to the bedroom. In the middle of the hallway, I partially open a walk-in closet door and peek inside. The kids are not there. I quickly close the door so I can proceed down the hallway into the office. Within seconds, I arrive at the office doorway. That's the only other room left I can access. I surmise if they're not in here, I won't find them.

I slowly open the door and enter the office and find flames at both windows and a small hole in the floor between them. There's a small fire against the exterior wall on the floor blocking the walk-in closet, but otherwise, the room is intact. There's some debris scattered about. But there's a lot more smoke in this room, and I need to get down on my hands and knees to crawl into it. I suspect that the hole in the floor and the small flames resulted from one of the blasts in the lower level coming up through the lower-level ceiling. I don't see the kids, but I want to look in the closet. I call out for them again and hear nothing. The flames are inching their way along the floor, but I can't put them out with the hose. There's no longer any water coming from it.

As I stand up to step over the small flames to reach the closet handle, the flames catch the bottom of my blanket. I quickly climb back over the flames to the doorway and realize there's a kink in the hose at the corner of the room where I entered. I immediately retrace my steps and undo the kink, and when water returns I immediately aim the nozzle at the bottom of the blanket and put the fire out. Smoke billows up, and I start to cough. "Good thing these flames were so small."

As I pull the hose farther inside with me, I wonder how far it will stretch but then discover that it's starting to melt and will soon burn through. I surmise that it must have been dragged through some small flames and wonder if the fire is expanding that fast from where I came in the great room already. I continue to alternately pray and call out to the kids but hear nothing except for the roar of the fire from the other parts of the house. I kick some debris aside and continue my way back to the closet.

I extinguish the small flames by the closet door with the hose, and through all of the smoke I reach over and try to feel for the door handle. But I can't open the door because the door is blocked. After quickly clearing the obstruction, I finally open the door enough so I can see inside. The kids aren't there.

The heat is becoming unbearable, and I'm finding it difficult to breathe with all the smoke in the room. In addition, my feet are hurting from stepping over some burning cinders and embers here and there. I pull out a handkerchief that I had been carrying in my pocket, cover my nose and mouth, and tie it behind my head. Soon it's saturated from the water from the hose. Now, only my eyes and hair are exposed. I turn around to leave the bedroom and quickly retrace my way back to the hallway. I feel the floor beneath me shake, and I sense it could collapse at any time. I again get down and crawl my way out of the room.

I alternately call out to the kids and pray. I have never prayed so hard in my life. I don't hear anything except for the roar of the fire from both ends of the house and an occasional siren from outside. I don't hear the kids. And I don't hear an answer to my prayers. I feel the water dripping over me from the blanket and wonder why the hose happened to be lying by the front porch. That can't be a coincidence can it? *If* it weren't for the hose, I would never have made it even this far. "Blessed be to whichever kid left it there."

I've been in the house for perhaps only a few minutes at the most, but when I make my way back into the hallway I discover that during the very short time while I was in the office, a wall has collapsed and the fire has spread into a larger area of the great room. Now there's so much smoke I can hardly see, and as a result, I almost stumble over a laundry basket with some clothes in it. I remember seeing it the first time but didn't pay much attention to it. I suppose the kids were playing with it earlier. Otherwise why is the basket in the great room? I'm coughing almost continuously now from the smoke and I again get down low to the floor to try to avoid it.

But when I push it aside, along with some clothes on the floor next to it, I can't believe what I see. There halfway hidden underneath the clothes is Emily in her pumpkin seat. "Unbelievable." I say a short prayer of thanks and pick her up. I'm nearly in shock that I found her. She starts to cry, but she seems unhurt. As I turn around, I suddenly realize that the only exit is the front door, and if I don't escape this instant, we'll be trapped. The fire is rapidly approaching from the side wall and the other end of the room and is nearly at the foyer and front door. The flames are fairly small but are growing in size. There's so much smoke I can barely see anything.

I come to the reluctant conclusion that Lizzy and Mikey were in another part of the house and didn't survive the explosions or have been burned to death in another room I can't reach. I realize I must abandon my search for them and find a way out of the house immediately. As fast as the fire now is spreading, Emily and I won't survive if we don't escape now. I start to make my way to the foyer.

I call out one last final time to the kids at the top of my lungs. A few seconds go by and I hear nothing. I say to myself, "I can't spend another second in here and must leave right now." As fast as the fire is spreading, the front entryway, the only escape from the house, will be a wall of flames within less than a minute at the most.

Then off in the distance, I think I hear a dog barking. "No way—that must be my imagination." Then I think I hear it again. It's a muffled sound and is hard to distinguish because it's drowned out by the roar of the approaching fire. I have looked everywhere where there's no fire, and I have not found Lizzy, Mikey, or Crackerjack. If I do hear Crackerjack, where's the sound coming from? I convince myself that it's my imagination because I have looked everywhere. But on a whim, I decide to backtrack and look in the hallway closet again. I had only quickly peeked in there before. If they were in any other part of the house, there is absolutely no way they could have survived.

I wonder if there's a miracle hiding behind the door, and I pray again to Jesus. At this point, the water from the hose stops flowing, and I surmise that this time it has stopped for good. As I approach the door, I think I hear a noise behind the door but quickly conclude again that it's my imagination. I really don't expect to find anything in the closet. I've already peeked in there once, but I pray with all of my heart and soul as I open the door. This time, I push aside some hanging coats and jackets and move a vacuum cleaner and carpet cleaner out of the way. It's dark in the back of the closet, and I turn the light on, but it doesn't work.

As I squint to look in the very back corner of the closet I cannot believe my eyes. There huddled together are Lizzy and Mikey. Crackerjack is stretched out between them apparently trying to protect them. They're crying hysterically. I say to myself, "I should have done this the first time instead of only quickly peeking in the closet."

When I brush aside the coats and jackets and they see me covered up in a steaming blanket with the white handkerchief over my face, they both immediately let out a bloodcurdling, scream the likes of which I've never heard. I suddenly realize that they don't recognize me and are terrified. I probably look like a ghost to them coming out of the smoke, covered up in a steaming blanket with handkerchief wrapped around my face. What a sight I must be to them after they have been in the dark of the closet and especially considering the circumstances. I can't imagine that the kids could be any more terrified.

I remove the handkerchief and call them, and they finally recognize me. I immediately hear, "Grandpa, Grandpa, Grandpa, Grandpa!" Crackerjack starts whimpering like crazy, and his big tail starts wagging in the kids' faces. As I bend over to them, Lizzy and Mikey instantly get up and try to climb up on me. This obviously doesn't work because I'm covered by the blanket and am also holding Emily.

I ask them what they're doing in the back of the closet, and Mikey says something that leads me to believe the kids were playing hide and seek before the explosions. Now I remember one of them telling me that earlier. The closet is about the only section of the house not affected by the explosions and fire. I assume they hid themselves in the closet just before the blasts and that it saved them.

I ask Lizzy and Mikey if they can walk. They're both crying. Lizzy adamantly says, "No." There's no way I can carry them all. When I get them up to the front of the closet, both let out another bloodcurdling scream. The flames have entered the end of the hallway, and they can see them. They immediately retreat to the back of the closet and want to stay there. I attempt to comfort Lizzy and lift her again to the front of the closet by the door, but as soon as I set her down, she again screams out one word, "No!" She screams bloody murder when her feet touch the floor. She again retreats to the back of the closet.

I then realize that the floor is hot and neither of them is wearing any shoes. They're both barefoot. "Where are your shoes?" Lizzy doesn't answer. By now, Mikey is screaming at the top of his lungs. There's no way that either of them can walk across the floor without any shoes. But more importantly they're scared to come out of the closet and won't as long as they see the flames and smoke. I ask them if they can close their eyes so they don't see the fire and they both say, "No."

I'm going to have to think of something very fast. Otherwise, as long as they see any fire or smoke, they will kick and fight to stay in the closet and they will want me to stay there with them. Time is rapidly running out, and they won't cooperate.

Now, I realize that the only way to get them to come out of the closet without fighting me will be to carry them and hide them underneath the blanket so they can't see the flames. Good thing I brought the blanket.

But I realize that the problem is insurmountable. I seriously doubt if I can carry two of them much less all three of them and negotiate my way around the flames and debris. I wish I was an octopus, but I only have two arms. I can't drag them out on the blanket because they won't cooperate as long as they can see the flames if their eyes are open. That would be too dangerous anyway. And there are too many obstacles. It just won't work. Am I going to have to leave one of them behind? Which one?

Crackerjack now is whimpering and is jumping up on me as if he wants me to carry him too. How's Crackerjack going to walk over the hot floor? By now the smoke from the fire has entered the closet, and everyone is coughing and choking. We're all having trouble breathing and are all gasping for breath. It looks like Mikey is about to pass out. Emily is gasping for air and can't breathe.

The incredible heat is getting to all of us. I turn around and peek out of the closet to look down the hallway and, to my horror, realize what caused them to scream. I now too realize that the fire now has not only spread across the great room but now has entered the hallway and is approaching the closet. There's no way we can go in either direction. There's no way out. What do I do?

I need to think fast. I need to think very fast. But there's no escape. We are all trapped. Within a minute, the fire will be at the closet door. Stepping over small flames and burning embers only several inches high at the most was manageable. But walking into an inferno of flames would be pure suicide. "How did the fire spread so rapidly? There's absolutely no way out."

There's only one option. That is to close the closet door and retreat to the very back of the closet and pray with all of my heart and soul. There is nothing else I can do. It now has been about four or five minutes since I entered the house. It's dark in the closet, and I can hardly see a thing. As I'm trying to comfort the kids and Crackerjack, they're climbing all over me and crying hysterically. I quickly get up and remove some large pillows from the closet shelf and lay them on the floor so the kids can lie on them.

Suddenly, there's a cracking noise, and I can hear a fireball erupt outside of the closet door. The kids scream. I sense that the fire now is just outside the closet door as smoke drifts in from underneath the door.

I remove the blanket and stuff it in the crack underneath the door to try to keep the smoke from coming in. When the kids hear the noise outside in the hallway, they shriek and now are absolutely hysterical. We are crammed in the back corner and trapped in the dark closet and will be consumed by the inferno within another minute or two at the most. There's absolutely no way out. I then remember I have a cell phone, but when I try to use it, there's no signal at all. The phone is useless.

I say to myself, "Hell can't be worse than this, and I can't believe that after all I went through, this is how we're all going to die."

Chapter 9

Outside, Julie has become entirely inconsolable, and she's crying uncontrollably. The entire house now is engulfed in flames. Flames are coming out of every window and doorway. The firefighters have hooked up their hoses and try to put the fire out, but it seems like all it's doing is generating more smoke.

She cries out, "They've been in there so long. They're gone!"

Some of the firefighters, equipped in firefighting gear, are running around the perimeter of the house trying to find a way in, but all doors and windows are engulfed in flames. The front entryway where Alex entered now is a blazing inferno. As Julie continues to yell and scream at the firefighters, one of them comes over and apologetically states they're trying to find an entrance to the house but can't. "There's no way into the house with these flames, and the only thing we can do is to hit what remains with water and try to put the fire out. Only then we can we go in."

Then as another explosion results in what appears to be the rest of the house falling apart and the remaining exterior walls and most of the roof of the house collapsing to the ground, she yells out at the top of her lungs "My kids are gone. They're gone forever. And my dad's gone too. Lizzy, Mikey, Emily, I love you so much! Daddy, Daddy, Daddy!" As the front of the house collapses to the ground in a blazing inferno of fire, it is quite evident that nobody could have survived it.

Alana and Sonja are huddled together, and Alana is sobbing, almost as uncontrollably as Julie. They have all come to the realization of what has just happened. "I just can't believe it, how did this happen?" she continues to say over and over again between the constant sobbing. Sonja looks to be completely stoic and stares at the burning house in horror.

Although all the neighbors are also visibly upset as well, they're doing their best to console and comfort the family. But it's difficult considering the circumstances. In the meantime, Garrett is busy gathering Andrew's kids as well as the neighborhood kids and taking them away to be with some neighbors for the time being so that they don't experience the realization of the painful death of their cousins and their grandpa. It's best that they be told later in the privacy of their own family.

He thinks, "They're too young for this. Hell, even I can't handle this."

Andrew, who was talking with the bystanders, sees him and comes over to help. But he's too late. As Andrew approaches, he makes a snide remark that at least his own kids got out of the house in time and are safe. Garrett just stares at him and doesn't say a word. Andrew offers no sympathies whatsoever regarding Garrett's loss of his kids in the fire. After a minute, Garrett then comments that at least Grandpa was there with his kids and that they didn't die alone.

By now, the news reporters are on the scene as well as more fire trucks and firefighters. There are police everywhere. The neighborhood residents and other spectators have risen to crowd proportions. The police do all they can to keep the crowd contained and away from the scene. The news reporters including the cameramen, however, are pushing their way closer. In the air, a helicopter can be heard as it hovers above.

It's now getting dark. The firefighters are still dousing the house with water as well as keeping an eye on the roofs of the surrounding houses. There are emergency vehicles consisting of fire trucks and police cars everywhere. Fire equipment is scattered around in the street, on driveways, and in the yards. Fire hoses are strung across the street in pairs. There is the constant sound of sirens. The flashing lights from all these vehicles are hypnotizing.

There is so much smoke that everybody can hardly see anything. The smoke drifts across the street and starts to swirl around all of the bystanders. People start coughing, and the police push the crowd even farther away up the street. The scene is haunting.

The families congregate together and are consoling each other. Crying and sobbing can be heard everywhere. As everybody comes to the realization that the kids and Grandpa didn't survive the fire, the discussion turns toward how it happened.

There's some speculation that somebody, perhaps one of the kids was playing with fireworks in the house that resulted in the explosions. But Garrett declares profoundly, "No way. No way at all. The kids were not playing with any fireworks, and there were at least three separate explosions coming from different parts of the house. They happened within seconds of each other. How can that happen? That wasn't caused by any fireworks! There weren't any fireworks in the house anyway!"

Everybody agrees and wonders what could have caused the explosion. One of the firefighters nearby overhears them and says "After we put out the rest of the fire and can see what's left and retrieve the bodies, we'll immediately start an investigation."

Another firefighter speculates that because there were multiple explosions, it suggests perhaps they may have been deliberately set. He comments that the investigation will look into the possibility of arson.

Julie comments, "I wonder if the Arab had anything to do with this? Do you think he may have set a bomb in the house?"

Garrett answers, "I don't know. But he sure is suspicious. I wouldn't be surprised."

Then the firefighter retracts himself. "I shouldn't have said that. I really don't know what caused the fire, and it's too early to say anything. We'll do some work tonight, but we'll be able to start a full-scale investigation tomorrow when it's light. I can't speculate what caused the explosion, but we can't rule out the possibility of arson. It sounds like we may be interested in this Arab person that we keep hearing about. First thing we need to do after we put out the fire though is to recover the bodies."

Chapter 10

After huddling in the dark in the back of the closet with the kids and Crackerjack, I can do nothing but wait for the raging fire to tear through the walls or door any second. I know the closet is near the center of the house and wonder if the firefighters have arrived and if there is any way they can get to us. But I know from the outside, it appears the entire house is on fire, and I'm certain they don't even know we're here and alive and that this closet in this part of the house has yet to be destroyed, but will be within seconds.

It's probably the only part of the house that is not yet consumed by the enraging firestorm, and I know nobody is aware of this but me. But I know all entryways into the house are a blazing inferno and there is no way they can come in to get us. The feeling is gut-wrenching. I know without a shadow of a doubt they can't come in to get us and we're doomed. I close my eyes and pray as hard as I can.

Suddenly, I hear what sounds like another explosion from the basement followed by a rumbling noise. Everything is shaking, and I realize that the floor is giving way. Before I can prepare for it, the floor collapses, and we all fall down about ten feet into the basement floor. All sorts of things are tumbling down all around us, and there are more burning flames. Debris and rubble are everywhere.

The lower-level ceiling, the main level floor, and who knows what else also come crashing down all around us, and I'm thrown down on top of it. The heat is intolerable. As I fall, I hit my head on something, and a massive pain erupts and shoots from my brain down into my body. I can't think and I lose consciousness.

As I'm totally oblivious as to what's going on, I'm curled up lying on part of the upstairs floor that now rests on the concrete basement floor in a corner of the unfinished section of the lower level. A few seconds later, I start to wake up and realize that I had indeed passed out. I slowly try to gather my thoughts, but my brain is very fuzzy, and I can't think. I suddenly remember falling when the floor collapsed. I wonder what caused the explosion and the floor to collapse and wonder if another explosion is coming.

As I gather myself some more and try to wake up further, my thoughts slowly return. I suddenly remember being in the closet and that we'd fallen. However, when we fell, only the closet area collapsed; and as I look up, I can see the flames through the hole in the ceiling and suspect that the remaining floor will collapse any second and fall in flames all around me. I also know that the remaining upper level as well as the roof above us may collapses on top of us any second. As I look up, I realize there are only a few joists, walls, and beams supporting what's left.

As I look around, I realize that the lower level is ablaze all along the exterior wall, obstructing both walk-out doors and all the windows. The steps leading upstairs are on fire. But somehow miraculously, there are no flames in the corner of the room where we fell. There is rubble and debris everywhere.

Similar to upstairs, I'm in the only area of the lower level of the house and basement where there are no major flames except for some very small ones here and there from burning debris that fell around me. Otherwise, there is raging fire and smoke everywhere else, and especially along the windows and doors leading to outside of the lower level. There is no escape here either. Again, I am completely trapped.

Parts of the upstairs floor continue to collapse around me and more comes crashing down against the far wall. There is debris and rubble everywhere. I'm in the corner of the unfinished area of the lower level, and there is about thirty feet separating me from the nearest visible large flames. But everything else outside the area where I fell is on fire and the flames are rapidly spreading toward me through all of the rubble and debris. The heat and smoke are nearly overwhelming. Some of the remaining walls upstairs also crumble and fall to the lower level a short distance away. I know it's only a matter of a minute or perhaps even seconds before what's left of the main floor and maybe even the roof collapses on top of us.

By now, I'm fully conscious, and I remember the kids. I look around, but the smoke is drifting towards me, and I can hardly see anything. They are nowhere. I don't see them anywhere. I call them, and there's no response. I start praying again and continue to yell out to them.

I call for Crackerjack but hear nothing. The only sounds I hear are the roar of the fire, the crackling of the cinders, and the crashing of the upstairs floor and everything that was on it as it continues to fall into flames across the room.

When I look across the lower-level room, there is nothing but flames and burning debris and rubble, and I can't see anything through the smoke. As I try to move, I realize that both the vacuum cleaner and carpet cleaner from the closet are lying on my legs. I had not felt that at first. With all my strength, I'm able to finally push them aside. I then realize I had probably broken at least one of my legs if not both of them in the fall. I can hardly move.

My back is wrenched, and I'm in excruciating pain. I think I'm paralyzed. My arms are so weak I can hardly move them either, especially after moving the two cleaners off my legs. I can hardly move any part of my body at all. I start to vomit, and I'm coughing so hard because of the smoke I can hardly breathe. I am also extremely weak and have a massive headache that hurts so much I can hardly think straight. The heat and smoke now are absolutely unbearable.

The closet door and blanket are beside me on the floor that collapsed from above. I look down at the blanket that was stuffed under the door when I was in the closet and somehow one end has caught fire as small flames appear. The flames are not yet large, but they are growing rapidly. I realize that within less than a minute the entire blanket will be engulfed in flames and will ignite the area where I lie. The heat and smoke are so intense I can't believe I'm still alive. But I know this won't be for long. I am sweating profusely.

I can't move. I call out again to the kids and Crackerjack and hear nothing. I look for the kids all around me. They are gone. There is nothing but fire, smoke, and smoldering debris everywhere. Everything is pretty much obliterated by the smoke. I can't make out anything anywhere. I am prepared to accept the fact that the kids didn't survive the fall and are buried in the rubble and flames somewhere around me. There's no way I can move the rubble to look for them.

If I don't leave right now, I won't make it. I have to get out immediately before it's too late. But then I realize even if I could get up, there's no way out. I can hardly see anything. My thoughts intensify as I know I must try to save myself and get out of the basement and make my way outside immediately. But I can't. I can't move. I can't even move the blanket. I have no feelings in either of my legs. In fact, I can hardly move any part of my body at all.

But that doesn't matter anyway. There's no escape. The entire perimeter of the lower level is growing into a roaring fire, and there is no way out anywhere. Every exit is blocked by flames, which now totally surround me. I am completely trapped by the raging inferno.

I yell out as loud as I can one last time for the kids and hear nothing. I yell out one final time for Crackerjack and hear nothing. The realization that they are gone for good is so devastating that I myself nearly lose any desire to live anymore. I try to move my body one last time, but I'm completely immobile. I'm paralyzed from the fall. I can't move a single part of my body. The small flames at the bottom of the blanket are getting larger and are starting to spread upward.

I start to cry and close my eyes. This is it. I know within seconds I'll be consumed by the fire. And the kids have probably already died from the fall or burned to death somewhere around me underneath all the rubble and debris. I can't even see them. I tried my hardest. I had faith. But I failed. I am trapped by growing flames that surround me and that encroach toward me, and I can't move any part of my body because I'm paralyzed. I now close my eyes and pray so hard that I pass out and lose consciousness as the flames spread up the blanket toward me and around me faster and faster.

Chapter 11

As things quiet down somewhat and people start to disperse after coming to the conclusion that Alex and the kids perished in the fire, suddenly, a bloodcurdling scream is heard in the crowd. Then another scream and another are heard. People are pointing at the smoke swirling from down the side of the house. "What is that?" People are shouting, "What is it? What in the world is that? What is it?"

Julie and Alana look up at where everybody is pointing, and they think they see a ghost. It's an obscure white object that is fading in and out of the smoke from the side of the house. It's hard to see because now it's dark and the smoke is hiding it, but it's definitely there. And it's getting larger as if it's moving toward them out of the smoke. It's on the side of the house, but it's too far away to see it clearly.

Julie, having realized that she just lost her kids and her father in the fire, is quite frightened and lets out a bloodcurdling scream louder than the one before. Being an emotional train wreck, she's convinced it's a ghost coming out of the darkness and smoke from the fire.

In the midst of the smoke, what looks like an apparition appears and then disappears to the ground again. It then reappears and again drops to the ground, out of sight once again. It's difficult for everybody to see it because they are too far away to see it closely in the dark and with the smoke, but it definitely exists. Everybody can see it. But what is it? What a haunting sight this is.

Then Garrett yells out, "That couldn't be Alex, could it? No way. Absolutely no way at all it can be him. There's no way he could have survived in there. But it looks like some sheets or something blowing around. That's not Alex! And it's not the kids either. I wish it was, but it's not. But I'm not sure what it is."

Alana stares at it with some wavering hope and then cries out, "It's not him. I wish it was too, but it's not. When Alex went in the house, he had wrapped himself in a blanket. Whatever this is, it's not the blanket. It looks more like some sheets blowing around in the wind."

The group's hope that it just might be Alex quickly vanishes. But everybody continues to wonder, "What is it?"

Somebody comments that it looks like a moving tent that is being blown over and then rising up again. "It's a ghost. It's an apparition arising out of the smoke." Everybody becomes extremely apprehensive as it gets closer. Or perhaps it's only some large debris blowing around on the ground in the breeze? It's hard to see in the smoke and it's dark.

Julie then cries out, "Those are the sheets that I just brought over today! I recognize the pattern. I know those are the sheets because I put them in the sink in the basement to soak to get some stains out. I did this after I showed them to Mom, but I forgot about them. They're definitely my sheets! What's going on? Why are they blowing around like that? They were in the sink downstairs!"

Then the smoke temporary lifts. The sheets stop moving and fall to the ground on the side of the house just down from the neighbor's front yard. The pile of sheets lies on the ground and now is still. Everybody is perplexed. There looks like there may be something underneath the sheets. Then the sheets wiggle a little. Unbelievably, out crawls Lizzy. She gets up and runs toward the crowd up the street coughing and screaming, "Mommy, Mommy, Daddy, Daddy." Julie and Garrett are absolutely beside themselves.

They both break through the barricade and run up to Lizzy, who flies into Julie's arms. They can't believe what's happening. They are totally stunned. Lizzy is coughing from the smoke.

They both look at the pile of sheets lying on the ground and out crawls Mikey. He also gets up and runs to the crowd coughing and is picked up by Garrett. Garrett and Julie are trembling and are incredibly overjoyed.

Julie cannot believe what just happened, and she is shaking with emotion. She frantically asks Lizzy and Mikey what happened. They're both still coughing, trying to breathe, but Mikey says a few words that sound like, "Grandpa carried us."

Lizzy then starts crying even more while still coughing and yells out, "Emily, Crackerjack, Emily, Crackerjack, Emily, Crackerjack."

Mikey then says, "Grandpa didn't carry Emily out. Only us."

Lizzy continues ranting until Julie shouts, "What are you saying?"

Lizzy is crying and continues to blurt out between her coughs "Emily, Crackerjack, Emily, Crackerjack."

Mikey again reiterates, "Grandpa didn't carry Emily out. He only carried us out."

Julie and Garrett understand this to mean that Emily and Crackerjack are still in the house and didn't make it out alive. They figure that Alex couldn't find them or that they didn't survive or that he couldn't carry them and had to leave them inside. They become panic-stricken at the thought of this.

They look at the pile of sheets lying on the ground and realize that it is still shaking a little. Garrett surmises, "That must be Alex, right?" Julie and Garrett pass off Lizzy and Mikey into the arms of Sonja and Alana and run toward the pile of sheets. They are still some distance away from it when out pops what appears to be Crackerjack, but if it's him, he looks different. He's all white with some spots and looks much larger. It's difficult to see him from the distance and in the dark.

But they know its Crackerjack because they can see his tail upright fanning the air. He's stumbling, appears dazed, and is panting like crazy. He takes a few steps, but then he's obscured by the blowing smoke again. Crackerjack immediately disappears back into the smoke blowing from the house. They lose sight of him.

Garrett reaches the pile of sheets and throws them off. They are soaking wet but are giving off steam from the heat. There lying on the ground underneath a single sheet is Alex. He has collapsed, is stretched out on his back, and is unconscious. His clothing has been burned, and his shoes are black and are smoldering.

Julie is looking desperately for Emily, but she is not anywhere to be found. Alex doesn't have her, and she's not in the sheet that covered Alex. She's not there. She's not anywhere. She assumes the worst and surmises that Emily didn't survive. She figures that even if Alex had found her, he had to leave her behind because he couldn't carry all three of them. Her emotions alternate between being ecstatic that at least Lizzy and Mikey were rescued but horrified that Emily didn't make it.

She's an emotional wreck and starts to cry thinking about Emily and what happened to her. Garrett comforts her. She leans over and says, "Daddy, where's Emily? You couldn't carry her too, right?" Alex lies on the ground still with his eyes closed and doesn't respond. He is motionless. Emily is simply nowhere to be found.

Garrett then calls for Crackerjack, and he appears out of the smoke and stumbles into plain sight. Crackerjack is wrapped in a sheet, which is also soaking wet and giving off steam. He's wearing socks over his paws that are stretched up his legs. They're wet but charred at the bottom. It looks like he was injured and is all bandaged up. What a sight. "What on Earth happened to you, boy?" Garrett says to him.

Crackerjack walks up to Garrett panting and wheezing and starts wagging his tail furiously. Garrett assumes that Alex wrapped him in the sheet and put the socks on his paws to protect him from the fire when they escaped.

Garrett then looks at Crackerjack more closely and yells at Julie. "Julie, look at this! Look at this! Can you believe it? You're not going to believe this! You're not going to believe this at all!"

There nestled on Crackerjack's back underneath the sheet wrapped around him and tied with a rope around his belly is Emily. She is softly crying, but she's very much alive. "Crackerjack carried her out! Alex must have covered her with the sheet and tied it around Crackerjack with the rope, and he carried her out on his back! I can't believe this!"

Garrett unties the rope around Crackerjack, carefully removes the sheet, and takes Emily in his arms. He then gives her to Julie.

Julie is absolutely overwhelmed by emotion and can't believe it at all. She is absolutely ecstatic and nearly speechless. "I can't believe my dad did this. It was impossible, but he did it!"

She then realizes that during all the commotion that they have forgotten about Alex. She then looks at Alex, and there is Crackerjack licking his face. She suddenly yells out for help. "Are there any paramedics? Can anybody help? Please help me! Help! My dad! My dad! Somebody help him!"

Alana, who is a nurse, comes over and does a quick evaluation of Alex. She immediately states that he is in critical condition and he needs to be taken to a hospital right away. She knows that Alex is not going to make it. Julie tries to take his vitals and wonders whether he's even alive.

Suddenly, Alex barely opens his eyes briefly and looks at Sonja, who by now has run up to be at his side. She smiles at him, and he tries to smile back. He says softly, "We did it. We did it." He then looks up at the sky, closes his eyes, takes what appears to be his last breath, and loses consciousness. He lies there motionless.

Alana asks, "Who is 'we'? I saw him go into the house by himself. What does he mean by 'we'?"

Within seconds out of nowhere, a person dressed in white pants and a white shirt arrives. He says nothing, but he appears to be a paramedic, perhaps with the fire department. He huddles over Alex and begins attending to him, and he motions for everybody to stand back.

Julie looks around for the ambulance and calls out for a stretcher. But, there is no ambulance anywhere. "Where is the ambulance?" she yells out. "We need an ambulance now! I can't believe there's no ambulance here! How come ambulances didn't come when the fire trucks and police cars came? Ambulances should have been here a long time ago!" Looking at the firefighters, she screams at them at the top of her lungs, "Why haven't you called an ambulance by now?"

She asks the paramedic, but he doesn't answer and he continues to motion everybody away. "Where is it? Somebody call an ambulance now! We need to get him to a hospital now! Now!"

Julie asks the paramedic, "Is he going to be okay?" The paramedic doesn't say anything but slowly moves his head from side to side as if he's saying no. Alana knows from her nursing skills that Alex is on his deathbed and he's not going to make it, but she doesn't want to alarm anybody.

As they stand there observing the paramedic and looking for the ambulance, another minor explosion is heard coming from the remaining rubble that is still on fire. A small fireball of debris comes streaming at them, falling only a few feet away. Everybody quickly moves away. Garrett, Julie, and Alana, who are all huddled together, run across the street to avoid the falling debris. Then Sonja reluctantly follows. Out of nowhere appears Officer Musty. "I'm available. Since there's no ambulance, I can volunteer to take Alex to the hospital in my police car. Is that okay?"

He no sooner says this than Crackerjack appears and starts barking. Garrett runs over and tries to calm down Crackerjack and wonders why he's barking. He never barks. Then Crackerjack does something he's never done before. He grabs the pants at the ankle of Officer Musty and starts shaking and tearing them.

Crackerjack starts growling and is shaking Officer Musty's pant legs furiously. Office Musty makes some smart-ass comment that Crackerjack has picked a bad time to want to play as he tries to kick him away. But Garrett knows that Crackerjack is not playing this time, but he can't figure out what's gotten into him.

Other police officers arrive and help kick Crackerjack away and free Officer Musty from the attack. Crackerjack lets go and runs off. Garrett apologizes profusely for his dog's behavior and attributes it to him being afraid of the uniform and all the commotion.

Surprisingly, Officer Musty takes it in stride. "That's okay. I can understand the dog's behavior considering what's going on. No problem. I'll make friends with him yet, trust me."

The police officers tell Garrett and the others to retreat behind the barricade and not to bother the paramedic. He needs room.

But while Crackerjack was attacking Officer Musty, an ambulance appeared out of nowhere, negotiated its way through the emergency vehicles, and pulled up on the lawn next to Alex. After this commotion ended and everybody turned to look back at Alex, they see somebody dressed in white putting him in the back of the ambulance. Being focused on Crackerjack and Officer Musty, they totally missed this.

Sonja cries out repeatedly, "I want to go with you," as she attempts to run toward the ambulance. But she is ushered back and restrained by the police who have reassembled behind the barricade. "Where are you are taking him?" she yells out.

Nobody answers. Sonja desperately wants to go in the ambulance with Alex, but she is restrained by the police who are trying once again to calm down the crowd of onlookers and push them farther away.

Within seconds, the ambulance takes off but without any sirens or emergency lights flashing. The ambulance drives around all the fire trucks and police cars and accelerates out of sight at the top of the street.

Julie, Garrett, and Sonja look at each other in astonishment. Things happened so fast. The ambulance appeared and disappeared in what seemed to be only seconds.

Sonja cries out, "We need to go to the hospital. I want to see my Alex."

Garrett in a hurry states, "We can take you. Julie, please round up the kids and put them in the car. I moved it up the street a little while ago. We'll be there shortly."

Sonja asks, "Which hospital did they take him to?"

Garrett says, "I don't know."

Sonja then asks some of the policemen to which hospital the ambulance went. They don't know either. She then asks some of the fire fighters, and they also don't know. Sonja then remarks that there are two hospitals close by. One is north and the other is south. One of the policemen asks what color was the ambulance.

Garrett says, "White."

The policeman looks at Garrett in disbelief. "What?"

Garrett again remarks "White. It was all white."

The policeman then says that the ambulance district used by the north hospital uses a red ambulance and that the ambulance district used by the south hospital uses a mostly red and white ambulance.

Garrett reiterates, "It was all white. There was no red on the ambulance. Only its lights were red, and they weren't even turned on."

The policeman asks, "Are you sure?"

"I am absolutely sure. It was all white. No red on it at all." Sonja and Alana agree and confirm this.

The policeman then calls over the commanding officer and the fire department chief, and they discuss the matter. He asks who called the ambulance. They both say that nobody had called the ambulance. They were getting ready to because it had not arrived yet from the initial dispatch but had not done so yet. They ask Officer Musty. He knows nothing. "I'm not aware that anybody uses an all-white ambulance around here either. I have no idea where the ambulance came from and where it went."

Garrett then complains and asks why an ambulance wasn't called as soon as they arrived with all the other emergency vehicles. The commanding officer and the fire department chief look at each like it is the other's fault. But the chief states that the ambulance should have been automatically dispatched when the original call came in. Garrett looks at both of them with disgust. Surely the dispatch was notified and should have contacted the ambulance district.

Sonja asks Julie and Alana whether the kids need to go to the hospital because they suffered from some smoke inhalation. "Do we need more ambulances for them too?"

But Alana states that she had looked at all of them and they seem all right and have stopped coughing. "We'll monitor them and we can take them in later ourselves if needed, but they all seem to be doing okay now."

They check with all the other emergency personnel on site, and nobody knows anything about the ambulance that took Alex away. Nobody called any ambulance. They all say that they are not aware of any all-white ambulance that they know of anywhere within a hundred miles.

The commanding officer then asks everyone to describe the paramedic. Everybody states that he was dressed all in white, but nobody was able to get a look at his face. For some reason, nobody bothered to look at him that closely. It was dark. There was a lot of smoke. He never said anything. Nobody could describe what he looked like, and nobody could identify him. Everything happened so fast.

Everybody is completely dumbfounded. Where is Alex? Where did the ambulance come from? Who called it? Who was the paramedic? Where is he? Where did the ambulance take Alex? Is he alive? What in the world is going on?

Andrew, who has been missing from much of the action, reappears with his kids. Alana greets him, and they discuss the status of things and note that Matthew, Daniel, and Hannah are tired. It's way past their bedtime, and they're having a hard time standing up. Alana gives Garrett a hug and tells him to pass his hug on to Julie. She then surmises it's best that they leave and get their kids to bed. There is nothing they can do. "Please let me know if you hear anything about Alex. Call me anytime tonight. I'll say a prayer and we'll be in touch first thing in the morning if I don't hear from you," she says.

In the meantime, the news media, especially the local TV networks, are trying to get to Garrett, Julie, and Sonja to get interviews for their nightly news. Garrett tells them politely that they have no comment and do not want to be interviewed right now. They're in a hurry and do not want to be bothered.

The media persists and tell Garrett that the nightly news will be coming on very soon and they want live interviews. Garrett again tells them to leave and that they will not be interviewed tonight. Soon, they are arguing with each other. The police break up the altercation, and the media retreats for a bit.

After things start to settle down and after everybody finishes answering questions by the fire department and police department and doing a little related paperwork, Julie, Garrett, Lizzy, Mikey, Emily, and Sonja all pile into Julie's SUV and leave as well. It now is late. The smoke is starting to clear as they drive away. The firefighters are finishing up their work.

As they drive up the street, the light from a full moon shines in the car, and everything is quiet. So quiet that it's like nothing ever happened. But everybody knows otherwise. As they get to the top of the street, Garrett makes a comment that the Arab and the old white van are gone.

He continues, "Before and during the fire, I noticed the van was there, but the Arab, for some reason, was not in it. But I noticed that the Arab returned to the van when Alex emerged from the fire. But the next time I looked when the ambulance arrived, the old white van had left. Now both are gone. Interesting."

Everybody looks at each other and silently wonder about this. Did the Arab have something to do with the explosions and fire? Did the Arab perhaps kidnap Alex or his body? If so, what does he want with him? Or does Alex have something that the Arab wants?

They decide to drive to the north hospital and arrive shortly. Garrett and Sonja enter the emergency room door and inquire if an ambulance arrived with Alex. They then ask if an ambulance arrived with anyone matching Alex's description. They are told that no ambulance has arrived recently and certainly none with Alex. They then check with admissions, and after hassling about patient confidentiality and privacy rights, they learn that Alex was not admitted. He is not at the north hospital.

They then drive to the south hospital and go through the same routine. No ambulance has arrived at the south hospital recently either. They also check with the admissions desk, and after going through the same questions, they learn that Alex is not there either. They inquire about who uses an all-white ambulance, and they are told that nobody uses an all-white ambulance that they know of. Perhaps the nearest ambulance district that might use such an ambulance is more than a hundred miles away.

They ask where the ambulance may have taken Alex. Nobody knows. They call the ambulance dispatch. The ambulance dispatch tells them they have not recently dispatched any of their ambulances. Being desperate, they call several urgent-care facilities in the area. They are told by each urgent-care facility that ambulances normally don't bring patients to these facilities and no ambulance has arrived at any of them. They don't know any ambulance district that uses an all-white ambulance.

They then decide to go to Garrett and Julie's house and make some more calls. The kids need to go to bed anyway since it's so late. They naturally invite Sonja to stay with them since she has no other place to go.

On the way home, they realize that they're being followed, not by one vehicle but by several vehicles. The headlights of the vehicles behind them are on high beam and light up inside of the car, especially as they make each turn behind them. As they turn into their driveway and enter their garage, all the other vehicles either swing in their driveway or come to a screeching halt in front of their house.

As Garrett, Julie, and Sonja get out of the SUV and unbuckle the children who all fell sound asleep while driving home, about a dozen people quickly descend upon them before they can close the garage door. It's the TV and news media. Bright lights now light up their garage, and even brighter lights are shown in Julie's and Garrett's faces. Almost immediately, there are cameras aimed at them as the cameramen compete to see who can get the closest to Garrett, Julie, and Sonja.

Microphones are thrust in front of them. The reporters start firing off questions. "What caused the explosion and fire? Where is Alex? Do they know where the ambulance went? Was he alive when the ambulance left the scene? What was it like to think your children were dead and then find out they are alive? Is what Alex did a miracle? Do they think the house was deliberately set on fire, and if so, by whom? And why? What is this story that's going around about a suspicious Arab? Did the Arab set the explosions? Did the Arab kidnap Alex or his body? What does the family think?"

Garrett says politely but firmly, "Please get out of our garage. We don't know anything and have no comment. We don't want to be interviewed right now."

But they continue relentlessly. "Please, everybody, leave! We will not be interviewed tonight!"

But they're unyielding and continue as if Garrett said nothing.

Garrett then puts his palm up, looks straight into the cameras, and sarcastically states "For all you people watching this on your TV, you should know that your news reporters have invaded our home and have no sympathy or understanding of what we are going through. Instead of waiting until later tomorrow, they insist on invading our privacy late tonight. They are ruthless and you should be ashamed of their insensitivity. You can honor our wishes by boycotting this station."

Not wanting any of this to air on their stations, all the cameramen and reporters retreat to the front yard and their vehicles. Garrett quickly closes the garage door, and the family enters the house. Inside, they ask themselves the exact same questions that the reporters asked. But there are no answers. But most importantly, they want to know, is Alex still alive? Where is he? Was he abducted? If so, who took him, and why?

Chapter 12

I find myself lying on the ground fading in and out of a semi-state of consciousness. But I realize that I'm outside and even though I can still smell the smoke, I catch whiffs of fresh summer air. My thoughts relive what I just experienced. Everything now is pretty much a blur. What I last remember is that I woke up lying on top of the rubble and debris that fell onto the basement floor after praying like I never have before. A spirit came over me and I suddenly had a burst of adrenaline and regained some strength. I try to remember more of what happened next but it's difficult.

I recall that I'm lying in the only area of the lower level where there are no flames except for some small ones at the bottom of the blanket, but the entire outside wall of the house is ablaze and that fire and smoke are rapidly spreading toward me. Smoke is blowing everywhere. There seems to be no escape and apparently, there is no way out even if I could manage to get up. I realize instantly that the flames at the bottom of the blanket are crawling upward and are spreading rapidly.

I slowly regain consciousness, and somehow enough strength returns that I'm able to reach down and grab the burning blanket and toss it away from me. Next to me is the closet door that is precariously balancing sideways in such a way that it would smash anything below it if it were to fall. With all my remaining strength, I push the door over and shove it aside. Underneath the door is a pile of jackets, coats, and pillows from the closet.

I slowly push aside the jackets and coats, and I again cannot believe my eyes. Underneath them are Mikey, Lizzy, and Emily! And underneath them are Crackerjack and more pillows from the closet that apparently cushioned them when they fell. Unbelievable! But they are not responsive at all. They are not even moving. I yell at them and shake them continuously for what seems like eternity.

In the meantime, I notice there's something directly behind and above me that's not on fire, and I grab it to try to pull myself up. I'm finally able to stand up. My legs are trembling and weak. I realize that it's the sink in the unfinished part of the basement that I pulled myself up on. It's full of water. I look in the sink and discover two sheets and four large mismatched socks that were mixed up with the sheets. I then remember that Julie took the sheets down here to soak earlier to try to get some stains out. I suppose that the socks were mixed in with the sheets and perhaps she didn't know it.

I again yell at and shake the kids and they slowly start to respond. I pull them off Crackerjack, and he starts to whimper. The kids now are lying on the rubble next to him, and he slowly starts to respond as well and he stands up. I take the wet socks out of the sink and think about putting them on the kids' feet but realize that the socks are way too big.

But I know that there's no way they're going to walk anyway even if I can get them up. They're not only barefoot, they're also scared of the flames and smoke. If they're going to get out alive, I am going to have to carry them. I can't drag them out on the blanket because it's now burnt to a crisp. It wouldn't drag anyway because of all of the rubble and debris everywhere.

Lizzy and Mikey start to wake up more, and it immediately becomes clear that they won't get up and leave as long as they can see any flames or smoke anywhere. Their faces are buried downward against the rubble, and they won't look up. I try to pick them up, but they kick and scream because they see fire and can sense the smoke, and they're terrified. I tell them to keep their eyes closed but that doesn't help. They aren't going to cooperate as long as they know they can see any flames or smoke if they open their eyes. I need to think of something very quickly.

So I very quickly put the socks on Crackerjack's paws and pull them up his legs. By some sort of miracle, they stay up and don't fall down. Perhaps this will help him walk across any hot cinders. He now is standing there and staring at me. "What in the world are you doing to me?" He looks at me with his big brown eyes. What a sight to see him like that. He's whimpering, but his tail is going a mile a minute because he is so happy to see me.

I then think I can cut a hole in the middle of one of the sheets so I can poke my head through it and then let the sheet hang down off my shoulders where I can wrap it around me to form a protective tent of sorts, similar to the wet blanket I used upstairs. Because they're wet, similar to the wet blanket, this hopefully may offer some protection from the flames; but more importantly, the kids may cooperate if I can carry them inside of it so they can't see the flames and smoke.

But how in the world am I going to carry all three of the kids? I failed to remember that I could hardly move my legs. There's no way I can carry all of them. I think I can carry one. I might be able to carry two, but certainly not three. I certainly can't carry all three of them while climbing over all the rubble and dealing with the flames on the other side of the room. There's absolutely no possible way I would be able to do this. Will I need to leave one of them behind? Which one?

I spot about six feet of small diameter rope coiled up behind the sink and a lightbulb comes on. I quickly take the other sheet out of the sink, lay Emily on top of Crackerjack's back and as fast as I can wrap the sheet around Emily to cover her and then wrap the rest of the sheet around his belly. Then I secure Emily and the sheet by using the rope to wrap it around Crackerjack's back and belly.

She slides underneath his belly, but after I rearrange her and the sheet and tighten the rope, she is pretty much good to go. She'll simply ride Crackerjack like a horse. By now, Crackerjack is wagging his tail intensely, and he's looking at me as if knows exactly what his job is going to be.

Lizzy and Mikey by now are fully responding and are starting to cry, "Grandpa, Grandpa! No fire, no fire!"

I ask them if they're hurt. In muffled voices, Lizzy says, "Don't know," and Mikey says, "I don't think so." I ask them if their legs are okay. Neither responds. I then ask them if they can walk, and Mikey says, "Grandpa, I don't want to." Lizzy says, "Me too." Their faces are still buried, and they refuse to look up or even try to stand up. I look up and am horrified to see what remains of the ceiling is about to give way and would send the inferno upstairs on top of us.

I pull the other sheet over me, poke my head through the hole I cut out, and pick up Lizzy and Mikey, one in each arm underneath the rest of the wet sheet, and look for a way out. Crackerjack is right by my feet carrying Emily on his back, trying to stay under the sheet as it drags in the rubble, but otherwise is right beside me. I tell the kids they can't see because they're under the sheet but to try to keep their eyes closed anyway.

Which way do I go? I can't go anywhere. There is nothing but flames in every direction. Both doors and all the windows are blocked by what now is nearly a raging inferno of fire. We're trapped. The only thing I can think of is to negotiate my way to the wall of flames and try to climb through it and the open window as fast as I can. I know that would be pure suicide, but that's my only option. If I wait another minute, we will be consumed by fire here anyway if the smoke doesn't kill us first. I wonder how fast a person can catch on fire by going straight through it.

I close my eyes and pray with all of my heart and soul as hard as I can. When I open my eyes, I can't believe what I see. The flames and smoke are rolled back on each side into separate walls of fire, and the flames in the middle die off, allowing me a pathway to the blown-out atrium window where we can climb out. We will need to climb over a lot of rubble and debris, but it looks doable.

I can't believe the fire has been rolled back and partially extinguished to create a pathway for me like this! And the smoke has subsided too! I immediately think of Moses parting the Red Sea as this is exactly what is happening now. The pathway created is littered with debris, some burning here and there, but I can make my way through as long as the fire doesn't start up again. I'll have to chance it. I'll need to move quickly, and hope I have enough strength. I hope my legs don't buckle.

I can't believe that I have regained some strength in my legs and can somewhat walk, but the pain in them is excruciating. I'm sure they're both broken. I sense a spirit above looking down on me through the smoke. I know the spirit is providing me strength and helping me. How else would the fire and smoke subside like that to create a flame-free pathway like that? How else would I be able to walk with what I think are two broken legs? How else could I move at all after being paralyzed from the fall?

I can't believe that the rubble I'm climbing over is not that hot. There was a fire here just a minute ago. How can what I'm walking on not be burning hot? There should at least be burning embers and cinders everywhere that would burn my shoes. But there aren't.

But then I think when the Red Sea was parted by Moses raising his staff, the Israelites walked on dry ground and crossed it. One would similarly think the ground would have been muddy and they would have sunk in it in the pathway created for them after the sea was rolled back. But the ground they walked on was dry. Similarly, here, why isn't the rubble and debris still burning hot on my feet? But they aren't. I can't help but think of this analogy. I suppose if the ground can be dry and free from water and mud in the Red Sea bed, then the debris once on fire here can be free from burning embers and cinders as well. This is truly a similar miracle happening right before my eyes. I pray again.

I then remember being able to escape through the window opening carrying Lizzy in one arm and Mikey in my other arm underneath the sheet, and with Crackerjack carrying Emily moving in unison right beside me underneath the sheet. I remember as we exited the window I turned back to look at the pathway from where we came and seeing the walls of fire that were rolled back collapsing and completely filling in the path with fire and smoke again. I got out just in time!

I can't believe that I just walked through that and there was no fire in the pathway created for me but now the pathway is ablaze again. Surely I had some divine help with this. A vision of Moses and the parting of the Red Sea remain in my mind as we climb outside and I stumble up the hill on the side of the house.

I last remember stumbling in the back yard, falling down, and getting up repeatedly trying to walk us up the hill away from the side of the house. I remember all of us constantly coughing and trying to breathe with all the smoke around us. I remember my legs feeling like they were on fire. I then remember getting far enough away from the house, falling one final time to the ground, setting Lizzy and Mikey down on the ground and telling them that we're outside now. I ask them if they can walk and the both say, "Yes." I then tell them to crawl out from underneath the sheet and run to their Mommy and Daddy as I lift the sheet for them to see.

Now it's all over. I'm lying there and feel Lizzy, Mikey, and Crackerjack leave from underneath the sheet. I'm all alone. I pray again. I can't believe how I was able to do this. My legs were gone but somehow came back.

I then sense that the spirit that was with me again was with me the entire time. I realize that every time I prayed, the sense of the spirit got stronger and something good happened. I don't know if it was Jesus or an angel or God Himself, but whatever it was it was definitely there. If it were not for the spirit and an incredible injection of adrenaline, we wouldn't have made it. I lie there and pray and again thank Jesus for helping me.

I apparently pass out again, but then find myself able to briefly open my eyes. I see Sonja. I remember saying something to her and then closing my eyes again for the last time.

I then sense somebody hovering over me and then carrying me into an ambulance. Everything now is becoming more of a blur, and I am finding it very difficult to think of anything. My mind goes blank. My eyes are closed, and I can't open them.

I cannot feel anything. However, suddenly I start to gain a very strange and unusual sense of everything. What a strange feeling this is. I feel myself floating and all of the excruciating pain I had is gone. Although my eyes are closed, I can see everything. It is as if I am hovering above everybody and can see everything below. I can see Sonja, Julie, Alana, Garrett, and Andrew among the neighbors. I can see all the kids. I can see the firefighters and the police. And I can see the ambulance with me inside leaving the scene. I am floating above them and looking down on everything that is happening below.

But at the same time, I sense myself floating higher and higher; and even though it's dark outside, I find myself floating through brightly lit clouds. I sense that I'm leaving my body, but I'm conscious of my mind merging with my soul. It's like I'm leaving this world and going to another. I pretty much know what's happening to me. The floating sensation goes on for several minutes. My ability to see what's going on below me gradually diminishes. Soon, I can't see it anymore.

As I float higher through the clouds, they change to different colors. It's dark, but the sun is shining on the clouds and it's producing the most brilliant colors of the rainbow I can imagine. The vivid contrast of the sun shining on the clouds and the colors against the dark of night is an incredible sight. The beauty is breathtaking. Then the most magnificent music within these clouds can be heard. The feeling of all this is indescribable.

But behind the clouds appear some dark clouds and I see lightning and can hear rumbles of thunder in them off in the distance. Soon, the rumbles of thunder gradually become louder and the lightning bolts become brighter. After a few more minutes, the dark clouds approach the bright clouds and the thunder becomes deafening cracking whips, and the lightning bolts are like strobe lights all around me.

Now, all the brightly lit clouds, the magnificent colors, the dark clouds and the lightning are intermingled with each other. The music and the thunder are competing with each other. I am in a state of confusion, and things get very blurry. It's becoming more difficult for me to think straight.

All the clouds start to swirl around. I'm floating higher and higher and moving faster and faster. I go through and then above all of these clouds and sense a feeling of both wonderment and fear. Then everything gets very quiet as I continue my upward journey. I then enter a void of oblivion as the clouds, colors, and lightning all dissipate below me. The music and thunder also dissolve and gradually disappear. I'm now in a vacuum. There is no light and no dark. There are no sounds. I'm in a space-time continuum of pure nothingness.

I can see a very faint light far off in the distance, and it looks like I am headed in that direction, but I have no control of what's going on or where I'm going. But I sense that I am being accompanied by a spirit. It's the same spirit who was with me in the fire.

"What's happening to me?" I think I know. Although I still have a feeling of utmost peace I gradually develop a sense of increasing fear at the same time. I soon become frightened and then I'm terrified. I know I've died, but where am I going? I sure would like to know.

Chapter 13

It's now going on about 10:00 PM. Garrett and Julie quickly put the kids to bed, which was easy because they all fell asleep in the car. Julie prepares their spare bedroom downstairs for Sonja and they all sit down in the great room. Everyone is still in a state of shock and distress following the events of the evening. Garrett turns on the TV as the 10:00 PM news is about to come on. Garrett and Sonja get on their smart phones and begin making more phone calls to try to locate Alex. Even though they visited the hospitals, they call them anyway. They call the police station. They call the ambulance district dispatches again. They call anybody they can think of.

Their calls to the two local hospitals reveal nothing new. Neither of them have any record of any ambulance arriving with anyone matching the description of Alex. They develop a list of all hospitals and urgent care centers in the entire county and in the city and they methodically call each and every one. Not a single hospital or emergency center has any record whatsoever of any ambulance arriving that evening with Alex. He is nowhere to be found anywhere.

In the meantime, the local news comes on and the featured story is "Grandpa saves kids but disappears! Stay tuned."

The local news reports on the house explosion, Alex saving the kids, and the abduction of Alex. The reporter says that he regrets not being able to provide live interviews with the family but hopes to have this tomorrow.

Garrett, Julie, and Sonja relive the events of the evening as they are played out by the news reporters and cameras that were on the scene at Alex and Sonja's house. The story is brief and ends by the reporter stating that if anybody knows the whereabouts of Alex Fisheramen, to report it to the local police immediately.

Garrett then states, "It's been almost eight hours since we've heard anything about the terrorists. I wonder what has developed since then. There must be new developments because things were happening so fast earlier today."

After a brief commercial, the news returns and the anchorman states that the rest of the news broadcast will be dedicated to the status of the terrorist activities and threats because of the magnitude of the situation. He goes on to say that this afternoon and evening, some significant developments have taken place. He says to stay tuned after the news for an extended news program with additional coverage and a round-table discussion on the crisis.

Julie changes channels and every network and some of the non-network stations are reporting the news focused on the threats made by the terrorists. She quickly changes the channel back as the reporter begins:

"In national and global news we have some critical updates on the activities and threats by the Islamic terrorists. The terrorists who have threatened the United States and other countries of the Western world are members of a separate sect affiliated with ISIS and who were thought to have previous ties with Al Qaeda. The sect is very well organized and well-funded, and up until now has been unknown and operating secretly for years. Certain members of the sect now are known to have been secretly planning major terrorist activities in the Western World ever since 9/11. The group that has infiltrated the United States is being referred to as ISA, the Islamic State of America.

"However, as a result of the magnitude and validity of the threats, the matter now has turned into a global crisis. The president of the United States has declared a state of national emergency. More on this later. In summary, here is what has transpired regarding the threats made against the United States.

"First, the terrorists have announced that they have planted nuclear bombs and other bombs at locations in the United States and within a few days they will reveal where some of the bombs are located. They claim that all of the bombs are tamper proof and cannot be disabled or moved. Any attempts to disable or move them will result in immediate detonation. They claim they can detonate these bombs remotely and plan to do so at midnight in three days after the location of the first bombs are revealed.

"They claim that the strategic location of one of the nuclear devices is so unique that it alone could render all of the United States being uninhabitable for years and possibly result in a global catastrophe as well.

"The terrorists have stated that they want to wait the three days and then detonate all the bombs at the same time instead of detonating them now because they want the people of the United States to have some time to think about their fate. But more importantly, the destruction of America by exploding the bombs all at once at the same time will achieve the highest glory to Allah.

"Any retaliation including any further air strikes against ISIS forces or on any Muslim communities in the Middle East or anywhere will result in immediate detonation of all bombs without delay.

"They claim that no less than twenty major US cities will be wiped off the face of the Earth, and there will be extensive collateral damage. Additionally, transportation, utility, and other critical infrastructure such as major bridges, electrical energy distribution, and water supply systems will be destroyed. The estimate of the population of the twenty largest cities including their surrounding metropolitan areas exceeds one hundred million people.

"They also claim they have clinically reproduced an extremely deadly and highly contagious disease they will spread across America. They claim they already have application systems in place in many densely-populated areas in various parts of the United States ready for release. They claim they have shipped samples of the deadly disease to the CDC in Atlanta to be verified.

"The CDC has stated the disease could be either a virus, bacteria, or spore borne illness but they will not know what it is until they receive the samples and can test them. Original speculation was that it may be Ebola because of the recent Ebola outbreak in northern Africa where many terrorists live and train. However, the terrorists have strongly hinted that it's both air borne and water borne which Ebola is not, and that it's thousands of times more deadly and contagious.

"However, testing may take days or weeks. Both the CDC and the WHO have stated that if the disease is airborne, the terrorists could easily distribute it, for example by aerosol application in air duct systems in buildings anywhere. If it can be spread by water, many major water supply systems would be vulnerable. It's possible that such a disease could take the lives of millions of people in a matter of days and then escalate more after that.

"The terrorists claim that the US government and military are incompetent, and there is absolutely nothing that they can do to prevent either the bombs from being detonated or the spread of the disease throughout the country. The US missile defense system will not work against these bombs. The bombs are already here. The terrorists state they will actually prove this and show how vulnerable the United States is.

"The terrorists are currently in the process of hacking into our cyber and communication networks including the Internet and network broadcasting systems. Some satellite and cable communications have already been compromised. In some instances, the terrorists have already taken control and have begun to broadcast their own programming in some areas. It's a full-scale cyber-attack.

"Do not be surprised to see an unauthorized broadcast from them in the near future on this station or on other stations. If you do, please note that it would be a hijacking of the station's broadcasting system and would be an illicit unsanctioned event and is not approved or endorsed by the media station or the United States government.

"The terrorists have announced that they have the capability of disrupting the distribution of electrical energy by hacking into the electric grid in various sections of the US. However, this has not yet been confirmed.

"The terrorists have declared that IF any other country announces support for the United States then they will immediately be subject to the same wrath that will soon come down on America. The terrorists have also declared that other countries of the Western World including all of Western Europe will be next after the United States is destroyed.

"The terrorists are adamant that all of these events *will* happen and they cannot be prevented. In fact, they are so confident they're already claiming victory.

"In addition to declaring a state of emergency, government authorities are trying desperately to locate the leaders of ISA who are responsible for the threats and full-scale investigations are under way. However, this is pretty much a lost cause. The terrorists are in hiding and are dispersed across the country. The president has conceded that all of this has taken the government by complete surprise and that for all practical purposes it is too late. Our military forces are of absolutely no use.

"The question of how the terrorists were able to plan and carry out this plot by escaping CIA and other government intelligence is profound. There are some reports that the CIA and other government officials have been aware of an extensive complex communication code used by what now is known to be members of ISA for years however have not been able to decipher it. There is speculation that ISA may have infiltrated the CIA working on the project who aided in keeping the code from being broken. Other reports speculate that Russia may be involved in the plot. But this is all mere conjecture.

"But there are some reports that certain government officials were actually aware of the plan however did not want to publicize it for obvious reasons, or were unable to thwart it. The government is silent and will not discuss the merits of the matter. It's obvious that they are completely embarrassed.

"Regardless, it is inconceivable that the United States government was not aware of this plan regardless of whether they wanted the public to know about it or whether they could have prevented it. Certain members of the executive branch including the president have been asked about this, but for whatever reason refuse to discuss it."

The news reporter, clearly upset, then provides his own editorial. He emotionally carries on.

"The fact that our government intelligence was not aware of this plan or was and did nothing about it remains a complete mystery. Were certain members of our own government involved? You know, with the exception of several isolated incidents, there have been no significant or major successful terrorist attacks in the United States since 9/11 that compare to the 9/11 catastrophe. It's no wonder. The terrorists had significantly more than a decade after 9/11 to plan all of this.

"This is what they've been doing this entire time since then. It's been their plan all along to wait and destroy America all at once in a planned action of immense magnitude in glory to their Allah. And they somehow were able to do it without our government doing anything about it. How, I have no idea.

"During this entire time, they have been secretly and silently planning and plotting this massive assault against us. They have built or acquired nuclear and other bombs right here in our own country and through cyber-attacks and against our electronic and utility infrastructure. And now they claim to have the additional biological weapon that they also plan to use. And where was our government during all of this?

"And to think, the United States government has been totally naïve and vulnerable to this or for whatever reason didn't act on it if they knew about it. Our government and military have been thinking left all these years when they should have been thinking right. The terrorists claim that the US government has been incompetent is valid. Regardless whether our government was aware of it or not, it failed us.

"How did the terrorists get into the US or recruit Jihadists here? Did they sneak in with the refugees? Was that possible because the government did not have an extreme vetting process in place at the time? How were they able to build or acquire all of these bombs right here in our own backyard? How are they able to produce and import a biological weapon? So, what about our national defense system? What about our national security system? What about our superior intelligence our government is supposed to have? They claim their budget was slashed, but one would think they would still have known. How could they know nothing about this?

"And soon the United States of America will be nothing as well. Our government is light years behind because it has had blinders on and refused to think outside of the box. And it has refused to follow up. The terrorists have been smarter than our government, and now it looks like the American people will pay the price. Big time! I suppose we'll have only a few days to figure out what can be done, if anything."

The news reporter is clearly disgusted.

Garrett is intrigued by the remark about one of the nuclear bombs being so strategically placed that it could destroy the entire country all by itself. "Well, how can one nuclear bomb all by itself have an impact on all of the US and possibly the entire world simply because of where it is? I wonder what is so unique and strategic about this location. I wonder where this place is!"

Julie gets up and turns off the TV. "I've heard enough, and can't take it anymore."

Sonja also gets up. "Me too. I cannot believe this is all happening."

Both exclaim they're going to bed; however, Garrett turns the TV back on and watches the remainder of the news and the round table discussion. Following that, he goes to bed as well.

As each member of the family goes to bed, nobody can sleep much. Everyone is still so emotionally charged; they can hardly think straight. There are so many things to worry about. What happened to Alex? What caused the explosion? And now the terrorists have invaded America and appear inevitably destined to completely destroy the entire country if not the entire world in less than a week.

Chapter 14

After being swirled around for what seems like eternity within the clouds, I've entered a void of nothingness. The music and the thunder have disappeared, and everything is deathly quiet. There is no light. There is no darkness. There is no sound. I am no longer floating, and instead feel myself moving through the void and increasingly faster at an incredibly accelerating force. Soon I'm moving faster than ever thought possible. Before long, I sense that I am traveling faster than the speed of light. There is no longer any sense of time. Time is standing still, but I'm literally flying.

The feeling is indescribable. I feel myself moving so fast that I'm shaking uncontrollably. The experience is both thrilling and frightening at the same time. But I sense I'm not alone. I can feel other souls around me and amongst each other, but each is alone and not able to see or communicate with any other souls. Are they all going in the same direction as me? I get a strange feeling that although most of them are, some of them are not. But I don't know for sure. I can't see anything, but I can sense them. I know they're there.

I look up and I can sense the spirit is still with me, but it's different now. I sense that it's both a good spirit and a bad spirit at the same time. Or are there now two spirits? I don't know if this is comforting or if I wish it would go away. But after briefly thinking about it, I decide I want it to accompany me regardless of what its intentions are. I don't want to experience this journey alone no matter what. Being here in this void alone is unbearable. Being all alone and not being able to communicate with anyone or anything is absolutely unendurable.

I don't know where I'm going. I develop a feeling of hopelessness, and I feel a huge question mark about how I lived my life. I know I've lived an honorable life and I had faith. However, I'm still terrified because I'm entering the unknown and don't know my destiny. But I know the possibilities.

In the far distance of the void I see a faint light. It's the size of a pinhole looking across an empty universe. There are no stars or other visible matter in the void. The light slowly becomes larger and larger as I move closer to it.

After a little time, the light is directly in front of me and I enter straight into it still going at an incredible speed. The void suddenly vanishes and the light becomes an enormous wormhole spiraling around and around as I'm thrust into it. I feel very dizzy. The feeling is indescribable. It's hard for me to think straight.

The spirals spinning all around me and moving me forward are all different colors similar to the clouds I saw before, but they contain an enormous amount of lightning forking off between the colors. It is an enormous vehicle of pure energy. It is absolutely spellbinding and almost blinding.

I know for sure I have entered another dimension and have left the universe that is home to Mother Earth. The spirals are traveling faster than I am, but I feel it hurling me forward at a rapidly accelerating pace. The dizziness abates somewhat and I can finally think more clearly again. I again wonder about the spirit and look up. It's still there traveling with me, and again I sense that it's both good and bad. I still can't see it, but I know it's there. I feel it's been assigned to me for some reason. I again wonder what's going on back on Earth. To my astonishment, I realize that all I have to do is think about it, and I can envision everything.

I can see Sonja, Julie, and Garrett at their home all watching the news. I realize that the terrorists are a very organized and funded sect that has secretly been planning the terrorist activities in the Western world for years and that their threats against the United States are real. I am aware that the president has declared a state of national emergency.

I can see the news reporting that the terrorists are poised to detonate bombs including nuclear devices in at least twenty major US cities in the near future and that they're attempting to launch a cyber-attack to disrupt everything from communications to the electrical grid across America. I know about their development of a biological weapon and smuggling it into the United States. I know that one of the nuclear bombs has been placed at a secret location that is so unique that it alone could destroy the entire country and perhaps the world. I am aware of the same things that Sonja, Garrett, and Julie are experiencing, and I am seeing the same thing that they are seeing on the news.

I can also see what Andrew and Alana are doing as well. What a strange feeling to feel like I'm at two places at once, but I don't have the ability to do anything or communicate in either place. I have no control of anything. I'm helpless.

I decide to think about myself in the ambulance to see where I am going back on Earth. I assume my body is being transported to one of the two local hospitals. I'm pretty sure that I've died and am not dreaming, but I want to know for sure. But I can't see myself or the ambulance at all. For some reason, I can envision everything else but not myself back on Earth. What happened to me is nothing but a distant memory now. No matter how hard I try, I can't see myself back in the world from where I came. I have no idea what my status is. Why can I see my family and know what's going on regarding the terrorists but not see myself back there?

Officer Musty and the Arab then come to mind. I can't envision them either, but for some strange reason, I feel their presence. I reason that I'm merely remembering my prior thoughts of Officer Musty trying to help and the suspiciousness of the Arab before I left Earth. I wonder what they are both up to right now. However, I realize that these are all muffled thoughts and I really don't know what to think about them.

I then think of my family again. And once more, to my astonishment I can see them. I know exactly what they are doing at this very instant. I can see the news and I know exactly what's going on in the world regarding the terrorists. I wonder why I can see my family and know what's going on with the terrorists and the crisis they've created, but I can't envision anything else. How strange this all is.

I see everybody praying for me back on Earth, that is everybody except for Andrew. When they all prepare to go to bed and say their prayers, Andrew is the only one who doesn't.

After flying through the incredibly fast swirling wormhole I can eventually make out the other end where I assume I will exit it. It starts off the size of another pinhole that gets larger as I approach it. Eventually, the exit from the wormhole rapidly comes into view.

I wonder what's on the other side and where I'll end up. I again look up and the spirit is still above me. I try to say something to it, but for some reason, I am not allowed to talk with it, and it does not talk with me. I cannot actually see it, but I know it's there when I think about it. I can feel it. I can definitely sense it. But is it both a good and bad spirit, or is it two separate spirits, one good and one bad?

Then the spiraling speeds up even more, and I prepare myself for my exit. With one final enormous burst of energy, I exit the wormhole and am thrown into another void similar to the first one. Again there's no overall light, no darkness, and no sound. It's a vacuum of pure nothingness. But this void is multi-dimensional and forks off into two separate distant glows, each on a separate plane.

On one plane off in the distance it's a very bright constant white light that is welcoming. It's very serene and is a very positive place. On the other plane it's a dimmer flickering light that appears to be a red and orange pulsating ball of fire. It's one of hopelessness and is a negative place. They are opposite from each other but are each in its own dimension.

Both lights are far away, and I know what each one is. I wonder if this place between the two lights is perhaps purgatory. It's 100 percent emptiness. I still sense the presence of other souls around me, but this time, each soul is in his or her own world as if the void belongs entirely to each soul alone. I certainly feel alone except for the invisible spirit that is accompanying me for some reason. Otherwise, the loneliness here would be absolutely intolerable. I cannot imagine spending eternity here at all.

I sense that I'm not moving anymore and that I'm merely waiting for something. But what?

I pretty much know that these two lights in the distance are the entrances to heaven and hell. I start to tremble with incredible fear. I find myself crying profusely, but there are no tears. I look down, and although I have left my body, I sense that I have been given a new one. I can feel it, but I just can't see it. I look up again and the spirit is still there, but I can't acknowledge it and it can't acknowledge me.

The wait is unbearable, but it's welcome. It's agonizing as well because it gives me time to contemplate the unknown that lies ahead of me and the possibility I may be sent to where I don't want to go. But I'm not sure if I want to stay here either. I can't fathom being here all alone for eternity, but for now staying here is okay because I'm so afraid where I could otherwise possibly be sent.

Then suddenly, my ability to think freely is taken over by a most powerful force of which I have no control. I'm allowed to ask myself certain questions and experience certain emotions but not others. Although I still have certain emotions I can sense what's happening. The control over me that's taking place is overwhelming. I know something is going to happen to me now, but what?

Chapter 15

Garrett and Julie have the day off following the holiday. But they would have taken the day off anyway as a result of the events of the previous night. Upon coming into the kitchen for breakfast, they immediately discuss and agree that they will not be interviewed by any news media. They will avoid them if they return today. It's a waiting game to see how soon they will arrive. Everyone is still in a state of shock over what transpired the evening before.

At breakfast, Julie turns on the TV. On every network and news channel the programming is preempted by news on the developments regarding the terrorists and their threats against America. It's more of the same, and there's nothing new to report about the threats since the evening before. There's some news about some minor panic and looting in the streets in various cities, mostly on the East and West Coasts, but it doesn't seem to amount to much. The National Guard has been alerted in case these situations become worse.

With the break in the news and nothing new to report, the majority of the channels have changed course for the time being and are addressing related topics. One common story showing up on many channels is a reference to the Apocalypse told in the book of Revelation. There is much debate whether the current events match those foretold in the Gospel; however, some theologians and other experts are speculating that what is happening just might be the beginning of the end of time.

The news states that amidst this speculation various religious cults and religious fanatics are springing up all around the world. Many of these appear to be taking advantage of the doom and gloom predictions resulting from the threats by the terrorists to gain attention for themselves.

The news then goes on to say, "But, there is one particular religious leader from the Middle East who has emerged who is beginning to draw huge support with many followers. He proclaims to be the Second Coming and savior. Not much is known about him in the Western world. However the number of people who are already following him is surprisingly large.

"Many of these 'pop-up' cultist leaders come and go, and now many seem to be taking advantage of the crisis begat by the terrorists and the speculation of some that Armageddon may be upon us. After all, the entire world as we know is suspect to total destruction if the extent of the nuclear bombs is as real as advertised by the terrorists. Are they merely seeking attention for themselves and want some sort of personal glory, or should we pay more attention to them?

"But this particular leader appears to be quite different, and he appears to be gaining a following that is increasing significantly by the hour. His following and worshippers are running videos of him on numerous cable and satellite stations to spread the word. Is he for real, or is he another hoax? Stay tuned for more news on this."

"Well, how about that?" asks Julie. "What else can go wrong? I can't believe any of this is really happening. After last night and now this? It's all like a bad dream, and I wish it would all go away! What can be next?"

Garrett and Sonja get back on their phones and continue to make calls to try to locate Alex, but to no avail.

Julie continues her emotional outburst. "I just don't understand. Just why would he disappear like that? Who took him? What do they want with him? Does he have something they want? What is so important about him that he has to be kidnapped? He's probably not even alive anymore. Why, why, why? I just can't fathom why they want him dead or alive. And what caused the explosion in his house?"

While they're eating breakfast, they hear a knock on the door. It's Officer Musty. "Good morning," he says in an upbeat mood as Garrett opens the door.

Everyone is surprised that he's holding balloons of all sorts of colors, waving them in the morning breeze. "Come on in," Garrett says. "What's with the balloons?"

"The balloons are for your children. I thought it may boost their spirits considering what they went through last night."

"You didn't have to do this, but this is so kind of you. Come on in."

Lizzy and Mikey are delighted, and it doesn't take long for them to warm up to him. He teases them in a friendly way.

Officer Musty then sits down and talks to Sonja, Garrett, and Julie about the status of things and the search for Alex. "I wanted you to know that word has gotten out about the suspiciousness of the Arab in the old white van and that he's been declared a "person of interest" in the cause of the explosion and fire and also in the disappearance of Alex. The police have an all-points bulletin out to apprehend him. However nobody can find him. The van has apparently vanished into thin air. It hasn't been seen since shortly before the ambulance appeared last night."

Garrett then shares his observation that the van was parked up the street during the fire, but without the Arab in it and that the Arab returned to the van after Alex came out of the fire. But the van was not there when the ambulance showed up and left.

Officer Musty finds this of great interest. "What you're telling me corroborates what others have said. Because the driver of the van appears to be an Arab, with all the news about the terrorist threats, the FBI and/or CIA will likely get involved. I want to let you know that there's a high probability either the FBI or the CIA, or perhaps both, may contact you all to ask questions. The Arab may be a prime suspect in what appears to be a case of arson and the abduction of Alex. Other than that, I need to find Alex as soon as possible."

Garrett looks at him wondering why he would say that and profoundly exclaims, "Yes, so do we!"

Officer Musty then gets up, and as he starts to leave, he gives Garrett, Julie, and Sonja his business card with his cell phone number. "If you get any word on where Alex is or if you find out anything, please give me a call. I'll be searching for Alex and may need to go out of town for a few days. You may not see me for a while, but be assured I have your back, and I'll let you know if I find out anything. If you learn anything, please call me before talking to anyone else first. If I don't answer, please leave a message and I'll get back with you as soon as I can."

Garrett, Julie, and Sonja thank him and promise to keep in touch if there are any developments. Officer Musty then looks around the room briefly and walks out the door. As he does, Crackerjack, who just came inside through the back door, spots him and freezes. Garrett puts a quick eye on him and tells him to sit. Crackerjack utters a soft growl, then sits, then lies down and watches Office Musty attentively as he leaves through the front door.

Officer Musty no sooner leaves than a few minutes later Andrew and Alana show up with Hannah. Andrew gets out of his car and knocks on the front door.

"Good morning, everybody," Andrew says as Julie opens the front door. "We just dropped off Daniel and Matthew at summer camp, and Alana will be going to work soon, so we thought we would stop by on our way back home and say hi."

"Come on in," says Julie. "You want some coffee?"

Andrew then motions for Alana to get out of the car, and she comes into the house carrying Hannah.

Julie greets Alana. "I'm surprised you're going in to work today after what happened last night. Also, don't most people have the day off as a holiday since the Fourth was on a Sunday?"

"Well, in my profession, I don't have much choice. You know, registered nurses are supposed to be committed to their work. Besides, I probably couldn't find anybody to take my shift anyway. Have you heard any more news about Alex or what caused the explosion?"

"Nope, not surprisingly. There are no developments that we know of regarding my dad or what happened."

"That's too bad. I was hoping for some good news. I must say, I really like your new house and what you've done with it."

"You want a quick tour now that we've rearranged everything? Come on, I'll show you both around."

After a walk around the house, they sit down in front of the TV with the kids off playing with Crackerjack.

Andrew remarks, "Your house is a lot like Dad's, but his house is a little bigger. And both are a hundred times larger than our house."

Clearly irritated, Alana comments, "A hundred times? Andrew, why are you always so concerned about what others have compared to what you have? You should be grateful to have what you have, especially since you don't do much to contribute anything."

The news on the TV turns to the topic of the person from the Middle East who claims to be the Second Coming. After some interviews with various prominent men of the cloth, the news station shows a video that was provided to them of this person.

It's a very short prerecorded video of somewhat poor quality. The video starts and shows a Middle Eastern man, perhaps in his thirties, dressed in a gray tunic or robe, wearing sandals who looks almost identical to traditional pictures of Jesus. He sits down on a log in the shade, looking out over an oasis in a sunlit desert.

Sitting next to him is an older woman who is dressed in a tan wrap with a scarf that is traditional Middle Eastern dress. The video is very short. It starts, and he very briefly addresses the viewers:

"My name is "Evedothlid Ammenofi. You can call me Ammen. As you may already know, I am of the sacred blood and have returned for you. You may have recently seen me in the Mosul region where Christians have been persecuted or driven out by the Islamic extremists. I have originally come from Jerusalem.

"The Holy Bible talks of the Second Coming in the book of Revelation. It talks of the day of reckoning. That day is very near.

"The tests will be passed, and through the blaze of glory above and through the fire below, I will be your light to your eternal end. Other angels will be beside me, but I am the last angel. Only the last angel of the father can save you. Please listen and take word and follow me so that you can survive and be saved. Like Jesus who came before you, I again come before you now. There is no other way."

The news then states that after the commercial they will join another round-table discussion to talk and debate the qualities of this person, as well as some other persons who are coming forward also looking for a following.

Alana is half-amused and half-mesmerized. "Is Ammen for real, or is he just another whacko looking for personal glory at an opportune time?"

Andrew proudly states, "I've been up since the crack of dawn, and this is about the third time I've seen this video."

Garrett then comments, "This must be the same person who the news states that a lot of people are starting to follow and take seriously. He sure is getting a lot of worldwide attention and so quickly."

Alana says sort of tongue in cheek, "Well, now that the world is coming to an end, it doesn't surprise me in the least that all of these goofballs now are crawling out of the woodwork looking for attention. But there does appear to be something appealing about this guy. I can see why he's developing such a following so quickly."

"You don't think he's for real, do you?" asks Julie.

Alana remarks, "I don't know. But if he's for real and if the world really is going to end, do you know where you will go after you die if you don't follow and worship him? That is, if he's really for real."

"The world is not going to end, dear," says Sonja softly. "I wouldn't be so quick to judge or agree with him."

"I wouldn't be so sure," says Andrew. "With everything else going on, nothing would surprise me now anymore. Maybe we should find out more about him."

Julie then exclaims, "I sure wish Dad was here. I would love to hear his opinion." She ends her comment in disgust, clearly shaken by the video as well by the events of the evening before.

Andrew, at odds with his sister, comments, "Sounds like you're supporting Dad's intense faith without even giving this Ammen person a chance. Personally, I'd like to learn more about this Ammen." He has a snicker on his face that hints if he decides to follow Ammen, this will be his way to upstage his dad (if he's ever found and is alive) who has been trying to convert Andrew to Christianity for years.

Sonja has a look on her face as if she can't wait to say something but remains silent. She lets her children continue.

Andrew adds, "Plus, what do I have to lose? Maybe, just perhaps this Ammen person is for real."

"But is he really the return of Jesus?" asks Alana.

"I don't know, but does it matter? He said we must follow him. He didn't say anything about following Jesus of the past. Either way, if I decide to follow him, Dad can't get on me anymore about Jesus, can he?"

Andrew strongly suggests he would then have his own savior to follow and would have an excuse not to listen to his dad anymore about following Jesus.

After spending a short time chitchatting with more discussion about Julie and Garrett's new house, Alana, Andrew, and Hannah leave. They all agree to keep in close touch.

As soon as they leave, within minutes, two late-model white SUVs pull up, and four men in dark suits all wearing the same style sunglasses walk up their driveway and then the sidewalk. Garrett sees them outside the window and speculates that this may be the FBI or CIA that Officer Musty was talking about.

Garrett is correct as they identify themselves at the door. Garrett and Julie invite them inside. Two are with the FBI and two are with the CIA. They tell Garrett, Julie, and Sonja they will be working together on the case of the fire and especially the disappearance of Alex.

They explain that the reason for this is that they have heard about the Arab and that he's a prime suspect, even though nobody knows much about him. Because of the terrorist threats and the government has reported that many terrorists have entered the United States from the Middle East, the FBI and CIA have a real interest in finding and questioning him. Julie asks about the issue of profiling, but the agents completely ignore her.

For about the next hour, they answer countless questions regarding the disappearance of Alex. A lot of the questions are the same, asked in different ways.

Garrett tells them what he observed regarding the van and driver the night before. Sonja then tells them about Office Musty and that he wanted the family to keep in touch with him regarding any developments.

As soon as Musty's name is mentioned, one of the agents emphatically states that they are already aware of Officer Musty and that he doesn't have any jurisdiction in the matter. The agents want the family to be in touch with the agents instead of Officer Musty.

One of the agents then tells Sonja that although it appears that Officer Musty may have good intentions, appears to be a nice guy, and wants to help them, he simply doesn't have jurisdiction. The FBI and CIA do instead. They provide Sonja, Garrett, and Julie their business cards with their cell phone numbers.

One of the agents then reluctantly tells Sonja, Garrett, and Julie that they have reason to believe that their lives may be in danger, especially Sonja's.

"Why?" asks Julie, startled to hear this.

"Is she staying here with you? It's possible that whoever abducted Alex may want something from you also. Until we know more information or can catch the person and resolve the issue, it's necessary that you take the utmost precautions."

Julie then mentions the news media. "You know, we were hounded last night, and we don't want to be interviewed. Can you do anything about that?"

"Maybe so. We're actually arranging for a security detail to watch over you and protect you. Later this morning or early afternoon, you can expect somebody else from the FBI to come and coordinate this. They will likely arrive in a late-model white van. The security will involve an unmarked car or van with various electronic communications and surveillance equipment. They will watch your house and can travel with you as needed. But they will pretty much operate undercover most of the time. We're particularly concerned about your safety at night. In effect, you can consider them to be your family's bodyguards. They can help keep the news media from bothering you too if you like."

Julie, although shaken somewhat, is very thankful. Garrett and Sonja chime in their thanks as well. "What time do you say you think they'll be here?" she asks.

"We hope they should arrive in the next several hours and by early afternoon at the latest."

After a few additional questions and paperwork, the agents leave.

Crackerjack is lying on the other sofa across the room and doesn't take his eyes off the agents during their entire visit.

When they leave, Sonja turns the TV back on. As soon as she does, there is breaking news about new developments. As a result of the crisis and numerous other factors regarding the state of the US economy, the news reports that the US dollar now is being devalued. The stock market is crashing, and the DJIA and S & P have lost nearly 30 percent of their values. Trading has been stopped on all exchanges.

But what was not expected is the speculation that some retailers and stores may no longer accept the US dollar as currency. Likewise, it's speculated that they may not accept credit cards or cash and may only accept payment if it's made with gold or silver. It's presumed that some stores will begin this policy within the next day or two. Some stores are starting to accept only gold or silver already. And some stores are closing because of the possibility of looting. The price of gold and silver is skyrocketing. The worldwide currency standard is in a state of flux. The threat of nuclear bombs to be detonated across the United States has resulted in a complete financial crisis.

As a result, there is more panic in the streets in some cities, more looting going on, and there is additional speculation that the National Guard will be called out in some cities.

Garrett, being the expert on economics and finance, doesn't seem surprised. "You know, with the massive debt run up by the country all of these years since the last administration after 9/11, as a result of the crisis, this was inevitable. Our country is losing control of everything. Do you know just how serious everything is getting?" he profoundly exclaims.

Julie answers "If this is true, we probably need to go to the store today and get what we need before we aren't able to buy anything anymore. I say let's go now. Mom, what do you think?"

"I agree. Since I lost everything in the fire, I need to get some things, but with what?

"Don't worry, I'll help you. We'll figure something out."

Julie then snickers with a forced smile on her face "Garrett, do you have a couple of hundred dollars' worth of gold somewhere that we can borrow?"

"Yeah, just like you do. If you want to go shopping, don't you think you should wait until the FBI security detail arrives before you leave? I don't think you should go until later. You know, if the world really is going to end in a couple of days, does it really matter whether you buy anything now or not? I don't think it's safe for you to go out anywhere, at least not until our FBI security bodyguards come. *If* you do go before they come, I think you're asking for trouble."

Chapter 16

An enormous mirror appears before me and as I look into it I begin to see, hear, feel, and relive my entire life from the day I was born to the time when I left in the ambulance. I now realize that my entire life is being evaluated. Looking in the mirror, I relive and experience every single second of every event and thought during my entire life in incredible detail. Nothing is missing or left out. Things that I had long forgotten about are remembered. I get the sense that absolutely everything about how I lived my life is under review and is being evaluated by a great and almighty power. And I know *Who* that is.

I relive everything going backward from my time in the ambulance back to the day I was born. Then the evaluation restarts going forward again. It is more extreme than going backward. Then my entire life flashes before me and everything comes together going backward and forward at the same time as my entire life is being assessed. There is no sense of time. Time is standing still. Not a single second of my life is missing.

I relive every sin I have ever committed or thought about. They include the most minor and inconsequential thoughts I've ever had. At the time I didn't think they amounted to anything. I can remember every good deed and all good things that I have ever done as well. The evaluation of my life is in such detail I am absolutely astounded at what I'm experiencing.

I then realize that every second of my life is counted as a variable in a monumental mathematical formula that is an equation that measures the good and bad in my life. Every action and thought in every second of every day from the time I wake up in the morning to when I fall asleep every night are assigned a plus or a minus. Each is assigned a multiplier, which is a different weight of application or importance depending on various factors. Even my thoughts lying in bed at night are being evaluated to some extent.

As my life is assessed a myriad of questions are asked that are so numerous they seem never ending. They're not in any particular order, and again each is assigned a different weight in the evaluation depending on the degree of both the questions and answers.

How often did you pray?

How often did you thank God for giving us Jesus?

How often did you thank Jesus for dying for our sins?

How often did you thank God for providing his bountiful goodness?

How hard did you pray? Did you pray with all your heart and soul or just in your mind?

Did you contribute to help the poor and help the unfortunate?

Did you donate money, property, or your time to charity? How much?

Did you ever short anybody, by money, tip, property, words, or in mind?

How often did you go to church?

Did you contribute to church offerings? Did you tithe?

Were you ever selfish, no matter how trivial you thought it may be?

Did you ever reject the needs of others, be it physical, mental, or spiritual?

Did you ever lie or deceive others?

Did you ever break a promise or not keep a promise?

Have you ever been critical of others to serve your self-interests or when it was not justified?

Have you been supportive and optimistic of others or unaccommodating and pessimistic?

Have you ever been negative and done injustice to one rather than be positive with a helpful attitude?

Have you blamed others for misdoings for which you are responsible?

Have you been a complainer? Have you whined about things in your life for which you are solely responsible?

Or have you accepted things the way they are and offered gratitude for what has been granted to you?

Have you been a nagger? Have you looked to harass others rather than praise them for their goodness?

Did you ever hurt anybody, whether with words, mind, body, or spirit?

Have you every slandered, insulted, or defamed anyone, even behind their back?

Have you ever applied unjustified threats or blackmail to anyone to gain self-benefit?

Did you ever cheat on anything, whether physical, mental, or spiritual?

Have you ever cursed either by word or by mind?

Have you been humble or have you ever bragged or boasted about yourself in action or in mind?

Have you ever taken advantage of someone at their expense or suffering?

Have you ever been negligent, disowning, or in denial?

Have you always exercised responsibility in body, mind, and spirit?

Have you accepted responsibility for your actions, or have you looked for ways to blame others?

Have you ever been confrontational without a truly justified reason?

Have you been openly, willingly, and sincerely apologetic for misdoings?

Where you always polite to others or were you rude? Did you always say please, thank you, your welcome, or excuse me when appropriate?

By now I'm distraught thinking about the nature of these questions. I've heard enough and want the questions to end. Although I don't think that most of these apply to me, I learn that they apply to not only me but to everybody, perhaps differently to each; however, they all do apply at least to some extent one way or another. But there's no time to relax. I'm mortified as the questions go on and continue relentlessly.

Have you always offered sincere thanks for gifts or rewards given to you?

When someone did a good thing for you, did you reward them and repay the favor?

If someone invited you to a meal and fed you, did you invite them back and feed them?

Have you ever failed to volunteer for something when you could have?

Have you gone out of your way to do your best and taken the extra step to do better?

Or were you satisfied with what you did when you could have done more?

Did you spend money or time on any bad habits that could have been used to help others in need instead?

Were you always willing to share good things received by you with others?

Have you worked to earn your living when you were capable, or did you seek handouts instead?

Have you exercised patience and tolerance with others, or have you been quick to judge?

Have you been conciliatory or have you instead exercised animosity toward others?

Have you tried to be cheerful and positive or do you bring others down by your pessimism?

Have you been a good listener, or were you more preoccupied with what you wanted to say?

Have you ever been sarcastic, cynical, or acerbic to others or gentle and kind instead?

Have you avoided conflict with others and been appeasing or instead have you been hostile?

Have you been distrustful of others when it's not justified?

Have you always been tolerant and flexible of doings or sayings of others which you disagree?

Have you always been willing to compromise or instead insist on doing things your own way?

Have you always been kind, sympathetic, and compassionate towards others?

Have you ever been arrogant, egotistical, or even belligerent?

Have you ever been disdainful, condescending or derisive?

Have you always accepted blame and professed guilt for all of your misdoings?

Have you asked for forgiveness from others for your misdoings, or did you let pride get in your way?

By now, I'm exhausted. I can't believe these questions. Are they really all that important in reviewing my life? I realize that during my life some but not all of these questions may have applied in one form or another, or to one degree or another, at one time or another. Perhaps it applied only once or perhaps it was a minimal or unintentional, but that all doesn't matter. I learn that they all still count. At this point, I can't tolerate a single additional question. But unbelievably, they continue in inexorable fashion.

Did you give up and sacrifice any material possessions to help others in need?

To what extent did you buy items of pleasure when the money could have been used for others in need?

Did you ever litter or not take care of things of nature that God had given to you?

Did you take care of God's creatures of nature or use or do harm to them without a justified purpose?

Have you contributed to society, or have you contributed more to yourself?

Have you ever been hypocritical, duplicitous, unfaithful, or disloyal?

Have you been self-centered? How often did you say *I* or *me* instead of *you* or *they*?

Have you been righteous, virtuous, and honorable in your life?

Have you ever been jealous of others or of their possessions?

Have you ever been revengeful, vindictive, spiteful, or unforgiving of others?

Did you truly love with all sincerity and with all of your heart and soul? Or was it superficial?

Did you truly forgive others for their trespasses against you? Was your forgiveness really willingly and sincere or was it only token?

Or were you bitter, or did you hold a grudge?

Have you passed judgment of others before judging yourself?

Did you pray for others or have you prayed for yourself more so?

Did you love your enemies, forgive them, and pray for them?

Did you leave the world in better shape than when you entered it?

Have you gambled when there is no benefit to others? Have you gambled with how you lived your life?

Did you place God and Jesus Christ first in your life, and then followed by your family, or did you place others first before them?

Did you truly and sincerely love your God with all of your heart and soul, or was it superficial?

Did you read the Bible?

Did you attempt to spread the word of Jesus?

The questions are absolutely overwhelming. I learn that these are all standard questions that apply to everybody. But after suffering through this for some time, I get the feeling they're designed just for me, although they are not. These questions go on what seems like indefinitely and it seems that they will never end. But once when they are finally over, then each question is repeated and expounded upon with additional questions such as how often, how much so, how sincere, to what extent, why, etc.

The questions continue, and by now, I want to cry, but I can't. The questions won't stop. I can't deal with this anymore. It is an absolute relentless barrage of questions about how I lived my life that appear never ending. The questions about my life are absolutely staggering. I again ask myself the question, how important is all this?

Although I would have expected the acceptable answers to far exceed the unacceptable answers, now I realize that this may be questionable. This is primarily because I become aware of volumes of lost opportunities to do better that I simply ignored during life. Oh, how I wished I had these opportunities again. I wouldn't have let them go to waste had I known the impact they would have on the evaluation.

But then I ponder. Can some of the answers be subjective and perhaps this is the reason why they're expounded upon? For example, what about loving my enemies and praying for those who persecute me? I ask what if my enemy wanted to kill me. Am I supposed to simply roll over and let my enemy take my life if that was clearly its objective? Is that what I'm supposed to do? I can understand loving and forgiving it and praying for it but the big question is, would I be allowed to harm or perhaps kill it to avoid being killed myself?

But then I remember the sixth commandment, so maybe not. However, maybe God would justify it if it is in self-defense of being killed. What would I have actually done if I was confronted with the situation? Can I really live with taking someone else's life? Now that I'm not alive anymore, I suppose I won't need to worry about it anymore. Or will I?

But I also consider the devil, Satan, to be my enemy. Am I supposed to love and forgive Satan and pray for it also? I assume not because Satan is what it is and is not human. But, just how should Matthew 5:44 be interpreted in this regard? However, now that I'm not alive anymore, what would I do if I a find myself before him? I sure hope that doesn't happen.

Chapter 17

Sonja, Garrett, and Julie discuss what to do and they decide that Garrett will stay home with the kids and Sonja and Julie will go to the stores. They need to buy groceries, and Sonja needs to buy clothes and other essentials since she has nothing after the fire. In case the media shows up again or if the security detail arrives, Garrett will be better suited to deal with them. It's more likely that the media will be looking for them at home rather than at the store, and the media can be avoided better this way.

As soon as they get organized and Sonja and Julie grab their purses to go, there's another knock on the door. It's a man and a woman both dressed in business attire and wearing sunglasses. They are both carrying briefcases. Outside is parked another late-model white SUV. Garrett wonders if perhaps this is the security people, and he answers the door.

The man and woman introduce themselves as agents from Homeland Security and they want to ask some questions about Alex's disappearance and the Arab and the old white van. Garrett tells them that the FBI and the CIA have already been here and have already asked a bunch of questions. Sonja then chimes in that Officer Musty also has talked to them from the local police department.

The agents then look at Garrett and tell him that as a matter of fact Homeland Security has jurisdiction over the case, not the FBI or CIA or the local police. They then start asking the same questions that Garrett, Julie, and Sonja answered earlier in the morning.

By now, Julie is so frustrated she could scream. She wants to go shopping before it's too late, and now these agents are going to be here for another several hours. Several hours were killed earlier in the morning with visits from Officer Musty, Andrew and Alana, the FBI and CIA, and it seems like the entire day is going to be wasted.

She stands up and looks at them and shouts out, "We don't give a rat's ass who has jurisdiction. We're tired of answering the same questions over and over again. I didn't even know that the FBI and CIA could even work together on any case and now you come in and tell us that you have jurisdiction and they don't? They asked the same questions about a dozen times."

"The FBI and CIA can't work together? Where did you learn that, in a movie?" one of the agents asks.

She continues, "Well, why aren't you working together with them on this? I have no idea what's going on and I'm getting sick and tired of it! We don't know where my dad is, we don't even know if he's alive, and we don't know anything about the Arab! If you want to know anything, talk to the FBI, CIA, or Officer Musty!"

Garrett then apologizes for Julie's outburst. He comments that they're all still shaken over the events from the evening before and the morning and that she has a quick fuse and is very emotional. The agents understand and then apologize as well. The agents tell them that they merely want to introduce themselves and will ask only a few questions and they will be on their way.

Julie then apologizes and calms down somewhat.

After a few minutes, the agents provide their business cards and leave.

Crackerjack is lying in the corner on a vent and eyes the agents during their entire visit.

After they leave, Sonja and Julie again head out to the garage from the kitchen. Julie comments, "I've had it with visitors today. I don't want to see anybody else. It's already been a very long and busy morning, and now it's past lunch. When I get back home, I hope to simply relax for a change. I sure hope that I can use my credit cards at the stores."

Sonja adds, "Or that the stores will take cash. I need to get some things. I also need to get on the phone when we get back to start taking care of some business. I need to contact my insurance company and make a bunch of other calls too."

Garrett then says, "Do you think it will really matter? What if the world ends in a few days? I still don't think you should go until our bodyguards arrive, but I'm not going to stop you. I hope that the stores and banks are open. They may all be closed. Good luck to you."

Sonja and Julie then go to the garage through the kitchen door. They will take Julie's SUV and plan to go to the bank and then the mall first.

Garrett meets them in the garage to say good-bye and opens the garage door. As he does, Sonja comments that she forgot something and needs to go back into the house for a minute. She then goes back into the kitchen while Julie and Garrett are kissing each other good-bye.

As soon as they open the garage door, a black van suddenly appears out of nowhere and backs into their driveway. It stops right at the edge of the garage.

Julie joyfully exclaims, "Good, our security people are here. This must be them."

Garrett comments "But, Julie, the FBI said that it would be a white van. This one is black."

But, in a blink of an eye, the back doors of the van swing open and out leap four men in jumpsuits. As they run into the garage, they're waving automatic weapons in the air and are screaming in what appears to be in Arabic. They quickly motion for Garrett and Julie to go back into the house, and they close the garage door behind them. It all happens in a flash.

Garrett and Julie are so shocked by the suddenness of what happened they have no time to react. The men are quick to act and throw Garrett and Julie on the couch in the living room. The kids start crying. Crackerjack starts growling. Some of their jumpsuits are partially unzipped, and underneath reveals what appears to be Middle Eastern attire. Some are wearing face masks or turbans. Some are not.

It's evident they are all terrorists. They are yelling in a language that Garrett and Julie do not understand, and they have no idea what they're saying.

One is a lot more radical looking than the others and appears to be the leader. Julie and Garrett both wonder if this perhaps is the Arab who has been in the old white van.

Waving their AK-47s in the air, they're yelling out, "Praise be to Allah, praise be to Allah."

The kids continue to cry, and the leader shouts out in broken English, "Shut the babies up, now!"

Julie starts to get up to get Lizzy and Mikey, and one of the other terrorists shoves her back down on the couch, scratching her face with his gun. The leader then says, "Sit down, you not get up and you do as I tell you."

The kids continue to cry, and the leader again tells Julie to shut them up. Before she can react, he shouts out that if she cannot stop their crying that he will stop it himself as he points his gun at them. He has no patience whatsoever. Julie is shaking. She cries out, "No, no, no! *If* you let me get them, I'll stop their crying! Please!"

She's afraid to get up though and then tells Lizzy and Mikey to come to her and Daddy. After a few seconds, they hesitantly walk over, sniffling, and then finally throw themselves into Garrett and Julie's arms.

Emily is asleep in her pumpkin seat on the floor but is starting to stir.

Lizzy cries out and wants her dolly bag as she points to it. Then she motions to her room and says, "Want Racky."

"The leader shouts out, "Who is Racky" thinking somebody else is in the house.

Julie looks at him and softly says, "Racky is a stuffed raccoon like a teddy bear that I once had when I was a child and passed it down to Lizzy. Her grandpa would always make it talk and told her that it would keep her safe. She finds comfort in it and holds it whenever she is scared because she thinks it'll help her. She named the raccoon Racky.

"So the raccoon talks? Can it tell me where Alex Fisheramen is?" he laughs.

"What?" cries out Julie. Confused about the leader's comment about her father, she doesn't know how to answer. "In order for Lizzy not to cry, she needs her dolly bag and her Racky."

The leader goes over and gets her dolly bag and throws it at her. He then shouts out, "No raccoon. They give me the jitters, and we certainly do not need it to help you now, do we?"

Crackerjack starts to bark, and Garrett stares at him and tells him to stop, and he obeys instantly.

"What do you want?" Julie asks, still trembling.

"We want to know where Alex Fisheramen is," the leader states.

Both Garrett and Julie simultaneously blurt out, "We don't know."

"What do you mean you don't know?"

"We don't know."

"Well, you do know and you will tell us."

"But really, we don't know. We don't even know if he's alive."

"Well, you do know, and you will tell us. If you don't, somebody here will die until we find out. We need to find him now." Again, he starts waving his gun around in the air.

"Why? Why is it so important that you need to find him? What did he do?"

"We cannot tell you. It is not your business."

"What if he's not even alive?"

"You let us worry about that. We need to find him now, dead or alive!"

One of the terrorists then says something to the leader in again what appears to be Arabic.

The leader asks where all their cell phones are. Garrett points to his lying on the coffee table. Julie tells him she lost hers. Unbeknownst to Julie is the fact that Lizzy had been playing with her cell phone and she had turned the phone off and put it in her dolly bag. Julie didn't know this and has not been able to find it all morning. In her haste to want to go shopping, she actually forgot about it.

The leader then looks up her phone number in Garrett's cell phone and tries to call her. The leader then asks her what her cell phone number is, and she verifies the number that he is calling. Everybody quietly listens for a ring in the house, but hears nothing. He calls once again. Again, there's no sound.

He then smashes Garrett's phone and throws it into the wastebasket. He then orders Julie to stand up. He frisks her looking for her phone, taking some physical liberties in the process, and asks again where her cell phone is.

"I told you, I lost it. I have no idea where it is."

He then finds her purse and dumps it upside down, and everything falls out. The phone is not there either.

Then one of the terrorists again says something to the leader in again what appears to be Arabic.

The leader then asks if anybody else is in the house.

Both Garrett and Julie don't respond.

He asks again.

Again they don't respond.

The leader starts waving his gun at Garrett. Garrett finally says, "No."

The leader then asks, "Where's Alex's wife?"

Garrett mutters, "I don't know."

"You lie to me. You wanna die, right now?"

"No!"

"What's her name? Is it Sonja?"

The leader then motions to the other terrorists to search the house to find her.

"If we find her, maybe I shoot you here." He pokes his gun between Garrett's legs. "Because you lie to us, huh? She will tell us where we can find Alex. If she doesn't, then I think somebody here will pay the price. Maybe you pay the price, or how about them?" He points his gun at the kids.

He then walks over and waves his gun over the kids, and they start screaming again. The terrorists are absolutely merciless.

Julie eventually calms Lizzy and Mikey down, but they're still crying softly.

After about ten minutes or so, the other terrorists return, and say that they can't find anybody else in the house. Apparently, Sonja is not there. The leader then is furious and again starts threatening to kill somebody if they don't tell him where Alex is. He also wants to know where Sonja is.

Julie again tells them, "We don't know. Turn on the news. Read the papers. Nobody knows where the ambulance went. We wish we knew where they took him. He's my dad. We want to find him too. Why do you need to find him? Please tell me why it is so important that you find him." She's trying desperately to remain calm and now is trying to reason with them.

The leader becomes even angrier. He then tells them that if they don't know, they will hold them hostage for ransom until Sonja or somebody delivers Alex to them.

"Why do you want him?" Julie again asks the leader.

Again the leader tells her "You do not need to know. It is not of your business. Don't ask me again, or I get angry and hurt you."

"What has he done?" cries Julie. "He just saved my kids!. He may already be dead. We don't know anything. We can't help you. Why do you want him? Please let us go and we won't tell anyone you were here."

The leader then puts his face right into hers. He smells like a dead skunk as it appears that he's not had a shower or bath in weeks. He looks right into her eyes, only inches away from hers. His heavy black beard rubs against her face. She is trembling and shaking all over. He growls "How you say in America…fat chance? Nobody here goes anywhere until we find him. You ask again and you will never be able to see again." He points his gun right into her eyes."

With that, a white van arrives and parks in the street in front of the house. Two FBI agents get out and start to walk up to the front door. But as they do, they spot the other van in the driveway. Suspecting that something is wrong, they each disappear around each side of the house. The terrorists observe this through the window and set up an ambush inside the house.

Within minutes, the FBI agents are trying to sneak into the house through the back door and the downstairs door. All the terrorists, except for the leader, run off and disappear into other sections of the house. Soon afterward, a barrage of gunfire is heard.

A few minutes later, the terrorists return and hastily engage in a heated dialogue with the leader that Garrett and Julie cannot understand at all.

Garrett and Julie suspect the terrorists killed the FBI agents as they entered the house before they knew what was going on. All the terrorists now are frantic and move very quickly.

Two of the terrorists run out to the garage, open the garage door, open the back doors of the black van, and come back in the house with several black bags.

They open the bags and remove rope, duct tape, and black hoods. Fearful that the gunshots drew attention, the leader informs Garrett and Julie that everybody must leave the house immediately.

Julie asks, "Where are we going?"

"Someplace where you will not know and where nobody will find you. Or us."

Julie and Garrett struggle to try to get free; however, are quickly restrained and threatened if they don't cooperate. They are bound with duct tape so they can't talk or make any sounds, and they're hooded so that they can't see. Their hands are tied behind them.

Lizzy and Mikey are also gagged and tied up, but they're not hooded. Emily is picked up in her pumpkin seat by one of the terrorists, and he spits on her.

The terrorists then usher them all into the garage, and they are thrown to the floor in the back of the van. Julie somehow is able to get part of the tape off her mouth enough that she screams out, "If you don't let Lizzy bring her dolly bag and Racky, and if you don't let me bring food to feed the children and diapers, they will cry. You can't keep them gagged forever. Do you want that?"

"Why does the girl need her dolly bag?" the leader shouts".

"Because it has her doll and doll clothes in it and she takes it everywhere. If you don't let her take it, she will not stop crying until she gets it. Do you want her to cry?"

At the last minute, the leader goes back inside and grabs Lizzy's dolly bag and shouts out, "No raccoon." He then returns back to the garage and temporarily removes the hood from Julie, unties her hands, and accompanies her into the kitchen. He gives her thirty seconds to put baby food, some other food, and baby accessories into a diaper bag to bring. Then she is gagged and retied again, is re-hooded, and is pushed out into the garage. She immediately is thrown in to the back of the van, and the leader throws the dolly bag and the diaper bag at her feet. The terrorists climb in, the doors are closed as they take off, and the van disappears up the street.

Crackerjack is hiding in the laundry room, and the terrorists ignore him.

Thrown on the back floor of the van, Garrett and Julie wonder, "Where did Sonja go? Where is she? Why didn't the terrorists find her? Why are they looking for Alex or his body? What do they want with him? Does he have something they want?" In the back of their minds, they also wonder about the nuclear threats, the possible coming of the end of the world, and whether Ammen is for real. But most importantly they are terrified and are preoccupied with their own situation, and they ask themselves "Where are we going? What's going to happen to us?"

Chapter 18

Overall, after suffering from the incessant salvo of all the questions and the incredibly comprehensive review about my life, the thought of possible doom and torment in hell for eternity nearly becomes overwhelming and we have barely even gotten started.

After these questions the seven deadly sins are addressed. Pride, greed, lust, envy, gluttony, wrath, and sloth are also reviewed. Each of these has multiples of questions relating to them that range from the minimal to the foremost. It's surprising how many of these apply when you think that they would not. If you don't think they apply to you, at least to some degree, then you are ignorant of your own self being. This is made known to me in a very profound way.

Additional sins and misdoings that I had not even thought about are addressed along with a barrage of other questions. Why does it seem that the negatives about my life are more profound than all the positives and good things that I've done? Is there a reason for this? I have certainly done a lot of good in my life as well. Why aren't these being addressed to the same degree as all of these questions? Am I imagining this? This just can't be. In some cases, the questions apply to the measure of good versus bad based on a simple desire or thought regardless whether one actually carries out the actions.

Then after these are addressed, the Ten Commandments are raised. These involve innumerable questions in varying degrees, many of which apply in ways nobody even thinks about.

As my life is reviewed, I find myself asking the question whether I considered the possibility that my life on Earth was a test to determine where I would spend eternity in my afterlife. Oh, how I wish I would have been more aware of this when I was alive. I surely had thought about it, but not all of the time and certainly not every second every day. I wish everybody else would understand the critical importance of this as well. It's so easy to get caught up in our everyday lives on Earth that we are totally unaware of this.

Why wasn't I more aware of this when I had a chance? One should not ignore the possibility that life on Earth is a test without any opportunity for a redo. The intent is to try to live a pure life but that is impossible. Nevertheless, any undesirable answer to merely any one of these questions now makes me feel ashamed. I sense it's a sin in itself to neglect that possibility because that means you don't care. But ignorance and self-denial are actions of the devil in disguise.

The extent of the review is so enormous it is beyond comprehension. The calculation of the equation is of behemoth magnitude.

Included in the evaluation are the most insignificant things I've done in my life, events that at the time I would have thought were entirely inconsequential and trivial. However, now I realize that these too all count. Many are lost opportunities to do good deeds when I had the chance. Others were simply instances where I could have done better than I did. Regardless how insignificant they are, they all add up. The mirror doesn't lie, and I can't believe what I'm reliving.

One time I didn't clean up after my dog in my neighbor's yard who never cleaned up after his own dogs. His yard was a disgusting mess. Even though it was only one time, I should have cleaned up after my dog anyway and perhaps offered to clean up after his dogs as well. This was a lost opportunity.

Once I ignored another driver who pulled up at the same gas pump from the opposite direction who was angry with me because I got there seconds before he did. Perhaps I should have realized that he was in a hurry, and I should have let him pump his gas first. Another lost opportunity.

When I was a child, I got a kick out of burning ants with a magnifying glass and the sun. The ants were out in the yard and not anywhere near the house. The ants did not harm anything, and there was no purpose in killing them. I had killed some of God's creatures for no reason.

Once when I was at a fast food restaurant, I inadvertently pushed the lemonade button, which was right behind the water button for a split second before filling my cup with free water. The lemonade that briefly went into my cup was only a few drops. Nevertheless, it flavored my water, even though minimally, and I realize now that was considered stealing. I should have paid for the lemonade.

Another time I drove by and ignored a disabled car with a flat tire on the side of a lightly traveled road. I was in a hurry and assumed someone else, a trusted person, would drive by and help instead. I should have stopped anyway to assist. Another lost opportunity.

In another instance when I was much younger I was driving on a two lane highway doing the speed limit of 50 mph. Suddenly, a car pulls out right in front of me, causing me to slam on my breaks and swerve to avoid hitting it. That car then proceeds to creep along at about 10 mph in front of me. I couldn't pass it for miles and miles because of oncoming traffic. That made me very late to my appointment. I was very angry, tailgated the car, and called the driver all sorts of bad things.

After a very long time I'm finally able to pass the car. When I do I see that the driver is about a ninety-five-year old woman who could barely see over the steering wheel. Perhaps she shouldn't be driving at that age, but nevertheless, my anger wasn't justified. I shouldn't have driven so close behind her and yelled at her.

Additional events even more inconsequential than these are raised. There are so many such events that I didn't give much thought to at the time, they are overwhelming. I realize that everybody has numerous such events in their lives. I just wasn't aware at the time that every single one was a lost opportunity that would count.

I'm told to think about everything: every single misdoing, failure to do the right things in actions or in mind or in spirit, the inconsequential but lost opportunities, the seven deadly sins, the Ten

Commandments, etc. I'm then asked if I'm satisfied with my life. Has it really been good enough? Could I have done better? Am I going to pass or fail? How do I really know?

These thoughts are forced upon me whether I like it or not. They continue as my life continues to flash before me in the mirror and the evaluation continues.

I'm then asked if I'd thought about when my time is going to come when I was alive. It could be years from now. It could be next week. It could be tomorrow. Or it could be only minutes or seconds from now. You really don't know when. Should you start to pay attention to all of this immediately or can you afford to wait?

Is it worth the gamble to wait when you are risking where you will spend eternity in your afterlife? Did I ever consider this? Did I ever care about it? Remember the possibility that life and every second of it may be the one test of a lifetime that you certainly do not want to fail. And when your life comes to an end, it can come at any time, or at any second.

If you wait it's pretty much like Russian roulette, right? But in your case, instead of one bullet in six chambers, there are five. In other words, are you waiting to die or are you going to die waiting? All these thoughts are forced upon me one after another. Some are applicable but some are not. I wonder when they will ever end.

On one hand, I wish I would have had these thoughts more often and was more aware of all of these when I was alive. Now it's too late. But on the other hand, I wonder why I'm being asked these questions. These questions don't all apply to me. That's because I've attempted to live a good life and had a strong faith for nearly all my adulthood. I did not wait. So why am I being asked and told these things now? The questions thrust at me are overwhelming, and I'm absolutely fatigued.

It doesn't take me long to realize that an objective of life on Earth is to challenge evil by doing good in everything, all of the time. One must apply love to everything. This applies to every second in a lifetime. Nothing in one's life is immune. It all counts. All else falls into place accordingly. But everyone doesn't know this while they are alive. It's an awareness that is stolen by the devil.

The ultimate goal is to do good and love all the time without any omission whatsoever. But again, that is impossible. But nevertheless, it is imperative to try.

I cannot actually see the equation that is evaluating my life, but I can sense that it is of immense proportions. It's as if this monumental formula is multi-dimensional itself. There are numerous symbols and operating factors in the equation. Some are recognizable and some are not. One symbol is a sideways number 8. Another one is a backward number 6. I know what the sideways 8 means. As far as the backward 6 goes, I assume that as the variables and derivatives are applied and the changes are made in the equation, the constant remains the same. Perhaps the constant in this equation represents that which is desired or expected from God.

Then I sense some other symbols in the equation such as three interlaced rings with a surrounding ring. There are also factors in the equation that measure the degree of temptation, willpower, or effort that impact the weight given to each variable. There are other symbols in the equation that I have no idea what they mean. In between all these known and unknown symbols are all of the millions of variables of good and bad, each weighted to different degrees that represent my life. I'm not aware of the degree of each weight that is given to each question and answer, but I know which ones definitely outweigh and are more important than others.

It's a calculation that is far beyond anything that the smartest of the smartest mathematicians and scientists on Earth could ever understand. The equation that measures good versus bad is absolutely immense.

And while all these are being addressed, I feel an overwhelming question that looms. Am I willing to suffer in hell for an undetermined amount of time so that others can go to heaven? One premise is that this is what Jesus did. This feeling comes over me that regardless whether I'm in overall negative territory or not when the final balancing is complete, this question may come into play. I remember Pastor Gabriel preaching about this. But then I realize how unrealistic this would be. I don't think God would ever ask us to repeat what Jesus did. Nevertheless, I really hope this question is not asked of me.

I have no idea how I would answer it. But as unrealistic as this is, I wonder why I'm thinking about this.

I now am completely terrified and am shaking all over. I'm trembling with fear as now I wonder if I have perhaps failed the test. I had no idea. Not even a clue. I was so sure before that I had lived a virtuous and righteous life the best I could. I was so certain about it.

I was so confident, but now after reviewing my entire life and having these myriads of questions asked, I'm not so sure anymore. I am numb and cannot act or say anything. My emotions are bound within. I feel very sick. I feel like I am going to literally explode with emotion, but I can't. I want a do-over, another chance, but that won't happen. It's too late for that now.

But after intently focusing on the review of my life in the mirror and the myriad of questions, I suddenly realize that the questions of whether I believed in Jesus Christ, had faith in Him and loved Him, and whether I repented for my sins have not yet been addressed. I know I believed in Jesus as our Savior, had a strong faith, and acknowledged my sins for a very long time during my life. When will the answers to these questions be considered? Have they already been figured in? Surely that must carry enormous weight.

As I think about this, my life fades from the mirror. The mirror stares back at me, but now it's blank. I am absolutely distraught because these questions seem to me to be the most important of all, but they have not been addressed. Also I have not been asked if I'd ever repented and asked God for forgiveness. I realize the answers to all these questions would help me. But the blank mirror lasts only briefly as a wavering white light then appears in the mirror. Then the following questions are asked of me:

Did you repent for all of your sins to God?

Did you account for each one?

Did you ask for forgiveness?

Were you really sincere in your repentance and asking for forgiveness?

Did you forgive your enemies? How much so?

Did you truly believe in the Resurrection of Jesus?

Was your belief and faith in Him real, or was it only superficial?

Did you truly love Him? Did you truly make an effort to follow Him?

How profound did you believe that Jesus died for our sins?

Just how strong was your conviction in your faith in Jesus? Just how sincere was it? Was it a little bit or only a moderate amount or was it a lot?

Have you accepted Jesus as your Savior with all your heart and soul, or was it superficial? To what extent? And did you truly love your God and everything He created for you?

I am so relieved. I then realize that these questions do carry the most weight of all. In fact, the weight of these questions alone is so great that it can trounce all evil and sin. It's the trump card. Did I play it during my life? I sure did.

But I then sense what is the most important and critical question is whether or not I played it with enough conviction. If the extent of my belief, faith, and repentance was not sincere or strong enough and was not sufficient, then I'm doomed. But if it was sufficient it could wash away any net balance of the bad in my life. That's why it's the trump card. I just don't know if I played it with sufficient enough conviction and sincerity during my life. I'm pretty sure I did, but I'm not the one to judge. I know that it's a gift from God and all one needs to do is believe and accept it. And I wanted to believe, have faith, and accept the gift with all my heart and soul. But did I? Was my faith strong enough? Only God can judge this.

Now I am comforted to know that this variable is yet to be calculated, but I still don't know what the outcome of the equation will be. Then the wavering white light in the mirror disappears, and the mirror is blank again. But within a very short time another vision appears in the mirror. This vision is a scale that measures the positives in my life against the negatives in my life. The good versus the bad. It also takes into account the extent of my belief in Jesus, my faith, the extent of my love for others, and my repentance of my sins. It's the wheel of balance that I sensed during the review of my life that will reveal where I go in my afterlife.

The scale is actually a wheel that rotates and spins in place. It is the massive equation that absorbs everything about my life including and most importantly whether and to what extent I played the trump card. As the variables and weights of each are entered into the equation the wheel spins and rotates. The right side of the wheel is positive. The left side is negative. A pendulum swings from above and slowly sways from side to side as my life is evaluated. The pendulum is the indicator that will point to the final result when it finally stops. Shortly after this vision materializes in the mirror, I can see both the wheel and the pendulum slowing down as the entire review of my life is completed. I want the pendulum to come to rest on the right side of the wheel.

Although I am confident the pendulum will stop on the right side of center, I'm not certain, and suddenly, the balancing act becomes absolutely frightening again. To what extent were my belief, faith, love, and repentance strong enough? Was it enough?

Now I am literally petrified again and the wait to know the outcome is agonizing. The pendulum now swings more slowly back and forth and finally hovers around the middle but doesn't settle on either side of the center line. Where's it going to stop? Everything that is accounted for about my life and the impact of the trump card are so immense that it far exceeds anything that can be understood. The wheel of balance now has slowed considerably and nearly comes to a stop. I sense the trump card will determine where the pendulum finally stops. This is the last measure to be evaluated.

But just as the pendulum starts to stop, the wheel of balance slowly fades away, and I can't see it anymore. The mirror is blank again. The pendulum never did finally stop before it disappeared. What is the outcome? Why won't it tell me the final result? I want to know.

After the wheel of balance fades away, the mirror is blank once again, but only briefly. As I wait to learn the final result I'm astonished to see something else materialize in the mirror. What I see now is totally unexpected. In the mirror a vision materializes of me when I was about five years old sitting in my father's lap wearing the special shirt when he would tell me stories and puzzles. The vision zooms in and focuses on the shirt.

The shirt is just like I remembered it. There are three horizontal lines on the shirt and there are faded symbols on the middle line. The mirror and vision are enormous but still I strain my hardest to try and read it. But as before, the symbols are faded into the fabric and I just can't make out what it says.

I ask myself, why is this image of me wearing this shirt when I was five years old in the mirror now and what does this mean? I again squint and try my hardest to read the symbols or letters, but I just can't read them. They're just too faded. I wonder again just what do these symbols or letters mean. Why am I being shown this in the mirror now? What's going on? Oh, how I wish I could read these on the shirt. Will I ever understand what they say? Why is this so important now?

The image is there only very briefly. Then the image fades away and the mirror is blank again. There is nothing else to see in the mirror. The evaluation of my life is over now. Nothing else materializes in the mirror and the mirror starts to fade away as well. Soon the mirror is gone and I'm all alone in the void. I then realize that my ability to think freely has been reinstated. I ask myself what all did this mean.

What is the outcome of the review of my life? How is it being finally evaluated? Did I pass the test? Why am I not being told? Why was I shown the special shirt I wore when I was a child as the last vision in the mirror? Why is that so important? I don't know the answer to any of these questions.

As the mirror disappears I become cognizant again that I'm still in the void and I can see the gates of heaven and hell off to the sides on separate planes again. They are opposite of each other. They are tiny lights off in the distance and with the exception of these I'm in a complete state of nothingness. The time has come. Which way am I going to be sent? Or will I remain in a state of emptiness all alone by myself forever? Although I'm fairly confident where I expect and feel that I deserve to go, I am equally so scared, because I really have no idea.

Chapter 19

Andrew and Alana have no idea what's going on at Julie and Garrett's house. Alana is at work, and Andrew is sprawled out lying on the couch playing with Hannah and watching TV. He's otherwise biding his time until he needs to leave to go pick up Daniel and Matthew from summer camp.

Andrew suddenly perks up and scrambles to turn the volume up on the TV. There is a high priority news bulletin that has interrupted his program. This one is so important that it's preceded by the national emergency signal. Andrew jumps up to watch. Within seconds, a news broadcaster comes on the screen and after some introductory remarks announces:

"The leader of the terrorists making the threats against America is Muhannad Eblis Qadir, also known to some as Muhammad. He is a high ranking member of a previously unknown affiliated group of ISIS who has invaded America. It has been learned that he had previous ties with Al Qaeda militants and other terrorist groups including members of the Taliban. He and his group are Islamic extremists, Jihadists to the extreme. He is the leader of what is referred to as ISA, also known as the Islamic State of America.

"The following is an excerpt of a video from him that he just recently released for broadcast. He is speaking from an unknown location, presumably from Syria. However the ISA group is located in the United States."

The video begins with Muhammad saying, "There are at least twenty bombs that have been hidden in twenty American cities and other places in the United States. All are hidden in the most strategic places. Some of these are nuclear devices of unprecedented magnitude. They all have electronic timing devices and can be detonated remotely. They are all scheduled to be detonated at midnight in five days. And there is one in particular at a secret location, a location that is so unique that it could wipe out the entire country all by itself. There is nothing that anybody can do to prevent any of this.

"If any are found, they cannot be tampered with. They cannot be disabled or moved or they will explode immediately. Some of the nuclear bombs are much bigger than any other nuclear bomb ever built. They will wipe out the city and surrounding area into oblivion. I will soon let everyone know where some of these are located. It will not matter that you will know where they are because they will be completely tamper proof. Each has sensors that will trigger the detonation of the bomb if you touch it.

"I suspect that people are not taking us seriously and that nobody believes us. So, to show you that I am telling the truth and that we mean business, we will play a game with you American people. One of these bombs is set to explode in three hours from right now. I will even tell you in what city it's located and give you some clues where to find it.

"It hides within a twenty square mile area of Washington DC or what you all call the District of Columbia.

"It's set to be detonated in three hours from right now. Mark your clocks and watches. If America can find it in time with these clues I will give you, then I will have a nice surprise for you. I will then delay the explosion for perhaps up to three days. But if you cannot find it in time, then *kaboom*! If you find it, then you need to immediately broadcast where you found it so we know. You have three hours, starting right now."

He then provides photos with clues of the whereabouts of the bomb as he points to a clock.

The photos are cut-out pieces of certain buildings, like corner bricks and a window, a few trees, the bottom of a post to a street sign, the sky with parts of buildings or trees in the background, and then a final photo with a bunch of scrambled numbers on it.

The photos can be of anywhere. It will take forever to match the photos with each and every building in the area or to otherwise decipher the clues. But America must find it fast.

Muhammad then is shown laughing in an eccentric way to mock America. He then goes on to say,

"Ever since what you call 9/11, America spends billions of dollars on its military, foreign intelligence, defense systems, and national security. It wants to fight us in our homeland but can't. But America is so stupid. Its government is so incompetent. It forgets about its own country.

"You fail to secure the important things at your home. How very stupid your government is. We now take control and destroy everything you have. You will soon not have anything. It is happening right now. America will pay. Destruction and disease to America. Praise be to Allah.

"Within a few days I will tell you where the other bombs are located. Remember, if you attempt to tamper with, disable, or move any of the bombs, they will explode. Remember three hours. Remember the days. I will speak again soon."

Apparently, this news came on earlier and this broadcast is a repeat, but Andrew must have missed it as this is the first time he's seen it.

After the end of the video the broadcaster advises the American public that if anyone knows the whereabouts of the bombs or encounters one, or suspects anything, to notify the authorities immediately. He adamantly states, "Do not, I repeat, do not get close to or attempt to touch the device in any way."

He then shows live streaming video of pure panic in the Washington DC area. People are trying to leave the city. There is total gridlock everywhere. All major and secondary highways are parking lots. Gas stations are closed. Not a car can move anywhere. The National Guard now has been called out but they can't do anything because they can't move either because of the massive traffic jams. The city and surrounding area is in a complete state of panic.

Authorities are looking for the bomb, and they ask everybody to study the photos, and if they can decipher any clues where the bomb is to let them know immediately. A hotline phone number is provided. But, nobody wants to look for the bomb. Instead they want to leave town. The government is in a state of flux and many high-ranking government officials are headed to underground bunkers or are flying far away. For all practical purposes, the president has disappeared, and nobody has heard from him.

He then comments that if it's the objective of the terrorists and if it's their intent to create total pandemonium and chaos in America, they have certainly accomplished that.

Shortly afterward, a local news segment comes on the screen. It proceeds to discuss the Arab and the old white van and that the authorities believe that he may be responsible for the fire and kidnapping of Alex. The public is notified that the Arab is suspected to be armed and dangerous and that if anyone knows the whereabouts of the Arab or the van to inform the authorities immediately.

Andrew then telephones Alana to see if she's heard the news. He reaches her and after a few minutes he hangs up and calls Julie to see if she, Garrett, or Sonja has heard about it. But when he calls their house nobody answers. He then tries to call Julie's cell phone. It is turned off, and he gets her voice recording. He then tries Garrett's cell phone. He doesn't answer his either because it was smashed by the terrorists. He then calls Sonja on her cell phone. Again, there is no answer.

Andrew finds this very strange that nobody is answering their phones. He sends them all a text message and asks each of them to call him right away. No response. Because everybody usually always either answers their phone or text immediately, he finds this alarming.

He senses something's wrong, and he calls Alana back. "Alana, I've tried to call Julie, Garrett, and my mom, and nobody's answering their phones. I then sent each of them a text and asked them to call me right away. Nobody has responded at all."

"Andrew, I'm going to leave work early and I'll stop by their house on the way home to check on them. I hope to leave in about a half hour or so."

A few minutes later, Alana calls Andrew back. "Andrew, I decided to also call Julie, Garrett, and Sonja, but couldn't reach any of them either. I'll tell you what, instead of going over to their house, I'll pick up Matthew and Daniel from summer camp and come home to be with the kids so you can go over and check on them. I think you should leave right away. You can take Hannah with you."

"I'm not going over there. If you don't want to stop by on the way home, then we'll discuss it when you get here."

Alana, clearly frustrated, hangs up. About a half hour later, she comes home. Alana and Andrew then proceed to argue because Andrew doesn't want to drive over there and neither does Alana.

"Andrew, you're just being lazy. All you want to do is stay home with the kids. You need to be a man and go over there. I'm ordering you to go! I'll take Hannah and pick up the boys while you go there. Call me as soon as you get there."

Andrew huffs and puffs, grabs his keys, and leaves.

Andrew arrives at Julie and Garrett's house and sees the white van parked out front. He's apprehensive about going up to the house and wonders what's going on. He knows that this is some free time for him and he wonders whether he should take advantage of things and just go to a bar for a while. As he's contemplating this while parked in their driveway for some time, Alana calls him on his cell phone.

"Andrew, it's me Alana. Where are you? Have you found them?"

"Not yet. I just now pulled up the driveway to their house. There's a van parked out in front. I have no idea who it is."

"Well, if you just now arrived, it sure took you a long time to get there. Is Garrett, Julie, and your mom there?"

"I don't know. I suppose so. Their garage door is open and their cars are still in the garage."

"Well, apparently they're still in the house and have some visitors. Maybe that's why the van is parked out front. Maybe that's why they've not answered their phones."

She suspects that he's procrastinating and tells Andrew, "Just go in there and make sure everything is okay and then call me right back."

161

Andrew, disgusted, doesn't want to go up to the house. He mutters "Okay", and hangs up on her.

He then reluctantly walks up to the front door. He rings the doorbell and knocks on the door, but nobody answers. He discovers that the door is unlocked. He slowly cracks the door open and peers inside. He doesn't hear anything. The house is eerily quiet.

Suddenly, Crackerjack comes to the door and starts barking. Andrew wonders why he's barking. "He knows who I am and normally he would greet me with his tennis ball in his mouth wanting to play," he thinks. "Something must be wrong."

Andrew slowly enters the house and calls out for Julie. No answer. He then calls out to Garrett and then to Sonja. No answer. Andrew starts to get frightened. Then Crackerjack runs into another part of the house and keeps barking. Andrew slowly follows him, and they enter the back room. Lying on the floor in a pool of blood is one of the FBI agents. Andrew is so startled that he runs back into the living room and screams. He's shocked and doesn't know what to do.

Crackerjack then runs downstairs and is barking some more. Andrew follows him and discovers the other FBI agent also lying in a pool of blood by the basement walk out door. He screams again and runs back upstairs. Nobody else is in the house.

At that time, several white SUVs pull up, and a swarm of FBI agents surrounds the house with guns drawn. Apparently, the agents who were killed had called before entering the house and said they may need backup. When they didn't respond, the FBI sent additional agents to the scene.

Several FBI agents enter the house and run into Andrew in the living room and tell him to sit down on the sofa as they disperse throughout the house. One of the agents stands over Andrew with a gun pointed at his head.

After a quick search of the house and discovering the agents who were killed by the terrorists, the agents tell Andrew to get down on his knees and to put his hands behind his back. He's immediately handcuffed as a suspect of the killings. Andrew starts pleading his case that he's innocent and explains why he's there. They don't believe him and tell him to shut up.

Then as the FBI agents are talking on their cell phones and amidst a flurry of activity they hear a noise coming from the basement. Several FBI agents then slowly and silently go down the steps with their guns drawn. As they peek around the corner, there in the shadows appears Sonja. The FBI agents take aim, but at the last second raise their guns straight up in the air. They recognize her.

They help her upstairs as she's absolutely hysterical. "What happened?" they ask her. She's shaking from head to toe and it takes her several minutes to compose herself.

"I was in the kitchen when a bunch of terrorists jumped out of a van and brought my daughter and son-in-law in the house through the garage. They had guns and were yelling at them. I was terrified and ran downstairs and hid in a crawl space in the back of a closet. I know they were looking for me but never found me. I heard somebody come in the house and then gunshots at the same time from upstairs and downstairs. Then I heard them take Julie and Garrett and their kids away. There was a lot of yelling and screaming going on. The terrorists were looking for Alex, my husband."

"We know about what happened to Alex. Do you know why they're looking for him?"

"No. Nobody knows anything. It's still a big mystery."

"So, who killed the agents? Do you know what happened?"

"What agents?"

"There are two FBI agents who entered the house to protect you all, but they were shot on the spot."

"If that's the case, I'm sure it was the terrorists. I heard the shots but didn't know what was going on. I really don't know much because I was hiding, but I'm certain it was them. Andrew didn't arrive until after the terrorists left and after I heard the gunshots. I heard Andrew scream after he came in, but I was afraid to come out because I wasn't absolutely sure if any terrorists were still in the house."

Andrew then yells out to the FBI agents, "See, I told you I didn't kill them! I want to call Alana, my wife. I want to talk with her right now!"

One of the agents puts his hand down Andrew's pants pocket to get his cell phone as Andrew is still handcuffed and then dials the number given to him by Andrew.

The agent holds the phone up so Andrew can talk with her. After a few minutes, the agent talks with Alana and after a few more minutes he hangs up and takes the handcuffs off Andrew.

Andrew stretches his arms in front of his body and slumps back into the couch, looking at the agent in disgust.

The agents search the house and find Garrett's cell phone smashed in the wastebasket. They can't find Julie's cell phone. Sonja then pulls her cell phone from her pocket and turns it back on. She had turned it off when she hid in the crawl space because she was afraid that if somebody called her, the terrorists would hear it and find her.

After doing some preliminary investigative work and assigning a security detail to watch over the house and clean up, they let Andrew return to his house. He takes Sonja with him since it would not be safe for her to stay at Julie's house. Two FBI agents follow Andrew and Sonja home in a white SUV.

When they arrive at Andrew's house, the agents come in and talk with Alana, Andrew, and Sonja. They tell them that they will provide a security detail for them. They explain it will likely be unmarked cars parked outside of the house.

They tell Andrew that they want to set up some remote surveillance cameras in his house and to wiretap all their phones so that they can monitor them in case the terrorists or anyone else contacts them.

Although Andrew agrees with the FBI providing protection, he reluctantly agrees with the cameras and telephone monitor. Alana on the other hand adamantly agrees with everything the FBI wants to do.

Sonja then remembers Crackerjack. "You know, we left Crackerjack back at the house," she says.

Andrew retorts, "He'll be okay."

Alana shoots back, "He will not be ok. Who's going to feed him? Does he have water? Who's going to let him outside? Andrew, I cannot believe it. How could you have forgotten him? You go back and get that dog now. Give him a biscuit as soon as you get there too."

"I'm not going back there. There were dead people in the house."

One of the FBI agents smiles at Alana and then looks at Andrew. "I'll go with you."

They leave in the FBI's SUV. While driving there, Andrew is fascinated by all the electronic communications and surveillance equipment in the car. He comments "This is all custom-built, right?" The agent doesn't respond.

When they arrive at the house, a few of the other agents are still there taking pictures, dusting for fingerprints and doing other investigative work. Crackerjack is nowhere to be found. But a walk around the house quickly finds him playing fetch with another FBI agent in the backyard. When Crackerjack sees Andrew, it doesn't take him long to come bounding up to him with his tennis ball in his mouth with his tail flying everywhere.

As soon as they all get in the SUV and Crackerjack jumps in the back, Alana calls Andrew on his cell phone. "Don't forget his dog food and dog toys."

Andrew hangs up on her then huffs and puffs and goes back inside to get them. A few minutes later, they return to Andrew and Alana's house with Crackerjack.

As soon as they arrive and Andrew sits down in his chair and turns on the TV, they hear the national emergency broadcast signal. They all know what that means. There has been another critical development in the terrorist activity and threats. Everybody huddles around to watch. In the meantime, the FBI agents go back outside and set up camp in their SUV across the street. A van pulls up and parks behind the SUV. Apparently, it is additional FBI support. By now it's getting very late in the day. It's getting dark outside as some black clouds roll overhead.

"I wonder what's happening now," comments Alana.

As they wait for the emergency news bulletin to come on, Andrew jokingly comments, "Maybe they're hiding another bomb where we live in our city that will also go off in three hours. Wouldn't that be something?"

Alana looks at Andrew sternly. "I can't believe you would say something like that. Will you hush and grow up!"

Everyone is very anxious to see what this new emergency news broadcast will say. Obviously, they expect it to be very bad news.

Chapter 20

As I gaze off into the distance and look at the two lights, I feel myself slowly moving again. I am petrified and then suddenly realize that I have every reason to be. I'm moving toward the pulsating orange-and-red ball of fire, and I am pretty sure I know what that is.

I am so scared. My sobbing has turned into a full scale hysterical meltdown as I cry out "No, no, no, this can't be happening! Why me? I've lived a righteous life. I've repented for my sins and asked for forgiveness. And I've believed in and had faith in Jesus. I did love others. I did love my God. I'm sure my faith has been strong enough. I can't believe this! Dear God, please help me! This must be a mistake! Why am I being sent this way? There has to be a reason! Why? Please! Tell me!"

As I'm crying uncontrollably I find myself floating again. The journey to the gates of hell takes some time. The light gradually gets larger and larger as I move closer to it.

I think again about the family back home and can see them, but they're starting to fade away. I know all about the terrorist crisis, ISA, the bombs and biological weapon threats, the FBI and CIA visits, what happened at Julie's house, their abduction, the changing status of the national economy, and the man named Ammen.

It's interesting that he's drawn such an incredible following so quickly. I have no idea whether he's for real or not, but my initial reaction is that I suspect that he's not. But I really don't know anything about him. Maybe he is for real. He looks just like Jesus. Maybe I shouldn't be so premature to judge. But even the image of him fades away for some reason. For some reason, when this happens, I become absolutely distraught.

I then try to see myself and where I am back home, and again I can't see myself at all. I then try to see what's going with the Arab and Officer Musty, and I can't see them either. Why can I sometimes see my family and know what's going on regarding the terrorists, the crisis, and the economy, but nothing else?

I then look above to see if the spirit is still with me. It is. But I feel more uneasiness about this spirit now. I feel something different about it but I have no idea why. I sense that it is still both good and evil, and the spirit is becoming unstable. Maybe it is two spirits and not one.

After spending time reminiscing about my life and wishing I could live it all over again and have another chance, I gradually arrive at the gates of hell. The entrance is an opening to a massive cavern that is guarded by Cerberus of gigantic proportions. It could not be any more monstrous and frightening, and I'm trembling with fear. I gaze into the cavern, and it has the appearance of a massive dungeon that is never ending in all directions. I keep crying out, "What's going on? I don't deserve to be here! Why?"

The cavern is so vast that it goes on forever in every direction all around me. But I sense that it is multi-dimensional as well although this is beyond my understanding.

I am led by some unknown force past the beast and into what appears to be a waiting room. I can sense other souls there, but I can't see them or talk with them. After a little while, I'm led to a hell viewing room where I learn about its infrastructure. There are no visible walls, but each room is separated by some sort of force field or window.

I can hear off in the vast distance the incredible wailing of multi-millions of souls crying out in constant pain and agony. The sound becomes louder and then deafening and is unbearable. The stench of a sulfuric odor and other odors makes me want to vomit. I can feel the heat radiating from the cavern. It's more horrific than I ever imagined. I'm already sick and shaking uncontrollably with fear, but I try to deal with it.

I look down at my body. Although I can't see it, I know I'm completely naked, and I can sense my flesh and body parts that will be subject to the pain and torture.

Again, I look up to see if the spirit is with me and wonder if it is an evil spirit or a good spirit. I wonder this because again I am getting the feeling that it's now different than it was before throughout my journey here. In fact, I get the bizarre sense that there is not one spirit but two spirits. "What's going on?" Maybe I'm imagining things.

What I learn about hell is through some sort of mental telepathy coming from this incredible powerful force that I can't see. Being in the viewing room is like an orientation before I am led any farther.

The viewing room looks out over a lightly lit massive cavern that goes past the horizon in every direction. In the middle is the Lake of Fire. There are demons that are frightening and hideous beyond description everywhere. Surrounding the Lake of Fire there are separate rooms that go off into the distance that seem to be never ending. Each room is intended to punish souls by unbelievable torture and torment depending on the type of sins that were committed and the extent of the sins. Each room is designated for a particular type of sin or bad or evil doing and the extent of it in one's life. Once a soul finishes its designated torment, torture, and pain in whatever rooms it is sent, it is cast in the Lake of Fire.

I'm allowed to see several rooms closest to the orientation room. The first room I'm allowed to see is that of hopelessness. As soon as one enters, one loses all hope of escaping and realizes that he or she will be tortured forever. There he or she learns what eternity is really like. This feeling is incurable and is so mentally agonizing that it alone is enough to result in consummate suffering.

The room is so hot that the souls catch fire and burn upon entering it, but don't burn up. The burn is a continuing process and no soul knows how long the incredible pain will last. They assume it will be nonstop and will go on forever. The torrential bawling alone coming from the torture that these souls suffer is incredibly frightening.

Souls that are being tormented in this room include those who have repeatedly lied or deceived others in their lives. I wonder if that means that the soul is being lied to when it enters the room but isn't aware of it.

The second room I see is that of failure. Souls in this room are suffering for being of greed and failure to help others in need. They are broiled above flames and are suffering thirst and hunger from the deprivation of water and food that it's so profound that they suffer an incredible sickness.

They have what is equivalent to a stomach ache and gastrointestinal illness that is so severe that their bodies continually writhe in excruciating pain. Then they are submersed in the boiling liquid. Even though they are desperate for food and water, the souls are all vomiting, and they swim in their own vomit and diarrhea. These souls were so greedy during their lives that they now are paying the price for not helping the needy by being deprived of the same things that they were.

The wailing coming from these souls is absolutely piercing.

The next room I see is for those who have severely disobeyed the laws of lust. Souls in this room include adulterers, rapists, and those who engage in child pornography among others who disobey the laws of lust. The longer or more intense the action or thought one has, then the more the sin. The more sin one has, then the more the punishment.

Here, souls are suspended above flames of fire, and various body parts are cut off one by one by demons with machetes and knives. The body parts reappear, and the process is repeated over and over again.

The gnashing of teeth and howling from the unbearable pain coming from these souls is unfathomable.

The next room I see is that of torment. The souls in this room are suffering for hurting others, whether deliberately or by self-negligence. Souls are thrown into an enormous vat that is full of wriggling snakes, worms, maggots, scorpions, leeches, and spiders.

The vat is boiling above flames of fire. When thrown in, the souls disappear and are completely covered by the soup of the squirming creatures. The souls eventually swim up to the top to try and breathe and escape but are then poked down and buried again by the demons with pitch forks. This goes on continuously.

I see their eyes are eaten out. I see snakes, worms, maggots, scorpions, leeches, and spiders crawling out of their eyes, mouths, noses, and ears after eating their internal organs. These all reappear and the process is repeated. I don't want to look, but I'm forced to. I have no choice.

The howling that comes from these souls is absolutely intolerable. I cannot believe just how gruesome this all is. I have never been so terrified and I am shaking in incredible horror.

I have only seen these four rooms. After seeing just these four rooms, I can't even begin to imagine what the other rooms are like. Then I understand there are countless rooms and that each is designed for each type of sin or other bad doing, and that the time that each soul spends in each room depends on the extent of the sin or bad doing that he or she committed.

And a soul may reenter the same room and experience the same punishment multiples of times after their time spent in other rooms. Many souls continually rotate between the various rooms in unbelievable agony before being cast in the Lake of Fire forever. I wonder if the extent of torture is dictated by the result of the equation that measures how one lived his or her life.

This all is so horrific that I want to pass out or die again, but I can't. I must endure this and there's no way out. There's no escape ever. While I'm trying to imagine what the other rooms are like and how they could be any worse than these, I then understand that all of these rooms are in what is known as the first level of the first chamber. Also, I learn there are nine levels to the first chamber. Each torture and torment that takes place in each subsequent level is more intense than that of the previous level. Therefore, there are countless rooms in each of nine levels in the first chamber, with each level being worse than the one before it.

I absolutely cannot fathom how the extent of the torture in just the second level can be any more horrific than the first level which

I have seen much less subsequent levels being even worse. This is absolutely unbelievable.

Then, I learn that there are nine chambers. In each chamber there are nine levels and in each level in each chamber there are countless numbers of rooms. The torture in each successive chamber is more intense than the preceding chamber. The last chamber, being the ninth, is reserved for the most wicked souls of all.

This is absolutely incomprehensible. I simply cannot imagine whatsoever what the other rooms in even the first level of the first chamber must be like notwithstanding the fact that there are nine levels in each of nine chambers, and that each level and each chamber is worse than the one before it. I think that there is no way that the subsequent levels and chambers can be more intense than the first level which I am viewing. But evidently they are. The thought is so staggering that I cannot understand how it's possible. It's totally unimaginable.

I then learn that the subsequent chambers are of different dimensions of torture, pain, and agony of which only God and Satan are aware. That's why I can't understand this. I wonder what those dimensions are like and what souls go there. But I certainly don't want to go to find out.

I can sense Satan overlooking all of hell, but I can't see him. I understand there are numerous demons everywhere attending to each room even though I can't actually see all of them or all the rooms. The demons are not only ugly beyond comprehension, but their monstrous appearance is terrifying beyond reality. I can only see some of the rooms in the first level of the first chamber. Just having to look at a demon is so frightening that it's a horrific torture in itself.

The demons seem to have various powers and there appear to be certain demons with special powers. I sense that the more demons there are, then the more power Satan has.

Then the orientation period is over and I'm led out of the viewing room. I'm being forced to go to one of the rooms to start my torture and the rest of my eternity. I feel myself moving again although it's against my will. I cannot stop it. I am trembling with fear that is so overwhelming that it's indescribable. I start to float away again. No stopping this.

I wonder what the first room will be like and if there is any way that I can tolerate it. I know that I won't and that I am doomed. I am so frightened I'm shaking uncontrollably. I still don't understand why I'm here. I again cry, but there are no tears.

Chapter 21

Julie, Garrett, and their children experience a terrifying ride that, although starts off smooth, ends as a jarring journey as they get jostled about. It's quite a rough drive. They can't see because they're hooded. They can't move because their hands and feet are tied. They're all on the back floor of the van rolling around with every turn.

During the ride, they can hear the terrorists talking; however, they can't understand anything they say. Both Lizzy and Mikey are trying to cry but only muffled sounds can be heard because they're gagged with duct tape over their mouths. Julie can feel them struggling but after a while they tire themselves out and settle down. Emily has fallen sound asleep and has withstood all of the bounces and the noises of the ride, both from inside and the outside of the van.

The driver is driving relatively fast and at times appears to be reckless. The van's shock absorbers are shot and the ride leaves them hurting all over. They figure that the trip takes somewhere over an hour. It seems like the van made a lot of turns and drove around in circles at times, but they have no way of knowing. They don't know if they're a hundred miles away or just a few miles from their house.

They believe that they've been on highways and some back roads, but they have no idea where they are. Finally, the van comes to rest and they can hear a noise that sounds like a large door opening up. The van then moves slowly and stops and they can hear the noise again. They assume the garage door has closed and they're in a garage somewhere.

They hear the terrorists open up the doors and leave the van, and can briefly hear additional noises in the background. They know they're inside a building somewhere. There appears to be additional people in the building and they presume they're more terrorists. Then the doors of the van are shut, and they remain in the van alone for some time. After a most uncomfortable ride, they're happy to be at a standstill, but they're very apprehensive as to what may be in store for them.

By now, both Garrett and Julie have been able to loosen the duct tape over the mouths somewhat by opening and twisting their mouths every which way, and with some difficulty, they can talk with each other. Garrett says to Julie, "Are you okay? Are the kids okay? I sure wish we had our cell phones. We could call for help if we could free our hands. This is the first time we have been left alone. Maybe the police or FBI could find us using a GPS from our phones or something."

Julie responds, "Well, they destroyed yours, and I have no idea where mine is. Maybe Lizzy was playing with it and it's under the sofa, or it fell behind a sofa cushion or something back home. I should've had you call my cell phone back home to find it before they came, but that's history now."

Julie has no idea that her cell phone, which was turned off, is in Lizzy's dolly bag which is sitting right by her feet. But even if she realized this, it wouldn't help because her hands are tied and she's hooded.

After what seems like an hour or so of silence except for the muffled sounds coming from outside of the van, suddenly they are startled when the back doors are abruptly opened, and they hear the terrorists yelling at them. They can't understand anything they're saying.

Suddenly they feel themselves being hoisted up and thrown out of the van onto a concrete floor. Then their hoods are removed, and they can see. But they're left there alone for a while. They ache all over.

It seems to be a large vacant warehouse of some sort. It's dirty and hot, and although the terrorists have some fans going here and there, it really doesn't help much. It's dimly lit. The garage door from which the van entered is an industrial sized door that is tall enough for large trucks to go through, but is not very wide. Guarding the door are two men with automatic weapons.

Off to the side inside the warehouse parked next to the van in which they were transported are several other vans. Most are old, and they are all black and appear to have been repainted. That is, except for one that is older and white. It's parked on the end and is hard to see.

Garrett and Julie immediately think this just might be the same van that Alex and Sonja had talked about. They think of the van that had been watching and stalking Alex for some time. But they don't know whether this is that same van or not.

The building is quite large and consists of mostly a vast open concrete floor with industrial sized overhead cranes on one side of the warehouse. The ceiling appears to have a retractable roof that can be opened up in the middle. There's no explanation why the roof can be opened except perhaps so that large industrial equipment can be lowered in and out. "How strange," Garrett thinks.

Everything is dusty and dirty. Off to one side they can see several tables set up with all sorts of computer equipment, numerous monitors, wires, cables, what appear to be antennas, and other electronic equipment. There are boxes next to all of the equipment apparently to transport the equipment when necessary.

In the middle of the room there is some sort of contraption encased in glass with a lot of wires and other electronic equipment hooked up to it. It's rather large, and there are metal railings that surround it several feet off of the ground. There are several terrorists working on the device but it's too far away to get a good look at it. But Garrett has an idea of what it may be.

Down the exterior wall a short distance from the garage door is what appears to be a vacant office that has a separate outside door that is presumed to be locked. If there are any windows, they're hidden behind curtains that reach the floor along the back side of the office.

There are a few windows outside of the office in the warehouse, but they're all boarded up and are at least ten feet above the ground. In the far corner of the warehouse is another very small room, which appears to be a bathroom.

A short distance away there are some ropes that dangle from the ceiling and some knives and other things on a small table. Underneath the ropes appears to be dried-up blood on the floor. Garrett immediately recognizes these as items used for torture. A large spider can be seen scurrying across the blood on the floor.

Garrett presumes the activity going on in this abandoned warehouse is perhaps a temporary subcommand post of a larger terrorist organization of which their kidnappers are a part. There are perhaps as many as eight terrorists all hovering around the tables working with the equipment and talking to each other or working on the glass encased device in the middle of the room. Many are clothed in Middle Eastern garb. Some of the terrorists have an AK-47 strapped over their shoulders as if it was a permanent accessory to their apparel.

When they talk with each other, they're very animated. Some are very flamboyant when they talk and others seem to have an angry disposition about everything. There are automatic weapons lying around everywhere, and additional weapons hang on the wall behind the large table.

Both Garrett and Julie are very uncomfortable. Lizzy, Mikey, and Emily are several feet away and are struggling violently to get free. Muffled sounds can be heard coming from their bound mouths. Garrett and Julie are very thirsty and need to go to the bathroom. But more importantly, they are distraught over what the terrorists are doing to their kids.

They look at their kids and start crying and try to get the attention of the terrorists. They need to take care of Lizzy, Mikey, and Emily. Among other things, it's time to feed them and they expect that Lizzy and Mikey will be wailing whenever their duct tape is removed.

They desperately want their own tape removed, but more critically, they want the gags removed from Lizzy and Mikey. They know how uncomfortable they are. Mikey has a runny nose, and he's having trouble breathing since he can't breathe through his mouth. They remember that only the evening before they were breathing smoke from the fire.

They also know that it's about time to change Emily's diaper and they need to check Mikey as well. They know there's something in the pants of one of them because they can smell it.

Finally, after what seems like eternity, the leader walks over to them. The first thing he says to them is, "Are you going to tell us where Alex is now?"

Both Garrett and Julie try to talk but are afraid to. They make muffled sounds through the tape over their mouths.

The leader then angrily says, "I'll take the tape off of your mouths and untie you if you promise to tell me where Alex is."

Julie promptly nods her head up and down. She will do anything to be able to breathe again and be able to talk normally.

The leader then removes her gag. Julie is sobbing. "Can you please take the duct tape off my kids and untie them? Please? Please? Look how you're hurting them. They're not going to go anywhere, you know that."

The leader says, "I can't do that. They will cry and somebody here will shoot them if they make any noise."

Julie then pleads with him. "Please? They need to be fed and have their diapers changed. If you let me attend to them, they won't cry. I promise."

The leader yells out something Garrett and Julie don't understand, but clearly he's agitated that they have to deal with the children. He makes it clear he wished they were never brought along.

After a few seconds, another terrorist who had been watching this comes over. Apparently he's another leader and he says something to the first leader that cannot be understood. The first leader then leaves and the second leader says in good English, "Okay. I will allow this, but if anybody cries or makes any noise or if anybody moves, I can guarantee you that you will wish you were dead."

He then unties Julie and removes the tape from Garrett's mouth but doesn't untie him. She then goes over and frees Lizzy and Mikey who immediately fly into her arms. The leader tells all of them to remain still and quiet and not to make any noise as he flashes his gun at them.

Garrett then asks if there's a bathroom. Julie says she has to go as well and that she needs some water for the kids.

The leader then gets angry and outright comments that he wishes the other terrorists had just left the kids back home. But then he reluctantly agrees and goes on to say that if Garrett and Julie don't cooperate, they will kill the kids.

He then calls over another terrorist with an AK-47 to watch over Garrett while he accompanies Julie to the bathroom with Lizzy and Mikey. He goes in with them and watches everything she does while waving his gun in the air. She changes a stinky diaper and gives them water.

They come back out and Julie then feeds all three of her children, depleting what she had brought in the bag by about a third.

Lizzy is holding her dolly bag and crawls into Julie's lap and falls asleep. Mikey sits next to Julie. Emily is in her pumpkin seat, and although her big blue eyes are wide open and she is staring at everything, she doesn't make a sound.

Garrett is then allowed to go to the bathroom and is given a water bottle. They are led to a corner near the torture apparatus and are told to sit and be still. The leader then says, "If anybody makes a move or makes any noise, you know what will happen," as he waves his gun in their faces.

They sit there for at least another hour while the terrorists attend to their business. In the meantime, several terrorists can be seen leaving the building in several of the vans. Now there are only about half dozen terrorists left and three vans in the warehouse. It appears that whatever work they were doing on the device and with the electronic equipment on the table has been completed.

The terrorists now are observed packing the computer and other electronic equipment in the boxes, apparently to be removed from the building. It looks like they may be leaving soon.

One of the leaders comes over. "I'm sorry I've neglected you. We've been preoccupied with some things." He sits down with them and asks them again but very calmly "Where is Alex Fisheramen?"

Garrett and Julie again explain that they don't know and that nobody knows. The leader asks again, but a little louder, "Where is Alex Fisheramen. Tell me now!"

"Why do you want Alex? What do you want with him?" Julie confidently says. "We are nothing but a hindrance to you. We can't help you, and we're just in your way. Why don't you just take us out in the van and dump us off somewhere? That will make it easier for you, right?"

The leader then remarks "Somebody somewhere knows where Alex is." He points to the torture equipment and says, "Do you know what that is?"

Garrett reluctantly nods his head up and down.

The leader smiles at Garrett. "We're holding you for ransom. If nobody comes forth and gives Alex to us, dead or alive very soon, then one of you will pay the price." He looks at Julie and then the children and exclaims, "Or worse!" as he waves his gun at them.

He continues, "Who will pay the price? I'll tell you what. I'll let you decide who goes first," as he points to the children and walks over to the ropes hanging from the ceiling and throws some additional torture devices and several knives on the floor by the ropes.

Garrett mumbles, "That will not accomplish anything. We don't know anything! We've told you that!"

"But it will because we intend to show the outside world." He then points to a camera system with camera lights other terrorists are setting up on tripods nearby. "We will broadcast very soon." He looks up at the dangling rope and then down at the knives. "Somebody knows where Alex is. You will tell me who goes first. Or if you don't, then I will decide!"

He again looks at the kids and then grabs Mikey by his neck, and he screams bloody murder.

The leader then lets go of him. Garrett then blurts out, "If you must do this, then do it to me. You can hang me up there, but don't you dare touch our children."

The leader then leaves and is on his phone. Garrett recognizes that it's not a cell phone but another type of phone, perhaps a satellite phone or powerful two-way radio of some sort. Garrett, Julie, and the kids are then left sitting there for another half hour or so.

They're all resting when they're again startled by the garage door coming back up and another van drives in. There's a flurry of activity, and then two vans leave. Why do vans keep coming and going? When the garage door is briefly opened, they can see that it's already getting dark outside.

They figure that now there are only four terrorists left in the building and two vans. One of them is the white one that they assume is the van that the "Arab" might be driving. But Garrett reasons if the Arab in the white van kidnapped Alex and is part of this group, then why would they be asking them where he is? So perhaps this is not the same white van, but he doesn't know for sure.

The leader comes over and sits down with them but doesn't say anything. Garrett then asks him what the contraption in the glass case is and points to it across the way. The leader then exclaims, "You do not need to know. You and a lot of other people will find out soon enough."

Garrett remembers what he had heard on the news and puts two and two together. The device is exactly what he thought it may be. He then screams, "My God! You wouldn't really do this, would you?"

The leader smiles at him, again in a smart-ass way, says nothing and gets up and leaves again. He then turns around and comes back and waves his gun in Garrett's face and startles everybody by yelling out loud enough to wake the dead, "Are you going to tell us where Alex is? Is anybody? If not, it looks like we are going to have some fun here!" as he points to the rope and knives on the floor. He then kicks the knives farther away and tells Garrett not to make a single move.

He smiles again at Garrett and leaves. They sit there a while longer alone.

After what seems like eternity, two terrorists come over and get the camera and lights ready. A third terrorist is on the phone with somebody, as if he is coordinating something.

The leader then comes over and asks Julie who they decided on. Garrett immediately gets up and says, "Me." Julie looks at him in horror.

The leader stares at Garrett. "Okay, have it your way this time. But this will not be the case next time." He makes a loop in the rope, orders Garrett to lie on the floor, unties his hands, and puts the loop around Garrett's ankles. He hoists him hanging upside down several feet off of the floor. Garrett is dangling by his ankles, and his face turns beet red as blood rushes to his head. He is moaning and starts to scream.

The leader then unbuckles Garrett's pants and he pushes them up to his ankles and ties them with additional rope. He takes a knife and approaches Garrett as he slowly swings back and forth. He yells something about Allah and slices Garrett's shirt and his underwear, partially cutting him in the process. Blood starts to drip on the floor. The leader puts a mask and a different turban over his head, and the camera lights come on. He then points to the other terrorist working the camera and lights who motions that he's ready.

The leader steps in front of the camera.

"Good evening to you, Americans. You have probably already heard from my good friend" (apparently talking about Muhammad). "As you know, in only a few days America will be destroyed. There are nuclear bombs planted in many of your cities and another one at a certain special place that would be of most interest to you. The devices are all hooked up to timers and are remotely controlled. You cannot dismantle or move them. They all have sensors. You do not believe me now, do you? I now am going to show you something to prove this."

The camera then swings towards the contraption in the glass case and then swings back.

"There are many of these across America. But this one is not like the others. The others have a clock, a timer set to explode several days from now. This one does too, but it also has something else which makes this one unique. This one will go off at sunrise tomorrow. There is nothing you can do to turn it off or remove it. Only I can delay the explosion, and there is only one way I will do this.

"I can reset the timer to a later time if somebody comes forward with a person named Alex Fisheramen. We need to find him. You can deliver him to your local news station, and they can immediately broadcast that they have him and we will then contact the station to get him. It doesn't matter whether he's dead or alive. We simply want him. This gentleman here has agreed to suffer the consequences until then if Alex is not turned over to us."

The camera then swings towards Garrett hanging upside down.

"If nobody comes forward with Alex Fisheramen, then this gentleman will suffer the consequences in a very painful way. The device goes off as planned at sunrise tomorrow. You have until then to find him for us. I figure you would like to know where this device is located. I will give you a hint. It's north of 37.251902 and east of -93.225861. It's not on the East Coast. Good luck in finding it. You won't."

The leader then waves his gun in the air and takes another swipe at Garrett with the knife, again slicing into his underwear and leg.

Garrett, kicking while suspended, screams out, "I didn't agree with anything, you bastard!"

The leader then spits at Garrett and waves off the camera and closes the session by saying "Find me Alex Fisheramen or he dies bad, and you die too. You have until sunrise. Then show time."

He then praises Allah, mutters something about enforcing the Sharia, and turns his back to the camera.

The camera and lighting are turned off, and the leader then takes off his mask, replaces his turban, and in disgust slaps Garrett with his gun, cutting him again. The leader then unties Garrett, drops him to the floor, and he and another terrorist usher him over to the device. Garrett pulls his pants back up. He's kicked by another terrorist. The terrorists proceed to tie Garrett, Julie, Lizzy, and Mikey to the metal railing that surround the glass case with a series of knots using several ropes. Emily is still in her pumpkin seat. The kids are close enough to Julie that she can comfort them, but Garrett and Julie are tied up so tight there's no way they can escape.

They are tied up in such a way that they can lie down or sit up, but not stand up. Garrett looks over at the device and sees a timer that's counting backward from 09:00 hours.

The leader retreats to help the remaining terrorists pack up the camera and lighting equipment and the remaining computer and electronic equipment. Boxes are then neatly stored away in the remaining two vans in the warehouse. The remaining terrorists get in their vans and can be seen on their phones talking with others about the status of what they are doing.

It's apparent that they all plan to leave soon. Garrett and Julie wonder if they're going to leave them and their kids alone and tied up to the nuclear bomb after they leave. They know nobody knows the whereabouts of them or the bomb.

Chapter 22

I look up again to see if the spirit is still with me. Suddenly, I feel that there now are definitely two spirits. I'm inclined to think that one is a good spirit and the other is a bad spirit. I sense that these spirits are in disagreement and are actually challenging each other. What are they doing? This is so strange. I surmise that the good spirit may be an angel from heaven and the bad spirit is an invisible demon from hell.

As I feel myself moving into the first level of the first chamber, I try to think again of Sonja and everybody back on Earth. I get a brief vision of Julie and Garret being abducted, but this quickly fades away. I know that is for real because of the intensity of the vision I had for a fleeting second, but the vision didn't last. I am so concerned for them and wish I was there to help in some way.

Now I can no longer see them at all. No matter how hard I try, the previous visions I had of what they were doing in real time have vanished and it's no longer possible to see them. I try to think again of the terrorists and the status of the crisis. Likewise, I no longer can see any of that either.

I no longer have any feeling of what is going on or any connection with anything back on Earth. The real-time visions I had previously now have completely faded away. I figure that now since my time in hell has officially started, any contact I previously had with the outside is gone and will be gone forever.

I now find myself becoming preoccupied with this spirit, or two spirits who now are accompanying me. The harder I think about them, the more I can sense what's going on with them. I look up and concentrate and can feel one is in constant uninterrupted prayer. I cannot feel the other spirit as much, but when I think about it, I sense fire.

They appear to be battling against each other, but I don't know the circumstances. Then I wonder if I'm simply imagining all of this. Of course this is hell, and I suppose hell can play all sorts of tricks on me. Maybe the spirits that I sense above me are nothing more than a figment of my imagination conjured up by the devil himself to play games with me as more torture.

After a while, I'm led by this force, of which I have no control, to a room on the first level of the first chamber. I am floating without any control whatsoever. I don't know anything about this room except that it's a first level first chamber room. It is supposed to be one of the rooms in the first level consisting of the least amount of torture and pain of any level or chamber. I continue to cry and shake with fear.

As I'm led into it, I can see it contains a river of hot burning lava, with bright orange-and-red flames, just like a lava flow from a volcano. I can't see where it starts nor to where it flows. It's several hundred feet wide and is so long I can't see either end. I sense that it might flow in a continuous circle.

I can hear several million other souls wailing and being swept within the flow while being poked by demons with their pitch forks standing on the riverside to make sure that none of the souls escape. But I can't see the screaming souls. There are demons everywhere. They are absolutely hideous. Their appearance is terrifying.

I look down at my body, and although I can't see it, I can sense it and I know that I'm naked and vulnerable. I'm not really embarrassed to be naked because I sense that the other souls who I can't see are also naked. I sense that likewise they can't see me either. But I'm just too plain scared to even think about it.

A force lifts me up in the air and sets me down and places me on the edge where I sit with my toes dangling just inches from the hot flowing lava as if flows by me. I can feel the heat. I think of my childhood when I'd sit at the edge of a swimming pool, wanting to test the water with my toes first to see how cold it is before getting in.

But in my case, I don't need to test the river. I can see it, smell it, hear it, sense it, and I know exactly how hot it is and what it will do to me.

I expect to be kicked in or jabbed into the river by a pitch fork, but I'm not. It's as if the demons don't see me for some reason. How bizarre this all is. I am sitting right there in front of them. But for whatever reason, they're ignoring me. I'm absolutely terrified. The wailing screams of pain I hear from the other souls in the river are so deafening, it's unbearable. There are no words to describe just how gruesome this all is and how terrified I am.

Then I hear very loud organ music of the worst kind. It's so profoundly sinister that I feel death and doom surrounding me. It makes me want to cry uncontrollably. But I already am.

Maybe the wait is Satan's way of torturing me further by giving me time to think about what it's going to feel like before he gives the go-ahead. This is torture in itself.

I look up again and concentrate on the two spirits to see if they have anything to do with what is going on with me and why I haven't been jabbed or kicked into the river yet. I get the feeling that before I'm sent flying into the river of fire I must wait for the spirits to come to terms or something to happen with them. How long is this going to take? If this takes forever, it would be okay with me. But I know better than that.

Again, it seems like they are challenging each other, but I can't figure out how or why or what is going on between them. All I sense is a positive and negative charge coming from above. I find myself pulling for the spirit who is in constant prayer because I assume that it is a good spirit and that the other is a bad spirit. I sure would like to see what they look like or talk with them, but I can't.

I can hear the souls yelling out in horrendous pain as they are continually bobbing up and down and being swept down the hot river of lava and fire and being poked by the demons' pitchforks. I wonder why they don't burn up. Apparently, they feel the incredible pain of being burned, but don't completely burn up.

Amidst hearing them screaming in pain, I can hear them all cursing. They're all cursing Satan because of what he is doing to them. To my surprise, they're also cursing God for sending them to hell. As I listen to the sounds, it becomes apparent to me that the more they scream in pain, the more they curse.

It's as if Satan dwells in the pain and agony and that he becomes more powerful the more they curse. It's like a dog chasing its tail. The more they scream in pain, the more they curse. The more they curse and scream, the more he enjoys it. And I sense the more power he gains.

I envision Satan turning up the fire when the souls curse him or God, as this is exactly what he wants them to do. Hatred breeds hatred. The souls scream and curse and he turns up the fire. They scream and curse more, and he turns the fire up some more, and this process goes on and on. I wonder if there's a limit to how much a soul can curse Satan or God for putting them through all of this agony.

I begin to wonder how demons are made. Perhaps when a soul gives into Satan's wrath and bows up to it and praises it instead of cursing it, the soul is made into a demon. Perhaps something like this would prompt Satan to release the soul from its agony. But, I'm not sure.

Maybe demons are made from those souls who praise and worship the devil because the soul finally figures this out and that it's better to dish out the torture instead of receiving it. Is it worth it to do this? I contemplate it. If this is true, do I want to become a demon and worship Satan to avoid the torture? Should I praise Satan to avoid the incredible pain and agony that is forthcoming?

But this doesn't make sense. So, just how are demons made? Where do they come from? Why are some more powerful than others?

As I contemplate all this, I continue to hear the souls curse Satan because he's putting them through their incessant misery. I don't hear a single soul praising either Satan or God or yelling out anything else to try to avoid the torture. I don't hear any souls asking God for forgiveness. They're cursing Him as well for sending them to hell.

Perhaps once they're submerged into the fire, they can only curse and that is the only thing that they can say. Maybe they lose their ability to do anything but scream and curse, even if they don't want to, which gives him his power. The more I think about it, the more convinced I am that is the case.

The more they curse Satan and God, the more Satan turns up the fire. The more Satan turns up the fire, the more they curse and scream, and the more powerful he becomes.

Perhaps it's a good thing that I have this waiting period that I can spend some time thinking about these things. I figure that other souls are thrown into the fire immediately upon arriving. But why am I being treated differently? I need to think and think fast. This may be the last time I can think independently before I become unable to do anything except wail in pain and curse Satan and God like the other souls do.

I wonder about this and somehow decide to think outside of the box and figure out that if I approach things differently as soon as I am sent into the fire, whether I would experience anything different. Perhaps I should not curse Satan or God like the other souls do and instead scream out something else. I figure it may be worth a try, and what do I have to lose? It is going to be pure torture anyway.

But what if I won't have the ability to do so? I'm scared out of my wits as to what will take place. I am trembling so much it's hard to even think straight now.

I again look up to see how the spirits are doing. Suddenly, I get absolutely sick to my stomach and feel very nauseous. I suddenly feel so sick my gut is wrenching in pain. I no longer sense the good spirit and can only sense a feeling of fire looking down upon me. Where did the good spirit go? Did it lose its challenge with the bad spirit?

Maybe the good spirit's prayer was not good enough? Or maybe the bad spirit had more power than the good spirit? At any rate the good spirit now appears to have vanished. Only the bad spirit remains with me.

Then I notice that I'm no longer sitting at the edge of the river. Instead, I feel myself being lifted above the river of fire. I have no control over the power that is lifting and moving me. It has complete control over my entire body.

I am naked, and I start to sweat like I never have before. The sweat from my body that is the result of the heat emanating from the lava flow and fire underneath me is running off my body like my body is a water faucet.

But I can feel the sweat is not normal. Instead, it is turning into sulfuric acid. It starts to burn my body. My sweat starts to burn me, and I am in incredible pain, and I have not even been submersed into the river of fire yet. But I look at my body, and there is no sweat. I can't see my body, but I can feel it starting to burn even more. The pain is excruciating beyond belief. I sense that I'll be dropped in the hot burning lava at any second. I'm crying hysterically. I look up and sense the bad spirit laughing at me.

I look down at the molten river of fire underneath me and start to cry even harder. But when I do, I can now feel the tears. Previously when I would cry, there were no tears. But now the tears are rolling from my eyes and down my cheeks. But my tears are not normal either. My tears instead are turning into a sulfuric acid, and my eyes start to burn fiercely from it. My eyes hurt so bad they feel like they're on fire. Now I can't see anything, and I am losing my ability to think. Now I'm blind. The pain is unbearable.

He has near total control over me now, and I figure that my time has finally come. I feel that any second now I will be dropped into the fire and it will all be over. But then I realize that it will not be over. It actually will only be the beginning. I start to think of what eternity is really like. I don't want to think about eternity now; however, I am forced to think about it by this power over me. Whether I want to or not.

The thoughts go through my head incessantly: river of fire, eternity, unfathomable torture and pain—forever. It goes on and on nonstop. I have no control to purge it. I cannot stop thinking about it. I am so scared I want to just pass out and die, but I can't. The force will not let me. Any second now I will be dropped into the river of fire and will begin to suffer the most incredible torture and pain for eternity.

Chapter 23

At Andrew's and Alana's house, everyone's very anxious to see what the emergency news broadcast will say. After a few minutes, it finally comes on. The news reporter states he has good news and bad news and then some more bad news.

First, he says that a bomb has been found in an abandoned warehouse in the vicinity of Washington DC and that the authorities have identified it as a bona-fide nuclear device of unprecedented magnitude.

The terrorists now have decided to reset the timer so that the bomb will explode in several days from now when the others bombs are scheduled to go off instead of tonight. A news clip of the device and timer are shown with numerous authorities standing around, trying to figure out what to do.

The authorities cannot defuse the bomb because it's encased in an impenetrable glass case that's wired with sensors to explode if there is any contact made with it. There are sensors wired inside as well as outside of it. It's affixed to the concrete floor by bolts that cannot be removed and is also wired with sensors. The bomb appears to be permanently sealed in place.

Nobody can touch it because if they do, it will explode on contact. In addition, the glass case apparently cannot be removed or taken away. It's miraculous that nobody touched the device before it was found.

Second, he says that the terrorists have claimed an additional nuclear device in another city and that they have set it to explode at sunrise tomorrow before the others are scheduled to be detonated several days from now. He then turns to a video provided to the network news.

The video starts with a masked terrorist leader talking and then the camera swings toward the nuclear device, and finally zeros in on a civilian strung upside down hanging from the rafters next to the bomb.

"My God!" screams Alana. "I can't believe this." She screams again in horror. "My God, that's Garrett!" Everybody becomes hysterical.

Sonja straightforwardly declares, "I can't believe this. The nuclear device must be right here, in our city! Garrett hasn't been missing that long! I just saw him a little while ago earlier today. They could not have taken him that far. Especially with all the traffic problems."

Alana tries to contain her emotion, but it's difficult. "We need to call the authorities right away and tell them! Otherwise, they'll be looking everywhere."

"Shall we call the police or the FBI?"

"How about if we call Officer Musty?" says Andrew.

In all of the commotion, they forget that the FBI is outside watching their house. Otherwise, all they would need to do is to go out and tell them.

Sonja wants to call the FBI and Andrew wants to call Officer Musty. After a mild argument, Andrew wins out and convinces them that since it's a local matter that they should call him first.

Sonja reluctantly agrees and calls the local police department and asks to be put through to Officer Musty.

The receptionist answers, "Who?"

"Officer Musty." She frantically tries to recall his full name and finally remembers it as Asad Namirha Mustafa. She describes him.

The receptionist states in a matter of fact tone "There is no Officer Musty or Officer Mustafa that works on our force here.

There are no officers on duty here with any of those names or of the description you gave."

"What?" says Sonja in disbelief.

"I'm sorry but the police officer who you named does not work here. We do not have any record of him."

Sonja is totally confused, hangs up, and decides to call the FBI.

While she is scrambling around to get their business card with their phone number, her phone rings. She answers it, and it's Officer Musty. She's shocked that he would call so soon and she's confused. Did he know that she just tried to reach him?

"Hello. Sonja. I just wanted to check in to see if you are all okay. I've been thinking about everybody."

"Officer Musty, I can't believe you just called me. I just got off the phone with your police department looking for you."

'You did? You called them? What's the matter?"

"The police department dispatch person or receptionist or whoever I talked with said they don't have any record of you working there."

"Well, well, well, I can understand that. The dispatcher is new to the force, and I've not met her yet. Apparently, she doesn't know about me, perhaps because I do a lot of undercover work."

Sonja contemplates his answer for a few seconds and comes to the conclusion that it's reasonable. She gives Officer Musty the benefit of the doubt. But she wonders about the coincidence that he would call immediately after she hung up with the police department. She proceeds to bring him up to date about the abduction and video.

"Well, thanks for letting me know about this. I've been busy in the field and was not aware of it. I'll follow up on this for you. Thanks again for letting me know. I'll take care of things from here and be in touch."

He proceeds to give Sonja his personal cell phone number and tells her if they need to call him, to call his personal number rather than call the police department or dispatch number. Although still finding it strange that Officer Musty called back so soon, Sonja is relieved.

But as soon as she hangs up, there's a knock on the front door and it's one of the FBI agents who was watching the house from outside. He reminds them they have all sorts of monitoring devices in their vehicle. He tells them about the news that just came on TV and asks them if they're aware of it.

Andrew excitedly but proudly states, "Yes, we just watched it. We just got off the phone with Officer Musty and he said that he would follow up and take care of things."

The FBI agent gets agitated and reprimands Andrew. "We know that. We told you that the FBI has jurisdiction and you need to contact us and not Officer Musty. We don't want you to work with him on this case. You need to work with us. Can you do that from now on? Do you happen to know who the person was who was hanging upside down on the rope?"

Alana cries out, "Yes, it was Garrett, my brother-in-law! He must be close by and perhaps in our city!"

The agent comments, "That's what we suspected, but we needed to confirm it. We'll be checking on a few things and need to follow up on this right away. We'll be in touch."

The agent knew all the time and appears to know a lot more but doesn't have time to talk. He thanks them again and hurriedly returns to his undercover car parked down the street.

Alana, Andrew, and Sonja return to watching the news. By now the news about the terrorists has subsided for a while and has turned its attention to the panic in the streets. The news reporter explains that everybody is trying to escape every major city in America, resulting in traffic gridlock everywhere and the screen rolls with video of mammoth traffic jams in about four different major cities in America.

In addition, there are intermittent power outages as electricity has been going off here and there in some places in America, resulting in more confusion and panic.

After showing this the news reporter says that Great Britain has announced its support for the United States and has offered its resources in an effort to combat the terrorists. The reporter then goes on to say that it expects the terrorists to next target England for supporting the United States. But what can Great Britain do to help?

The news addresses the discord and tensions between all countries that have a nuclear arsenal. This is believed to be the United States, Russia, the UK and France, China, India, Pakistan, North Korea, and Israel, as well as the Islamic extremists. Because of numerous issues between these countries there is widespread concern that any detonation of a nuclear device anywhere in the world could result in an immediate escalation involving all countries and a worldwide nuclear holocaust.

As soon as one nuclear bomb is unleashed anywhere, there is a reasonable possibility that other countries will follow suit and launch their nuclear warheads immediately. The tension between many countries is extremely high for many political and economic reasons.

There is a short commercial and during that time, Alana begins to weep not believing any of this is actually happening. "It just goes from bad to worse!"

After the commercial, the next news segment addresses whether the events are the beginning of the Apocalypse and turns to a discussion with theologians about the book of Revelation. During this segment, the news focuses on Ammen. Although there is much speculation that the current events do not match what has been prophesized, nevertheless a possible imminent end of the world has resulted in Ammen receiving an incredibly growing following.

The news shows massive congregations of people supporting and following Ammen throughout the Middle East and comments that now he has a following in the tens of millions and that many people feel that he is actually the Second Coming. His following now has rapidly spread across North America and Europe.

All of the other people who have proclaimed similar status seeking a following for their own personal glory have pretty much disappeared, but Ammen has managed to remain in the spotlight. His following is growing by the tens if not hundreds of thousands every hour throughout the world. The news then shows another video clip of Ammen.

Ammen is again sitting on a log overlooking an oasis in the desert somewhere in the Middle East, dressed in a gray robe. Again, the older woman sits beside him and appears to be wearing a tan wrap of some sort. Ammen looks just like pictures of Jesus. He speaks softly.

"My name is Ammen. As you may already know, I am of the sacred blood and have returned for you. You may have recently seen me in the Mosul region where Christians have been persecuted or driven out by the Islamic extremists. I have originally come from Jerusalem.

"Your Holy Bible talks of the Day of Reckoning. That day is very near. Your Holy Bible talks of the Second Coming in the book of Revelation. The prophets said I would return, and I have. There is only one way to survive a pending holocaust that will take place in the very near future. You must believe in me as I am before you now. As the tests by my father will be passed, through the blaze of glory above and through the fire below, I will be your light to your eternal end.

"My father has proclaimed an order in which I will be the last angel to come before you. Other angels of the same blood will be beside me, but I am the last, the sacred angel of the father. Please listen and take word and follow me so that you can survive and be saved. Like Jesus who came before you, I again come before you now. Only through me before you now can you live everlasting. There is no other way."

Andrew becomes uncommonly shaken by all the news and what is transpiring in the world has suddenly sunk in. He now realizes that this is all very much real. For the first time in his life, he takes an interest in something that is of a cerebral nature instead of succumbing to the mundane.

He suddenly has acquired a deep realization that there *are* nuclear bombs that will destroy America. They *are* here, and are essentially very close to him. A deadly and highly contagious disease *will* be unleashed across America. Now he profoundly realizes that his life, as well as his family's lives, is in imminent danger. He has the look of a deer caught in headlights, and Alana has to snap her fingers at him to get his attention.

Andrew is mesmerized and captivated by Ammen. "You know, I think Ammen is for real. I think all of us should follow him. I certainly believe in him. How about you?"

Alana is shocked. This is not like the Andrew she knows at all. It's like suddenly he's a different person. But she's also shaken by the news. She comments, "All these years I've believed in Jesus and you have not, and now here comes this Ammen guy. And now you're convinced that he is the Second Coming in only such a short time?"

"He's not a guy. He's an angel. In fact, he's the last angel! He said he's the angel of the father."

Sonja asks him, "Now, my son, how do you know that? Andrew, after all of these years, after what your father and I did to try to raise you to be a Christian, how can you be so sure in a matter of minutes to believe that Ammen is the last angel of God and will save you?"

"Because he said he is. He said that he is going to be last angel, that he has returned for us, and that the only way to be saved from everything is to follow him. I think that's good enough for me."

Alana is perplexed. There is something about Ammen that is welcoming to her too. He does look just like Jesus. She appears to be vulnerable. Perhaps she can be convinced as well. But for now, she's on the fence and wants to learn more. After all, she has been a Christian for her entire life, as has the rest of the family, except for Andrew. But she feels her soul also being captivated by Ammen. Just maybe he is the return of Jesus.

She ponders aloud, "If I were to follow and worship Ammen, will I remain a Christian? Is he really the Second Coming? Is he really the return of Jesus?"

Alana wonders about these questions and finds herself interested in him as well. It seems that when Ammen speaks, somehow he's able to spiritually connect with the people listening to him. "I can see why he's developed such a massive following," she goes on to say.

Ammen certainly is becoming the hot topic everywhere.

Chapter 24

I now can feel my body being lowered very slowly ever so close to the river of fire. How agonizing. I have an insatiable desire to start cursing Satan, and this is exactly what I think he wants me to do. Am I going in on my stomach or on my back? Or will I go in feet first or headfirst?

I feel my body being turned around, but I can no longer see as my tears have turned to acid and have burned my eyes out. The stinging sensation is unbearable. Everything is dark. I don't know if I'm upside down or right-side up. But then I realize that I am being lowered ever so slowly so that my toes and feet will touch the burning lava first.

As I'm lowered and the very end of my toes touch the molten liquid, a pain that feels like a million volts of electricity shoot from my feet throughout my body and straight into my head and I scream at the top of my lungs. The pain is indescribable.

But I prepared myself for this and just as my mind is completely taken over by the devil, instead of cursing Satan like the others I instinctively yell out as loud as I can, "Jesus, I still believe in you, please have mercy on me!"

Perhaps I should curse Satan and God instead like every other soul does, but something comes over me, and this is what I scream out instead. I don't know what makes me say this. I have just enough energy left to yell it out one more time, "Jesus, Jesus, Jesus, I still believe in you and have faith in you! Please, Jesus, help me! I praise you in the highest glory!"

I can hear all the other souls cursing the devil, and my scream seems for a split instant to drown out their sounds. "Wow," I think. Then my mind briefly goes blank except for the incredible pain.

But as soon as I yell out "Jesus" for the last time, I feel my body suddenly being yanked back. I'm no longer being lowered into the river of lava but instead feel my body being turned around and now fear that I am going in headfirst. I fear this will be my punishment for mentioning Jesus in hell and not cursing Satan.

However, instead I am being pulled from the river by an unknown force, I find myself hovering several feet above it. I remain in this position for a little while, and then suddenly, I can think again. Then my eyesight comes back. My sweat and tears come to a stop as well. The pain also diminishes. I wonder what's going on.

I look above, and to my astonishment, the good spirit has returned. I sense that it's much stronger now. But I can feel the bad spirit as well. It's clear that the bad spirit is very angry with me. But the good spirit is with me again. I know I have angered the bad spirit by saying *Jesus* and asking Him for mercy. I get the sense that this is his domain, and by saying "Jesus" in his home has caused him to become even more irate. I can feel his anger throughout my body.

Once again I can sense the good spirit and the bad spirit challenging each other in what appears to be another duel. The good spirit is using prayer as his weapon. The bad spirit is using fire as his bludgeon of choice.

But although I anticipate hovering over the river of fire until there is an outcome, instead I feel my body moving again. I am lifted away from the flowing river of lava and high up to the top of the cavern where I can see more rooms. I'm on some sort of invisible platform very high up. There are enormous hellish bats flying all over and in my face.

From there I can see the beginning of level two in the first chamber. Level two appears to be quite different than the first level, but I can't make out exactly what it's like. It's too far away.

Suddenly, I feel the presence of Satan. He is glaring at me down from the top of the cavern, from the sides of the cavern, and up from the pit of the cavern. He is everywhere. He is so powerful that he is overbearing and absolutely horrific in every sense. Although I can't see him, I know he's like a gigantic monster built out of fire and is incredibly terrifying. I can feel the heat from his breath even though I can't see him.

I know that I've not only angered the bad spirit but have also angered Satan by saying the word *Jesus*. This is Satan's domain and apparently by saying what I did was taboo according to his rules. But I realize that perhaps I said the magic words which hit his weak spot. Maybe it did. Maybe it didn't. I don't really know.

But I realize that I have angered him so much that now he wants to punish me even more. I have a feeling that he will send me to another room that is more horrific than the room with the river of flowing lava.

At this time for some unknown reason I think of my granddaughter's stuffed raccoon. I gave it to Julie when she was a little girl, and she passed it down to Lizzy and to Mikey. It was a creature of comfort and always made them feel secure when they were afraid of something. It took the place of the teddy bear that she had previously.

I remember telling them that it would always be there to protect and help them when they were scared. Now I wish that I could hold that raccoon myself. I'm like a crying baby and think half in jest that if I could talk to it now, I would ask that old raccoon to do something—anything, anything at all—to help.

Although I realize this is nonsensical thinking, it's briefly pleasant to dream to get away from what I'm experiencing. I suddenly come to my senses and realize that I'm on the move again. I expect to be sent to another room of horror in the first level, but, he doesn't send me there. I feel myself going in the opposite direction and wonder where I'm going.

Then I realize that I am floating to level two of the first chamber. The intensity of my fear grows proportionately to the degree of torture anticipated. I assume now that I have angered him a lot. He is exercising his discretion. As I sense myself moving, I hear Satan tell me that I can never ask Jesus to help me again while in hell, and if I do, I will be subject to even worse punishment. I am to be bound by his words literally. I cannot ever again ask Jesus to have mercy on me.

I'm immediately thankful that I'm still in the first chamber and not in the second chamber which would otherwise be even more intense. But, I'm still overly terrified at what level two will bring. The force then takes me into a room in level two that is similar to the room I was in previously. It's also a river of fire, but it's somewhat different. I am floating above, and as I look down, I can see it.

The river is a soup of flowing lava that has a white hot glow instead of an orange or red glow found in level one and there is electricity like lightning running through the flames. The lava consists of pure acid that has flames coming from it. The stench is unbearable.

I can see the demons, but this time I can also see the souls submerged and bobbing in the river as it flows by. There are not as many as in the first level, however there are still millions of souls suffering here. The souls are screaming their lungs out in pure agony and are cursing Satan and God. The moaning is frightening enough. I could not see the souls in level one. But I can see them now in level two.

The souls are all deformed bodies that are burned to a crisp and are so ghoulish looking that they are a hundred times more frightening than the zombies found in the most gruesome horror movie ever made. The souls are fed the burning hot soup of the flaming lava with huge ladles. One demon holds the soul and another pries open its mouth and another demon pours the white hot lava in the soul's mouth and over the soul's face.

The soul then goes into convulsions as the soup eats the soul's internal organs and the electricity runs throughout the body. Then the soul is thrown in the river for a swim. The souls struggle to breathe and wail and curse in unfathomable pain. After a while, the soul is plucked out again, the body is restored, and the process is repeated each time the soul circles around.

The wailing and gnashing of teeth from the pain along with the endless moaning is ear piercing. The cursing of the devil and God by the souls in this level far exceeds their cursing in the first level.

So this torture is worse than the intensity of level one? I believe it. My fear factor has jumped and I am shaking so much that I am already having convulsions. I am losing control of my body and my mind as I float above and watch what happens below.

I simply cannot imagine how the next seven levels can be worse than this. And I absolutely cannot imagine how subsequent chambers are even more intense than the first chamber. This is impossible I think, but deep down I know that this is all very real. I wonder what sort of different dimensions the subsequent chambers are. My curiosity runs rampant, but then I suddenly grab a hold of myself and I tell myself that I don't want to find out.

As I'm floating above, I again look up and still sense the good spirit and the bad spirit. I can feel them still fighting; however, I become aware that the good spirit now has lost some strength and that the bad spirit has gained some strength. I sense Satan sending the bad spirit more power to use against the good spirit. But I feel that the power that he's sending to the bad spirit is coming from his anger at me for saying *Jesus* and asking Jesus to have mercy on me in his domain.

I hope that I didn't cause the good spirit to lose the battle because I did this. But I think that saying the magic word *Jesus* saved me from going into the river at the first level. Now that I think about it, I wonder if that brought back the good spirit. I start to think of what my plan may be when I am lowered to the embankment of this river in the second level.

I surmise that if I again scream out, "Jesus," or better yet, "Jesus, I still believe in you, please have mercy on me," perhaps I will be spared again. But I was told never to say that again. Will that anger the bad spirit and the devil even more? If I yell out the name of Jesus, would that perhaps anger Satan enough to send me to the third level? Or maybe it could be worse. Maybe I'll be sent to the second chamber. I know I can't pray to Jesus out loud to help me. Satan clearly told me I couldn't do this, and I don't want to find out the consequences if I do. I then learn that even if I wanted to, I will have not even have the ability to ask Jesus to have mercy on me. So, doing that is out of the question.

I need to think of something before it's too late. My ability to think independently is weakening now, and I must try and stay mentally strong as much as possible and as long as possible.

When I now look down, at this level I can see my naked body clearly. Interesting, previously I couldn't see my body or see it as much. My toes are burnt from the first level but appear to be healing to be ready for the next round, but other than that, my body still has a somewhat pure nature about it. I marvel at it, but then quickly return to reality as I know what's about to happen.

All of a sudden, I feel myself moving again. I'm being lowered slowly at an antagonizing tortoise-like pace down toward the flowing river of hot lava. I look up and sense that once again the good spirit has vanished and is no longer there. "Oh no! No! No! No! Please come back. Why does the good spirit keep leaving me?"

I again sense the bad spirit is laughing at me. But this time I sense the devil laughing at me also. I figure that the bad spirit won the duel. Perhaps this is because he was given additional power from the devil because I had angered him by saying, "Jesus, please have mercy on me."

So, what do I do this time? If I say the exact same thing as in the first level, it could definitely backfire on me. I don't want that to happen. My punishment would be even worse. But I won't have the ability to say that anyway. Do I instead praise Satan and bow up to him and become a demon? If I did that and was converted into a demon, then I would dish out the torture instead and I would no longer have to suffer from it.

Maybe it's worthwhile to do this. But if I did that, I would be abandoning Jesus and my God. I do not want to do that either. But maybe it's too late to worry about that anyway? I'm confused, and it's harder for me to think straight.

Maybe this is why all of the souls simply curse Satan and God instead. But maybe they are forced to curse them and perhaps they don't have the ability to scream anything else, even if they wanted to. I am desperately trying to figure out what is the best plan, but the energy I have and my ability to think for myself is gradually being sapped out of me.

So that is probably why the other souls don't say anything except to curse them. That is the only thing they have the ability to do or say. I assume for some unknown reason no other soul has figured this out or has the ability to do it. Their minds were weakened just like mine.

I now am getting closer to the river as I am lowered. This time the demons are looking at me and they're waiting for me. One of the demons dips his ladle and scoops up the lava to feed me and stares at me waiting for me to land at his feet. I can see lightning shooting out from the ladle and flaming acid dripping from it. Another waits to grab me as soon as I am lowered to the embankment and to throw my head back and pry open my mouth.

I am only a few feet away from the demons now. I have never been so scared in my life or in my after life for that matter. I'm already convulsing in complete horror as to what I'm about to experience. I am shaking and crying uncontrollably.

Chapter 25

After Garrett, Julie, and the kids had been asleep for some time, the terrorists get out of their vans and the leader comes over to Julie and Garrett to check on them to make sure they're still tied up and can't escape. The leader picks up the knives on the floor and puts them in a bag to be put into one of the vans. But he leaves one of the knives and places it in the middle of the table sitting about ten feet from Garrett.

The leader wakes them up and tells them that they are going out to get something to eat and will be back soon. He glares at Garrett with a look that would kill. "When we get back, if there is any evidence whatsoever that any of you tried to escape, I'll immediately put a bullet in one of your heads. I'll give you the choice as to who it will be. If you don't choose anyone, then I'll decide, and then I may kill two of you instead. Your choice. Who will it be?"

Garrett doesn't answer and simply hangs his head down.

"I need an answer now, not when we get back! Pick somebody!"

"Me."

"No, that won't do. You pick somebody else this time. Now!"

"Look, we don't intend to escape, so there is no reason to even pick anybody. You have us tied up so tight and in such a way, there's no way we can get away, even if we wanted to. You know that!"

"If you don't pick one of your family now, then it will be two of your family who'll pay the price if I decide. Is that what you want?"

Garrett is speechless.

"Okay then. I don't want to see any attempt whatsoever when we get back. If I do, then I'll decide which two of you it will be. Don't any of you dare to try anything. That includes your kids!"

All the terrorists pile into one of the vans and the industrial garage door is raised. The van disappears out of site into the night and the garage door comes crashing down. The click of the lock can be heard as the door hits the floor with a thud. They're now all alone in the warehouse.

Garrett and Julie immediately start to struggle to try and get free from the ropes but it's useless. The ropes are wrapped around their legs, arms, and bodies and are secured to the railing in such a way that it's absolutely impossible for them to do anything, except to sit there on the floor. It's absolutely hopeless. They can't untie the ropes at all. All they can do is stare at the nuclear device and listen to the tick-tick-tick on the timer counting down.

Garrett spots the knife on the table, but there's no way he can reach it. It's about ten feet away from him. Garrett and Julie begin an incessant conversation as what to do, what they can expect, if they can try to plan anything when the terrorists return, and a myriad of other topics. This goes on for perhaps fifteen to twenty minutes or so.

Julie looks over to check on the kids and lets out a scream. "Garrett! Where's Lizzy? Where's Lizzy? She's gone! Did the terrorists take her? I thought she was here just a little while ago sleeping when they left! Lizzy! Lizzy! Where are you?"

Suddenly, Lizzy appears from the other side of the glass case. She somehow managed to free herself from her ropes. Garrett can't believe it but becomes frantic because he knows that the terrorists will be back any minute. They will certainly kill one of them and probably two of them when they discover she's free. He contemplates telling her to bring him the knife but is apprehensive in doing this for several obvious reasons.

Suddenly, the garage door opens up. Garrett screams at Lizzy. "Lizzy, run! Run into the office and try to get away through the door and get help! Run!"

But Lizzy returns to Julie and starts crying. Julie, fearful that the terrorists will kill her for untying herself, screams at her, "Lizzy, if they find you not tied up, they'll kill us. You're our only hope. Run into the office and try to get away outside! You gotta do this, now! I love you! Run! Run!"

Lizzy, scared, instinctively grabs her dolly bag and scampers into the office just down the wall just as the van pulls into the warehouse. It's somewhat dark in there. That's probably the best and only hiding place in the warehouse, but it's evident that she'll soon be found there.

As soon as the van pulls in and the garage door is shut, the terrorists get out and congregate in the corner. They're all eating sandwiches and talking but don't realize that Lizzy is missing.

Several minutes later, the leader walks over to Julie and realizes that Lizzy is missing and is not tied up any more. As soon as he notices this he yells out to the other terrorists. Julie can see Lizzy opening up the office door to the outside and running into the darkness. However, she has left the outside door open. None of the terrorists are aware of this, at least for now.

The terrorists are all yelling at each other and running all over the warehouse trying to find Lizzy.

"Your girl is missing! Where is the girl? Do you remember what I said I'd do if I found any of you trying to escape? Do you? Do you? How did you let her get away? I want to know now!"

Garrett points to their ropes. "We didn't untie her! We couldn't have! See, we're still tied up! She got away all by herself!"

Julie adds, "We didn't see her leave. We have no idea where she is. We thought you took her with you!"

"You will pay for this, just like I said. You'll see!"

It doesn't take long for the terrorists to discover that the office door to the outside is ajar and that Lizzy has escaped outside. But they know she can't go far and that they will find her. The abandoned warehouse is actually part of a much larger complex that contains several locked buildings of which the entire complex is fenced with barbed wire with a closed gate to its entrance. There is nowhere she can go or hide.

In the meantime, Lizzy is running between the warehouse and the fence trying to find a way out. She is a frightened little girl.

Tears are running down her cheeks. She's running and stumbling, looking for a dark area to hide in the shadows away from the parking lot lights.

Julie quietly says to Garrett, "If by a miracle Lizzy finds help, I pray to God that he'll give her the ability to talk and help them find us." But she then reluctantly sobs, "There's no way she will say anything. She won't even talk to us yet. Only if she could say more than one word at a time."

Chapter 26

It's getting late and Andrew, Alana, and Sonja are in their living room eating ice cream and waiting desperately for a phone call or news about any developments. They're discussing what their plans will be in the morning.

"Andrew, do you think they will be holding summer camp tomorrow with everything going on? Even if they are, do you think we should take the boys or let them stay home?"

"I haven't heard anything, so I suppose summer camp will be open."

"Well, I don't think they should go. In fact, I plan on staying home if I can. I'm going to get on the phone and see if I can get a replacement."

"I'd still like to go shopping if I can. Since I lost everything in the fire, there's a lot I need to get," says Sonja.

Andrew opens up the front door to let Crackerjack outside, and sure enough the FBI undercover car is parked up and across the street. But this time, it is not a car but instead is an SUV with darkly tinted windows. He supposes that they changed shifts during the night.

The FBI sees him, and one of the agents gets out of the SUV and approaches him. The agent waves hello and Andrew waves back. Alana then comes to the door and invites him inside.

They briefly discuss the status of the abduction of Julie and Garrett. The agent comments that they never found Julie's cell phone in their investigation and search of her house and they suspect that she perhaps may have it with her. But they don't want to call her phone because if she has it and has concealed it, the kidnappers will hear it ring and they will confiscate it.

The agent goes on to say that their technicians are working with the cell phone carrier to monitor the phone. Apparently, it's been turned off. They suspect that if Julie has it, she turned it off to keep it hidden and has not been in a position to use it to call for help yet. That is if she can.

If the phone is turned on, they may be able to track it and locate the position of the phone by using GPS and cell phone towers, but the phone needs to be powered up long enough to do this.

Andrew comments, "Well, that makes sense."

The agent then states that the FBI and CIA have been searching all night for the terrorists and the bomb. They've analyzed several factors including the location from where Garrett and Julie were kidnapped, and the timing between their abduction and when the TV video was provided to the network. They've taken into account road accessibility in view of road and bridge closures and massive traffic jams that still persist.

Unfortunately, after studying all of the logistics, what they determined is that the bomb and the family are within about a sixty-square-mile area of where they live. That is still a massive area to search for something in such a short time.

They're inspecting the video to see if it reveals some clues, but so far, they have not uncovered anything.

The agent explains that the bomb is close enough that he fears the deadly radiation fall-out from the bomb could well expand for many miles from the epicenter and therefore that could very well include their house, even if the bomb is miles away. Andrew, Alana, Sonja, and their family are at risk if the bomb explodes at sunrise as the terrorist indicated. There's a reasonable probability that they could die in the explosion as well.

Alana wonders, "What should we do? All the kids are in bed, and they're all very tired, but we won't be able to sleep at all worrying about all of this."

Andrew declares, "We should all leave right now and drive as far as we can. I say we wake up the kids and leave right away. Now!"

The agent states, "You won't be able to do that."

"Why, who's going to stop us?"

"After the news came out, everybody in every major city has been trying to escape the city limits, and there are massive traffic jams everywhere. This includes where you live. All major roads for miles are gridlocked, and the bridge across the river is closed. All gas stations have closed, and a lot of the traffic lights are not working as a result of some electrical outages here and there. Nobody can go anywhere. You couldn't get more than a mile or two at the most once you get out of your subdivision."

Alana adds, "Even if we could get away, we wouldn't be able to go anyway. Both of our cars only have about a quarter tank of gas and we would need to fill up. You said all of the gas stations are closed, didn't you?"

Andrew is distraught. "You're kidding, right?" He stares at the agent. "You sure the gas stations are closed?"

"Yep, we were one of the last ones to fill up just a little while ago before they closed. We have a surplus reserve, but nobody can use it but us. There's no way they're going to open back up again."

Sonja dejectedly comments, "Well, I guess we're just stuck here then, right?"

The agent says that he has to go back to his vehicle and make some calls, and he wishes everybody a good night. Andrew says to him, "If the bomb is going to go off at sunrise, are you still going to stay with us until then?"

The agent says, "Well, now that you ask, probably not. We'll likely leave during the early morning hours. We're calling in some choppers."

"Can we go with you?"

The agent looks at him and confidently states, "Probably not."

As Andrew continues to stare at the agent, the agent then says, "Well, we'll see, but I'm sure there won't be any room." As he turns around to go back to his SUV, Crackerjack comes back into the house.

"We'll be in touch," the agent says.

Andrew turns on the TV, and the news is mostly about the terrorist crisis. The news is on twenty-four hours now and is preempting all other programming. After several minutes, the local news comes on and the local reporter is commenting about the massive traffic jams and closed gas stations and other closed business establishments in the area.

The reporter states if anybody has not attempted to leave their houses yet, to stay put. They're advised to reevaluate the situation in about four to six hours from now.

He announces that there is a possibility that the local news station will close down later tonight because they will also need to evacuate.

Andrew says, "Well, they won't have any problem doing that. They all have helicopters they can use."

Sonja and Alana decide they will try to get some sleep and go to bed. They both say they will probably get back up again in a few hours to see if there are any new developments.

Andrew says okay and then channel-surfs and finds another TV station that is addressing Ammen. He slumps back on the sofa and intently watches the program. Ammen now has commanded a following of gigantic proportions and his following continues to grow. "That's my angel" he exclaims.

He decides to do some research on him. He wants to know about Mosul, the persecution of Christians there, Jerusalem, and other things that Ammen has mentioned in the various videos of him that he's seen.

He has heard in the news about the persecution of the Christians by the extremists in Mosul and elsewhere but never paid attention to this before. He decides that if he can verify this, then that will help confirm Ammen is for real. He gets out Alana's laptop and does a Google search. After about twenty minutes of researching and watching the news about Ammen, he believes that Ammen is telling the truth. He then remembers what Ammen said about being the last angel of the father, that a test will be passed, that other angels will be with him from a sacred bloodline from the days of Jesus, and that he has returned to save those who believe in him. Andrew now is pretty much convinced Ammen is for real.

Chapter 27

Lizzy is out of breath after running from the warehouse. She's about four buildings away and turns around to see if anybody is following her. The complex is dimly lit. She sees the terrorists running out the door to search for her. She finds some Dumpsters and tries to climb in, but they're too high. She then runs along a fence and hides behind some bushes.

There she's secure for a while. She's in the shadows, and it's dark there. She can see the terrorists looking for her at the other end of the complex, and they're relatively far away. Suddenly a raccoon emerges from along the fence in the shadows. It had an apparent interest in the Dumpster behind her. The raccoon walks up to her and stops.

She doesn't see it at first and then suddenly realizes that it's only a few feet away. When she spots the raccoon, it frightens her, and she screams. The raccoon looks at her and slowly ambles toward the fence.

Lizzy looks at the terrorists who heard her scream. Now they're running in her direction, but they're not exactly sure where she is. She figures they will find her within a minute or two.

She looks back at the raccoon, which has stopped and is sitting there a few feet away looking at her. Being totally scared, she's vulnerable to anything. She looks at the raccoon, and the raccoon sits on his haunches and looks back at her. It appears to be smiling at her. She pauses and says softly, "Racky, is that you?" She thinks that perhaps the raccoon is her stuffed animal that came to life to help her. Her grandpa and her mommy always told her it would comfort her when she was scared.

It's still dark behind the bushes. The raccoon then slowly ambles along the fence some more but stops every few feet and looks back at Lizzy. It's as if the raccoon wants her to follow it. The raccoon eventually crawls under the fence through a hole dug out in the ground underneath it. She gets up and slowly walks behind the raccoon, dragging her dolly bag behind her. She then discovers the hole underneath the fence where the raccoon apparently came and went. It's just large enough for her to fit through to get to the other side and out of the warehouse complex area.

"Racky," she calls out softly again. "Is that you? Racky?" She sees the raccoon on the other side of the fence. It has stopped again and is sitting there looking at her. She thinks the raccoon is coaxing her to follow it.

She gets down on the ground and crawls under the fence and gets to the other side; however in the process, her doll falls out of her bag in the hole. She's unaware of this. She runs along the fence on the other side for a while and then finally sits down to rest on the other side by some more bushes. She sits there and looks in her dolly bag in the moonlight and realizes that she lost her doll. The raccoon has disappeared. She's devastated.

She decides to backtrack and look for her doll. She finally finds it sitting in the hole underneath the fence. She grabs it, but the clothes on her doll are stuck on the jagged fence bottom in the hole. As she struggles to get it free, one of the terrorists approaches and starts to look behind the bushes for her. He will undoubtedly see her. He's only a few feet away. She continues to pull on her doll, but its clothes are wrapped in the jagged fence bottom and the doll won't come loose.

She temporarily runs several feet away and hides behind a bush, but then suddenly, the raccoon reappears and goes back under the fence from where she came and disappears behind a bush a few feet away from the terrorist.

Just as the terrorist approaches and turns around to look at the hole under the fence where her doll is, the raccoon reappears a few feet away on the other side of him and hisses at him. He's startled, jumps, and turns the other way toward the raccoon. He curses and chases the raccoon away and now is on the other side of the bush away from the fence. He continues to search for her, but now he's looking on the other side of the bush away from her.

Lizzy is convinced that Racky saved her, and she briefly thinks of her grandpa.

Lizzy returns to the fence and pulls and pulls and finally frees her doll, tearing part of the doll's clothing on the fence. She runs away on the other side of the bushes on the other side of the fence, carrying her doll in one hand and her dolly bag in the other. She's free of the complex and, for now, has successfully escaped outside of the warehouse complex.

The bushes get thicker and turn into woods. The full moon has come out from behind the night clouds. It has provided a little bit of light in the dark of night, and she's barely able to see where she's going.

She follows a pathway and stumbles along in the shadows from the moonlight and comes across a creek. There's about a foot of water in it and it's about three feet wide. To a little girl her age, in the dark it looks like a raging river. She decides to sit down and rest and sits on a log. As she puts her dolly back in the bag, she feels the cell phone and pulls it out. She had forgotten that she had put it in the bag.

She gets an idea that she can call for help but has no idea exactly how to use it. When she played with Julie's cell phone at home, it was always pretend. She doesn't even know how to turn it on.

She talks into the phone like she would do at home when she was in pretend mode, but obviously there's nobody on the other end because it hasn't been turned on. She eventually realizes that it needs to be powered up. Everything is very quiet now and things seem to have settled down. Lizzy takes a deep breath to relax.

As she fumbles around with the phone, a bullfrog suddenly lets out a strident "Ribbit, ribbit, ribbit" just a few feet from where she's sitting. She's startled and jumps up, and in the process, she drops the phone on the ground. The phone disappears within the sticks, rocks, leaves, and other debris in the dark.

She looks down and feels for the phone but encounters a spider web and is met by a large spider. She screams again, grabs her dolly bag, and runs down the creek several feet away and sits on a large rock. She figures that the cell phone has been lost for good.

There's no way she's going back there to try to find it. Not with a big frog and gargantuan spider there. In addition, she wouldn't be able to see it anyway. It's dark and she figures that after moving several feet away the phone is pretty much lost now and can't be found.

She sits there and starts to cry, but at the same time she's thinking of what she should do. Knowing that her mommy and daddy are tied up back at the warehouse, she wishes that her grandpa was there to help her, or that Racky would come back and be with her. She has no idea where she is, what is around her, or where to go. She is very much afraid. The darkness of the woods and the sounds of the night coming from the woods are frightening. And she can hear the terrorists on the other side of the fence coming closer looking for her.

Chapter 28

Back at the warehouse, the terrorists return and tell the leader they can't find Lizzy anywhere. He becomes angry, and they all start screaming at each other. Julie and Garrett have no idea what they're saying, except they hear the words "Praise be to Allah" every now and then.

The leader starts swinging his gun around and accuses Garrett of letting Lizzy escape. "Somebody here will pay for this," he shouts.

Garrett again tells the leader that he didn't do it and that he couldn't do it. He points to the ropes that still have him tied up.

One of the other terrorists then says something to the leader and points to his watch.

The leader then quickly checks on the ropes that have everyone tied up and yells something to the others, again which Julie and Garrett don't understand. He then grabs the keys to one of the vans, runs into the office, and closes the door that goes outside and gets into the van.

Another terrorist climbs in on the passenger side. The other terrorists pile into the other van. The garage door goes up and the vans disappear into the night, apparently to look for Lizzy, who they now suspect has somehow left the complex area. As they leave, the garage door is closed and hits the floor with a thud and locks in place.

Now alone again, Julie and Garrett immediately start struggling again to try to free themselves, but to no avail. They are bound like moths in a spider web. While they struggle they talk with each other again to try to figure out what's going on. They wonder where Lizzy is, if she is okay, and what they're going to do. They question what will happen to them.

They fear that the terrorists will find Lizzy and will kill at least one and maybe two of them. Garrett presumes he's a goner when they return and tries desperately to free himself, but it's a lost cause.

As they continue to struggle, Julie looks over at Mikey and lets out another bloodcurdling scream. "Mikey! Mikey! Garrett, Mikey's gone!"

"I can't believe this! Did they take him? I could have sworn he was just here still tied up! Mikey! Mikey!"

"Mikey, Mikey, Mikey, where are you?"

After about the third time they call his name, they spot him playing on the other side of the nuclear device. He had freed himself and climbed up on a stool and is just about to turn the handles that secure the case. Julie nearly has a heart attack. They both know from what the terrorists told them the device is wired with sensors and will explode upon any contact with it.

"Mikey! Mikey! Don't touch that! Get away from there, come here, right now!" she blurts out.

Mikey can understand a lot of things and is just now starting to talk more and more but refuses to obey sometimes, especially when he's unsure of what is happening. Julie says to Garrett, "Typical of him but now's not the time for this! What do we do?"

Mikey slowly climbs down from the stool on the other side of the nuclear device and then goes over to the table where the knife is.

Garrett tells him calmly, "Mikey, can you please bring the knife to me?"

Mikey picks the knife up by the sharp end and barely cuts his hand. Although it's only a drop of blood, he's terrified. He thinks he's done something wrong. Mikey drops the knife and it bounces on the floor just out of reach of Garrett and Julie. Mikey, thinking he's in trouble, runs off. Mikey runs into the office and disappears in the semi-darkness in there. Julie calls for him, but he won't come out. Mikey thinks he's in trouble for cutting himself with the knife because he knows he's not supposed to play with them and doesn't want to come out of the office, even though his daddy told him it was okay.

Garrett reaches for the knife, and by stretching his body to the limit, he's finally able to kick it closer and is able to turn around and grasp it with his hands behind him. He tries to cut the ropes that bind him, but it's difficult because of the way he's tied up. However, he eventually cuts through and frees his hands. He then attempts to strategically cut the rest of the ropes so that he can wrap himself up again if necessary to make it look like he's still tied up, although he may be able to escape with some effort.

After a little time, he succeeds and is finally completely free from its restraint. He stands up to stretch. He contemplates what to do next. His first thought is to get Mikey, but he's unsure what to do with him. As he starts to run over to him, both he and Julie observe Mikey come out from hiding behind the curtains in the office, and open the door to the outside.

Mikey's ability to unlock and open the door does not surprise either of them. Mikey finds handles and locks of great interest. For a three-year-old little boy, he finds these fascinating. The handle on the glass case in which the bomb is located is what lured him over there in the first place.

Garrett and Julie had to acquire special locks at home because of his uncanny ability to open all of the doors no matter what sort of handle and lock that they had. They watch Mikey walk outside but then immediately he comes right back in, closes the door, and hides behind the curtains again.

"What are you doing, Mikey? Please come here right away. Everything's okay. Please?"

"Julie, I wonder why he came back inside so soon after opening up the door?"

Garrett continues to call him to come out from behind the curtains as he runs over to him. However, Mikey stays there and soon Garrett knows why. The garage door starts to go up. Apparently Mikey saw the terrorists coming back. Garrett now realizes that the terrorists have returned and that he needs to act fast. He needs to act very fast.

He forgets about Mikey and scrambles back to the rail and rewraps the ropes around him to make it look like he's still tied up. One of the vans pulls in, and the garage door again is closed. He quickly finishes retying himself, but just as the terrorists get out of their van Garrett realizes that he has left the knife at his feet.

He knows that the terrorists will expect the knife to be on the table where they left it. The table is a good ten feet away. Garrett has no time whatsoever to untie himself and put the knife back on the table without being seen.

He quickly loosens the ropes around one of his hands and picks up the knife. Just as the leader turns around to walk over to him, with the ropes halfway restraining him, Garrett flings the knife into the air toward the table. The knife hits the side of the table, flips up, and happens to land almost exactly in the middle of the table where the terrorists had left it. "I can't believe I did this! That has to be a miracle." He then rewraps the ropes around his hands just at the leader turns their way.

The leader walks over to Julie and Garrett and is so angry he's lost control of himself. The terrorists have not been able to find Lizzy even though they have driven all over the entire industrial complex and around it. He screams at Julie, "Where is Alex Fisheramen? Where is the girl?"

He then walks over to the table. He momentarily looks at the knife. He then looks at Garrett. "I have absolutely had it with you all. Now time has come and somebody pays!"

Garrett thinks that the leader has noticed that the knife is out of place from where it was when he left. He believes that the leader thinks they were up to something while he was away. The leader starts to reach for the knife and looks at Garrett.

Then instead of taking the knife he reaches for his AK-47 hanging from its shoulder strap and proceeds to fire at least a dozen shots that just barely miss Julie but end up hitting the curtains in the office. The shots rip the curtains to shreds from the floor up about six feet high from one wall to the other.

The curtains can be seen swirling around from the bullets hitting it and then falls to the floor in a pile. The bullets hit the curtains inches apart from each other from the floor level on up. It's filled with bullet holes. The curtains continue to wiggle about as it comes to rest in a heap on the floor. The boarded up windows behind the curtains are riddled with bullets.

The leader is infuriated and lets go another half-dozen shots up in the air and into the office. The bullets can be heard ricocheting all over the metal beams and falling to the concrete floor. The shots continue to echo throughout the building for some time. He's out of control because he's so angry.

Julie is shaking with fear. She's thinking of Mikey behind the curtains and thinks the absolute worst. He's been shot to death. She wonders if perhaps that the leader knew that Mikey was hiding behind the curtains, and she assumes this is the leader's way of retribution for all of the trouble they've caused. She is absolutely devastated and starts to cry uncontrollably.

Then the garage door opens back up and another van pulls in.

The leader now realizes that Mikey now is missing. He yells at Garrett and Julie. "What happened to your little boy? Where is he! Tell me now!"

He is so mad they fear another round of gunfire.

Garrett emphatically shouts back, "We don't know! We didn't untie him! Look! We have no idea how he got away and thought you took him when we weren't looking!" They continue to plead their case that they had nothing to do with his escape and point to their own ropes that bind them.

Julie doesn't want to say he was behind the curtains because she's afraid to find out and learn that the leader shot him to death.

The terrorists search the warehouse and can't find him anywhere. One of them goes into the office and looks around, steps around the pile of curtains on the floor, and returns but doesn't say anything.

The leader approaches Garrett and tells him when they find the kids, they will kill both the kids and one of them. But he then tells them that maybe he will reconsider and save them if both he and Julie denounce and condemn Jesus Christ and convert to the teachings of the Sharia law of Islam. They will need to do this in another video to be shown to the world. They will have only a little time to think about it. Or they can reveal where Alex is. Otherwise, their children will be shot when they're found, and maybe Garrett and Julie too.

They are told as soon as they find one of the kids, they will need to make an immediate decision. The leader then goes over to Julie and tells her, "Your choice." The leader then spits on the floor between Garrett and Julie and leaves to talk with his men.

The terrorists then see that the office door to the outside is slightly ajar again and think that Mikey escaped too. The leader and the terrorist who went in the office engage in a heated discussion. They grab the remaining automatic weapons that are hung on the wall and return to the vans to go back out and resume their search for Lizzy and Mikey. Julie and Garrett assume Lizzy is still missing outside and that Mikey is lying in a pool of blood underneath the curtains.

But this time, two of the terrorists remain inside to keep an eye on Garrett and Julie.

Emily sits comfortably in her pumpkin seat. But she starts to stir from her sleep. In a few minutes she will be wide awake and will want her diaper changed and a bottle. It's just about her feeding time again. Julie can't believe Emily slept through all of the gunshots and commotion.

Julie just stares at the curtains and sees it all shot up and lying in a heap on the floor and again breaks down into uncontrollable tears. She is convinced that underneath the curtains lie a lifeless Mikey with bullet holes in his body.

Garrett looks at the timer on the bomb. What was once 9:00 now is a little under 6:00. He can't believe how fast time is going by. He hears the tick tick-tick-tick as the timer on the clock continues to wind down.

Chapter 29

The woods are very spooky. Now in addition to the crickets, occasionally an owl can be heard off in the trees somewhere. Lizzy is again startled when she hears the croaking of the bullfrog, as it appears to be only a few feet from her. She lets out a scream because the silence of the night immediately around her was so suddenly interrupted. What a scary sound for her to hear just a few feet away from her in the dark.

As it turns out, it was not good for her to scream. Although she is unaware, a countryside highway runs along the other side of the creek and the terrorists are driving and walking the road in search of her. They hear her scream and now are hot on her trail.

She hears the van coming and can see its headlights from across the creek. But much more upsetting to her is the fact that she can see one of the terrorists walking along the roadside with a flashlight and another with a spotlight. They heard her scream.

They're shining their lights into the bushes along the road. Lizzy crouches down behind a big boulder-sized rock and a couple of times, their lights swings by her and just misses her. One of the lights illuminates the ground just inches from her and stays there momentarily, but the terrorist doesn't see her. Lizzy is so scared she's gasping for breath.

Then she spots one of the terrorist negotiating his way down the embankment to the creek below. He now is only a few feet away from her but still doesn't see her. The moon now is going in and out of the clouds as they float by. She's hiding in the shadows.

Now she's trying to hold her breath. He's swinging his light all around her, and then he turns it off. Now it's very dark. The moon has temporarily gone behind the clouds. She can barely see him in the shadows looking at the spot where she was sitting on the log just a minute or so ago, only a few feet away.

She looks back at that spot and there on the ground is a faint light. It's Julie's cell phone that apparently powered up on its own when it hit the ground when she dropped it there.

The terrorist turns off his flashlight to better see the glow on the ground and then goes over to it. He sees it and stoops over to retrieve it. As he holds up the phone, it now is brighter after he lifts it out of the leaves on the ground. He says something that she doesn't understand and immediately turns it off, shoves it in his pocket, and starts looking more intensely for her. He knows that she must be around there somewhere very close.

He calls the van over and the van parks on the side of the road at an angle. It then drives very slowly up the road with its headlights on aimed into the area of the creek and bushes. If that was not bright enough, on come the high beams. The light is blinding and the headlights light up the hillside on the other side of the creek. The entire creek area below is just barely outside of the light and is still in the shadows. However, a separate spotlight being carried by one of the terrorists is aimed at her and the light lands right on her as she's trying to hide behind the rock. It's like she's the star of the show. The light stops, and she is encompassed in the spotlight.

The terrorists see her and immediately call out to her. They run down toward her. Lizzy panics and runs down the creek and tries to run into the woods. However, the embankment is too muddy and steep for her to climb. So she crosses the creek and stumbles up the other side and runs through some more bushes. Her shoes and clothes are wet. The bushes are some very dense thickets and they scratch her enough to draw blood as she runs through them.

She's dragging her dolly bag behind her, and after a few minutes she's in the dark again out of sight of the terrorists. She's short on breath and needs to stop and rest. She hides behind some trees, but she can hear the terrorists getting closer to her. They keep calling to her. They're hot on her trail now.

It's only a matter of time before they catch up with her and get her. She can see their lights hitting the area all around her. So far, they've not yet spotted her again.

She looks in her dolly bag and realizes that her doll had fallen out again. She's devastated and terrified. She wonders whether she should go back and try to find her doll, which would certainly allow the terrorist to find her, or whether to continue to run ahead.

She reluctantly trudges ahead and comes upon the road around the bend where the van had parked. She desperately wants to follow it because it's safer than the woods and it's not as spooky. But she's afraid that the men in the van may come and see her. She spots what appears to be a closed gas station down the road and goes back into the woods and follows the tree line to try to get to the gas station.

She starts to run through some tall grass and stumbles over a log and falls to the ground. Her leg, now all scratched up from the thorn bushes, hurts her and she can't get up. It appears she may have broken her leg in the fall. She tries to move and get up, but can't. She lies there clutching her dolly bag with one hand and her leg with the other. The lights from the flashlights of the terrorists now shine all around her, but she's still hidden in the tall grass and bushes. She can't run because her leg hurts and may be broken. In fact, she cannot move at all and she starts to cry as the pain sets in.

The moon has come out again and partially lights up the area where she lies. It's simply a matter of only a minute, and perhaps only seconds before they find her. They're closing in fast and are only several feet from her. It's deathly quiet, and the terrorists are so close now that any movement or the slightest sound at all from her will pinpoint exactly where she's hiding. She holds back her tears to be as quiet as she can and desperately tries to remain as still as possible. She holds her breath and tries not to move a muscle. She knows she cannot move or make even the slightest sound whatsoever because it will give away where she's hiding.

She feels something on her leg and looks down to see what it is. The moon emerges fully from the clouds and provides just enough light that she sees a spider about half the size of her hand crawling up her leg and disappearing inside the front of her shorts.

Chapter 30

I'm finally lowered onto the embankment of the river of fire and slowly and gently placed there in a kneeling position. I feel like I am going to be executed. I can't move. One demon approaches me with his talon-like claws to grasp my head, throw it back, and open my mouth.

The other demon raises the ladle and I can see the hot lava spilling out of it with flames and lightning shooting out everywhere. I can't believe just how hideous, gruesome, and frightening these demons are.

Drops of the flaming liquid fall within inches of my face. A few specks barely graze my cheeks and I can instantly feel the pain radiate down into my body like lightning bolts as the droplets turn into a few blisters on my skin. Both demons stare down at me, and I can see their eyes which are glowing red with fire. I am in complete horror mode.

The only thing I can hear is the horrid screams of terror coming from the other souls all around me that drown out the sound of the rushing river going by and the crackling from the lightning and fire from within.

Suddenly, in a flash, some thoughts and questions go through my mind that would otherwise take me minutes to think about. The thoughts are a reverie of a sequence of questions and ideas that pass in an instant but are crystal clear.

For some reason, I think of these other souls and wonder about them and their history. I feel so sorry for them. How did they get here? What did they do or not do? Do they really deserve to be here and suffer this way? Do they deserve to be here more than me?

Is there a possibility that perhaps some of these souls may not have even had the opportunity to know Jesus because they never heard His word? Perhaps His word was never spread to them? Is the reason why they're here because they never had the opportunity to profess their faith? Maybe they were never told about Jesus. Or what if they were told of Jesus but didn't believe in Him? Is that why they are here? Or perhaps they were unknowingly recruited by the devil. But why would I think of these things? I don't even know if any of this is the case or not.

But if so, I can't believe they would be punished this way for those reasons. Is the devil responsible for this somehow? Are any souls who were deprived of the Word of Jesus here also? Or do they go somewhere else? I wonder what happens to these souls that never knew of Jesus. I can't believe God would allow them to be punished in hell, but if he wouldn't, then how do they get into heaven if they never knew Jesus? Maybe they're the souls that end up in purgatory?

Regardless, I am so forlorn for their misery and pain that suddenly I'm overtaken by incredible emotion listening to their wailing instead of thinking about my own fate. All these thoughts go through my head faster than a blink as if some unknown force is making me think about the misery of all of the other souls in this room.

Just as the demon lowers the ladle to start pouring the liquid inferno down my throat and over my face, with all of the remaining strength I have, in pure instinct and impulse, I scream out as loud as I can, "Jesus, please have mercy on all of these poor souls! I believe in you, and I always will! Please have mercy on all the souls here, not just me! I still believe in you and have faith in you! I give praise to you!"

Anticipating my face being eaten by fire in an instant, there is nothing. I wait in agony, and wait and wait. I try to open my eyes and see what's happening and am astonished that I can see. The demons around me are frozen in place like statues!

I cannot believe this. A sudden rush of euphoria overtakes me. I look up to see what the bad spirit is doing. Last time I saw it, it was laughing at me. I expect it to be so angry with me that now I sort of wish that I had not yelled out what I did. In fact, I don't understand what came over me to say what I did, but nevertheless, I did. Expecting an absolutely enraged spirit angry at me for screaming the words of Jesus, my euphoria instantly turns to fear again.

But the spirit is not there. It's gone. I then sense the good spirit again. It's back and it's strong. I am absolutely elated. Did my scream asking Jesus to have mercy on the other souls make it come back? I wonder if my expression of mercy for the other souls as well as me had an even better effect than when I was in the first room.

I look back at the demons and to my horror they are again starting to move. They are no longer frozen in place. It's like they are slowly waking up. They again are staring down at me and I can see anger in their eyes the likes of which no one could imagine. They start the process again, but there's something wrong with them.

The one demon who was about to grasp my head is shaking and for some reason can't touch me. For some reason he's weak. The other demon stumbles and spills the ladle of fire and also appears weak. But they're slowly regaining their strength, and it becomes obvious that within seconds they will have their full power back and I will again be doomed.

Now my ability to think independently again returns. I can feel my weakness fade away and I can start to feel some strength myself. I can feel the blisters on my face heal and go away.

As one demon refills his ladle and the other starts to grab my head again, I suddenly feel myself being raised above them. I now am floating above them and feel myself being lifted to the rafters of the cavern again. I suspect I'm going to be persecuted by a most angry devil who this time will subject me to an even more intense torture.

Is this just because I screamed out for Jesus to have mercy on all of the souls there? I can again sense Satan staring at me from all around as I float closer and closer to him. He's pulling me toward him by a powerful force.

I'm not looking forward to this at all and begin trembling with absolute fear again. As I near him, I close my eyes and start a prayer with all of my heart and soul. I did follow his instructions literally and did not ask mercy for myself but sense that now I have done worse by asking mercy for all of the other souls instead. What does he have in store for me now? I am so scared.

Chapter 31

At Andrew and Alana's house, everybody's sound asleep. Sonja and Alana are in the bedrooms and Andrew is lying on the couch in the living room. Suddenly, the silence is broken by the sound of a telephone ringing. Andrew awakes with a jump and scrambles to answer it. It's the FBI outside. They need to talk with them right away. Andrew tells them to come inside and he goes over to unlock the door. He then goes to the bedroom and calls for Alana and Sonja to wake up and come to the living room.

A few minutes later, one of the FBI agents knocks on the door and he's greeted by Alana. He comes in and sits down on the couch. They fear that he has some really bad news. But instead he says, "We just got a signal."

"What?" remarks Alana.

"A signal, we got one. Somehow Julie's cell phone was powered up and a signal was received. Our tech unit is working with the carrier and they're tracking it by using the GPS and cell phone towers. They're trying to locate its position, but that will take a little time. The signal was active for only a short time and then was lost."

The agent then tells them he's waiting for a phone call but in the meantime he has some more questions for them. He proceeds to ask a lot of questions about Julie's cell phone, what they know about it, how often they called her on it, whether she used text messaging, and so on.

Andrew asks the agent, "Why can't you simply call Julie's cell phone?"

The agent stares at him with a blank look on his face. "Did you really just ask me that? We've already talked about that. Did you forget already? Our protocol forbids it. We don't know the circumstances surrounding Julie and are afraid that if we call or text her, her captors will hear it and confiscate and destroy the phone if she has it. I've already told you that! In addition, it will not work to call her on her cell phone." He starts to explain but stops as he's interrupted and gets a call on his cell phone.

The agent answers the call on his phone, and it's the FBI Tactical Unit. They advise that they have positioned the phone within several miles from where Andrew and Alana live. But they weren't able to get a precise reading or location because it was only powered on for such a short time, which was not long enough to get a more accurate position of its location.

The agent suggests that either someone turned the phone off right after it was powered on or perhaps her battery went dead before they could complete the cell search for it.

Alana says, "Well, that's better than a sixty-square-mile area to look for it. I can't believe that they're only a few miles from here. I wonder where they are."

Andrew reminds everybody, "That means that the nuclear bomb is also just a few miles away."

The agent then explains, "Assuming the nuclear bomb is only a few miles away, not only just about everything within this range would certainly not survive from the fallout but the blast would probably ignite everything in an inferno that would kill every living thing and completely demolish all buildings instantaneously. Everything will be burned in flames and nothing will survive. All property, all living things, everything will be obliterated. That includes this house and anybody in it."

"Wow," both Alana and Andrew exclaim together.

The agent then gets on the phone and is on a conference call to help organize and coordinate a local search within an area of some coordinates that he obtains in the call and reads aloud and repeats again.

He then asks Alana and Andrew to list every building or enclosure or other area that they can think of within several miles from their house where they think that the terrorists could possibly be hiding. They're told to focus on vacant buildings, vacant houses for sale of which they might be aware, secluded wooded areas and the like. They should list anything they can think of which may be suspicious.

"That's impossible," Andrew remarks. "Several square miles is still a pretty large area."

"It's not impossible," both the agent and Sonja say simultaneously. The agent then goes out to his SUV and returns with some electronic communications and surveillance equipment and hooks up a conference with other FBI agents to start reviewing every location they can think of.

They begin to build a list and call in more FBI backup. The agent then calls the CIA. It's evident that the FBI now is setting up a communication center from the living room of their house instead of using their SUV. The FBI now will use Andrew and Alana's living room as a command post.

"How did Julie's phone suddenly turn on?" they wonder. "Why did it turn off so quickly?" Their curiosity builds.

They're happy that at least it was on long enough for the FBI to get a partial reading of its position. A couple of square miles is certainly better than sixty square miles. Hopefully they can find them very soon. But then on the other hand, they're scared because the nuclear bomb is also only a few miles from them as well.

Then the agent gets another call. He walks outside to the front porch to take the call privately as he doesn't want anyone else listening to it. After quite a long time, he then goes out to his SUV and returns. He sits back down on the couch and stares at everybody. He drops his head in his hands and then looks down and rubs his eyes. He then slowly looks up at everybody. He dejectedly says, "I have some more news to tell you."

He has a very stoic look on his face as if he has the most terrible news in the world to tell them. Alana, Andrew, and Sonja appear devastated. They sense this is not going to be good. Not good news at all. They do not want to hear what he has to say, but they need to know.

Chapter 32

Garrett and Julie are increasingly uncomfortable and they call one of the terrorists over to ask permission to go to the bathroom and get something to drink. Julie also tells the terrorist that she needs to feed Emily and change her diaper.

The terrorist doesn't understand her because he doesn't speak English. Julie then goes through some charades to get her point across. It's difficult to do so being tied up. Garrett then realizes that if the terrorist unties him he will see that he is already free from the ropes although it still looks like he's tied up. So he then changes his mind and tells the terrorist he doesn't need to go and Julie can go first.

At that time the garage door goes back up and two more vans drive in. There now are perhaps six terrorists in the building. One of them is the leader who comes over to talk with them. The one terrorist talks to the leader, but Garrett and Julie don't understand what he's saying. The leader then walks by Garrett and spits on him, but unties Julie so that she can take care of her business.

He again follows her into the bathroom and then after a few minutes they return back to the railing where he ties her up again but allowing some room for her to maneuver to feed and change Emily.

In the meantime, several terrorists are searching for Lizzy outside of the compound and more terrorists are searching for Mikey inside the compound. As the garage door is closing, Garrett can see the lights of one of the vans outside as it swings around and lights up the building.

The leader then proceeds to tell Julie if they don't find Lizzy and Mikey real soon, they will all need to leave and they will not be coming back. Julie asks, "Why?"

The leader then points to the nuclear bomb, looks at his watch, and says defiantly "You don't think we want to stick around when this goes off, do you? My boss is thinking about advancing the timer because he's so angry with everything. He's thinking about killing you all as well."

"What do you mean?" asks Julie.

"He is outraged that you or anybody else will not reveal where Alex is. He is outraged that your little girl has escaped. He is infuriated that your little boy has escaped. He is ready to kill him right now." He points to Garrett. "He is angry because we need to attend to you and your baby's needs. Do I say more? You are all nothing but a giant bunch of trouble!"

"But you're the ones who brought us here! If you go, what's going to happen to us?"

He responds to her, "I don't know. We'll probably leave you tied up here, or we'll kill you all so that you will not have to suffer until sunrise."

Garrett desperately wants to say something but refrains from saying anything in fear it will backfire.

Obviously, the terrorists don't like him at all.

The leader then turns around and temporarily walks away.

A few minutes later, the garage door goes back up and another van rolls in. A laughing terrorist climbs out of the van dragging a little girl on the concrete floor kicking and screaming behind him who he has tied up. It's Lizzy. He throws her on the ground in front of Julie. She falls to the floor and tries to climb on to her lap but can hardly move. She's absolutely hysterical. It looks like she might have broken her leg. She can walk, but barely.

The terrorist then retrieves her dolly bag from the van and throws it at her. He then pulls Julie's cell phone out of his pocket and tosses it to his leader and points to Julie, saying something to him with great emotion that she can't understand.

234

The leader then as angry as he can be looks at Julie and shouts out, "What is this? What is this? You say that you lost this but your little girl was hiding it all of the time for you! You remember what I said if you lie to me? Do you? Do you?"

He then removes his AK-47 from his shoulder, clicks it, and shoves it into Garrett's forehead between his eyes and grimaces as he's about to pull the trigger. Julie is hysterical and is crying, "No! No! No!" She struggles to try to cover her eyes and ears. She closes her eyes and buries her head in her lap. Julie's an emotional train wreck.

With the gun thrust into Garrett's head, the leader puts his finger on the trigger and a gunshot is heard that echoes and vibrates throughout the building. Out of the corner of her eye, Julie sees Garrett's head jerk backward and then his body slump down to the ground as the gunshot continues to echo throughout the warehouse.

Chapter 33

Mikey runs down the side of the building and then runs the same path that Lizzy ran earlier. Although Lizzy was clearly trying to escape, Mikey on the other hand is too young to understand and decides to go on an exploratory field trip first. Typical little boy behavior. He doesn't seem afraid of anything and ambles down the partially lit alley and comes upon the Dumpster.

There he spots the raccoon climbing out with some garbage. The raccoon stops in its tracks and looks at Mikey. Mikey thinks the raccoon is cool and wants to pet it. He's not startled or afraid of it at all. He is accustomed to large and wild animals. He's ridden Crackerjack like a horse when he was a little younger. He likes to go to the zoo and get close to the animals, and the larger the animals, the better.

The raccoon looks at him, waddles off, and heads toward the fence stopping periodically to look back at Mikey. Mikey follows him. The raccoon comes up on the hole under the fence, stops and looks at Mikey again, and then turns around and scurries through it. Mikey gets down and crawls through the hole under the fence following the raccoon. He stops for an instant to look at the torn doll clothes on the fence. He then continues on just as Lizzy did, but halfway crawling and halfway walking.

Mikey then follows the raccoon for a while until he can't see it anymore. The farther he walks away from the complex, the darker it is. Mikey follows the bushes for a while, stopping along the way to inspect some huge spiders building giant spider webs between them that glisten in the moonlight. He can barely make them out in the shadows. He picks one up and admires it in the moonlight. Surprisingly, the spider doesn't attempt to run off. Mikey smiles and lets it go.

He continues to walk some more and eventually comes upon the creek. He hears the croaking of the bullfrog, is amused, and tries to find it. He eventually gives up and plays in the water for a few minutes and then ambles up the other side to the road. He's at about the same spot that Lizzy was when the van appeared.

Mikey now is getting tired, and it's darker again because the clouds have reappeared, which have obscured the moon. He decides to follow the road and walks slowly along its shoulder.

Within minutes, a van with several terrorists approaches and spots Mikey. Mikey is oblivious to the terrorists and continues to walk right into its headlights. The van stops, and several automatic weapons are stuck outside of the van's windows aimed right at Mikey. He has no idea what's happening. Mikey just continues to waddle along.

Suddenly, an SUV approaches from the opposite end of the road. It's the FBI on a routine patrol scouting out the area trying to look for suspicious buildings where the terrorists could be hiding. They are following a map with coordinates set for the new perimeter that was set upon the cell phone signal.

The terrorists aim their guns at Mikey, but the lights from the SUV shine on them. The guns are then pulled back into the van and the van accelerates at a high rate of speed nearly running the SUV off the road as it passes it by. The FBI turns around and chases the van. Both vehicles disappear into the distance around the bend of the road.

Off in the distance around the bend, screeching tires and a barrage of gunfire can be heard. The gunfire continues for several minutes and then becomes more intermittent. After several minutes it stops. In the meantime, Mikey decides to sit alongside the road.

He just sits there, spots a praying mantis that has flown down on the road next to him. He picks it up and admires it under a dimly lit street light. After a while, he lets it go and then is intrigued by some noises he hears in the woods. He gets up and goes back into the woods where it's dark. He's unfazed by the gunshots and appears to be oblivious to them but starts to wonder if he should hide.

A few minutes later some headlights appear from where the gunfire was heard. Mikey is no longer there. He's hiding in the woods behind some fallen trees, but he's watching the road and he sees what's going on. The vehicle slows down and flashlights can be seen aimed at the bushes and trees along the road. Somebody is searching for him.

Then a spotlight comes from the vehicle and lights up the countryside. But Mikey is completely hidden. He is hidden so well that not even the brightest lights will reveal him. He has no idea whether it's the terrorists or the FBI.

Chapter 34

I feel the presence of Satan enveloping all around me. I wait to hear what he's going to say. I know for sure that he's so angry with me for praying that Jesus have mercy on all of the other souls in hell. I ask myself why I said this. What made me do it? Something came over me and prompted me to shout that out, but what? Have I now sealed my fate in hell to an even worse torture? I fear the ultimate punishment.

I look up again and the good spirit is there, and the bad spirit has vanished. If there is any hope for me, it has to reside in this good spirit.

But just as I start to feel some relief that the good spirit has returned, I feel the presence of Satan ever so close that I could almost reach out and touch him. I can sense fire from him as he wraps himself around my body and surrounds my soul in such a way that I feel he has just about gained complete control of me.

Now I know that he's so angry with me he wants to torture me even more. I feel his fire in my eyes and I'm blinded. Then I can feel myself suddenly being hurled out into the lower cavern of hell again. In the process I'm told by Satan that I can never again pray for the other souls in hell and that if I do, I will suffer an even worse torture forever. Again, I must take him literally. So I cannot pray for myself and I cannot pray for any other souls either. I know I will not be able to do either of these, even if I tried.

I land at the entrance of another room and my sight returns. But this time I can't determine the level. I get the feeling that this is either the third level of the first chamber or it may be the first level of the second chamber. I would like to know but either way the torture here is going to be more intense than that of the last room I was in. That is for certain.

A massive door to this room is unveiled and I'm tossed into the room. The door closes with a thundering thud. It's pitch-black and I can't see anything. I have no idea how large the room is, if there are any walls and if so how close they are, or what if anything else is in the room. The experience of being in total pitch-black darkness in hell and not knowing what else is there or what is going to happen to me is more terrorizing than anything I can imagine. It is deathly quiet.

I then somehow sense that this is the room of the "unexpected." It is used as a torture room for those who have harmed or played tricks on others and is also used for those who have angered Satan.

I'm floating in this room in total blackness and start to get dizzy because I can't maintain my equilibrium while in the dark. It's as if the room is rotating in several different spherical motions or orbits at the same time and I'm floating in weightlessness. I can't figure out if I'm upside down or what position I'm in, but I could not be any more uncomfortable.

I find myself slowly spinning around which makes me so dizzy I feel nauseous. I feel so sick I feel like I'm going to vomit. Then I'm startled and horrified by the loudest and worst organ music ever that starts off with some bass notes that are so low it shakes the darkness with violence. It's so loud that my eardrums are bursting, and I have a massive headache. The organ music again is absolutely sinister and frightening. It's worse than what I experienced in the first room. It's shaking everything.

I then can sense other beings in the room, but I can't see anything. I have no idea how close they are or what or who they are. With the organ music pounding in my head, I can hardly think straight. Such an experience if one can imagine this cannot be any more horrific and terrifying.

Then a bright light instantaneously blinks one time like a strobe light. In that split second, I can very briefly see dozens of demons approaching me with pitchforks. Others are approaching me with huge ladles dripping with melting hot goo of some sort. Others are approaching me with rods shooting out flames of fire, lightning, striking snakes, and other despicable things. Interesting that I can't see the lightning and flames of fire in the dark, but in the split second of light, they are very real.

Knowing what these demons are about to do to me has me absolutely horrified because now it's dark again and I can't see them, but I know they are coming after me. I know they are approaching me in slow motion which further intensifies the horror. The ultra-slow motion of what's happening is horrific.

The room is multi-dimensional and the demons are coming at me from every direction and from directions that I didn't even know existed. Because it's dark and I can't see, I don't know where they are, but I know they are approaching me and getting very close. I can sense them. It's so hideous and terrifying that I scream in horror. I'm literally shaking all over with fear.

I feel a tickle like a feather on my neck and impulsively reach around to swat it away in the darkness. Then I feel another on my cheek, then another high up my leg and then another much higher up my leg. It's pitch-black darkness and I am petrified. I am shaking from head to toe in absolute terror. I'm shaking and swatting my arms around me so much I am convulsing in absolute horror.

In a split second, I wonder whether I'm still in the third level of the first chamber or perhaps the first level of the second chamber. Either way, the intensity of this torture and torment is without question more terrifying than what I previously experienced. I do not even want to think about how bad the pain will be when they eventually torture me. This time it appears it will be a very slow, agonizing torture rather than a sudden influx of unbearable pain that would put me out of my mind. The ultra-slow motion of what's happening and what is going to happen to me is absolutely terrifying.

I feel that the demons are within a few feet of me now, moving in an ever-slow motion, and again I think very quickly that I need to scream something because in the next few seconds I am going to lose any control of my mind to complete and utter fright. I will lose total control of myself and will no longer have any free will to think for myself except to try to withstand the unbearable pain and agony.

Just as I feel a cold wet slimy substance grab my legs and arms, something comes over me and for whatever reason by total instinct I find myself yelling out at the top of my lungs, "May Jesus have mercy on all of you demons for you do not know what you do! Jesus, please have mercy on all of the demons in hell! They are all merely lost souls, and I pray for them. I still have faith in you, and I always will! I sing praise to you in the highest glory!"

Suddenly, the organ goes silent, a dim light emits from around me and stays lit; everything is silent, and I can see that each and every demon is again frozen in place, like statues. Some of them are within inches of my body. The sudden sight of them so close to me in the light terrifies me even more, and I again scream in immediate panic. The demons being frozen in place is similar to what happened in the other room I remember. I slowly regain my composure as I continue to survey my surroundings.

Very soon, the demons unfreeze and start to move and resume their actions again. Everything is in agonizingly slow motion. The light starts to dim as if whatever was in store for me here is going to still take place anyway. I look up and the good spirit is with me and for the first time I can sense some emotion from it. It's smiling at me! There are no words to describe this feeling. Why is it smiling at me? Is it because of what I said?

I then find myself being lifted towards the door. As I'm floating upward, I brush against some of the demons and try to recover from the shock. The door opens and some unknown force leads me out of the room. I'm again floating in the cavern up and away. I'm now being hurled once again toward Satan. I cannot imagine what could be worse than the last time I was within his grasp. I fear the worst and know that he's undoubtedly infuriated with me for screaming the words that I shouted.

But what can be worse than what I've already experienced here? I just can't believe that it can be any worse. But it can. Much worse and many more times to the extent that trying to speculate what the additional rooms, levels, and chambers are like is impossible to comprehend. But what will I shout out next time? I have pretty much run out of options considering what Satan told me specifically I can't say and wouldn't be able to say.

Just as I can sense the wrath of Satan to come down on me, I look up again and for some reason I can feel the good spirit talking with him. I wonder what this is all about. Is it negotiating something? What's going on?

While this is going on, I somehow gain confidence and feel like telling Satan himself that I will pray for him and ask Jesus to have mercy on him as well. But, after thinking about it I decide that would not be a good idea. I don't even want to begin to imagine what that may accomplish if I were to actually do this. Gaining more confidence, the more I think about saying this and wanting to actually yell this out, I sense the presence of Satan fading away. It's almost as if he knows what I'm thinking. But I would not do that.

I then sense myself floating in what again appears to be across the upper section of the cavern. I try to see the ceiling but can't. Although I know I've been lifted far up into the cavern, if there's a ceiling, it's still far away. It's never ending. After a while, I sense myself floating and moving again. But at least I didn't have to confront the devil as close as I did last time. I suddenly get a feeling that I may actually leave hell. My terror turns into excitement as I find my body floating towards the viewing room.

Why was I allowed to leave and why was I not thrust into an even worse room of torture? Perhaps the good spirit had something to do with this? Did it negotiate something with the devil? I wish I knew.

Perhaps Satan perceives me as a bad influence in hell and doesn't want me? Perhaps Satan doesn't want to risk any influence I may have on other souls there. That must be it I think. But if anything was negotiated on my behalf, what will Satan receive in return if anything? Maybe it will be for "future considerations." Maybe I will never know.

But as a result of whatever happened I feel somewhat optimistic and blessed. I suppose there is even room for Jesus and our God in hell, if the right things are said and if one continues to have faith.

After some time, I'm returned to the viewing room. There I remain for a very long time, left there to witness the horrific torture of millions of other souls. This experience is torture in itself. I feel so sorry for all of these other souls, and the feeling becomes unbearable.

There's nothing I can do but watch and listen to millions and millions of souls wailing in the most unbelievable torture and pain. I start to actually feel what they feel and I start to actually share in their anguish and misery. The experience is absolutely overwhelming. But just as I get to the point when I can no longer tolerate it, I am lifted up and start to float again.

The floating process is agonizing slow and leaves me with time for deep thought. I'm eventually led back to the waiting room. There I sit again for the longest time where again I have additional time for deep reflection and contemplation. I wonder what's going to happen to me. Am I going to leave hell? If so, where am I going? What force has control over me? Is it the devil? Is it the bad spirit? Is it the good spirit? Is it an angel? Is it Jesus? Is it God Himself? Or is it something else?

But as I sit there and think of these and other things, suddenly I get the awful feeling that my experience in hell is not over. The feeling is gut-wrenching. Perhaps it's just the beginning? I have a definite sense that if I leave hell, that I am definitely going to return and will experience things that will go far beyond what I have seen and experienced so far. I can't understand this feeling that I will return here but it's very real. It is very real indeed. The feeling that I will return to hell is so definite that it overwhelms me. I know for sure it's going to happen, but I don't understand the circumstances or what's happening.

Now although I've had a period of respite I start to get scared again. But for now, at the same time I'm also so relieved. I feel blessed. I feel very blessed. I think hard to try to reconcile everything that has happened to me and I have difficulty trying to understand what's going on. I'm both relieved and scared at the same time.

I look up and the good spirit is there, and it is very strong again. I wish I could see it. I wish I could hold it. I wish I could give it a hug. I wish I could kiss it. I wish I could talk to it. But I cannot. But for some reason, I feel the good spirit holding, hugging, and kissing me instead. I feel that it's going to talk with me. But so far, it has not. Perhaps this is all my imagination. This entire experience has totally overwhelmed me and I'm confused.

After a while, I'm led out through the gate. As I pass Cerberus out of this forbidden place, I can feel its wrath on every soul going through the gate that it guards.

I now am slowly floating again in the void. Although there is no air, the mere fact that I'm no longer breathing the foul smelling sulfuric acid is refreshing. I feel rejuvenated. After what seems like a very long time, I float to the point in the void where I relived my life in the massive mirror. I'm forced to stop. I hope that I don't have to experience that all over again.

As soon as I think of this possibility, the mirror reappears, and again I become terrified. But instead of reliving my life and having a million questions asked of me, I see the vision of me wearing the shirt with the three lines with the faded symbols and lettering on the second line again. It remains for a few seconds and then the vision vanishes and then the mirror disappears.

Again, I'm astounded as to why I'm being shown this vision. Why am I being shown this vision of me wearing this shirt again? What do the symbols or letters say? They appeared to be bolder and not as faded this time, as if they were materializing into view, but the shirt was not visible long enough for me to try to read it. I sure wish I knew why I'm being shown this and what it says. But I have no clue.

After the mirror disappears, I float in place for a while and don't move. I wonder what's going on.

After going into deep thought again about my life I look out and far away in the distance I can barely see two lights. They are so far they're like pinholes at opposite ends of the universe. One is a very bright constant white light that is welcoming. It is very serene and is a very positive place. It is a place of hope.

On the other side it is a dimmer flickering light that appears to be like a red-and-orange pulsating ball of fire. It's one of hopelessness and is a negative place. I know that place. It's where I just came from. I wonder what the other place is like. I certainly would like to find out. In the meantime, I'm back in the void of nothingness, except for these two lights so far away.

I look up hoping to see the good spirit again. It's there. I then think of my family back home on Earth. I am literally shocked that I can see them again. Not much as the visions are somewhat faded but it seems like their reality is starting to reappear again. I get the sense that these visions will become clearer. I hope that continues. I will revisit these visions again a little later.

Then I think back about my experience in hell and can't help but feel what Jesus went through when He died for our sins. To think He suffered like He did just for us. Wow! There is no way anyone can praise Him enough for suffering for us as He did. Now that I've experienced hell and actually feel what He did when He died for us, I simply cannot praise Him enough.

But for now, I wonder what's going to happen to me. Although I'm relieved I am still shaking uncontrollably from what I just experienced. Am I going someplace else now? If so, where am I going? I can think of four alternatives. One is very acceptable to me. One might be acceptable perhaps if I could predict the future. The other two are not acceptable at all. One of those I just came from and I absolutely don't want to go back. But, the feeling is overwhelming that I will go back there, but why? That feeling is absolutely definite. But for now, where will I be going next? What's going to happen to me?

Chapter 35

Julie, sure that Garrett has been shot to death, buries her face in her lap even more and cries uncontrollably. She is shaking. She refuses to look up. Lizzy and Emily are bawling so loud that she knows it's upsetting the terrorists. She thinks that they are all going to be put to death unless they stop their crying immediately. With her eyes closed, she prays for Garrett again.

Suddenly the leader runs toward the other terrorists and in the process brushes against her back. She raises her head, looks over, and sees a lot of commotion and a flurry of activity. She reluctantly glances over at Garrett and expects to see his lifeless body lying in a pool of blood. She doesn't want to look at him fearing she won't even recognize his face. Instead, he's slumped over moaning.

She is absolutely beside herself. "Garrett! Are you alive? Are you alive? Garrett! Garrett? Didn't they just shoot you in the head?"

Garrett slowly raises his head, looks around a bit, and softly says in a whisper, "What happened?"

Julie now is sobbing with even more uncontrollable emotion, is overjoyed, and says "I don't know. I thought they just shot you!"

Garrett then says, "I heard a click when the gun was shoved into my head and then I heard a gunshot from over there." He points to the office door that leads outside. They can both still hear the ringing in their ears.

After looking around and watching things, Garrett and Julie slowly realize that over by the office door, one of the terrorist guards outside had busted the door open and fired a warning shot to alert the others inside that trouble was coming. That's the shot they heard and thought was blowing Garrett's head off.

The guard outside heard the gunfire on the road on the other side of the industrial complex. It was the same gunfire that occurred when the terrorists, who were looking for Mikey, encountered the FBI on the road. The guard assumes that somebody, whether it be the local police, FBI, or whoever will be on their way and in the complex soon. So he fired a warning shot to alert the other terrorists in the warehouse. Then several of the terrorists' cell phones ring and it is evident that they have been alerted that the FBI are on their way.

Things start to happen very fast. There's a flurry of activity everywhere. Now there's about eight men running around carrying boxes to and from the vans, pulling automatic weapons that were hanging on the wall, talking on cell phones, and hooking up equipment. One terrorist walks over to the nuclear bomb and checks the timer. Garrett looks at it.

Now it's under 04:00 hours and is counting down. One of the terrorists comes over and sets an electronic device on the floor beside it that's a little larger than a cell phone but has all sorts of lights on it. There's a large red button and a smaller red button on it. The leader comes over, picks it up, presses one of the buttons once, and puts it in his pocket.

Another terrorist emerges from one of the vans and is dressed in a coat that appears to be covering something. He's restrained by a leash. They've not seen him before. "Why is he on a leash?" wonder Garrett and Julie. He's accompanied by two other terrorists who are walking him away from the van.

Apparently, he was locked up and hidden in one of the vans this entire time. The terrorists lead him over to the nuclear bomb and tie his leash to the railing down just a little bit from Garrett, and just out of his reach. One terrorist opens his coat to check on something and Garrett and Julie are aghast at what they see.

He has dynamite strapped all around his body with wires coming out in all directions. The straps are all secured with belts that buckle in the back so that there is no way he can undo everything himself. His arms are strapped inside with one hand sticking out. It's as if he's wearing a straitjacket.

Strapped to his back is another electronic device similar to the one lying on the floor hooked up to the dynamite with wires. It doesn't take them long to figure out he's a suicide bomber and the terrorists have a remote triggering device.

The leader comes over and briefly talks with Garrett and Julie. Julie asks, "What's going on?"

The leader then tells them that they are re-setting up surveillance equipment because they fear that somebody has discovered them and will be here soon. "All because of you and your kids," he screams. "I should kill you right now for that!"

He tells them that all of the terrorists are probably going to be leaving very soon and if they do they will not be coming back but he says the suicide bomber will stay. He has volunteered to jump on the nuclear device and push the button in the event that anybody else comes into the warehouse.

In the meantime, if anyone comes in before they can leave, they are setting up an ambush and they're all willing to die if that happens. The suicide bomber will detonate the nuclear device no matter what. They want to make sure that the nuclear device will explode whether anybody else enters the building or not. Either way it *will* explode. That is a 100 percent certainty.

"Why do you need a suicide bomber to jump on the bomb if you can simply detonate it remotely? Wouldn't that be overkill? Why do you also need the explosives? How do you know he'll really do that? How do you know he'll really kill himself to set off the bomb?" asks Julie.

The leader proudly declares, "Because he wants to do it in praise of Allah. He has been trained to do this for the last four years. It's not overkill. By setting off the explosives, he's merely enhancing his praise to the almighty because he is doing it for himself. There's no way you or anybody can talk him out of it. In fact, he wants to do it right now and it's been difficult for us to restrain him. That's why we have him on a leash. He can't wait to do it. Plus, although we really don't need it, its insurance for us to make sure the bomb goes off.

"That's how much he wants to do it and that's why we know he'll do it. As soon as I release him he'll do it without even thinking about it. I can release him remotely with this other device. In the glory of Allah, he will be blessed upon high when he jumps on it and detonates it and he knows it. I'll be leaving the trigger with him before I leave, although he really won't need it.

"But if for some reason he fails, then I have complete control with this remote device. Between the two of us and the others, we will make sure it will go off. Right now, we don't need to do anything. It's on a timer and will go off by itself, unless I stop it with this or set if off early. Only I know the code to do that.

"Anybody else who may get a hold of this who does not enter the right code within a certain time or enters the wrong code will lock the engagement and that will be it. *Kaboom!* Otherwise, it will go off anyway at sunrise when the timer gets to zero. So no matter what happens, there is no way it's not going to go off."

Garrett comments, "So, if he jumps on the bomb, it will go off, even though the timer has not expired."

The leader spits on Garrett and says, "Precisely. And if I die before then, it will then certainly go off because nobody else knows what code to enter and when to enter it to prevent it from going off."

Julie asks the leader, "How are you going to get away before it explodes?"

The leader retorts, "We have special ways to get far from here very fast. Plus, we know our way out of here to get around the traffic jams. But that really doesn't matter. We have choppers and airplanes ready for us. I and a few of the others are due in another city by morning to engage another bomb that needs to be set to explode."

Garrett comments, "So you're the ones who are setting all of the twenty bombs?"

"Of course not. I'm only responsible for two things. One—I need to engage three of the bombs. I only have one more to do. There are ten others with teams who are setting the other bombs. Each coordinator has three or four bombs to engage. We've all been setting these for the past week or so. Two—I'm required to find Alex

Fisheramen. He has not shown up yet. Therefore you will die a most unpleasant death."

Julie intently asks, "What do you mean ten men doing three or four bombs each? That adds up to thirty or forty bombs, not twenty bombs. The news and you have been saying there're only twenty bombs, not thirty or forty."

"I know. You are correct and you are so perceptive. You American people will be surprised when you learn that. Maybe double the show!" The leader sarcastically smiles at her.

"So, that's why you're setting them to all go off at midnight at the same time three days later rather than now or separately in order to give you enough time to set them all up to go off at the same time in each city, right?"

"You got it. When they all go off at the same time, it will be in the highest glory to Allah. In some cities like yours, there may even be two, or maybe even three, bombs in various places, not one. That's why I gotta go. I got more work to do."

The leader then leaves to join the others in setting up the ambush.

Julie and Garrett look at each dumbfounded.

Garrett whispers again to Julie, "You know, it sure is creepy having this idiot with explosives strapped all around him tied to the same railing that we are. He's only a few feet away from me, and he stinks. I guess as soon as they all leave, they will release his leash and then he'll be free to jump on the bomb whenever he wants after they're gone, right?

"But I'm not so sure how he's tied to the railing. They have this contraption tied to a hook on his leash behind him with another electronic device attached to it. Maybe he's not kidding when he said they can release him remotely after they get far enough away."

Julie whispers back to him, "Yeah, but they still don't know that you're really untied and just acting like you are still tied up, right?"

"Shhh," whispers Garrett. I really don't want to have to do anything with him. Boy, I really need to go to the bathroom."

"I'm sure glad I'm not in that position right now," Julie says back to him.

By now Lizzy's and Emily's cries have been reduced to sniffles, and they're semi-asleep.

The terrorists continue their flurry of activity. With the FBI on its way and an ambush being set up, it's evident that something very big is about to happen in the warehouse and Julie, Garrett, Lizzy, and Emily will be right in the middle of it.

Chapter 36

Back at Andrew and Alana's household, they're waiting intently to hear what the FBI agent has to say. They fear the worst news. The agent tells them that he was just relayed some additional news from the government and has some other information to tell them.

"CIA intelligence has revealed that there are actually closer to thirty or forty bombs being planted in various cities across the US instead of twenty. Some cities may contain two or three of these bombs. We're told that your city is one of those where it's suspected that there may be at least two bombs and perhaps three. They fear that some of the nonnuclear bombs may be strategically placed and hidden so that they will destroy critical infrastructure as well as masses of people. Not all of the bombs are nuclear, but some are believed to consist of massive explosives planted at critical infrastructures."

"Like where?" asks Andrew.

"They may be places like water supply systems, electrical distribution facilities, major airports, refineries, major bridges, or government buildings. Speculation is that some could completely destroy the electric grid in parts of the country, such as the entire New England area or west coast. Places like that."

"Wow, how can they be able to do that without getting caught?" asks Alana.

"It is a complete mystery how they've been able to do it. But they have. I suppose they had well over a decade to plan all of this. There is also reason to believe that some of the bombs are dirty bombs meaning that they are not anywhere near as powerful as a bona fide nuclear bomb, but still destructive. They will still result in some radioactive fallout.

"They believe that some of the other bombs may be the most devastating nuclear devices ever built. The magnitude of these is several times larger than anything the US was even aware of."

"I just can't believe they are able to do this!"

"But what is really disturbing is the terrorists' claim that one bomb in particular has been placed or will be placed at a location that is so unique that it alone could destroy the entire country if not the entire world. They claim it would render the entire country and perhaps additional vast lands throughout the globe uninhabitable for years."

"Where do you think that is? How can one location be so unique to make that happen?"

"Well, the only thing we could think of is that it may be an EMP, but there's no way ISA has the capability of launching something like that."

"What's an EMP?"

"That's short for a kind of nuclear bomb that is detonated at a level in the atmosphere that provides an electromagnetic pulse that would obliterate the entire electrical grid across much if not the entire country. Imagine the entire country not having any electricity for months or even years."

"Wow! You're kidding, right?"

"No, I'm not. But the experts tell us they don't have the capability of launching that and therefore it must be another location here in the US where they are planting it, but we simply don't know where it is or what's so unique about the location to make its impact so expansive and deadly."

"Wow, I can't believe all of this!"

"Well, they're more than surprised the terrorists were able to find or produce the amount of enriched uranium or plutonium and equipment needed in the US to build the bombs. How they got it is anybody's guess. If they were imported, they don't know how they did it. But they just recently arrested an individual actually not too far from here who they suspect knows a lot about this.

"Apparently, he's an Islamic extremist who's an American citizen who at one time or another had connections with nuclear research personnel at Los Alamos, Livermore, and Oakridge, among several other places where nuclear research has been conducted. He has connections with ISIS, ISA and other Jihadists. In addition, he has contact with high ranking Russian government officials as well as some Iran and Pakistan officials.

"It's speculated that Russia has helped ISA in funding, building, and placement of the bombs. It's also speculated that ISA may have purchased the nukes from North Korea and perhaps Pakistan and smuggled them into the US. You may recall that the United States in effect gave Iran about $ 150 billion in the nuclear Iran deal and in part in return Iran pledged it would not build any nuclear weapons for a period of time. Well, there is some speculation that Iran gave that money to North Korea and that North Korea built the bombs for them. Any of these scenarios is a possibility.

"Also, they suspect that some if not many of the bombs are not made conventionally but with some other materials. Some are believed to be made of ammonium nitrate, but some of these nuclear bombs are considered catastrophic and would destroy everything for miles. The radiation fallout from the nuclear bombs will be tremendous. Although CIA Intel has revealed the information to us, the general public is not aware of this. There are also current investigations into the possible participation of some government officials since about 2009 in all of this. Unbelievable! To think I work for them!"

The agent is clearly disgusted.

"If I can ask, why are you telling us all of this?" asks Andrew. "I thought you guys keep this kind of stuff all a secret and it's one of your government cover-up sorts of thing."

"Your question brings me to another bit of information. There's no way that anybody including us or any other FBI agents around here can evacuate before sunrise now. The city is for all practical purposes surrounded by rivers and the major bridges across all of them have been closed. In fact, we just received word that a bomb has been found attached to the understructure of your bridge that crosses the river right here. As you know, that's one of the main interstate highways that connect the east and the west in this part of our country. It can't be defused or removed. It's got sensors on it. In fact, the bridge is now closed. There's no way to escape and evacuate anywhere.

"The traffic jams from everybody trying to leave the city is now at such a critical level that there is no way it can be alleviated before sunrise. It cannot be eased at all. People are running out of gas in the middle of the road, blocking traffic. All gas stations are closed. There are accidents everywhere blocking traffic. Because of the massive volume of people on the road trying to escape the city, nobody and I mean nobody is going anywhere. People are getting angry. A lot of them even have guns and that's not good with all of the emotion out there, people trying desperately to get far away, but can't.

"Some have been in the same spot and haven't moved for over six hours. They're hungry, thirsty, need to use facilities, and are absolutely desperate. Like I said, many have brought their guns and now there is rioting going on with everyday people shooting others because they can't move.

"We just found out that our choppers probably can't get here until after sunrise. If they can't get here within the next hour, they're not coming at all. We will be stuck here just like you.

"You cannot blame them. Who wants to be here? So, that's why I am telling you this. It doesn't look like any of us will be around after sunrise to tell anybody anyway. It's safer to stay here and pray. So, it doesn't really matter."

There is a moment of silence. Sonja, Andrew, Alana, and the agent just stare at each other in disbelief.

Alana is absolutely distraught. "This really cannot be happening, can it?"

Andrew then forces a smile. "It looks like Ammen sure came on the scene at the right time."

Everyone looks at him not knowing whether he is honestly serious or if he's being facetious.

"I am dead serious," he says, as he senses the sudden tension in the room.

Then the agent drops the bombshell. "There are two more bits of information you may want to know. The CIA has learned that ISA wants to accelerate the time when the bombs will explode because Muhammad is concerned that at least one other nuclear power will strike first which will result in a domino effect and immediate global thermonuclear destruction. Russia fears that the United States will target it and Russia has Western Europe in its sights. The Chinese, North Korea, and Pakistan as well as other countries with a nuclear arsenal are also on edge.

"Our government has pledged that as soon as one nuclear bomb is detonated, it will launch its arsenal against Russia. Russia has declared if that happens, it will launch its arsenal as well. As soon as one country lets go even just one nuclear warhead, the others will follow suit almost instantaneously. The political circumstances involving all of the countries with nuclear warheads and the ability to launch them are complicated. They are extremely complex. Government officials of each country are walking a tightrope. Even though the bombs here in the states will go off anyway, regardless of who launches the first nuclear warhead, ISA wants to initiate everything because of their pride in doing this for the glory to Allah.

"And finally, there's one more thing. Does this little boy look familiar to you?"

The agent then pulls out a downloaded photo that he just received.

Alana jumps up and cries out "Yes, it's Mikey! Where did you get this? What's going on?" She recognizes the boy walking along the road as Mikey. "When was this taken? Where was this taken?"

"Just a little while ago, our agents in the field saw him walking alone on a country road not far from here, but when they turned around, he was gone. This is a cell phone camera shot taken from the window as they passed him by. The agent thought it was Mikey all along but wanted to confirm it.

"They said that there was some shooting in the area too. They're investigating it, but for now, they don't have any further information. "I cannot comment any further," he says.

"Is Mikey safe?" cries Alana.

The agent looks down and again buries his head in his hands. He moves his head from side to side as he quietly whispers, "I'm afraid to tell you what's going on and what's about to happen."

Chapter 37

Mikey is still hiding behind the fallen trees and remains there for a long time. He's scared to come out because he sees all the flashlights shining in the bushes all around on both sides of the street, and he has no idea who they are. He knows they're looking for him.

Although he was in inquisitive-little-boy mode when he escaped from the warehouse, now he's feeling somewhat alone. He's hungry and thirsty and has decided that he wants to be with his mommy and daddy again. It was only a matter of time.

Before they were looking for him silently and were not calling for him, but suddenly, he hears his name being called. The FBI agents got confirmation that the boy on the road is Mikey after Alana confirmed it from the photo uploaded to the FBI agent at her house.

He hears, "Mikey, Mikey, is that you? Your mommy and daddy sent us to get you. We can take you back to them. Mikey, Mikey, where are you? Where are you, Mikey?"

This is sort of like hide-and-seek Mikey played at home. He instinctively thinks that he needs to hide some more but stops and thinks a little bit.

Mikey is a little hesitant, but the more he hears them, the more he's inclined to reveal himself. He remembers there are bad guys about, but he gets the feeling that these are not them.

After about ten minutes or so, the FBI agents have moved farther down the road and are disappearing out of site. He's had enough and decides that if he waits any longer they won't come back.

So he decides to chance it and come out. He slowly crawls out and ambles back on the road.

A few minutes later he's picked up by the agents in the SUV. One of the agents, Agent Freeman, immediately tries to make friends with him. Agent Freeman desperately tries to comfort him so that he'll cooperate and help them. This is such a far cry from what he has been through that Mikey very quickly becomes cooperative.

The agents ask him where he came from. Although he can talk a little, he's unable to tell them and instead he motions to the woods. He keeps pointing to the woods back where he came from. The FBI agents talk among themselves and decide to let him take one of them there by foot.

Agent Freeman gets out of the SUV, lets Mikey out, and follows him. Agent Freeman is armed and carries various electronic and communications equipment. Mikey becomes very inquisitive of the equipment and the agent does all he can to get Mikey's attention back to the task at hand. The other agent parks the SUV on the side of the road and calls for backup.

Mikey leads Agent Freeman down the road past the trees, into the woods, down an embankment, across the creek, and up to the bushes on the other side. Mikey hears the croak of the bullfrog and wants to find it. The agent distracts him in order to keep him moving and tells Mikey that he'll give him a frog after they get back. They finally make their way to the fence, follow it down a ways, and come across the hole in the bottom of the fence behind some more bushes.

Mikey crawls under it, but the hole is too small for the agent to get through. There's no way he can crawl under it. He's too large. And he would not be able to carry his equipment through it either. Mikey starts to wonder off into the shadows on the other side and the agent desperately starts calling Mikey to come back. But Mikey has vanished out of site. Now Agent Freeman wishes he didn't let Mikey get too far ahead of him and go through the opening first.

The agent immediately calls for backup on his phone. Within several minutes another agent makes his way to the same spot with some wire cutters and they cut the fence so they can get through. They walk around the bushes and see the industrial complex. It consists of multiple buildings including several warehouses on about forty acres or so.

In between the buildings there are other structures and various other things such as Dumpsters, a huge row and stacks of propane tanks, out-buildings, stacks of skids, and fifty-five-gallon drum barrels scattered here and there.

There is a parking lot with several dimly lit lights on tall poles and alleys between each building. Most of the windows in all of the buildings are boarded up or have a covering on them and there is no way to peer inside any of them.

The parking lot is fairly large and wraps around each building. It seems to be mostly empty except for a lone car parked here and there. On the far end of the parking lot in the dark behind another building there's an old white van parked similar to the one that was stalking Alex, but nobody sees it. It's like a ghost hiding in the corner.

The entire complex is surrounded by a very tall barb wire fence and a gate that is closed. They figure they are in the right spot, but have no idea which building it is. There are so many. And they don't know where Mikey went. There are bushes and shadows everywhere. They gingerly call out to Mikey but get no response. Although they need to find Mikey they don't want call for him too loudly because if there any terrorists around, they don't want to alert them of their presence.

They sneak along behind the bushes while getting on their phones to coordinate more back-up and suddenly come across Mikey sitting on the ground behind another bush near a parking lot light poking a stick in a large spider web. Several feet away from him is the raccoon sitting on his haunches looking right at him.

The raccoon is casually eating something that it apparently retrieved from the Dumpster, or perhaps from the creek. If the spider web was not enough, the agents are startled to see the raccoon, just sitting there so close to Mikey.

They try to shoo the raccoon away, but Mikey says, "No, no no."

They try to shoo it away again, but the raccoon just sits there, minding its own business. They wonder why the raccoon isn't hissing at them or running off. They can't believe it's just simply sitting there next to Mikey, as if it was his pet.

Again, Mikey says, "No, no, no. Leave him alone. He's our friend."

"Our friend? Why do you say that?" Agent Freeman asks.

"Because he knows Grandpa," Mikey responds.

"What?" both agents exclaim in unison.

Then trying to still stay on the good side of Mikey, Agent Freeman says to him, "I suppose the raccoon told you that, right? What's his name? Did you name him?"

Mikey looks at him slowly and says "Racky." Mikey then smiles and gets up to walk again. They make their way to another bush and peek out from behind it. They can see most of the buildings from there. The raccoon follows for a bit and then waddles off into the bushes again.

They ask Mikey which building he came from. They want to know where his mommy and daddy are.

Mikey points to the last building on the other side about two hundred yards away.

As soon as he points to the building, the agents spot two guards with AK-47s patrolling the grounds. Then they see the garage door go up, a van come out and leave through the gate that is remote controlled, and the garage door go back down again. With his binoculars, one of the agents gets a glimpse of the inside and says, "Bingo."

After watching the terrorists and the activity around the garage door, they turn around, and Mikey is gone again. He was there one minute and the next minute he's not. The terrorists patrolling the area now are running their way. They're holding their automatic weapons out in front of them and are pointing them in the direction of the bush where the FBI agents are hiding. It's apparent the terrorists have spotted either them or Mikey. The agents fear the terrorists spotted Mikey and are after him.

The raccoon can be seen scurrying away and then crawling under the old white van in the back corner of the parking lot.

Chapter 38

After floating what seems like aimlessly for a while in the void, I begin to wonder again where I'm going. Maybe I'm not going anywhere and will spend the rest of my eternal life here. Is this perhaps purgatory? But I had thoughts of that earlier when I could sense other souls around me. Here I don't get the same feeling.

This is a very lonely environment that consists of pure nothingness. I cannot see or hear anything except for the two faint lights that are only pin-points across each end of the void. That is it. It's total stillness. No sense of time. Nothing else exists. No stars, no other lights in the cosmos, no sounds, nothing.

I'm in an abyss of absolute isolation and solitude all around me. It is neither hot nor cold. I am numb and cannot feel anything. But I can think and still have my mind, or soul I should say. What a lonely place. I cannot imagine staying here forever.

Having eternal time to contemplate my life and why I didn't live better I would lose my mind in short order. But that can't happen. Even though I'm all alone here in total emptiness, I can't turn off my mind or my emotions. This just makes it harder to cope with. And to think this might go on forever here.

I look up and the good spirit is still there. I can't see it, but I can definitely sense its presence. I am glad it's here with me. It's the only thing of comfort in this space of uncertainty. I wish I could communicate with it, but I can't. If this spirit was not here with me, I just can't imagine being here forever without it.

Then suddenly, I start to spin around, slowly at first, and then faster and faster. Then I stop and I can see the faint red orange pulsating light but not the brighter white light. Why is this? I wonder. The light at the gates of hell seems to be getting a little larger as if I'm moving back toward it again. I get the most awful feeling and I start to get very scared again. Am I going back there? Why? What's going on?

Then I start spinning again, this time even faster, and I start to get very dizzy. I close my eyes to try to resist the dizziness. After about a minute or two, I open my eyes and find myself being pulled backward like a slingshot and being hurled toward the white light. Because I was facing backward, it appeared that I was going back to hell. I am literally in shock. I'm hurled toward the bright white light. I turn around and watch the light at the gates of hell diminish to nothing, but I know it's still there.

The dizziness gradually subsides. I'm able to turn around and watch the bright white light get closer and closer. I start to sense a feeling of restfulness, peacefulness, optimism, and hope. The closer I get, the more exuberant I become. Soon there is a feeling of wonderment and I get a feeling that I'm being beckoned by an invitation. Everything is positive. What a stark contrast from where I came. The closer I get, this feeling intensifies immensely. I have never been so happy. I feel like I'm going home.

After a little while I arrive at the gates of heaven and I'm greeted there by an angel. I'm accompanied inside the gate and led to a waiting room. There I can feel other souls around me. But at this point, I can't see them. There aren't as many souls in the waiting room here as there were in the waiting room in hell. In fact, there are a lot less.

But as soon as I enter I develop a very awkward feeling that I don't belong here. I feel like a fish out of water and suddenly I become very apprehensive. I know that I'm not going to stay here. That feeling is definite. In fact, the feeling is as definite as the feeling that I had that I would return to hell.

On one hand, I'm so relieved to be out of hell, but on the other hand, I get the feeling that where I will spend my eternal life will be decided here. I could be sent back to hell. I wonder why I was sent to hell in the first place. When I left it, I had a very strong feeling that I would return there. But I don't understand why. The feeling that I will return to hell is still overpowering. And the feeling that I won't stay here in heaven is equally overwhelming.

Is my life on Earth going to be evaluated again? I really don't want to relive that all over once more. That experience was harrowing because it seemed to me that as the wheel of balance was slowing down, I was left with the feeling that perhaps I deserved to go to hell and not heaven after seeing my entire life in the mirror, despite the fact that I thought I had repented enough, and that my belief and faith was strong enough. Oh, the lost opportunities I had. That must be the reason why.

In the end I at least thought that the trump card was in my favor. But I don't know why I was sent to hell, and now I don't understand why I'm here.

Moral of the story: Don't take your life and what you think is sufficient enough belief and faith for granted. You had better try harder with the remaining time you have even though you think your past and your level of belief and faith has been acceptable. Because if you don't you'll be wrong which will be confirmed when you look at your entire life in the mirror. And then, well, surprise! It's too late. You may end up where you certainly don't want to go. You only get one chance and you don't know how long you'll have it. I can't get these thoughts out of my mind.

After I'm in the waiting room for a bit I'm led to what appears to be a viewing room. I assume this is similar to the orientation room where I was in hell. I assume here I will get a lesson on the infrastructure of heaven.

I look up and the good spirit is still with me. I still can't understand why the spirit is with me sometimes but I'm so happy when it is because it's certainly comforting in a world of uncertainty. Although when I look up but can't see it, I know it's there.

I look down and although I can't see my body, I can sense that I am clothed again. I'm no longer naked. What a relief this is. That really didn't matter in hell, but I suspect it may matter here. I then realize I'm wearing a robe and assume all other souls here are as well.

I think briefly about what's going on back home. To my surprise, now I can see my family and again I know what's going on there in real time. I can't believe the events that have transpired back on Earth since I last had a vision of them. But rather than spend my time looking at them, I'm more taken in with my own experience here. My thoughts return to the here and now.

Looking through what appears to be some sort of force field, like an enormous window, I can see a very small part of heaven. What I see is the entrance and a long hallway that connects the waiting area with the main part of heaven. Both the entrance and hallway are majestic in every sense; however, they're simple at the same time. I can't understand how something so simplistic and plain can be so magnificent.

In hell I could hear and sometimes see the poor souls wailing in torture, the most awful of all places. Here it's the complete opposite. I've heard it said that heaven is pure paradise. Well, that's the biggest understatement ever. No words can describe the immense rapture, the incredible peace and love that I see and feel here.

Looking through the entry and down the hallway there is a backdrop that is a pure bright crystal white, but a color white that is unlike anything I have ever seen. The color actually has a feeling, an incredible sensation to it. It is more than just visual.

There are pulsating colors around it and they are so brilliant, and vivid they're more than breathtaking. Here the colors far exceed the spectrum as we know it on Earth. There are so many colors I didn't even know could possibly exist. It's like a whole new dimension of colors. Each color exudes its own feeling and sensation. And each is absolutely spectacular. Each of these colors radiates its own positive feeling and that feeling blends in with the others and encompasses everything here in complete harmony. The colors are inherent in everything. Everything is of light. Everything is of love.

I can hear the most serene and beautiful music. The music is being directed by the colors. It's like a ten-thousand-piece orchestra that is perfect, flawless, and precise in every way.

I can sense angels throughout. Some are going and some are coming. From and to where I wonder, but I can guess. Everything emanates from light and colors, but is very real as to what it is.

It's the most peaceful place of pure splendor and tranquility. There's a completely unspoiled nature about it. The music that is playing consists of the most pleasant sounds that are beyond imagination. It's an orchestra of an absolutely amazing harmonious reverberation that is choreographed by the colors.

The instruments that create the sounds are not recognizable and are unlike anything on Earth. I think I can hear harps and the most beautiful organ music, but these are only a miniscule piece of an immaculate orchestra of merging melodies.

The music and colors blended together seem to be a mode of communication. What a difference where the primary noise in hell was the wailing, screaming, and cursing by the poor souls and the most awful and sinister organ music playing at an intolerable volume that no one can imagine.

The colors and music vibrate and echo together and even more colors and sounds are produced and the process goes on and on. But it's so mellow at the same time. Everything I see is so pure I would be afraid to get close to it because it appears that the purity could be spoiled so easily.

It seems to be a most fragile environment but at the same time it is strong and resilient and cannot be ruined. I'm told by the angel that the purity is guaranteed by the souls who are here.

At the entrance are plants, trees, flowers and everything else of nature that is unlike anything on Earth as well. It is God's garden and it is indescribable. When I look at it, I just can't imagine anything that could be any more beautiful.

Then I get a glimpse of some of the souls who are in heaven. I can see them in spiritual form. They are all so pure and clean. There is no illness. There is no sickness. Every soul is in perfect health and is in their prime. They all know each other and get along with each other in such a pleasant atmosphere that they contribute in mass to the majestic splendor of everything that's inherent here.

There is no sin, no remorse, nothing negative anywhere. The power of everything being positive is immense. There is complete harmony and love in everything. Happiness abounds everywhere.

I learn about the souls who are here. All of the souls in heaven have each been assigned a different status which provides them varying degrees of access to the experiences of heaven. Although all are equal in love and spirit with God, there is a reward sequence that corresponds to what a person did with what he or she was given on Earth.

But everyone is satisfied because they know that their status has been assigned according to certain factors that include what type of life they lived on Earth and the degree of their love and faith in Christ and repentance. They have had their chance and no longer have any control over that now. Each accepts his or her status and nobody complains.

I suspect that the status level assigned to each was determined at least in part by the massive mathematical formula and equation calculated in the mirror of reliving one's life that I experienced.

Then I realize that the same formula applies to those in hell. The more one sins, the worse the torture is depending on what level and what chamber one is assigned.

Here, the stronger the faith, the more one repents, and the more good deeds one does on Earth, then the higher the ranking one receives in his or her status here.

When I think about it, such ranking in the afterlife makes sense. For example, if a person, say who prayed less than five or ten minutes a day barely had what was required to enter heaven, then why should he or she be entitled to the same status and the same things here as another person who had an extremely profound faith, who repented much more strongly, who lived perhaps a near sin free and vastly better life, who prayed hours and hours each day, and who went out of his or her way to spread the word of Jesus to many? It doesn't make sense that they should share the same entitlement here when their qualifications are so vastly different.

And likewise if one person barely made it into hell because although he or she tried but just barely missed the mark of what was required to enter heaven, then why should he or she be punished to the same extent of torture as another person who say was a mass murderer or a serial killer and who denounced Christ altogether?

Therefore such ranking and the varying degrees of status in heaven or punishment in hell make absolute sense. Otherwise, it wouldn't be fair considering that their lives were so vastly unequal in terms of sin, repentance, and faith. It is reasonable that a soul should be rewarded for extraordinary belief and faith compared to another soul who barely had enough.

In hell there's a separation of rooms, levels, and chambers that all feed into the wickedness of the devil. All souls suffer independently although they are together. Their curses of Satan feed into the hatred of him and cause him to be more powerful. And their cursing of God for allowing them to go to hell enhances their hatred and Satan's power grows even more.

Here in heaven there are no separate rooms and all souls live together in peace and harmony and they all make up the power of God as one entity. Each soul is separate, but is intrinsic in such a way that they all form a single harmonious body of one. One is all and all is one here. Their mere existence resonates into an unconditional love for God and everything that he has created.

What is most profound is that the extent of one's repentance of sins and one's level of faith, love, and belief in Jesus Christ also determines the status of each soul here. I confirm that this is the trump card in the wheel of balance. It carries the most weight of all.

I then learn that if there is any question whether one's repentance and faith was strong enough to outweigh the accumulation of bad and sins in one's life, then it results in an equilibrium anomaly. In such case, the soul did make an honest effort to play the trump card in its life but it was insufficient even if just by a little bit. The effort was either not quite strong or sincere enough or was compromised with respect to the life lived. Or that perhaps the person continued to sin significantly after he or she repented and his or her sincerity of faith withered afterward.

This results in a question mark within a prescribed margin of error. It appears that perhaps these souls may still enter heaven, but may need to pay a price first. This decision appears to be subject to a much deeper discretion of God.

I start to think of a zillion questions. The first thought I have after learning this is I wonder if God has the ability to free the souls from purgatory and hell, and is it possible that the Second Coming can accomplish this?

I learn that if a soul pays the price, unless the price merely equalizes his sin, then the higher the price paid then the higher the status it may receive in heaven. I pretty much know what this all means, but I'm surprised because it was my former understanding that nothing could break eternity in hell, but now I realize that this may not necessarily be true.

Of course, now I remember. I recall the room of hopelessness. It appeared that many souls spend time in this room in hell first. Perhaps the hopelessness that the souls experience in this room may be a lie in itself. If this is true, then how cruel for the devil to play such a trick on those poor souls. What an unusual torment that would be.

I don't understand the reasoning behind all this, or if I'm even understanding this all correctly. I'm not told anything more about this discretion of God and wonder whether anyone would be required to pay the price to enter heaven. Does the Bible say this? But I get a strange feeling that I may learn more about this later. But as for now, here in heaven, an incredible sense of hope and optimism emanates from the souls that are here and is absorbed by everything within.

But despite the varying levels of status, there is absolutely no animosity among any of the souls here. There is absolutely no jealousness among any of them. There is absolutely no envy among any of them. All souls are content to be in heaven no matter what their status is and all souls are content with their status in heaven.

They don't care that any other souls may have a higher status. How everybody got here is no concern to any soul and each and every one of them understands that. Each has had their chance and understands that and now that time of opportunity has expired. This is universally understood and accepted.

It appears that most of the higher-ranking souls are those who were meek and the downtrodden on Earth, the poor, the sick, the hungry, the outcast, the forgotten ones, those who were the most unfortunate on Earth, but those who believed and had the most faith. Not surprisingly in many but not all cases these are the same people who probably did not have the same opportunity to sin as much as those who were more fortunate in what they had.

Sometimes but not always, the more fortunate one is on Earth, for example the more wealth one has or the more power one has, then it appears the more opportunity or temptation he or she has to sin, whether he or she knows it or not, and especially the more lost opportunities he or she has. Again, there's the concept of lost opportunities. I wasn't aware of this, and I'm surprised to learn this.

Then I remember, Jesus said, "It is easier for a camel to go through an eye of a needle than for a rich person to enter heaven." A rich person has more opportunities to do good, but what will the person do with the opportunities? What will the person do with all of his or her material possessions? If he or she fails to use the wealth or power for the good of others, they will be doomed.

But if this is the case, then I wonder if it could be justified that these souls should be shown more mercy because it was more difficult for them to combat the temptations from the devil that others such as the meek didn't have to endure. But perhaps they may have been expected to give up more in a material sense, repent more, and have more faith as well, because they were given more responsibility to do so when gaining their wealth and power. Now I can understand why it's so difficult for a person who has wealth to enter heaven. Now I know why one must sacrifice his or her material possessions.

The higher-ranking souls also appear to include more members of the cloth, although I can sense that members of the cloth make up a portion of the lower ranking souls as well.

In hell, there's a separation of the souls and Satan. Hatred is bred by hatred among other things. Here in heaven, the souls actually are absorbed into and become part of God himself. There is an unconditional love of God and everything created by Him.

I cannot see God, but his presence, power and glory is felt everywhere. God is omnipresent. This is what actually makes up heaven. His power is enhanced by the souls here that praise him, and by the angels that serve him.

At His right side is Jesus Christ through who the power is manifested. This is because He is the reason why the souls are here. God and Jesus Christ are separate but are one and the same. It is a complete perfect circle.

I want to learn more about the angels. They are perfect in every sense. After learning about the souls, I get the feeling that I will actually meet with another angel who I can talk with and have a closer experience or encounter here, just as I did in hell. I hope for a tour of heaven so that I can see it myself. I am anxious to see the activities or what the souls actually do here. I so much want to spend eternity here. I feel like I've come to my final home, and I don't ever want to leave.

But I still have this definite feeling that I don't belong here, and that my visit here is only going to be temporary. I again develop a sense of apprehension and trepidation. I get the sense that I won't be staying here, but I don't understand the circumstances.

I wonder what my next experience is going to be like here.

Chapter 39

As the terrorists scurry about preparing for what they fear will be an invasion by the authorities, all Garrett and Julie can do is sit there and watch. Julie continues to think about Mikey. She can't believe that her little boy lies dead under the pile of curtains. She has no idea that Mikey had walked out of the office door to the outside before the curtains were blasted away by the terrorist.

Garrett keeps a very close watch over the suicide bomber who at any moment when released could jump on top of the nuclear bomb and detonate his explosives and the nuclear device. He is only a few feet away from him, his leash tied with the electronic release device to the same metal railing to which Garrett and Julie are tied. They are all just a few feet from the glass case that contains it.

Garrett looks at him but turns away when he looks back. He has dark beady eyes that peer above the thick dark beard on his face and he appears to be in a trance. Without a shadow of a doubt, he has a look about him as if he wants to jump on the nuclear bomb right now. He's anxious and looks like nothing is going to stop him. It's a good thing that he's restrained by the leash that secures him to the electronic device and metal railing, at least for now.

Garrett wonders when his restraining device will be triggered to release him, allowing him to do his thing. He looks over and sees the leader who still has the other remote device sticking out of his pocket. He assumes this is the triggering device that will release him.

Garrett looks at the suicide bomber again out of the corner of his eye. His eyes are on the nuclear bomb, he's still in a trance, but now he is chanting repeatedly, "Blessed be Allah. Glory be to Allah."

As if he's not creepy enough, his constant chanting gets on Garrett's nerves as it reminds him of just how very real the situation is. Garrett now won't take his eye off him, speculating that at any second it could be the end of everything.

Suddenly, the garage door goes back up and a van pulls in. Two terrorists jump out of the van and talk with the leader. From what Garrett and Julie can figure out, they assume he's telling the leader that they've looked everywhere and can't find Mikey anywhere. One of the terrorists then points to his watch and it becomes evident that many of the terrorists want to leave the facility immediately.

Apparently, they're arguing whether to set up an ambush or to leave. The leader is adamant about staying put, but most of the others appear scared to be around when the FBI or whoever arrives or when the bomb goes off.

Their flamboyant arguing in what appears to be Arabic is actually somewhat comical, but the intensity and nature of their disagreement is not.

Suddenly, several muted gunshots are heard outside in the parking lot somewhere and everything goes quiet. The terrorists stop arguing and become silent to listen. One of the terrorists walks over to the office, kicks the pile of curtains lying on the floor, and tries to open the door to the outside to peak out. When he kicks the curtains, it appears that this foot gets stuck in it, as if something is under them, but he then kicks it again and removes his foot.

The door is stuck from the earlier incident, but he's finally able to open it enough to peer outside. He apparently sees nothing. Then another gunshot is heard, and he drops to the floor. As he falls, it can be seen that his face for all practical purposes has been blown off. The back wall of the office is spattered with blood and it's running everywhere.

This prompts the other terrorists to grab their guns and four of them take positions in each of the corners inside the building. Another goes into the office, kicks the body out of the way and closes the door to the outside. He now is hidden in a dark corner there, using the pile of curtains and the body to hide behind. Another terrorist hides behind the nuclear device. The leader takes refuge in the van, and another terrorist jumps in on the passenger side.

Then everything is quiet. There is tension in the air as it's speculated that at any moment the garage door will go up and there will be gunfire everywhere. Garrett and Julie are exposed next to the bomb. Garrett looks around and the only entrance into the facility that he sees is the garage door and the office door. Maybe someone could enter the bathroom from the outside if the boarded up window can be removed. It's also questionable whether the window is large enough. The wait is agonizing.

Five minutes go by. Ten minutes go by. Then twenty minutes. Everything is still and very quiet. The terrorists are becoming agitated and impatient. One of the terrorists in one corner of the warehouse yells something, waves his gun in the air, and starts walking toward the van.

Surprisingly he falls to the floor. He's motionless. What happened? After about a minute, a pool of blood can be seen running from underneath his body.

Another terrorist emerges from another corner and walks slowly down the wall with his gun in the air. Julie hears a muffled *phtt* noise and then he also drops down to the floor in a pool of blood. Garrett and Julie look at each other.

Julie says to him, "Did you hear that?"

"No, what?"

Julie then makes a *phtt* expression.

Garrett whispers "I think the FBI or somebody is here and is shooting at the terrorists. They must have silencers on their guns. But where're they shooting from? The office door is closed and the garage door is closed and the leader and another terrorist are in the van." I'm not aware of any other entrances to the warehouse. All of the windows are boarded up."

Then another *phtt* is heard and the last terrorist along the perimeter drops to the floor. He's wiggling and squirming and then starts writhing on the floor in pain. He rolls over to grab the gun that he dropped when shot, and another *phtt* puts him away. Now he lies still like the other terrorists who were shot. As with the others, blood can be seen running from underneath his body.

There are four terrorists left plus the suicide bomber. One is in the office, another is hiding behind the nuclear bomb, and the leader and another terrorist are in the van.

Garrett scans the warehouse to try to figure out where the shots are coming from, while keeping a sharp eye on the suicide bomber. Another several minutes go by and there're no more shots. Then Garrett figures it out. There's a FBI sniper on top of the building and he's shooting from a very small opening in the retractable roof. But this sniper apparently has a limited vision because of the angle of the opening. Garrett can see him leaning over the opening trying to peer inside.

Garrett suspects that there may be another sniper hiding in the bathroom. If so, perhaps he came in through the boarded up window in there. Garrett eventually gets the attention of the sniper on the roof but doesn't let anyone else know that he sees him. Although he has ropes all around him, he's able to strategically signal to the sniper by pointing with his hand to the nuclear device, the van, and the office. The van partially blocks the office from the sniper's view, so Garrett is not sure whether the sniper knows about it.

Another several minutes go by. More silence. Then suddenly the garage door goes up and there sitting in front is a SUV with its bright lights shining dead straight into the building. The terrorist behind the nuclear bomb jumps up and lets go several rounds with his AK-47 right into its windshield, shattering it into a zillion pieces.

The sound of the shots from his weapon hitting the windshield echoes throughout the building waking up both Lizzy and Emily. They're now into full-blown screams. However, when he does this he reveals his location and another *phtt* drops him to the floor.

Garrett and Julie are beside themselves knowing that if a bullet hits the bomb, they will all be goners. They're also afraid a stray bullet may hit them as well.

This now leaves the two terrorists in the van, one in the office, and the suicide bomber.

More silence. Apparently, the shots into the SUV either killed its occupants or the SUV was vacant.

Then the lights on the van inside the warehouse come on, and in a blink of an eye, it starts up, swerves in place, and heads out of the garage door. It runs straight into the SUV, knocking it aside, and the van with the leader and other terrorist disappears into the parking lot. A helicopter can be seen hovering not too far away.

For the next several minutes, there's more silence. Garrett takes advantage of this time and loosens the series of ropes that is wrapped around him. Several minutes later, he notices that the red light on the electronic device that is securing the suicide bomber to the rail is now blinking, but the suicide bomber isn't aware of this. The leader must have triggered it with the remote device that he was carrying. The suicide bomber now is free to jump on the device and end everything whenever he wants.

After a few more minutes, two FBI agents peek around the corners of the garage door from outside and enter on each side with their guns drawn. They slowly approach the suicide bomber who now has his eyes closed and is chanting quite loudly, "Praise be to Allah, praise be to Allah, praise be to Allah," over and over and over again. The FBI agents think that he's the only terrorist left.

They're a good forty paces from him and try to talk him out of jumping on the bomb. But the suicide bomber not previously aware that he was totally free from the rail opens his eyes, now knows he's free. He gets up and takes several steps along the railing to get closer to the bomb. Now he's close enough that he can jump at any time.

All of a sudden, the last terrorist emerges from the corner of the office and aims his gun at the FBI agents who are walking toward the suicide bomber. The FBI agents don't see or hear him. The terrorist shouts out at the top of his lungs "Drop your weapons you FBI or I shoot! Now! Now! Now!"

The agents freeze and stand there. They can't see the terrorist because he's behind them.

The terrorist then sees the other FBI agent aiming at him from the bathroom and instinctively shoots about a half dozen rounds at him and fells him to the floor in a pool of blood. The bullets go whistling by the agents. They think the terrorist was aiming at them and intended the shots to suggest that he means business. They're taken by surprise.

Both quickly lay their guns on the ground and raise their arms in the air to surrender. Then the terrorist walking up to them spots the FBI agent leaning over on the roof and fires another half-dozen rounds at him and this agent falls thirty feet to his death on the floor, missing the nuclear bomb by only inches.

The terrorist tells the agents to kick their guns to him, which they do. He tells them to kneel and put their hands behind their backs. While aiming his gun at the agents, he walks over to the suicide bomber, who now is free from his leash, and places in his open hand the triggering device.

The terrorist then yells out to the suicide bomber that on the count of three he will shoot and execute the agents and that the suicide bomber will jump on the nuclear bomb and push the button at the same time. They will do this simultaneously. By doing it this way, it will please Allah the most.

Then now realizing that he's out in the open and vulnerable, he retreats back into the dark of the office and stands behind the pile of curtains and the body. He doesn't take his aim off the agents.

The suicide bomber cries out, "Okay, praise be to Allah, praise be to Allah, glory be to Allah," and he takes a step toward the bomb and puts his finger on the button that now is blinking red.

"One." The suicide bomber takes another step; "Two." He climbs up on the rail. "Three." He jumps a good three feet in the air. The electronic device on his back now sports a red blinking light and in his hand he's clutching the other device that also shows a blinking red light. He is in midair headed right toward the top of the case holding the nuclear bomb.

At the same time, several gunshots are heard coming from the terrorist in the office. Both of the agents who were kneeling fall down to the floor. Garrett and Julie, who are trying to pray, are crying uncontrollably and screaming, "No! No! No!"

Chapter 40

Andrew and Alana fall asleep on the couch and Sonja returns to the bedroom. The FBI agent now has been joined by another agent and they set up additional electronic equipment in their living room. It's apparent that a lot of this is communications equipment and some monitoring and surveillance equipment of some sort.

After about a half hour or so and after several conversations with other FBI agents in the field, one of the agents wakes up Andrew and Alana.

"I have an update on things. I thought you may want to know." he says. "We've identified where Andrew, Julie, Lizzy, and Emily are located. They're being held captive by the terrorists in a warehouse in an industrial complex only a few miles from here. That happens to be the same place where the nuclear device is located."

"Well, we knew that," remarks Andrew as he stretches after waking up.

"Our agents have stormed the warehouse and there's been a shootout. We've lost several agents. All of the terrorists have been shot except for two who got away in their van and in a chopper and another still hiding in the warehouse and another who you are not going to want to hear about."

"What do you mean" asks Alana.

"Well, he's a suicide bomber, and he's threatening to blow himself up including setting off the nuclear device."

"Wow," comments Andrew.

"Where's Mikey? Has he been found yet?" asks Alana.

The agent then continues, "The agents found Mikey, and it was he and somebody else who led them to the warehouse. But…"

"But what?" asks Alana softly. Andrew and Alana have a horrified look on their faces, expecting the worse. They're anticipating that Mikey got shot during the shootout.

"He's gone again," continues the agent.

"What do you mean gone?"

"He's missing again."

Visibly relieved but still trying to hold back tears, Alana asks, "What do you mean he's missing again?"

"He disappeared right before the shoot-out. We don't know if one of the terrorists got him or if he ran away. They can't find him. But we hope he went back in the woods.

"Wow," again exclaims Andrew. "This is just like a movie."

Alana stares at Andrew. Alana then asks, "Who else was with Mikey when he led the agents to the warehouse?"

The agent comments as if he has no idea, "Somebody named Racky."

"Racky?" asks Alana.

The agent answers, "Yeah, I don't yet have any further information on him. All I know is that another agent put in his report that somebody named Racky helped Mikey when he first escaped and went missing. The report says here"—he shuffles through some papers he just printed out—"that Mikey said this Racky was a friend and that his grandpa knew him."

"You're kidding, right?" asks Alana.

"No," comments the agent with a straight face. "That's what Mikey said."

Both Andrew and Alana who both know all about Racky and how Grandpa would make it talk to his grandchildren simultaneously burst out laughing.

"Who is this Racky guy," asks the agent. "Do you know him?"

Alana doesn't answer, but just giggles. "You wouldn't believe it if I told you," she finally exclaims.

Andrew looks at the agent. "Well, I'm going to go out and look for Mikey. I'll drive over there. I know that area well. That's the place where they store all the propane tanks."

Alana stares down Andrew. "Propane tanks?"

"Yeah, you wouldn't believe all of the tanks they have stored there. There's a bunch of them, and they are all stacked next to each other. There're all usually full."

"Now how would you know about that?" she asks.

Andrew, realizing that perhaps he shouldn't have said that, slumps back in the sofa and says nothing.

"You're not going anywhere," she adamantly declares to him.

As things settle down somewhat, the agent then turns very somber. "I have one more thing to tell you," he tells them. "We suspect that the terrorists just might come here."

"You're kidding," says Alana. "They might come to our house?"

"Yes and no. We don't know where the escaped terrorists went. We don't know how many more there are. But there's a real possibility they could come here. Maybe they'll want more hostages, who knows? Anyway, we will need to take precautions here. And we need to do so very quickly too. It's obvious that your family has something they want or need. Why would they be looking for Alex or Sonja? What do they want with them? Or is there something else they possibly might want or might want to destroy perhaps? Are you aware of anything that Alex had that they may want or want to get rid of?

"You need to wake up Sonja and be prepared in an instant to retreat to the basement if we tell you. We will set up a perimeter around your house, but these terrorists are very good at things like this. Anything can happen."

Andrew says to the agents, "I think it's time to turn the TV back on. That won't bother you, will it? I'd like to know if there're any further developments on the global front. I'd also like to see how my good friend and savior Ammen is doing."

Alana and the agents look at Andrew. They're all stunned. They don't know what to say.

Andrew then gets up, grabs an apple, takes a bite out of it, making a distinct crunching noise, and leans over the shoulders of the agents to look at the monitors and other electronic equipment they've set up on the table beside them.

"I wonder if I could be an FBI agent," he says. "I think that would be the coolest job in the world. Do you all need any help?"

The thought that the terrorists may be coming to their house is gripping to Andrew, but Alana and Sonja are afraid for their lives.

Chapter 41

Another angel floats over to me and introduces itself as one of God's angels. I sense this is a very high ranking angel. Like the other, it communicates to me by some sort of mental telepathy. The exquisiteness of this angel is breathtaking. It will be my tour guide so to speak.

I immediately think of a million questions I want to ask the angel, but can't. I always thought that when one enters heaven, he or she is met by his or her passed loved ones and relatives, but in my case I was not. As I'm thinking this, the angel tells me that the hallway I saw has an entrance at both ends. The other end is where the souls normally enter heaven and is where they're met by their loved ones. When I wonder why I didn't enter at that end, as if the angel is reading my mind, I'm told that I entered heaven at this end of the hallway because I'm not ready to enter heaven. I'm here for a different reason.

Now this prompts more questions. The obvious question is why? Why am I not ready to enter heaven? And if that's the case, then why am I here? Am I simply a tourist? Perhaps that may be the reason why I somehow have this feeling that I don't belong here. Now, my feelings are a mixed bag of wonderment and trepidation. I'm very nervous because I'm confused. I sure would like to know what's going on. I wonder if perhaps I'm merely here because the spirit who was with me needed to stop here for some reason.

I start to wonder about the angels and demons and again and as if the angel can read my mind, it tells me about them.

"Both are spirits and separately serve their creators. They both have the ability to transform, transcend, and perform acts both on Earth and in their domains in the name of their creators. The spirits can operate in any form, including body, mind, or spirit.

"On Earth their presence, intentions, and messages may be manifested in whole or other form, within a person, within a dream, a song, or even perhaps within another living creature such as for example an animal. Their presence may be visible or invisible."

When I hear this, I think of shape-shifters. But in actuality, the transformation of an angel is through their spirit and not their body, although they can enter the body of anyone or anything for that matter.

"Whether it is heaven or hell, their home is their domain, but both angels and demons cannot be at two places at the same time. For example, an angel may either be here in heaven, or on Earth, or traveling somewhere in between. Although God is omnipresent, angels are not.

"A difference though is that a demon can be deceitful. It may want you to see and do one thing while its purpose is to accomplish something else to its benefit. It can operate in complete disguise, the person having no clue. It can be convincing and compelling without the person realizing it. It can manifest its intention through temptations and deception. It can change the course of events through unwanted manipulation.

"On the other hand, an angel is forthright and honest and only has your best interest in mind through the will of God. It may or may not operate in disguise, but without deception or guile. By nature, an angel is merely a messenger of God and cannot necessarily change the course of events by itself. That would be a function of God's will and not theirs. But, they serve God's will and God can exercise His power through them.

"Angels and demons are obviously at odds. Demons wish to exterminate angels and they attempt to do that from time to time, especially in certain situations. On the other hand, angels do not wish to exterminate demons because they realize that they're merely innate lost souls, but they can act to reduce their capabilities or extinguish their powers.

"A demon has a desire to succeed because that may elevate its standing and status in hell. On the other hand, an angel has a desire for you to succeed, not them. An angel has no interest in attaining a higher status because it serves God in the capacity granted to it and it understands that.

"The more souls in hell and the more demons there are, then the stronger the devil becomes. The more souls in heaven and the more angels there are, then the more glory there is in praising God.

Remember, in hell a soul wants to die but is incapable of doing so. In heaven, a soul wants to live and does."

I'm more interested in angels, and I wish it would tell me more. Again, like it's reading my mind, it continues my orientation.

"There are many different kinds of angels. There are angels that originate from male souls and from female souls. There are angels that originate from adults and from children. There are angels from all backgrounds, races, and ethnic groups.

"For example, an angel may originate from the soul of a deprived Christian sheep herder in some remote mountains, or a nomad in the desert of an undeveloped country. Or perhaps it may be from the soul of a pastor of a church or perhaps someone else in a developed country.

"Some angels come from special sacred blood lines that go back thousands of years to when Jesus was on Earth. God may release extraordinary power through them in unique or special situations. These high ranking angels must go through a very difficult and trying extraordinary ordination process and it is that process that enhances God's will. If they pass the ordination process, God can manifest His power of unprecedented magnitude. This is extremely exceptional, however.

"But it's God's intention to normally maintain an equal balance of all types of angels with respect to their race, background, ethnic origin and other factors. It's balanced to maintain an equal representation of the souls present in heaven. However, these particular angels are the lone exception.

"Perhaps you have heard about saints, seraphims, cherubims, ophanims, dominions, virtues, authorities, principalities, archangels, and angels?"

I respond, "I think I remember reading about these a long time ago, but I don't know anything about them." I'm now tempted to ask questions, but am afraid to. I finally get up enough courage and start to ask, "How are angels made?" But before I can speak, I'm again told the answer.

"Most of the angels come from the purist, of those who were with very little sin, and who profoundly believed and had extraordinary faith in Jesus Christ in the highest degree. But some angels are chosen by God, but they may need to pay the price. This involves special circumstances of which I don't expect you to understand."

I suddenly remember what my father told me when I was a child, and I'm tempted to ask about this, but I'm afraid to. But this prompts me, and I start to build up enough courage to ask, "Are there special angels?" Again, before I can actually say anything, the angel reads my mind.

"You may refer to them as such if you want because they may be special in what they do or the message that they may deliver may be special regarding the impending situation at hand, but no angel is any more special than any other. It's the will of God and not angels that have the power to do things. But God exercises more power through them than others, after their ordination process.

"Those who I mentioned earlier from certain sacred blood lines who are eligible to become what you refer to as special angels must endure an ordination process that is most difficult and is nearly impossible to complete. The bloodline of them is sacred and must be unbroken. And it requires special prayer from chosen blood lines to make it possible. If the required special prayers are not sufficiently made or are not made the prescribed number of times, the process will fail. The requirement that the chosen one must pray as prescribed is as important if not more so as the ordination process.

"At this time, God desires two of who you may refer to as special angels be ordained. Have you heard about what some on Earth refer to as the Apocalypse?"

I'm suddenly taken by surprise by this comment. I start to respond, "Yes," and want to ask, "Is this what's happening right now on Earth with the Islamic extremists planting nuclear weapons and spreading a deadly disease everywhere?" But again, the angel is ready with an answer before I can ask.

"There is great turmoil on Earth at the present time. Many on Earth believe that such extreme disorder has been the word of the prophets. But Satan has dictated the event by creating chaos on Earth at this time. By doing so, he has a plan to recruit many more souls into hell, and he will gain unprecedented power. Additionally, as a result the existence of Mother Earth is at risk. There is a high probability it will be destroyed in its entirety.

"But God is angry with the devil for instigating this. It is before the time as set forth by the Scriptures. If and when there will be an Apocalypse, it will be God's will and not that of Satan's. What is happening on Earth at this time is a singular event. It actually is not the Apocalypse as foretold by the prophecies in the book of Revelation, but may be the beginning of additional events that may lead to such. This will depend on what happens.

"God is outraged that Satan has defied Him and that Satan has instigated the current events on Earth. God does not intend for any Apocalypse to happen at this time. It is not time for that yet. God is contemplating how to deal with this without accelerating the prophecy foretold in the Scriptures. God is not ready for all of the events foretold to happen yet. But he must deal with the crisis nevertheless.

"But there is one way He can accomplish this in order to prevent Satan from gaining power and without the events of the prophecies of Revelation to come to be at this time. God contemplates that two new angels to be ordained to complete the first order of the Council that is required in this particular case. You may want to refer to them as very special angels if you like. If these two new angels are successfully ordained, God will utilize His extraordinary power to deal with the crisis.

"But the ordination process will be most difficult. And, it will require special prayers from a chosen one. That in itself will be an almost impossible task because although the chosen one will be told when to pray, will not know how to pray. The chosen one must pray as prescribed a certain number of times without knowing and without being told to do so. If the chosen one fails to do this, the ordination process will fail.

"These two angels must be ordained before the nuclear devices and other bombs are detonated and before the disease is spread. The ordination process takes three days in Earth time. The process is extremely challenging. But in this case, the world may depend on it. It is crucial that the two souls can be found and that the ordination process can be accomplished in time. Therefore this must be accomplished immediately in order to prevent what Satan is trying to do. Otherwise, Satan will gain extraordinary power on Earth and in hell, and Mother Earth will be likely destroyed.

"I will take you to God's Council Room where you can learn more about this."

Now this gets me thinking. If what is happening on Earth is not the real Apocalypse as foretold in the book of Revelation, then how can the world be destroyed by the terrorists at this time? This must mean that the terrorists will not be successful and the world will survive. But as I understand it, if God's plan does not work, then Earth will be destroyed by them even though the events are not the same as what has been prophesized regarding the end of time. But nothing can change what has been prophesized. So how can that happen?

However, if God's plan is successful, that also does not conform to the prophecies either. I'm not aware of anything in the Holy Bible that mentions special angels or that one must pay a price or any such ordination process or extraordinary power or a special prayer or any such design. So, how can this all be? As I understand it, the Gospel makes no reference to these events and certainly not out of the order as what is written, or any such plan. Certainly the Bible must be true and taken for its Word. The prophecies cannot be added to or be subtracted from. So, either way, I do not understand and am confused. How can either of these happen and not violate the Scriptures? This all seems so unrealistic. How can this all be for real? I sure would like to know what's going on.

Chapter 42

As the terrorist counts to three, Julie is trying to pray, but can't, and is crying hysterically. She's holding Lizzy and Emily and screams, "Garrett, Lizzy, Mikey, Emily, I love you so much." She briefly glances into the office where she thinks Mikey is lying dead underneath the curtains, and then clutches Lizzy and Emily as tight as she can. The curtains are riddled with holes inches apart from each other and she is confident that Mikey was shot multiple times and died instantly.

Garrett who semi-buried his head in his lap, eyes the suicide bomber. After the terrorist yells out two, and the suicide bomber starts to jump, in pure instinct mode, Garrett throws off the loosened ropes around him and jumps on top of the railing and dives into the terrorist. He hits the suicide bomber head on in midair and knocks him to the side. They both land on the floor inches from the nuclear bomb.

Simultaneously, the terrorist in the office raises his gun to shoot the FBI agents, but he trips and falls down and his gun goes off into the ceiling sending a string of bullets that ricochet off the office walls instead.

The FBI agents then get up and each instantly pulls another handgun from their coats. Immediately, one runs over and assists Garrett to tackle the suicide bomber, and in a brief struggle, they disarm him and secure him back to the railing. Garret immediately grabs the detonation trigger device from the terrorist and disengages it before the trigger is pressed.

Simultaneously, the other FBI agent takes aim and kills the terrorist in the office before he can get back up.

After several seconds of silence, one of the agents asks Garrett and Julie, "Are there any more, or is this all of them?"

Garrett exclaims "Wow! I'm not believin' any of this! As far as we know, that's it. There're no more terrorists in the warehouse."

"What happened to the guy in the office?" the other agent asks. "Why didn't he shoot us?"

Julie looks over at him lying on the floor. "He fell down. I don't know what happened. It was like he tripped in the curtains or something when he pulled the trigger. Maybe he tripped over the pile of curtains and that's why he shot into the ceiling instead of at you."

"How could he have tripped by himself?" asks the agent. "He was just standing there aiming his gun at us. That's impossible. I don't understand it."

As they look at the terrorists lying on the floor in the office, the pile of curtains on the floor next to the bodies starts moving. A corner rises up a few times and goes back down.

The agents fear that another terrorist may still be alive under the pile of curtains. They quickly aim their guns at the pile of curtains and are about to blast it with several more rounds of bullets.

Just as they start to pull their triggers the pile of curtains goes up a little higher and Mikey pokes his head out. He's just lying there and looks at everybody, just like he is playing hide and seek. Peekaboo.

"You gotta be kidding me," says one of the agents.

"I'm not believing this," says the other agent. "We thought you were still outside playing with a raccoon or something somewhere this whole time."

"Outside?" cries Julie. "Outside?"

"Yeah. He brought us here. If it wasn't for him, we wouldn't have found you. But he walked away when we got to the building, and we couldn't find him. We couldn't look for him because of the other terrorists outside roaming around, and we needed to get into this building as fast as we could."

"You mean he's been outside this whole time?" Julie cries and is overjoyed with tears. She can't believe it.

"Yep, the whole time," the agent fires back.

Garrett explains, "Mikey must have slipped out the door to the outside before the terrorist blew the curtains away and then slipped back in and hid under the pile of curtains afterward. The terrorist probably tripped over Mikey when he moved, not knowing he was under there."

"I can't believe it," says Julie. "So Mikey saved you when he moved under the curtains and tripped the terrorist?"

"I guess so," responds the agent. "Actually, he also saved you and perhaps millions of others too."

The agents then untie Julie. Garrett runs over, and Mikey jumps up into his arms. Mikey has a grin on his face from ear to ear. Garrett and Julie start to thank the FBI agents, but they're already attending to a more critical matter.

They walk over to the nuclear bomb and look at the timer. It now reads 2:45 hours and is still ticking away and counting down.

One of the agents makes a call on his phone and files a brief report, explains the situation, and calls for immediate backup and more resources.

While they're waiting for others to arrive, they study the nuclear bomb and try to figure out what to do. They discuss all of the sensors on it, the impenetrable glass case, the electronic trigger device, and how it's bolted to the floor.

"Impossible!" one of the agents comments.

Garrett comments, "The terrorists stated that they can detonate the bomb remotely any time they want."

Within about fifteen minutes, other FBI agents arrive bringing all sorts of equipment. A mobile unit had come earlier and was actually already close by carrying all this equipment and patrolling the area when it was learned that the bomb was located here.

Nearly a dozen FBI agents, CIA agents, and other authorities arrive on the scene and immediately hook up all sorts of electronic monitoring devices, cameras, computers, and communications equipment. One agent brings a Geiger counter and other similar handheld devices. When he holds them near the bomb and turns them on, they go off the scale and emit a constant noise that is so loud he immediately turns it off.

"Unbelievable!" he says.

Then they unpack other electronic equipment and start scanning the glass case. Two of the agents almost simultaneously exclaim "Wow!"

One then comments, "This bomb is real. And you're not going to believe just how big it is. This thing will blow up everything for miles and miles. I don't even want to think about the fallout from it. And the sensors, they're real too, perhaps not quite as sensitive as I expected, but we still have to be careful not to disturb it."

After one of the agents finishes a phone call with authorities in Washington DC, he comments, "This one is almost identical to the one found in DC but appears to be larger. In addition, the bolts that secure the device to the floor are also rigged with sensors. There's no way it can be diffused or removed. We can't even get close to it without setting it off.

The authorities have been studying the one in DC for a long time now and just can't figure it out. They've never seen anything like it. They just can't find any way at all how to disarm it, remove it, or disengage the sensors without blowing it up. They're still scratching their heads.

"The glass case cannot be touched or the bomb will go off. The glass case can't be moved because it's adhered to the concrete floor by dozens of massive bolts and because they also have sensors. The case can't be opened to disarm it because of the sensors both inside and outside of the glass. The bolts to the flooring cannot be disturbed because there are sensors there too. What are we going to do?"

The timer now reads 2:15 hours. And it continues to count down.

Garrett walks around studying the floor and comments, "Look at these expansion joints in the floor. It looks like the bomb sits on a separate slab of concrete, like a platform. See the drains that surround it." He bends over and looks inside the drains. "There appears to be a cavity under this floor section. Wouldn't that mean that the only thing holding up this section of the floor is these metal support beams?" He points to one of them inside of the drain. "Does somebody have a flashlight?"

He then points to the ceiling. "You know, this place has a retractable roof. I don't know why. Perhaps it was used to bring large heavy equipment in and out using the overhead cranes for some reason at one time. Maybe that's how they got this thing in here in the first place."

"What are you getting at?" asks one of the agents.

"I know this may sound far-fetched but..."

Garrett is interrupted by one of the newer agents who has arrived. "Look, we don't want to hear about far-fetched, we need to figure out what will work to disarm this thing."

Another agent then looks at him. "Let him continue. The DC people have had a lot more time looking at the same bomb there and they can't figure it out. We should listen to anything. Any idea at all is welcome."

Garrett then continues, "Thanks. As I was saying, I know this is far-fetched and is probably something that can't be done, but I have an idea that I thought I would share with you for whatever it's worth."

"Go on," comments the agent.

"There's a small door cover over there." He points to an oversized manhole cover on the floor. "Maybe if we can remove it, we can see if it leads to a basement or an area underneath here. The slab is not much larger than the bomb. If this section of the flooring is being held up only by these support beams, maybe the beams and sections of the drain can be cut away and this section of the floor can be lifted out with the device. See all of the drains that surround it? The flooring here appears to be a separate pad or platform for some reason. It's not that large."

"You mean lift out the section of the floor with the case and bomb all together?"

"Yeah."

The other agent then sarcastically remarks, "So, then what? How do we lift it out? Even if we could lift it out, where do we put it? Over there?" He mockingly points to another section of the floor a few feet away. "Even if we could lift it out, how do we get it out of here?"

Garrett then amusingly comments, "I don't know. You guys have access to a big helicopter? If you do, then maybe you can use the steel cable over there and lift it out of here." He points to several reels of industrial steel cable wire in a corner of the warehouse and then points to the retractable roof.

"And then what?" comments the same agent.

Garrett then comments, "I don't know, fly it up high in the sky by the helicopter and let it explode up there or fly it out to the country where there is much less people. I just thought about it. I'm only brainstorming here. I told you it probably won't work."

Another agent has overheard the entire conversation comes over and declares "You know, he just might have something here. I'm aware that there's a fleet of CH-47C Chinooks on their way out west carrying supplies. Based on their schedule, they should be relatively close or perhaps may even be passing overhead anytime now."

The agent does some quick calculations to get an estimated weight of the floor and bomb and Googles *payload capacities.* "A Chinook should be large enough to lift this out of here. The weight appears to be close to what it's capable of lifting, but I think it's doable.

I wonder if we can contact them and see where they are. If they're close enough and if they're available and if we can get some equipment here to cut the beams and drains away quickly, just maybe his idea will work. Hell, we don't really have any other option, do we? We're running out of time."

"Pure genius," says one agent.

"No way," says another other agent.

"It's worth a try," comments another agent.

"You got a better idea?" He points to his watch. "We are running out of time and we're all going to die if we don't try something."

The agent who mentioned the helicopter then says, "How do we get below the floor?" He walks over to the big manhole cover in the floor and tries to turn the handle on the door, but it won't budge. He tries several times. The handle won't turn and the door can't be opened. He then tries to pry it open with a crowbar that he finds close by. It still won't budge.

Several other agents also try without any luck. They try to turn and pull the handle in both directions. It's stuck and won't move at all.

"Well, that shoots that idea down," the one agent sarcastically comments. "I told you this wouldn't work. There's no way we can get down there. You'd think a kid could figure out how to open this handle."

"Maybe Mikey can figure it out," comments Agent Freeman halfway in jest. Everybody laughs. "Hey, Mikey, little buddy, come over here for a minute."

All the agents take a minute to laugh, some uncontrollably. The comic relief in a time of crisis and incredible stress is welcomed by everyone. "Yeah, right, no way he's gonna do this," chuckles another agent. "Any bets?" another agent inquires.

Mikey waddles over, and Agent Freeman points to the handle. "Can you open this?" Mikey bends over and looks at it. He then pushes the handle in, turns it one way, then pulls the handle out and turns it the other way and then pushes the handle back in again. He then looks up at everybody looking down at him and laughing at him. The expression on his face does not change whatsoever. He simply stares at everybody.

After a few seconds, one of the agents bends over and tries to lift the cover, fully expecting it to be still stuck in place. But to his surprise, he's able to lift the cover right off as if it was a piece of paper! Everyone is absolutely astounded.

"Doesn't surprise me at all," says Garrett.

After opening the cover, Agent Freeman sees a small metal ladder in place that goes down about six feet to a cavity underneath the flooring section. He climbs down the opening and looks around with his flashlight and then pokes his head up through the hole in the floor.

He states that there's an opening about six feet high underneath the entire section of the floor. But then he dejectedly says the bolts go through the flooring, and there're sensors everywhere. "There is no way to undo it or remove it because the bomb is sitting on top of it. There's a second row of dozens of enormous bolts all around it. There is absolutely no way to get to it."

But then he enthusiastically continues, "But it's doable. It's definitely doable. In fact, this should be a piece of cake. We can remove the floor with the bomb and everything in one piece. All we need to do is cut these support beams and joists and the drain surrounding it and the entire section of this floor can be lifted out in one piece. The floor and the nuclear device can be lifted out together."

"But how do we lift it out? What do we hook it on?"

"The railings that partially surround the device."

"Are they strong enough?"

"They appear to be. They're made of solid steel and go through the floor and are supported underneath. For some reason, it's like the flooring where the bomb sits is its own platform. All we need to do is cut it away. Maybe that's how they got it in here. We just gotta get the right equipment in here right now and get the chopper here. We need to get on the phone and act fast!"

Another agent then in a smart-ass manner asks "So, who's going to fly the chopper? That sounds like a suicide mission to me. Even if the pilot can get the bomb high enough up there and parachutes before it explodes, there's no way he can get out of the way of the explosion in time. Who in the hell is going to even want to try it?"

Another agent comments, "Doesn't matter anyway. If we don't try something here fast, we're all going to die anyway. Sunrise is only a few hours away now. Anybody else have a better idea?"

"Maybe if the pilot had a suit wing, I mean a wing suit, or whatever it's called," comments another agent in another smart-aleck remark.

Suddenly, Julie looks at Garrett and stares at him and says defiantly. "Don't you dare."

"What's that all about?" asks one of the agents.

Garrett comments, "I used to fly helicopters and did a lot of parachuting when I was in the service. I experimented around a little with the wing suits then. But this was a long time ago. I haven't done any of that for many years."

"Don't you even think about it," Julie says again. "Not gonna happen."

Another agent tries the controls on the wall, and after a lot of creaking and screeching of metal, he's able to open up the retractable roof. "Plenty of room," he says.

While they continue to discuss the matter, several agents are quick to get on the phone to try to get the right equipment delivered.

He continues "But the problem though is that now it's past 3:00 AM. Who is going to be available at this hour? Also, if the equipment is going to come from more than a few miles away, there's no way they will be able to get through the traffic jams, especially if it comes from the other side of the river. The bridge is closed. I just heard that it's worse than ever.

"And just about everybody and their grandmother have evacuated anyway. We'll never get it. And what's the status of getting a chopper here that's large enough and a pilot who will do it?"

Another agent states, "I just got a report that the Chinooks are long gone. We can't rely on them at all."

"So, the Chinooks aren't available? Well, that takes care of that. What does the timer say now?"

"Only one hour and fifty-nine minutes to go and counting down!"

Chapter 43

As things settle down somewhat, Alana decides to go back to bed. Andrew on the other hand decides to stay up and watch TV. It's somewhat apparent that he's bothering the FBI agents who have set up camp in his living room. They prefer to be alone and not be in the presence of a wannabe agent who is somewhat of a loose cannon, especially in the wee hours of the morning. But they have no other choice. It's Andrew's house.

Andrew changes channels repeatedly on the TV, trying desperately to find some breaking news or additional developments regarding the crisis or any news about Ammen. But being the early hours of the morning before sunrise, there's nothing on except repeats of earlier broadcasts.

Eventually, Andrew finds a few offbeat channels that interest him, but he keeps flipping back and forth between them. On one channel, he finds a clip of a very old *Three Stooges* show and a couple of cartoons on two other channels.

The constant *nuk-nuk-nuk* coming from the three stooges and the high-pitched voices and cartoon music coming from the cartoons over the course of about fifteen minutes or so has irritated the agents who are trying to keep busy watching their monitors and focusing on their communications with other agents in the field.

The noise from the TV finally reaches the agents' tolerance limit. One of the agents turns around to say something to Andrew when Andrew, looking at the front of the living room, catches him off guard and comments "Knock, knock, who's at the door?"

The FBI agents immediately draw their weapons and jump up looking at the front door. Since it's the early morning hours and they're not expecting anybody, except for possibly a visit from the terrorists, they've been on edge all night.

Andrew taken back somewhat with the sudden movement of the agents and their drawn weapons says, "I'm sorry. I really am. I was just going to tell you a really funny knock-knock joke that I just thought of."

That aggravates the agents even more but at the same time relieves some of the tension in the room. Andrew then says, "I know I'm bothering you, and I'm really sorry. I'll leave you alone so you can work."

He then turns the TV off and goes into the kitchen and rummages around for something else to eat. For several minutes, he paces back and forth like a caged tiger but doesn't bother the agents any more.

After some time goes by, one of the agents gets a call and a further update of the status of what's going on at the warehouse.

Andrew runs back out to the living room. One of the agents instructs Andrew to get Alana and Sonja. He has a new update and information that they need to know about right away.

Alana and Sonja join the others in the living room and the agents proceed to give them an update.

"All of the terrorists at the warehouse now have either been shot to death or apprehended, except for at least two who escaped. We still suspect that these or other terrorists may come to your house because they know you're a relative of Julie, and they may also know that Sonja is here."

"What about the suicide bomber?" asks Alana.

"They've captured him before he could detonate any of the explosives or the bomb. Apparently, Garrett had a struggle with him and saved the day. I mean night."

The other agent adds, "Actually it looks like he saved your lives and our lives and perhaps a million other lives as well, at least for the time being!"

C. J. RYSEN

"Wow!" exclaims Andrew. "Garrett did that? He's always been the family hero."

Alana looks at Andrew and says sarcastically, "Andrew, if you would grow up and take some responsibility, maybe you could do something to be a hero too sometime."

Andrew slumps back in his seat. He says nothing.

The agent then proceeds to give them a complete update explaining that Julie, Garrett, Lizzy, Mikey, and Emily have all been rescued and are in fairly good shape. They should be coming to the house soon.

But then he goes on to tell them that the situation is still very volatile and at a crisis level because the nuclear bomb timer is still counting down and now is less than two hours before it will explode. He explains to them that there are a number of authorities on the scene trying to figure out what to do.

He explains that this is the same type of bomb found in DC that has inside and outside sensors, or some type of electronic trip device. Nobody can figure out how to disarm it or remove it without it going off. And apparently, it's much larger too.

But he goes on to say that they're implementing a somewhat radical strategy proposed by Garrett that just might work, but that it would require getting some other equipment on the scene right away. Problem is that it's unlikely that they will be able to do this in less than two hours before the bomb will go off.

"Garrett?" asks Andrew again.

The agent fires back, "Yeah, Garrett has thought of a strategy that appears to be the only possible solution. Nobody else in the FBI, CIA, or other government agency has thought of this or anything else that would work, so they are going to give it a try. One of the agents called Garrett's idea pure genius. They are working on it now. Garrett is directing everything there."

Andrew comments "Boy, that Garrett—"

Alana interrupts him. "Andrew, don't even start it."

As the agent is providing a further update he gets another phone call and takes it privately as he turns around and walks away to the other side of the room. The other agent joins him.

300

Andrew whispers to Sonja and Alana, "Do you know that each agent has three different smart phones and three different kinds of guns? They're hiding them in their pants, coats, and briefcases. Isn't that cool?" he says.

Alana again tells Andrew softly, "Shut up and behave."

Then the agents turn around and advise them that there have been two additional developments that they need to know about right away.

"We've intercepted a message left by an unknown wireless caller to Alana. The phone number is on our black list and the caller wanted to know if Alex was here. Are you aware of this?"

Alana responds "No, I was asleep. Who was it from?"

"That's under investigation. We believe it to be the terrorists. We obtained the number from a list provided by Intelligence."

"Who would call at this hour of the night? Why do they want to know where Alex is? Why do they think I know?" Why do these people want to find Alex? I just don't understand it. Haven't they been following the news or reading the papers?"

"For some reason, they're obsessed with finding Alex either dead or alive, but nobody can figure why they want him. We've also received a report there's been a shooting only several blocks away from here and that a van suspected of having terrorists was spotted in an adjoining neighborhood just minutes ago. I think it's time for you all to wake up the kids and retreat to the basement where it will be safer. We don't know if the terrorists intend to come here or not, but we think it's very possible."

Suddenly, they all hear some squealing of tires outside and some gunshots close by. Everybody jumps. The FBI agents draw their weapons and turn off the lights in the house and Andrew and Alana run to get the kids. Sonja makes her way down to the basement.

A minute later, Andrew and Alana appear with the kids, fumbling around in the dark. The kids are taken downstairs by Alana. There are more gunshots heard outside of the house and Andrew runs like a scared rabbit. One of the agents says to him, "So, you still want to be an agent, right?"

Andrew is frightened and runs into a wall in the dark and then eventually finds the top of the stairs. As another gunshot is heard just outside he's startled again. In his haste to run down the stairs to the basement he trips and tumbles head over heels down about fourteen steps, landing on his head which hits the concrete floor below with a thud. A lone lightbulb comes on in the basement.

Andrew is out cold and not moving. A pool of blood forms under his head.

In the meantime, more shots can be heard coming from around the house. The terrorists have arrived and are in a shoot-out with the FBI. Andrew is lying at the bottom of the steps on the basement floor and is completely motionless and unconscious.

Chapter 44

Suddenly I become very apprehensive. What started off as an interesting orientation now's turning into a mysterious journey into something totally unexpected. I have no idea what the Council Room of God is, but I follow the angel as it leads me there. I'm told that it's a special place where God and the angels have very important meetings. I am absolutely bewildered because I'm not aware of anything in the Scriptures that mentions any of this is possible. This is certainly not what I expected heaven to be.

We circumvent heaven proper and go through a mysterious but short space and time continuum. I assume the Council Room is a private part of heaven that only angels are allowed to go. I'm led to it through some sort of secret passageway. We come upon a door that's an invisible gate of what appears to be mammoth size. I gather it's another force field. It opens, we enter, and I'm seated in a viewing area. There's another force field between this area and the Council Room like an enormous window that goes in every direction. I cannot see the ends of the window or the ends of the room I'm in anywhere.

I am absolutely awestruck at what I see. The Council Room is the magnificence of all of the greatest cathedrals on Earth all put together in one. All of a sudden, I become both absolutely enthralled and terrified at the same time with the immeasurable magnitude of what I see and feel here. I cannot believe what I'm experiencing.

There's a giant glowing oval shaped table at one end and a glowing round table at the other end. Both are connected. There are numerous high back chairs that surround them. I can see some angels sitting around the oval table and other angels coming in to join them. They're all in spiritual form. It's evident that a very important meeting is about to take place.

As each seat is filled and angels are sitting down here and there I notice that above them is what appears to be a throne that is in three parts but is all blended together into one. Although the throne is majestic and absolutely magnificent, it is very simple and plain at the same time and lacks any sense of value or wealth. It's in the form of a cross. How can it be so simple and plain yet so magnificent?

I'm pretty sure that this is where God and Jesus Christ sit. I'm not sure who or what the third part is for, but I assume that it is for the Holy Ghost because it's merged with the other two parts, and all three parts encompass the throne as if they're one.

I can sense God and Jesus Christ to his right, but both are not only also in a spiritual form but are invisible. At least to me. I don't know whether the angels can see Them, but I cannot. But I do sense their powerful presence. It is the spirit of both, but the power and love of one that emanates from the throne and envelopes all of heaven. All three are one. It is absolutely of another dimension and defies description. There are no other words to describe what I'm experiencing. I'm absolutely overwhelmed so much I find myself shaking from the experience.

As the angels take their places in the room, I'm told that certain angels of the highest order who are assigned to this event sit immediately below at the round table, and the other angels sit around the oval table. I'm surprised to see how many angels of all types there are. I cannot communicate with them but for some reason I can sense their backgrounds. Although I can recognize their backgrounds as to ethnic group, race, age, and other things, each are of an equal spiritual nature.

As each seat is filled, I sense that the angel who was accompanying me has suddenly left me. I look up and to my dismay realize that the good spirit that has been with me has also just left me. I suddenly come to the conclusion that it is also an angel of God and is joining the others. However, I'm not able to see where this angel is sitting. I mutter to myself "So this is why I'm here. The spirit who's been with me needed to attend this meeting."

All the seats are now filled with the exception of four empty seats immediately below God at the head of the section at the round table. This is where the angels of the highest order sit who are assigned to this event. One angel then enters and sits in the first seat but it is invisible. Although the angel is invisible, its spirit and presence are profound. The last three seats at the end are vacant. I know that for sure.

Why can I sense the backgrounds of the other angels but not this angel? How strange. It's as if these four seats are reserved for very special angels, but I'm not aware of the reason. I look around to see if any other souls are with me. I am left all alone in this room. I wonder why?

I look around to see if I recognize anyone who has passed before me but I do not. Then I remember that these are all angels and that they're not simple souls like me. Anybody who I knew who died before me who made it to heaven would be just like me. They're not worthy to be angels. They would be merely simple souls, and I would not expect that any of them would attain a status of angel. Therefore I would not expect any of them to be in this meeting. They wouldn't be here in the Council Room. They're probably elsewhere in heaven doing whatever it is that they do here. Just as I hope that I would be.

I then think of the remarkable opportunity that is being granted to me to observe the Council Room of God. I think to myself that perhaps other souls may never get the chance to experience this and how lucky I was to be assigned the grateful angel who made this possible for me to witness this. But then I realize why I'm here. The spirit who was riding with me needed to attend this meeting and this is perhaps only a temporary stopping place for us before it takes me to wherever we will be going.

I sense that when I came here it happened to be just at the right time. How lucky I have been. I could not have timed this any better. Otherwise, I would have missed this. I wonder why I have been blessed to witness this.

The three empty seats each have stitched on the front of the back sides of each chair three interlaced rings encompassed in a circle. Just below that and to the right are stitched three sideways numeral eights and immediately below that and to the right is a symbol that looks like a backward number six. Immediately below that, and to the right, is the roman numeral one. There are other symbols that surround these, but I do not know what they are or what they represent. There are additional symbols that look like a binary code, but I have no idea what it means. These are all superimposed by a cross.

Why these symbols are embedded on these particular chairs, I don't know. I sort of wish I had looked at the other chairs before the angels sat down to see if they also have these or other symbols, but I failed to do so.

Then one additional angel enters and takes the seat next to the invisible angel. This angel is also invisible and I don't know anything about it either, but again I know it's there because of the power of its spiritual presence. Although for some reason I don't recognize the background of this angel there is some mystique about it that catches my attention. A feeling of awareness and calmness comes over me. I try to think why, but then pass this off as an over-stimulated imagination in a world of wonder. There is simply too much to take in at the moment. After this angel takes a seat, that leaves two last vacant seats for angels of the highest order to be filled.

How very strange this all is. Although I don't know for sure, I assume that these two remaining vacant seats are reserved for the two new angels who need to be found and go through the special ordination process of which I was told.

I then notice that all of the angels are sitting in what appears to be a pattern or staggered sequence according to their backgrounds. There's a pattern of alternating male and female, alternating ages such as alternating adult and child, alternating ethnic groups and races, and alternating backgrounds. None of any specific group is sitting next to each other. It seems to be that this all meets an equilibrium balance. I can't help but study this pattern of where the angels are sitting.

Although I'm not positive, by studying this sequence and pattern, I'm inclined to speculate that the second to last angel will have a background of being an adult female, probably an older woman, and apparently from Turkey or perhaps some other Eastern European country or somewhere in that region of the world.

From this alternating sequence and pattern, it appears to me that the last angel will have a background of an adult male who was or is a lone Christian nomad and who is poverty stricken from an undeveloped country, possibly in the Middle East, but I cannot envision where. I can see this from how they are all sitting. "How interesting," I say to myself. And to think that these two may be related somehow and of the same sacred bloodline.

I don't know if I'm correct, but all of a sudden, I feel proud of myself for figuring this out. I want to pat myself on the back. I tell myself that I'm not going to say anything about it, but then who would I tell? Anyway, it will be my own secret that I think I figured out who these last two angels will be.

I sheepishly glance up to make sure that God or Jesus is indeed in the room. Although I cannot see them the power of their spiritual presence is immense and overwhelms me. Even though they're invisible, I now am blinded when I attempt to look at them.

I then learn that the meeting is to review the qualifications and ordination process of the two last angels who will be needed to help defeat Satan's reign of terror on Earth and to avoid Earth's destruction. The meeting comes to order. The communiqué, although not loud, reverberates throughout the room and is so powerful that I'm nearly blown off my seat.

It begins with a most powerful voice that comes from everywhere and that transcends everything. The message is revealed in a telepathic way, but it is crystal clear. The voice goes on to say, "This conclave hereby comes to order. This assembly is a follow up to our previous meetings to summarize and re-review the order at hand.

"There is great turmoil on Earth at the present time. Such extreme disorder appears to many on Earth to be the word of the prophets. But it is not the wish of God. Satan has dictated the event and wants to gain power by creating chaos on Earth at this time. By doing so, innumerable souls will succumb to the devil. In addition, the risk of total destruction of Mother Earth is very real and will happen unless something is done to stop it. However, the time is not yet and this does not conform to the prophecies that have been written.

"We are in the midst of an extraordinary event. We are all aware of the severe gravity of the matter and the extraordinary measure required to resolving it. It falls into the category of the first order. As we are all aware, the last time the first order requiring such a change in course occurred was a little over six thousand years ago in Earth time.

"What is happening on Earth at this time is a singular event. The necessary power that can accomplish the saving of the souls and prevent the destruction that is being created by Satan can be exercised after the ordination of two new angels in the first order of the Council. This is the will of God.

"These angels must be found and ordained before the nuclear devices and other bombs are detonated and before the disease is spread. The ordination process takes three Earth days. Therefore this must be accomplished immediately. Otherwise, the souls will be lost to Satan and he will gain extraordinary power on Earth and in hell. Additionally, the survival of the planet Earth is at stake.

"In order to change the course, it is required that two new additional angels of the first order be ordained. Accordingly, a full quorum of a new first order designated for this event is required.

"The ordination process will take three days. It is imperative that this be completed well before midnight of the third night. Our Mother Angel of Glory of the first order will oversee the first part of the ordination and will assist by transcendence within a chosen one on Earth.

"We have previously reviewed the ordination process for the second to last angel who is also of the first order. The soul who is designated to be the second to last angel has been identified and that ordination is in process, but has not yet been completed. However, it is imperative that the ordination of the last angel begin immediately rather than wait for the completion of the process regarding the second to last angel. Following is the process required for the ordination of the last angel. This process will be identical to that of the third to last angel and will also be identical to that of the second to last angel with the exception of the number of guiding angels who will assist in the ordination process.

"But it will be the addition of this very last angel who will complete the order. Only at that time the power will be exercised to change course and save the souls and Mother Earth who will otherwise perish under Satan.

"It is absolutely imperative that the following requirements be met exactly as set forth regarding the ordination of the last angel.

"First, the angel candidate must be of the same blood line as the preceding two angels of the first order. That blood line must be from the holy sacred blood line determined by Jesus, and identified to the Council. The angel, once ordained, will sit in the last vacant seat next to the second last angel who will sit next to the third to last angel.

"Second, the angel candidate must pass an extraordinary physical, mental, and spiritual test of faith in Jesus Christ and God. The requirements of the test will be identical to the test to be passed by the second to last angel and identical to the test which the third to last angel has previously passed. Those have already been reviewed.

"Third, the test must be by death on Earth and must be initiated by the devil or one of his demons. It cannot be initiated by the angel candidate, any person, soul, or angel. It cannot be initiated by Jesus and not by God.

"Fourth, the test will be in two parts. The first part of the test must be passed in the presence of the family of souls and must be passed in the blaze of glory to God on High. The second part of the test must be passed in a conflagration in the presence of Satan. Both will require extraordinary faith.

"Fifth, a demon of the devil must be found within and when it is discovered it shall be exorcized in the name of the Father, the Son, and the Holy Ghost by a guiding angel of the first order.

"Sixth, the ordination process must adhere to the specific sequence of events and actions set forth in the order. The specific sequence of events is separately being revealed to the current angels of the first order of the Council. It is possible that the demons of the devil will also be aware of some but not all of these specific events and the sequence of the events.

"Seventh, the candidate angel shall not know of the circumstances of the ordination and shall not have any knowledge of the ordination or the process or the sequence of events whatsoever until the process is completed or until determined by the will of God.

"Lastly, the ordination will require extraordinary prayer by at least one chosen one on Earth. The chosen one will not have any knowledge of the ordination process until told by God when the time is right for his or her prayer. The chosen one will not know who the angel candidate is. The chosen one will also be from a specified blood line as determined by the Order. The chosen one must pray three times for the success of the ordination, however although will be told when to begin its prayer, will not know and will not be told to pray three times.

"If the prayer is not sufficiently made or not made three times by the chosen one, the ordination will not be completed even though the angel candidate and the protector angels may have been successful.

"The angel candidate who will be the last angel must be promoted and assisted by the last two angels of the same order and of the same sacred blood line in passing this test who have previously passed the same test without their knowledge. The test must be passed within the same ordination process without his or her knowledge. It is the mission of the assisting angels to protect and guide the last angel candidate during the process, but the extent of the assistance and guidance will be limited by the order.

"The Mother Angel will assist in this ordination by overseeing the calling through transcendence as explained. Only she knows the final element of the code that is required to complete the order.

"There are two reasons for the need for two angels and not one to assist regarding the ordination of the last angel. It is prescribed by the ultimate consequence, the power of the order, and the power granted by this extraordinary ordination. The last angel candidate will require additional protection and guidance because all three angels will be subject to extensive attempts of final extermination by

Satan and his demons until the ordination of the last angel has been completed.

"The devil and his demons will become aware of the ordination process however will not know all aspects of it. They will attempt to stop it and end the process. They are very capable of accomplishing this. The demons can stop the process and are capable of extinguishing all angels of assistance and the angel candidate.

"The survival of the angel candidates and the angels of assistance, as well as the success of the ordination processes will be in grave danger until the completion of the ordination process. Remember that the guidance and protection by the angels will be limited by the order.

"If any of the foregoing does not take place exactly and specifically as hereby set forth and written, especially the precise events, actions, and their specific sequence that are required, or if the angel candidate becomes aware of the ordination while in process before the prescribed time, or if the special prayer is not sufficiently made, or not made three times by whom is chosen, then the ordination will be invalidated, canceled, and shall become null and void immediately. In that event, the order will cease.

"The only way for the order to be fulfilled is for all three of these angels and the Mother Angel to accomplish their mission as set forth by the strict order in transcendence through the name of the Father, Son, and Holy Ghost, and for the special prayer to be made as set forth herein.

"After these requirements are accomplished, the candidate angel will then be subject to the regular ordination process that is customary for the installation of all angels, pursuant to the will of God.

"The requirement must be completed prior to midnight of the third night."

The meeting is then adjourned. At the adjournment the ceiling of the massive cathedral-like room opens up to the cosmos and the cosmos turns into a blinding light and sound display similar to the one I encountered in the hallway upon entering heaven.

The colors are directing the most wonderful music. And within this there is a glorious melody that sings out in rapture that sends shivers down my spine. I sense it is being sung in every language on Earth as well as perhaps other languages not on Earth, in complete harmony as if it were speaking in tongues. Letters in a language unknown to me appear as a near blinding light in the cosmos, but which I understand to be "myAbwJ."

The sight is so grandiose but so subtle and humble at the same time that I am completely mesmerized. I have no idea whatsoever what is happening. I am absolutely awestruck. I cannot believe what I have just experienced and witnessed.

But most importantly, I am thoroughly perplexed because everything I just witnessed is not anything that even remotely resembles any iota whatsoever of what I understand is written in the Gospel or the events to take place per the book of Revelation.

I'm not aware that the Bible says anything about special angels, that such a meeting with angels would occur, that there would be an ordination process, that a special prayer would be required, or that any plan like this would take place, or that this is required for God to exercise extraordinary power to change course to defeat Satan and save the world. Why is this all needed for Him to gain special power? Doesn't God already have unlimited power anyway? Or would it be to enhance God's will perhaps? At any rate, the Bible doesn't mention any of this. I simply don't understand. If this is for real, how can this all be?

Chapter 45

At the warehouse, Garrett now is actively interacting with the agents and nobody would know he's not one of them. In fact, he's making a lot of the decisions and is ordering some of them around and telling them what to do, as if he's their commander. They follow suit, and it's evident that many respect him.

Julie is off in the corner feeding and attending to Lizzy, Mikey, and Emily. One of the agents comes over and tells her that two agents are prepared to take them back to Andrew and Alana's house, but they can't right now because of what's happening there.

"What?" exclaims Julie.

"Oh, I thought you knew," comments the agent. "There's been some shooting in their neighborhood, and the FBI is chasing several vans that appear to be full of terrorists. The agents think the terrorists know Andrew is related to you and they may go to his house in search of Alex or something he has or had. Therefore, it's not safe there."

Julie is surprised, but considering what she's just been through and considering how tired she is and what time it is, she somewhat takes it in stride. "They can't possibly go through what we have gone through. At least there are agents there to protect them. We didn't have that luxury here."

Suddenly, one of the agents who is on several phones jumps up and motions that he has some news. Another agent joins him. They have an update on whether they can get the equipment and the choppers.

"As far as the good news goes, an angle grinder with an assortment of blades, several oxyacetylene torches, cable cutters, and other equipment were found in one of the other industrial buildings in the complex by some of the other agents. They should be here any minute. We should have all of the equipment needed to cut away the flooring slab to allow it to be lifted out together with the bomb.

"The bad news is we got confirmation that the Chinooks choppers passed over about forty-five minutes ago and their pilots don't want to turn around to come back. In addition, they're all full and weighted down with supplies and the contact chief said that they didn't know if the chopper could handle the weight of the floor anyway."

"Where are they going?" one of the agents asks.

"They're taking supplies to the National Guard out west to help in a riot situation that has turned out to be a real crisis."

The first agent asks, "How can that crisis be any worse than this one?"

"Because they found another bomb. It's about an hour and a half from here by air."

"Really?" several agents exclaim.

The agent then explains when he talked with their commander he speculated that none of their pilots would want to come back here anyway. He's starting to lose men as are many command posts. There are more and more men in the military, National Guard, FBI, CIA, and other agencies who are abandoning their jobs to evacuate and be with their families. Nobody wants to be within a hundred miles of any large city or anywhere else where it's speculated that one of these bombs may be.

Another agent comes over and says he's found some local helicopters but can't find any pilots who are available who know how to fly them. But they're much smaller and would not be large enough to lift the concrete floor anyway. These are for example, a TV news chopper, a local police chopper, and an emergency medivac copter.

"Way too small for this. They're just puppy choppers compared to what we need. We've checked with the National Guard and military and no other choppers are available."

Within minutes, the other agents run through the garage door with the angle grinder, the oxyacetylene torches, cutters, and other tools.

The agents agree to start cutting away the metal beams anyway, just in case a large enough helicopter and pilot can be found in time. Several minutes later, the sounds of the equipment can be heard echoing from the floor below.

Garrett comes over and screams for everybody to stop. He's concerned that the sparks and vibration just might trigger the sensors on the bomb. After a few minutes, the hole is covered and after a strategic placement of some tarps, old towels, and other materials around the flooring, the effort resumes with only muffled noises heard now from underneath the floor. "How much time is left on the timer?" he yells" out.

"One hour and twenty-eight minutes and counting down!" is the response.

Other agents begin discussing whether they want to stick around to help or whether they want to leave and try to go home or try to catch up with their families. Several of them indicate that their families have already tried to evacuate but are stuck in traffic jams and that they could not be reached or joined anyway. Some of the cell services are being disrupted. These agents then agree that there's no other place to go for now. So, they stay put.

After about a half an hour, they finish cutting the last beam and drain away and they have the floor balanced on the foundation supports ready to be lifted out.

The other agents are frantically calling to try to find a helicopter large enough and a pilot, but have not been able to do so. If this was not a crisis situation and shortly after 4:00 AM, ordinarily they would not have any trouble getting such equipment. But at this hour and considering what the payload is, it appears to be next to impossible.

Before long, the counter reaches 0:59 minutes and now there is less than an hour before doomsday.

In the meantime, four other agents come over after inspecting the cable wire. Apparently the cable was already precut into several pieces and they don't know if they will be long enough. Another comments that if a chopper can be found, although the flooring section and bomb will fit through the roof, the helicopter probably won't. Therefore they would need to attach the cable to the helicopter first outside, unless it has its own hoist system that would work.

They roll the cable reel outside and measure each piece while two other agents climb on the roof to measure the distance to the floor. As they do this, they work on the ends to attach the steel hooks they found with the cable. As expected, the cable pieces are several feet too short.

One of the agents then shouts out, "Well, it looks like we're doomed. We have less than an hour and no chopper and no hoist system. Well, an excellent idea and a lot of work for nothing! That's because nobody out there wants to help us!" he screams out sarcastically.

The Chinooks, the only chopper around capable of doing the job, are long gone and are too far away.

They return inside and everybody continues to work and talk about the matter. "What can we do?"

The timer now shows thirty-five minutes to go and continues to count down.

Suddenly, a call comes in from another command post. It turns out that one of the Chinooks in the convoy was empty and the pilot heard the news and has turned around and is coming back. He was the last one in the convoy and didn't hear the need for the helicopter until several minutes after the report was broadcast for it. His commander had spoken for him without telling him.

The pilot took about fifteen minutes to think about whether to risk flying back but decided to anyway. It turns out he has terminal cancer and is not expected to live past another several months or so anyway. After much mulling over the situation and some deep prayer, he's decided to fly the chopper back to help.

He would also be willing to risk flying the bomb out as well, as he indicated he's going to die anyway and would rather save millions of lives in the process if he could.

In a few minutes, one of the agents is on the phone talking directly with the pilot. Unbelievably, he has a hoist system that when combined with the cable should be long enough and strong enough. And he has parachutes in the chopper as well as several wing suits and jet packs.

The agent on the phone with the pilot can be heard discussing the logistics of the lift. They figure out that once the chopper gets here, it will take perhaps ten minutes or more to hook everything up and at least another ten minutes or so to get the helicopter far enough up into the air into the farthest reaches of the early-morning sky and out into the country to be effective before the bomb goes off.

That means that they need at least twenty minutes once the chopper arrives, and probably more like at least twenty-five or thirty minutes.

"How long before you can get here?" asks the agent to the pilot.

"I'm about fifteen or twenty minutes out" is heard from the other end.

"That means that we need at least thirty-five or forty minutes and probably more than that for the chopper to get here, hook up the bomb and get it far enough away before it explodes."

"What's the time left on the counter?" another agent yells out.

"It's under twenty-five minutes and it's still counting down! We're not gonna make it! There won't be enough time! We need at least ten to twenty more minutes than this and probably more than that! And it's starting to get light outside! Sunrise will be here in less than half an hour!"

Chapter 46

I sit there both aghast and amazed of what I just experienced in the Council Room. I'm still trying to get a hold of myself. I'm in somewhat of a trance and I think of the enormity of the crisis on Earth. I was aware of the developing nuclear crisis back home and the threat of the deadly disease; however, I didn't realize the magnitude of just how profound and serious it is. I was not fully aware that the existence of Earth itself could come to an end. I can't believe that the world not only may soon be completely destroyed, but in all likelihood it will.

But how can it at this time? But more importantly, how can it be prevented? I understand it was not God's will for this to happen at this time. It is not the prescribed time per the events described in the book of Revelation. And I don't understand how God's plan can happen either. The Bible does not mention any of this. Nevertheless, at least for now I must assume that what I just witnessed is for real because of what I just experienced. Additionally, I suppose I have no other option.

I cannot believe what these two poor souls must endure to pass these tests and risk being terminated forever by demons at the same time. And I can't believe they are to be totally unaware of the process. And in addition to passing these impossible tests, they must avoid being terminated by the devil's demons that will be out to get them. And it must require special prayer by at least one unsuspecting soul who I suspect will be a person on Earth. How will the chosen one know to pray three times when not told to do so? If he or she fails to pray three times, the entire process will be a failure.

Obviously the demons do not want these angels to be ordained. I sense that this is not only a monumental task but an absolute impossible one. Even just one part of the test is hopeless. I do not see any way that process can be completed to the exact specifications. The sequence of events that I separately became aware of during the communiqué is of astronomical proportions. The entire ordination process appears to be simply unachievable. I don't see any way how it can be accomplished.

The words *stunned* and *shocked* do not justify how I feel. The more I think about it, the more I can't believe that I've just witnessed this meeting. Assuming this is all for real, then how will this all be accomplished? Even if the ordination is successful, just how will God be able to stop the crisis situation on Earth? Just how would that happen? What will He be able to do with His power? Does He simply make all the bombs, disease, and terrorists disappear? That's impossible. How will He prevent Satan from acquiring additional souls? I don't understand at all how any of this can be done. Just exactly how would He do this, and at the same time not violate what is written in the Gospel?

I'm probably not permitted to fully understand everything that just transpired and I'm confused. But, I'm aware that God works in mysterious ways, and ways that we do not always understand.

So then who are these three angels that will make this happen? Where will they be found? What is so special about their sacred blood line that is required? I sure would like to know what sacred blood line this is. I just hope that the last soul can be located, whoever he or she is, and that the ordination process of these last two souls into the special angels can be completed in time. That's what most important right now. And who will be the chosen one to provide the special prayer? Who will that be? And how will that person know to pray three times when not told to do so? It all seems absolutely unachievable.

I don't really care who they are, but then on second thought, I believe I may have figured out who the last two angels may be from the backgrounds from the alternating sequence of where all of the angels sat in the Council Room. I wonder if I'm right. Nevertheless, I have no idea how they can do it. And not only must one soul pass these seemingly impossible tests but two souls must pass the same test, and at different times. I don't see how one can do it much less two. I don't have any idea how it can be done. The entire solution proposed by God seems to me to be just simply impossible. It is also not realistic based on my understanding of what has been prophesized. But maybe it's the only way, but just how can it be?

Nevertheless, I just hope the souls can be ordained into angels in time, at least for the sake of my family back on Earth. Especially for Andrew who will surely go to hell because he refused to repent his sins and have faith in Jesus, and because of the type of life that he had, notwithstanding his refusal to follow Jesus. Now that I know what to expect in hell, my heart goes out to him more than ever now because I know what's in store for him there.

How lucky I was that I happen to time it just right to be here and be able to experience this. I am so overtaken and transfixed by what I just experienced that I didn't even see the angels get up and leave their seats. I then exit my trance and come to my senses. Then I sense two other souls in attendance in an adjoining viewing room but also closed from the proceedings. Are there other viewing rooms besides the one I'm in? But these are not ordinary souls like me or the others. After looking over to the other viewing room, I see a vision. I feel their presence.

How strange this is. I cannot see them well, but I get just enough glimpses of them in a vision before they're led away by another angel. One appears to be an older woman from Eastern Europe or Western Asia about my age or a little older and the other has a very similar appearance of Jesus. They certainly look like they could be related and of the same bloodline. If that's the case, I wonder what's so sacred about it. But am I imagining all this? Then I realize that both these conform exactly to who I thought the last two angels would be when I thought I figured out the pattern of how the angels sat around the tables! They are identical! Wow!

I am startled and jump back in my seat. Will these two souls eventually be the last two new angels? I wonder. Why did I just receive this vision? Or is this my imagination? This must be who they are! An older woman from the Middle East or Western Asia will be the second-to-last angel and a middle-aged man also from the Middle East who looks like Jesus will be the last angel. I can't believe that I think I figured this out!

Suddenly, I feel the presence of the angel who has been accompanying me. It has returned. I wonder what will happen to me next. The angel then tells me because I witnessed the meeting, God has decided to include me on the list of the possible chosen ones who He may select to pray for the success of the ordination process when the time is right. However, now is not the right time. Furthermore, I will not remember this. If chosen, I will be told when the time is right and what to pray for, but I won't know to pray three times. He values my prayer, but why am I on the list of possible candidates He has chosen to pray? I am nevertheless humbly honored.

I realize that this favor certainly is encouraging and becomes a positive reinforcement for me at a time of uncertainty. If I'm chosen, I wonder where I'll be. And if I'm chosen, I just hope I do what I'm supposed to do. I feel so honored, but at the same time I'm terrified of the responsibility. If I'm chosen, how will I know to pray three times when I'm not told to do so? If I don't, I'll fail.

Now that this meeting is over, my enthusiasm builds with excitement as I anticipate taking a guided tour of heaven. I so much look forward to this. I've only seen the entrance and hallway, the waiting room, the viewing room, and the Council Room. Now, I want to see heaven itself. I want to see all of the souls that are here. What do they do here? What sort of activities are there? What pleasures of paradise do they experience here? I'm so anxious to find out.

But instead, the angel leads me back through the very brief space-time continuum and into another room, which I learn is a review room. I am seated and hear the power of a voice that is both the most intimidating but welcoming voice that is totally unimaginable. I am startled by the abruptness, clarity, and authority of the voice. I listen intently. The voice states: "Your life résumé has been reviewed. There is one final question and you will have two options:

"Question: Do you believe that you deserve to go to heaven for eternity? Do you believe you are worthy in the eyes of the Lord? In other words, have you done what is required to enter heaven? Have you fulfilled God's purpose and truly followed Jesus Christ? *Yes* or *no*?

"Choice number 1: You can let God make a decision right now whether you remain in heaven or go back to hell. But you will not know the decision until after it is made. That decision will be *irrevocable*.

"Choice number 2: You can return to your life on Earth, but that is no guarantee of your final destiny. It would require an extreme change of course to be able to enter heaven if you choose this option. However, there will be a requirement imposed on you of which you will have no knowledge. *If* you choose to return to Earth, you will be required to do what you will not be told. There is a great possibility you will fail the will of God unless you do what is expected. You will not know why you were sent back there and you will not be motivated to do what is required. There is a significant possibility you would fail that test. Also, your time on Earth could end at any second.

"Most importantly, if you choose to go back to Earth, you will also forget and have no knowledge whatsoever on your own of your visit to and experience in heaven. You shall not remember anything on your own regarding the Council Room or your being witness to the circumstances of the ordination of the two remaining angels. You will not remember what you have heard in this review room. Although you may recall visiting heaven, you will not remember anything experienced here or any details of your visit on your own. Failure to do what is required when you will not know what to do and not be told what to do and considering you will not be motivated to do so will result in your spending eternity in hell."

I now am very much afraid and find myself trembling violently. This came on so suddenly. I was not expecting this at all. I don't know how to answer, but I know that I must respond quickly and without delay. Why would I be on the short list of the potential chosen ones to say the special prayer but then have to go through this? It doesn't make any sense.

I am thinking as fast as I can. I don't know how to answer the question. If I answer yes, perhaps I may be perceived to be arrogant and condescending when I should be more humble, and God may not agree. If so, that would spell doom for me. But on the other hand, if I answer no, I may be taken at face value and deemed forthright, which would also seal my fate.

I think I'm pretty much screwed either way. I wish this was an essay-type question rather than a *yes or no* question. I would like to elaborate on my answer, but I'm not allowed to do so.

Regarding the choices given to me, I feel inclined to want to have another chance on Earth. But the odds if I decide to return to Earth are no better. How will I know what is required of me when I won't be told what it is and considering I won't be motivated to do so?

However, more importantly, I realize that I'll not remember my experience in heaven on my own. So if I return to Earth, because I won't remember this, either way, how will I be motivated or encouraged to do whatever it is that I'm supposed to do? If I return to Earth, I will in all likelihood fail because I will not know to do whatever it is that is required of me. And my time back on Earth may be very short.

So how do I answer? But this all doesn't matter. While I'm all caught up in these thoughts, apparently, I was taking too long to answer. I suddenly hear the almighty powerful voice reverberate throughout all of heaven by declaring that I will not need to choose and that God will make the decision for me. It is done. God will decide. But I don't know what His decision is.

I am then led out of the review room and back to the waiting room. I'm so nervous because I don't know what decision God has made. But I'm not positive that any decision I would have made would have been any better.

I want to talk with the angel. I have a thousand questions I want to ask it. However, it's now thanking me for my visit and tells me that it must leave me now. I want to thank it, especially for letting me attend the Council Room meeting; however, by now it's gone.

I'm terrified once again. I get the same wretched feeling again that I did not belong in heaven in the first place and I was unworthy to be here. It's the same feeling I had when I first arrived here. But now I also get the same overwhelming feeling that I had when I left hell that I would go back there as well. What an absolutely overwhelming experience this has been.

What a cruel joke to tease me with a brief look at heaven, give me just a sample taste of it, and then send me back to hell if that's going to be the case.

I exit the gates of heaven and find myself floating again. The same void reappears. Now I'm really bewildered and start to question this entire journey. I become more and more confused. It was my understanding that our God is a loving and forgiving God. I did have faith. I did repent my sins. I did love Jesus and God with all my heart and soul. Or at least I thought I did. But I just don't understand. Is it because I failed when I had opportunities to do better that I simply ignored? What's happening to me?

I continue to float for a while, but then suddenly, I stop, and the mirror of life once again reappears. This is totally unexpected. "Now what?" I gaze into the mirror as I have no idea what I will see. But to my astonishment, once again the vision appears of me when I was five years old wearing the shirt with the three lines. Why? And again, I strain to try to read the symbols and letters on the second line. To my amazement, it seems that the symbols and letters seem brighter. But are they? They again appear somewhat bolder and not faded as much. But is it my imagination? I still cannot read them. I try my hardest, but I just can't make out what it says.

"Why am I being shown this shirt again? What does this mean? What do the symbols and letters say?" I am totally perplexed. But within seconds the vision disappears, the mirror vanishes, and I find myself on the move again, floating though the void. After a while, I can see the faint pulsating light of hell getting closer and closer. I can't believe what's happening.

I look up and am quite surprised that the good spirit has returned and is with me again. I ask myself the question why does it keep leaving and reappearing? Where does it go and why? I still can't talk with it, and it still doesn't talk with me. I begin to wonder if the emotional contact I had with this spirit before was nothing more than a figment of my imagination. Is it really there? I think it is. I can't see it but I can sense its presence.

I look out and the light of hell now is much closer. I am moving faster now. I find myself once again absolutely terrified as to what will happen to me next. It appears that I am headed back to hell but I'm not sure. The terror that runs through my body is unbelievable. Again, I am shaking and start to go into convulsions because I know what to expect in hell. I am so scared. I'm also totally confused and perplexed as to what is happening.

Despite the fact that the good spirit is with me, I feel abandoned and deceived. I had faith, but Jesus appeared to have abandoned me. It even appears that God has abandoned me. I even remember my father telling me when I was a child that he would always be with me and guide me throughout my life, even after he died, but he deceived me. Where is he when I need him? He said he would be with me and guide me, but he is long gone. He has also abandoned me. I feel abandoned by everyone. I'm all alone. And the spirit who rides with me won't communicate with me and continues to leave me.

I almost feel like I should just give up on my faith altogether. I question now whether it does me any good. I was tempted by Satan to bow to him. Now that everyone has abandoned me, perhaps I should consider this and become a demon to avoid the torture in hell if I'm sent back there. But this would mean entirely abandoning my faith in Jesus. Do I really want to do this? If I'm being abandoned, then I need to think if any faith I had really matters any more. The temptation to become a demon becomes overwhelming. I really don't want to suffer any more torture. Maybe it would be better to dish it out as a demon instead.

The only thing that has me holding on to my faith now is the spirit who has accompanied me. But it doesn't stay with me and I cannot talk with it. When it is with me, it doesn't communicate with me. When it leaves me, it abandons me also. It's as if it's just going along for the ride when it wants. Maybe I've just simply been imagining it all along. Maybe it really doesn't exist.

As I look up to sense it to obtain a feeling of some comfort, I feel the spirit has left me once again. Now it has abandoned me as well. I'm all alone and on my own. I'm absolutely terrified as to what is going to happen to me now. The light at the gates of hell appear to be getting closer and closer. It appears that I'm definitely headed in that direction. Why? Now what's going to happen to me next? And why?

Chapter 47

In the basement, it's dark except for the lone lightbulb in the corner that Sonja turned on. It dimly lights up a portion of the basement, but the corner by the stairs is much darker. She was the first person down there and pulled the chain when the other lights went out. In the semi-darkness, Alana huddles over the children who now are fussy because they were just woken up in the middle of the night and are coping with a cold and musty basement.

The older children have experienced coming down to the basement before at night when there were tornado warnings, but this time, it's different. This time there have been gunshots heard outside.

Sonja hurries over to Andrew to see if he's okay from his fall. "Andrew, are you okay? Andrew? Andrew? Andrew! Alana, you need to come over here right away! Andrew hurt himself really bad when he fell down the steps. In fact, he's not even moving. He's unconscious! Andrew? Andrew!"

"Maybe he's just pretending to be out. It would be just like him to do that," Alana says from the other corner of the basement.

"No, really, Alana, you need to come over here right now," Sonja says more emphatically. "He's bleeding from where he hit his head. He's not moving. He won't respond at all."

Sonja then hurries over to watch the kids to allow Alana to exercise her nursing skills to see what's wrong with Andrew. She comes over to him. "Andrew? Andrew? Andrew, are you okay? Please say something! Andrew? Andrew! Andrew!"

She gently rolls him over to see where he's bleeding from and is startled to see such a large cut on his forehead. She takes his pulse and listens to his breathing. She tries to get him to wake up, but he won't. She suddenly becomes frightened. Andrew is out cold. She calls upstairs to the FBI agents who now have dispersed throughout the house.

Finally, one of the agents hears her and comes to the top of the steps holding a flashlight. Alana yells up the stairs, "Andrew fell down the stairs and is unconscious! We need to call an ambulance or go to the hospital right away!"

The agent is very sympathetic but resolute. "I understand, but we can't do that right now. Nobody can go anywhere. There are terrorists outside around the house trying to get in and the other agents are in the middle of a gunfight with them outside."

Suddenly there are some noises heard upstairs, and the agent quickly says, "Gotta go," and rushes away.

Several minutes later there's a flurry of more gunshots outside, and the squealing of tires can be heard again.

Soon afterward, one of the agents comes downstairs and tells the family that it's safe and they can come upstairs now. They all come up except for Alana who is sitting by Andrew. The agent finds some towels, and Alana applies pressure to try to stop the bleeding. The agent then goes back upstairs.

"What happened?" Sonja asks.

The agent explains, "Apparently one of the terrorists at the warehouse plus three additional terrorists were trying to break into your house but were thwarted by our agents. Some were on foot and some were in their vans. Nobody was shot, but the terrorists fled when additional FBI agents arrived on the scene."

Sonja looks outside and cannot believe how many SUVs are parked all over the place.

One of the agents then states, "There were actually two more, but they took off to chase one of the vans of terrorists. They will not be coming back, not with all of us here now."

Alana calls back upstairs to the agents to inform them that Andrew has regained consciousness to some extent. He's very woozy, but she fears that he may have a really bad concussion. He's still oozing some blood and needs his head stitched or bandaged. An agent goes downstairs to help her bring Andrew up and lay him on the couch.

In the light, Alana can see the real extent of Andrew's injury and decides he still needs to go to the hospital. Although she's been able to slow down the bleeding considerably, he's still unstable and needs proper medical attention. She's very worried about Andrew losing consciousness for an extended period.

But one of the agents tells her that's not a good idea. With the terrorists still out there, it isn't safe. They are much safer to stay put with the FBI on the scene.

The agent then asks Alana, "I understand you're a registered nurse. Can you do something for him? There's no way you can go to the hospital at this time. And did you forget what time it is and what is about to happen at sunrise? Sunrise is almost here."

Alana gets a cold compress from the refrigerator and puts it on Andrew's forehead. She gets a first aid kit from the bathroom, cleans the wound, and applies an antiseptic. She then holds a new towel over the wound and applies more pressure and finally stops the bleeding. After doing so, she puts gauze over it, wraps it, and tapes it. Andrew is so woozy he feels no pain and is oblivious to what Alana is doing.

Sonja asks the FBI agents why they're there instead of the police. One of the agents comments, "Several reasons. First, they do not have jurisdiction in the matter and second, they are all a bunch of wussies and cowards because they have all gone home to be with their families or are trying to evacuate the city instead of staying here to do their job."

"Like you." Andrew muffles as he holds the compress over his forehead and gives a thumbs-up sign. Andrew is making it clear that he is proud of the FBI agents for staying to help them.

Then another agent comes over and tells them "Garrett, Julie, Lizzy, Mikey, and Emily are being brought over by some of the other agents at the warehouse. Garrett decided he's no longer needed at the warehouse and that the agents there can handle what needs to be done. Garrett and Julie want to come back to be with the rest of you before the sun rises. They should be arriving very soon."

Alana looks outside and is surprised that it is starting to get light already. The birds are chirping, and she can see the morning clouds in various shades of pinks and grays floating against a sky that is brightening by the minute. What a most beautiful morning. But that won't be for long. She asks when the bomb is supposed to go off. In about twenty minutes she's told. Alana starts to cry and calls her kids over to her.

Just then, two more SUVS pull up and Julie jumps out from one of the vehicles, and then assists Lizzy, who can barely walk, into the house. Julie is carrying Emily. Garrett and Mikey get out of the second SUV along with Agent Freeman. Mikey is holding hands with Agent Freeman, who he made friends with when he led him to the warehouse. As they step on the porch, the agent spots a frog in the bushes, grabs it, and gives it to Mikey as they enter the house.

Mikey is absolutely ecstatic. He's overjoyed. He immediately shows everybody as they all greet each other in the living room. Lizzy screams when Mikey shoves it into her face, and Julie tells him to take it back outside. Alana then comments, "Julie, let him hold it in here, it's okay, it can't harm anything."

Crackerjack sits in the corner on a vent and eyes the frog. Garret looks at Crackerjack. Garret knows that Crackerjack desperately wants to check it out. Perhaps he's naming it *breakfast*.

After a few comments about the night that everybody had experienced, they all sit in a circle and hold hands and watch the clock. Tears are streaming down everyone's faces in anticipation of what is expected to happen in a few minutes. Garrett has synchronized his watch with the timer on the bomb before he left the warehouse, and he's counting it down. He says that now there's about ten minutes to go. Everybody is in such shock that nobody wants to say anything. The silence is broken by the tic-toc-tic-toc of the clock. It's like the click-click-click-click heard on the timer on the bomb.

The FBI agents all go outside and are standing around by their SUVs, talking with each other or are on their phones. Some of the

SUVs leave. It's now much lighter, and there's a glow in the sky in the east. The sun us just about to peek over the horizon.

Just then, the kids are frightened by a horrendous noise above the house. Julie and Alana also jump. Andrew is still too woozy, but Garrett recognizes the noise. It's the sound of the massive rotors of the Chinook flying over. He wonders if it's just now arriving or if it's leaving with the payload. He looks at his watch again, gets up, and runs outside to look. However, the chopper has already disappeared behind the trees.

He knows if the Chinook already has the bomb and is carrying it away, then there's a chance that it just might make it far enough away in time before the nuclear bomb goes off. But on the other hand, if it's just now arriving, then he figures there's no chance it will have enough time to land and hook up the bomb and get away in time.

He thinks for a minute and realizes that they would have heard it once before if it had already arrived, so he thinks that it's just now arriving. If so, that would spell absolute disaster. He figures that otherwise, if it's now leaving with the bomb, they would have heard it twice, coming and going, which is not the case.

But then he thinks perhaps it arrived from the other direction and that's why they didn't hear it if it's leaving instead of arriving. But if that's true, then why was the Chinook flying in the direction of the city instead of out to the country? And why was it flying so low over the houses instead of up as high as it could?

He knows that the warehouse is only within a few miles of the house, and that's in the other direction. He fears the absolute worst-case scenario.

Garrett comes back inside and tells everybody what the noise was and explains what the helicopter was doing. He looks at his watch again and says six minutes to go.

Sonja, Alana, Garrett, and Julie all start praying like they never have before. Now coming out of his wooziness from the fall, Andrew looks at them, comes to his senses, realizes the reality of what is about to happen, and for the first time in his life he bows his head and also prays. But, he is praying to Ammen instead of to Jesus.

They all continue to pray, and they all tell each other that they love one another. The final words heard from them in muffled sobbing voices as they all hug each other are, "I'll see you in heaven." After Garrett says this, he looks at his watch and counts down—five, four, three, two, one.

Then they are blinded by a flash of a brilliant light coming through the windows and a few seconds later, the explosion of the nuclear bomb can be heard, a deafening earsplitting crack of thunder. It's as if lightning hit the house. Nearly every window in the house shatters, the mirrors on the walls shatter, things start flying off the mantel, bookshelves, and tables and the house shakes as if a 10.0 earthquake erupted right under the house. The vibration is immense.

The house violently shakes and vibrates for a few seconds and then an enormous roar like a freight train follows with a tremendous wind that rocks the house. The noise and wind continue as the blast sweeps over and through the house and the neighborhood. It echoes throughout. Simultaneously, it gets hot, and a second flash of light illuminates the house like a thousand suns. Everyone gasps to take in their last breath of air.

Chapter 48

As it appears that I'm headed back to hell and being in a state of shock, I start asking myself many questions.

How can it be that I didn't have enough faith in my life? I thought the level of my faith was more than adequate, but apparently, I was wrong. I did not think my life was that bad. I thought God was a kind, loving, and forgiving God and that He would have mercy on me. So why? I would give anything to live my life over again, but I suppose that's not going to happen. I want another chance. I'd make good on all of those lost opportunities. I just wish I knew I was supposed to do this when I was alive on Earth.

Then thinking about just how bizarre all of this is, I get a radical feeling and wonder if perhaps I'm actually in another room in hell and perhaps I never really visited heaven? Perhaps I was sent to the second or another chamber where I'm told that the level of torture can encompass other dimensions of pain and torture. Maybe this experience is just to tease me and that this is just a hoax played by the devil and is another form of torture?

Maybe this was not really heaven at all but instead a tantalizing joke played on me in hell. Am I still in hell and is Satan simply playing with my mind? Perhaps is this a torture of another dimension in a higher chamber of hell? After all, what I experienced in heaven, or thought I experienced, did not conform at all to what I thought the Bible stated. I'm not aware that the Gospel stated that any of this was possible. So perhaps I never really did visit heaven. Perhaps everything I thought I experienced about the meeting with the angels, the special angels, and ordination process required for God to use extraordinary power when He already had it anyway, etc., never really happened and I've been in hell this entire time. I sure wish I knew.

If that was the case, then what room of torture and torment will I be sent to next? I cannot even fathom it. But regardless, I anticipate that I will soon be suffering in unbelievable agony somewhere in hell soon anyway.

The more I think about all this, the more confused I get, and I just really don't know what to think. Now, I'm totally dazed and perplexed. I cannot think of anything anymore that makes any sense.

But for now, I can sense myself being thrown back into another level of hell, and I really don't want to go there. The more I think about this, the more frightened I get. In each passing second I get sicker, dizzier, more confused, and more terrified. I realize if I actually visited heaven, I still don't understand the events that I witnessed in God's Council Room. How can this all be? None of this is making any sense at all.

In fact, I find myself so horrified as to what is about to come and happen to me, I decide to start praying to God and to the spirit who is riding with me. But the spirit is not there. I decide that I'll still try to have faith even though it seems like I've been abandoned by everybody. Why, I don't know, but I'll try anyway. It's either that or become a demon to avoid the torture.

This entire journey of getting a little taste of hell, and a little sample of heaven if this is the case, before my eternal conviction, now has become an absolute nightmare. But it's not a nightmare or a dream because it is so real. I want to go to sleep and dream to escape the reality of all of this. I need some time off.

I happen to think of the TV documentaries about the various controversial topics that I enjoyed watching before I died and just how far-fetched and out of this world some of their conclusions were. Well, now I cannot imagine anything being any more out of this world or any more unreal then what I've experienced the last several days. I now know that multi-dimensions are real. Heaven and hell certainly are. I just wish I wasn't part of all of this now. I keep asking myself, "How can any of this be real?"

I think of my family back home and wonder if I can still see them. I first get a vision of what's going on in real time. But for whatever reason, it lasts only a few seconds and that vision changes to another but is starting to fade away again. When I approached heaven, these visions materialize; but when I approach hell, these visions seem to evaporate.

It's like there is some static electricity interfering with my ability to see them. Before it fades completely away I briefly see an image of my family all going to the hospital for some reason. But I don't know why. I can briefly see Andrew who appears to be in a coma and being attended to, but that's about it.

Am I imagining this, or maybe perhaps I'm going crazy?

The vision now is gone, and I can't see it anymore. Perhaps I'm reliving the night of the explosion and fire when I was put into the ambulance and it's only a figment of my imagination. Or perhaps they're going to the hospital is for some other reason? Is it because of Andrew? Or is because of me?

I look up to see if the spirit has returned. I want to plead with it to please not let me go back to hell. This is so real. Please put me to sleep and let me dream about something else. Please. But when I look up, the spirit is gone and hasn't come back. I don't know if it will return or not. I'm horrified to be alone and headed to a most forbidding place all by myself. I've been abandoned by everybody and everything.

Why does the spirit continue to leave me? Where does it go? Is it going to come back? Because I've been abandoned by it, I think perhaps this really has not been a good spirit at all but instead has been a bad one. Perhaps another hoax played on me by the devil?

This horrific journey is so real; I can't handle it anymore. I'm now literally shaking and trembling in fear and the fear is becoming overwhelming. I wish I would die and not experience any of this anymore, but I know that's not an option. So, since I can't die to get away from this, the only other option is to go into a dream to escape this reality. But I can't do this. Only God could let me do that, I suppose.

Suddenly, I get the urge to listen to music. Probably just to get away from all of this. I realize that I miss it so much. It would be so comforting in this abyss of pure silence and knowing that I will return to hell. For whatever reason, I think of the hymn "All Creatures of Our God and King" and the lyrics and rhythm go through my head. Oh how I would just love to hear a full choir and orchestra do that song. The refrain "Alleluia" and "Oh, Praise Him" take over my mind. It is overwhelming and most soothing.

But then the rhythm and lyrics fade away, and a more contemporary song, a rock-and-roll song, "Don't Stop Believin'" pops up and starts to go through my head. How interesting that a Journey like this can produce a song like that at this time. The lyrics don't seem to be relevant to me, but then for whatever reason, I realize I'm merely a lost soul wanting to find my way. How uplifting this is. Normally, when an earworm emerges like this, you want it to go away, but I hope this one doesn't. My emotions from within run rampant, and I want the rhythm and the words of the title to go on and on and on. It is most comforting. But eventually, it dissipates as well.

Then everything becomes deathly silent and I come back to reality and realize that I just want to get away from this adventure. I can't handle the uncertainty anymore. And I know I absolutely will not be able to tolerate going back to hell. The empty feeling and silence in this abyss of nothingness becomes absolutely unbearable.

So I pray to God to please let me fall asleep and dream about something else. I need a respite from this reality of horror. At least just for a little while perhaps to give me a short break. I now am in such deep agony; since I can't die again, I just want to go to sleep and not experience any of this anymore.

The gates to hell now are within sight and are getting closer.

The reality of what I've experienced over the past couple of days has finally sunk in, and I've reached my breaking point. Nothing is making any sense anymore. I am tired and just want to go to sleep.

"Please, dear God, I still believe in you. Please let me. Please just let me enter a dream so I can experience something else. I need a break from all of this, if at least just for a little while. I can't take it anymore. Please let me go to sleep and into a dream to get away from this."

Chapter 49

As it turns out, the pilot of the Chinook had come from the other direction and arrived at the warehouse with thirteen minutes to go before the bomb was to explode. But because the agents were ready, it only took about three minutes to hook up the floor section and bomb. It did get a little nerve-wracking though when the floor section and bomb almost hit the roof when it was lifted because it was swinging so much.

After taking off with the bomb, the pilot had to swing the chopper toward the city first to avoid hitting a hill and some trees because of the low-hanging payload. It then flew behind the hill and then swung around to lift the bomb up and away out into the country.

The Chinook was able to climb several miles up and quite a few miles out into the country and then higher still, and about ten minutes after it took off from the warehouse, the bomb exploded far above the clouds and away from the city.

It is unknown if some people did not survive the blast. However, the explosion was far enough away that most if not all people survived although there was still extensive damage done to buildings and structures for miles in every direction.

After several minutes the intense vibration, light, wind, heat, and echoing sound waves dissipate, and the air becomes consumed by smoke and dust. Everything is quiet now.

Everybody slowly lift their heads, and they look at each other in amazement. Garrett thrusts his fist into the air to claim victory. "Yes, yes, yes!"

Off in the corner, Crackerjack barks three times, gets up, and runs over into the middle of the circle. He is a very happy dog greeting each and everyone in the family, and his tail is wagging in everyone's face as he attempts to jump up and lick everybody. It's a welcome invitation back to reality and the realization that they are all still alive and that they survived the blast.

The family slowly gets up, hugs each other, and starts to look around at the destruction. It's deathly quiet. Although their house is still in one piece, the windows are gone, there is broken glass everywhere, and debris is scattered about. Outside there's a lingering haze in the air. Above, the sun is shining brightly, however it is shadowed by the eerie miasma that lingers below.

The family spends all morning cleaning up the mess. They immediately sweep up the shards of glass on the floor, but the broken glass in the carpet and outside in the yard is more difficult to clean up. Garrett finds several sheets of plywood and some tools in the garage and some additional plywood leaning against a wall in the far corner of the basement. He boards up as many windows as he can, leaving some open for some light. Julie and Alana take care of the kids, and Sonja and Garret finish cleaning up the best they can.

Andrew, still sitting on the couch recovering from his head injury, starts to stir. He decides to get up and turn on the TV to watch the news. Certainly, the news will be talking about the nuclear bomb going off, he thinks. He also wants to know more about the other bombs that have not gone off yet.

And he wants to see more of Ammen. He wonders whether his prayer to Ammen saved him and now he is convinced more than ever that Ammen is for real.

But obviously the TV doesn't work. Garrett was going to say something but decided to let Andrew find out for himself. Andrew goes into the kitchen to find something to eat and discovers that the refrigerator isn't working. It doesn't take too long to learn that all the electricity is out. News of this spreads quickly through the household.

Both Julie and Alana then try their cell phones. They want to call their friends and check up on everybody they know and see where they are. They each have different cell phone carriers and both find out in short order that neither of their phones work either.

The explosion has disabled all electrical service and communications in the area and for miles. They try the water and to their relief they still have water pressure. Whether the water is fit for consumption is another story though.

Sonja looks outside and tells everybody that all the FBI SUVs are gone. They have no idea when the agents left, where they went, or if they plan to come back.

After spending the morning cleaning up the debris outside and repairing the house, it's now early afternoon and everybody stops to take a short lunch break. Some leftover food items and other things are pulled from the refrigerator and freezer that could spoil now that they are no longer working and Julie and Alana prepare several dishes for everybody to eat now and later.

Andrew, feeling much better now, is up and about. He looks at Garrett. "You know, I'm going stir crazy and need to get out of the house for a while. While you and Julie enjoyed your adventurous times out and about over the past several days, I've been tied up in the house working with the FBI this entire time to try to find and save you all."

Garrett looks at him like he's crazy. "You've been working with the FBI? You've been helping them to save us? We've enjoyed having adventurous times?" Garrett is more than amused. He's in disbelief that Andrew has no idea what he and his family have gone through for the last several days. He can just imagine what Andrew has been doing the entire time they were gone.

Andrew then announces, "I think I'll take the car and drive around a bit. I'd like to see what sort of damage has been done around the neighborhood."

Alana stops him. "Andrew, that's not a good idea. You're not going anywhere. You're still recovering from your head injury, and you don't know what's out there. Plus, I need you here in case the terrorists return."

"That won't be any problem. Garrett will be here. You can handle things while I'm away for a while, right?"

Garrett just stares at Andrew.

Andrew then says, "I also want to go to Mom and Dad's house to see what it looks like in the daylight after the fire was put out by the firefighters. Mom, are you interested in going? Anybody else?"

That catches Sonja's attention. "Yes, I would like to see what's left of my house too. Maybe if there's anything left I can salvage it. The clothes that Alana gave me do not all fit well, and I still need some clothes to wear. I know I won't find anything there since I am sure it all got burned up in the fire, but I want to go and see anyway. I can go with you, Andrew. Alana, I'll watch over him."

Julie adds, "Well, if you're going out, why don't you drive by our house too and check it out. I have no idea what's going on there after we were taken away by the terrorists. I don't even know if it's still standing and in one piece after the bomb went off."

Andrew is very quick to come back. "I'm not going over there. There were dead bodies in your house. Garrett can go over there and check it out."

Garrett continues to stare at Andrew. "I'm sure that the FBI has cleaned the place up by now. Perhaps I can go over there later if you're afraid." Garrett then gets up and heads to the garage to retrieve some more tools and goes out back to do some more repair work to Andrew's house and clean up more of the yard.

Alana states, "I don't think it's safe for anybody to go out anywhere just yet. Don't nuclear bombs come with a radiation fallout?"

As Garrett leaves to go into the garage, he turns around and responds, "If there's any fallout it won't matter whether you're outside or inside at this point. But I agree it's safer to stay here and not go anywhere just yet. But whether Andrew goes anywhere is not up to me."

Andrew grabs the key to their car and says, "We'll, I'm going anyway. I'll be okay. Mom, you want to come with me? We won't be gone long. Come on, let's go."

Andrew and Sonja head out to the garage, get in the car, and take off.

Alana stands up and stretches. "You know, nobody here except for the kids has had any sleep for two days now. All of the kids are napping now. I just might lie down and take a nap for a bit."

Julie wholeheartedly agrees.

———◦———

Andrew and Sonja slowly drive up the street and out of their subdivision. Debris from the blast litters the street, but it's not bad enough that they can't drive around it. The windows in every house have been blown out. But outside of the broken windows and the debris, it appears that each structure withstood the explosion and is in pretty good shape.

After traveling for several blocks, they get the sensation that it's a ghost town. Everybody either has tried to evacuate or they're still in their houses, either dead or alive. Nobody is seen outside anywhere. There's no life anywhere, and it's deathly quiet.

They slowly travel down the main road, and they're the only car on the road. Sonja gets the jitters and wants to return home, but Andrew is driving and she's at his mercy. After several more blocks, finally, a few people can be seen walking around their homes, apparently trying to figure out the damage and how to repair it.

Sonja makes a remark how proud she is that Garrett already has Andrew's house halfway put back together. Andrew steams but doesn't say anything.

All the traffic lights are out and aren't working. After a little while, they arrive at Alex and Sonja's house. There's nobody there. The scene is one of complete devastation. There is nothing but rubble, burnt debris, and ashes everywhere. There are posts with yellow ribbons attached to them that form a perimeter that surrounds the lot. On the ribbons are the words repeating every few feet *Do Not Cross—Crime Scene.*

Sonja looks at the sight and cries uncontrollably. "My house, my Alex, my house, my Alex."

Andrew shows no emotion and stops the car and gets out. He decides to cross over the sealed off area. He ducks under the ribbon and walks around in the rubble rummaging for anything that he can find. There's nothing left. Sonja remains in the car and is too distraught to get out.

After some time, Andrew eventually comes across the metal chest that contained Alex's treasures that he inherited from his father. It's lying in the middle of the rubble almost where the living room was. It's intact and hasn't melted but is charred somewhat and covered in ash. Andrew wipes away the ash and sits down on it to rest for a minute and looks around. He doesn't recognize the chest and doesn't pay any attention to it all. He has no idea what's in it, but Sonja does.

When Andrew sits on the chest and looks around, Sonja sees him, and for some unexplained reason she suddenly is overcome with an emotion of hope and joy, but she doesn't know why. She simply watches Andrew from the window of the car. Then she immediately recognizes the chest and knows what's in it. She leans out the window of the car. "Andrew, we need to retrieve the chest you're sitting on. Can you carry it or drag it over here?"

Andrew simply stares back at his mother and appears to be in a trance. Then he collapses and falls to the ground and lies there motionless.

Sonja is shocked and screams out the window of the car. "Andrew, are you okay? Andrew? Andrew, talk to me! Andrew!"

Just as Sonja opens the car door to get out, he then slowly moves and pulls himself back up to sit back down on the chest. Seeing that he apparently passed out for a minute or two, Sonja asks him again, "Andrew? Are you okay?"

"No. Mom, I have a massive headache and feel very sick. I'm so dizzy. I think I'm going to lose it. My head hurts so much I think I may pass out again. My head is starting to hurt like it did after I woke up after I fell down the steps, and I'm feeling very nauseous."

Sonja realizes that Andrew is not in good shape. He stands up and starts to wobble and struggles to keep his balance. He halfway crawls but slowly makes his way back to the car. She tells him to quickly get in on the passenger side as she gets out and gets in on the driver's side of the car. He finally climbs in, and she takes off.

"I'm going to get you home right away. Or maybe we should go straight to the hospital."

"No, I'll be okay. Just take me back home. I just need to lie down and rest for a while. I should be okay."

They eventually return home and find everybody asleep. Even the kids are asleep. Some are sitting back in chairs, some are lying on the sofas, and some are in bed. Some are sprawled out on the floor.

"Mom, I think I'm feeling getter now. Perhaps if I rest for a bit, I'll be okay."

"Are you sure? Alana wanted you to go the hospital earlier. Let me get Alana and maybe we should do that."

"No. I'm not going to any hospital. It might not even be open anyway. I'll be all right. I just need to lie down and rest a little."

He ambles inside holding his head and he lies down on a couch and falls asleep. Sonja goes to the guest room and lies down to nap as well.

Everybody sleeps well into the evening hours. Nobody has had much sleep for several days now.

After several hours Alana finally wakes up and sees most everybody is still asleep. At the same time, Sonja also awakes up and comes out of her room. They meet in the kitchen. Sonja and Alana strike up a conversation about their drive, and Sonja tells Alana about Andrew passing out and complaining about a headache he had and that she had to drive him home.

"Really?" Alana comments. Alana then goes out and tries to gently wake Andrew up to see how he's doing.

But he's sound asleep and doesn't stir. She continues to gently touch him and call to him. After a while she's shaking him. He will not wake up. Alana suddenly gets frantic. Being a nurse and knowing about concussions, she speculates that perhaps his head injury is worse than she originally thought. Perhaps much worse.

Perhaps he had some internal bleeding or brain hemorrhage or has some other very serious brain injury from his fall. She tries again and Andrew is totally unresponsive. She takes some quick simple vitals and gasps. Julie and Garrett wake up and come over to see what's going on.

They all realize that they need to get him to the hospital fast. Alana comments that the hospital may even be closed because of the conditions everywhere and she doesn't even know if anyone is there.

Garrett looks at her and nods. "The hospital has emergency generators, but I don't know who if anybody is still working there. Perhaps everybody evacuated because of the news regarding the bomb."

"Well, we can't call an ambulance or the hospital because the electricity and phones still don't work."

"An ambulance may not even be available anyway. What do we do?"

In the meantime, Andrew is passed out and is completely unconscious. Alana takes his vital signs again and begins to cry. She finds out the Andrew is in really bad shape and in fact she's afraid he's not going to make it. He is out cold and won't respond to anything. She can barely find a pulse and a heartbeat. His vital signs are weak at best.

"We'll have to take him there ourselves and just pray they're open."

Garrett picks Andrew up over his shoulder and quickly carries his limp body out to their car. Alana helps lay him into the backseat, and they speed off to take him to the hospital. Julie and Sonja pack up all of the kids and follow in separate cars. Garrett decides to go to the larger of the two hospitals that are close by.

As they're driving, Garrett comments that they will find one of several possible scenarios:

"One—there may still be some people working there on emergency generators and they can help. Two—the hospital is abandoned and nobody is there because everybody tried to evacuate when the news of the bomb was broadcast. Three—there are still some people working there on emergency generators but they're too busy because there are many other injured people there seeking treatment from the blast."

Garrett suspects either scenario two or three is probably what they will find.

Within several minutes, they pull up to the emergency room doors and everybody breathes a sigh of relief that the hospital is operational. A sign on the door with instructions includes a message indicating that the ER and hospital are operating with a limited staff and resources.

Garrett turns off the car and Alana runs inside and immediately screams for help and returns with a wheel chair. Garrett and Alana pull what appears to be a lifeless Andrew from the car and place him in the wheelchair and wheel him as fast as they can inside. By now, Andrew's face, which has been as white as a sheet, has turned blue. Alana is holding his hand as they enter the doors and again screams for help as soon as they get inside. The staff reacts and a nurse immediately comes out to attend to him. In the meantime, Alana puts her head on his chest and screams out, "I don't think he's breathing anymore!"

The nurse quickly wheels Andrew into a treatment room as other staff comes over to assist. Alana and Garrett follow. They immediately transfer him on to a hospital bed and begin resuscitation procedures. He indeed had stopped breathing. But for how long? While the staff try to resuscitate him, Alana and Garrett are told to return to the patient waiting area and find a seat. The staff will be in touch as soon as they find out anything. As Alana walks slowly back to the waiting area, she starts to cry even more and sobs. "He's not going to make it. Even if they can bring him back to life, what if he has such a serious brain injury from his fall that he never regains consciousness? Why won't Andrew wake up? Why? Why? Why?"

She sits down in the waiting room area, bows her head, and prays that they can revive him.

Part II

Chapter 50

It now has been three days and there still is no sign of a brain wave or any brain activity at all. Not even a delta brain wave has appeared. Several doctors, nurses, and Reverend Gabriel from the church congregate in the hallway, just outside the patient's room.

The room number is 888. The door is closed, and there's a sign on the door that reads Family Only.

The doctors and medical staff are discussing the process in which to remove the life support system that is keeping the patient alive. The constant sounds of the ventilator and monitoring equipment inside the room is all that can be heard except for the muffled chatter coming from the hallway.

The sight of the tubes and wires coming from the near lifeless patient and going into all the medical equipment and monitors was previously relieving and comforting. Now it's frightening. After reading the health-care directive for about the third time, the family has decided to remove the life support system. Two doctors and three specialists have all concluded that the chance for recovery is zero percent.

Numerous tests have been conducted and none of them suggest that any recovery or even partial recovery is possible. The cost to keep the life support system and for every additional day in the hospital is significant and burdensome, even with insurance. After three days without any brain waves, it now is 100 percent hopeless, they are told. The patient has barely been hanging on to life the entire time.

The first to arrive are Garrett and Julie. One or the other has been here every day and night in the room. They come in holding hands, lean over the bed, and pray. They then take seats set in the corner.

Lizzy, Mikey, and Emily are being watched by a volunteer down the hall in a visitors waiting area. It was thought that this experience would just be too dramatic for them to watch.

Then Sonja arrives, bends over, says a prayer, and then takes a seat. She too has been at the bedside for nearly all of the last three days and nights.

Alana who was watching her kids and instructing another volunteer on how to attend to them down the hall finally arrives. She also leans over, says a prayer, and takes a seat next to Sonja. Like the others, she has spent considerable time at the hospital for the last three days and nights.

Then Reverend Gabriel comes in and does the same. He goes over and stands behind Alana and puts his hand on her shoulder. He then holds Sonja's hand.

Standing at the door all by himself is one lone figure, a tall slender man who is equally visibly shaken over what is about to take place. It's as if he doesn't want the others to see him standing there. But his presence is felt by everybody. Everybody sees him and acknowledges him.

Julie asks the doctor, "How long will it take after you turn off or remove the respirator?"

The doctor responds, "I seriously doubt if he can breathe on his own. It varies, sometimes within only a minute or so, sometimes several minutes, sometimes an hour or more. But considering the shape that he's in and the already extremely weak vital signs, I suspect he'll be gone within a matter of minutes at the most."

"Are we really sure we want to do this?" asks Alana.

Everybody hesitates for a few seconds, but responds, "Yes."

Sonja adds "You know, the doctors and tests concluded that after three days of no brain waves, and the fact that the life support system is the only thing keeping him alive, he would not recover or survive anyway. He has been declared brain-dead, so there is no reason to force him to stay alive any longer under these conditions. It would be against his wishes per his health-care directive."

"Ready?" asks the doctor.

Everyone is sobbing but say yes.

Sonja gets up and slowly walks over to the small table in the corner and unfolds a white blanket and then refolds it so that it is exactly three layers thick in a triangular shape. She then lays it on the chest of the patient with one corner facing the head and the other corners facing sideways. She then takes a Bible with a white cover that was sitting on the table, kisses it, and then gently rests it on top of the blanket. She then takes a bouquet of orange blossoms that she brought from home and lays it on top of the Bible, with all the flower petals pointed upwards. She nods to the doctor and to Reverend Gabriel.

The doctor slowly walks over and disengages the respirator. The monitors are left on to gauge the patient's status. The equipment that monitors the brain waves had already flat-lined three days ago.

The monitor for the heart rate and blood pressure is barely even showing a reading, but then it starts to drop rapidly. Shortly, the sound of the beep-beep-beeps turns to a steady nonstop tone, and the monitor shows level lines that reflect no activity at all anymore. It only takes about a minute or so.

The doctor looks at Reverend Gabriel and nods his head. Reverend Gabriel says a prayer and some additional words of comfort and ends by saying, "It is done."

Everyone in the room says almost simultaneously either "May you always be with Jesus" or "May Jesus Christ always be with you."

They then all hug each other and prepare to leave the room. There's no need to stay any longer now.

Then from the front of the room by the door way, a separate but very distinctive man's voice is heard after everybody else. He softly says, "May Ammen always be with you."

Within seconds after he utters these words the monitor beeps once and then remains silent. Then after a few seconds, it beeps again and remains silent. Then it beeps twice. After a few seconds, it beeps three times. Then it starts beeping continuously and is showing a reading again. The steady tone now is beep-beep-beep-beep. Everyone is startled. The sudden surprise of this shocks everybody. There is a sense of jubilation and hope, but some trepidation as well in the room. What's going on?

Within a matter of seconds, the doctor and a nurse come over and start taking manual vitals and attend to the patient. A nurse elevates his head on a higher pillow.

Everybody in the room is absolutely astounded. They never in their wildest dreams imagined that this would happen. Nobody has ever seen anything like this.

The monitors rapidly show an increasing improvement and within a few minutes all of the readings are normal. He's breathing on his own.

Then the patient moves one hand and then another. Then he opens his eyes. He is staring straight up into the lights and is trying to focus on what appears to him as a blur. He has come out of the void and now finds himself in another world. After a few seconds, the blur of lights fades away, and he slowly can focus on the sights in the room.

He knows where he was, and so suddenly now this. How different. It's a total different sensation and feeling. Everything now is simple and plain, so intensely different than where he came from. Now there is a sense of time. There is gravity again. He can hear voices again. He recognizes the voices. He can see things in plain sight right before him. No more visions and no more hearing and seeing things through his head. What was so complicated and convoluted now is so simple.

He has had his eyes closed for three days. Now his eyes are open and they are glassy looking. In an instant, Sonja is right there holding his hand. She removes the orange blossoms, the Bible, and the blanket and leans over and kisses him and tries to hug him.

Alex then lifts his head up, turns toward Sonja and smiles. With a raspy voice, he struggles but softly exclaims, "Thank you, Lord." He looks at Sonja and says, "I love you Sonja, so much. You are truly my angel." Then he says, "Lord, please do not let me wake up from this dream. I asked you to let me dream, and you granted my wish. How can I thank you?"

He then closes his eyes, but it's evident that he no longer needs the life support system. Alex now needs to rest and have a little time to recover. He is resting comfortably and very soon will open his eyes once again. He is moving his arms and legs freely and appears to have gained his strength back in a matter of minutes. He starts to make facial expressions, whereas for three days, he was motionless. What an incredible transformation in only a matter of a few minutes.

"Unbelievable. It is absolutely unbelievable. A miracle," can be heard being exclaimed throughout the room, the hallway, and the nurses' station several rooms away. The doctors are in disbelief.

Andrew, still standing at the doorway after praying to Ammen, then asks Sonja. "What did he mean by saying he doesn't want to wake up from this dream? Does he think he's dreaming now and that we're all simply an imaginary world to him?"

Chapter 51

After a little time, the doctors decide it's best for the family to leave the room so they can attend to Alex, run additional tests, and let him rest. Everybody reluctantly obliges, but Sonja stays with him. She tells everybody, "You all go home. It's been a most difficult day. I'll be in touch with you and let you know how he progresses."

She sits down in a chair and for the next half an hour the doctors and nurses come in and out and attend to him. Then they leave for some time. Eventually, Alex opens his eyes again. He's ready to talk.

"Oh, Sonja, what an incredible, beautiful sight you are. This is the best dream anyone could ever have. You are truly an angel sent from heaven."

She comes over and gives him an extended kiss and she breaks down with emotion. She is so elated that Alex is not only alive but appears is recovering and recuperating quickly.

Feeling her lips on his and her emotions inches away from his face, now suddenly, Alex shows emotion himself. He's somewhat confused and bewildered.

Alex starts babbling, "Where am I? What happened? Is there anything left of our house? Where are you living now? How is Andrew? Is he alive? Is Julie and Garrett and the kids okay? Did they survive? Why are the terrorists looking for me? Did anybody else survive the blast?

Before he can say another word, Sonja stops him dead in his tracks. "Stop, stop, you're not making any sense at all. What are you talking about?"

She fears that he has some sort of mental condition after being unconscious for three days and tells him to rest and that she'll be right back.

Sonja leaves the room for a minute and goes to the nurses' station where she talks briefly with the doctor. She tells him that Alex is awake and talking, but that he's talking utter nonsense. "He's talking about witnessing a bunch of events that took place over the last three days that didn't happen."

The doctor says, "Well, you must remember that he was in a coma and then pronounced brain-dead for three days. I suggest that you let him talk, but don't challenge him much at first and let's see what he says. We need to know how he progresses. No telling what he's going through. He certainly didn't dream anything because he had no brain waves since the afternoon of the Fourth. Not even a hint of a delta wave."

Sonja returns to the room and is astounded that in only the short time she was away, Alex has pulled himself up to a halfway sitting position in bed and has found the TV remote and is turning the TV on.

She comes over and gives him another kiss and gently takes the TV remote from him and asks him if he wants some water or anything. As the TV screen comes into view, she turns down the volume and says, "Alex, sorry I had to leave for a minute. You were saying?"

Alex, now pretty much fully cognizant of his surroundings, comments, "Okay, I know I'm in a hospital, but I'm confused. Why was Andrew here? I thought he hit his head and died. What happened?"

Sonja says, "Alex, you don't remember, do you? You took a nap on the afternoon of the Fourth of July before everybody came over for the BBQ and fireworks and you never woke up, until now. It's been three days. You don't remember putting the white blanket on your chest and falling asleep? You wanted to read some verses in the

355

Bible that you brought down from the attic, but for some reason, you couldn't open it up. You made a comment about how your Bible is so old and is falling apart and how you wanted a new one, but when you held the Bible with the white cover, you got this feeling that you should wait and not get a new one now. You got tired and took a nap instead.

"After about three hours, I tried to wake you, but you wouldn't wake up. I tried yelling at you and shaking you and everything. I rattled and shook you so much that you fell to the floor. You still didn't wake up. You were lifeless. So, I ended up calling an ambulance, and that's how you got here. You were in a coma and then after the doctors ran some tests they said you were brain-dead. If they had not hooked you up to life support when you got here, you would have died on the spot.

"You've not had any brain activity since they brought you here three days ago. The doctors and tests concluded that there was no hope for you to recover. But they have absolutely no idea what happened and why you went into a coma and wouldn't wake up. They ran more tests and declared you were brain-dead. And they have no idea how you went into that condition or how you came out of it."

Sonja then briefly stops and looks at Alex's eyes and says, "Your eyes are very glassy or bloodshot or something. They don't look right."

Alex then asks, "Well, have I had my eyes closed for three days? Is this the first time I have opened my eyes since Sunday?"

"Yes."

Alex then asks Sonja about their house and where she's living. Sonja is confused. "What on Earth are you talking about? I've been living at our house of course. It sure has been so lonely there without you. But, actually I've been here in this room with you for most of that time and have not been home much. Why are you asking me where I've been living?"

"What about the explosion and fire?"

"What are you talking about? There wasn't any explosion and fire."

Alex looks at her in disbelief and adamantly states, "Our house exploded and burnt down to the ground in a horrendous fire. The kids were trapped inside."

"No, it didn't. Alex, you've been dreaming. Everything is fine, everything is okay."

Alex slumps back in his bed. "Wow, wow, wow, wow. Now I know I'm dreaming."

Sonja emphatically exclaims, "I told you that you were dreaming. I'm so glad you believe me now. I think you were having a nightmare."

"No, no, you don't understand. I am dreaming now. I was actually living a real nightmare, and now I'm dreaming. You got it backwards."

Alex then continues, "So I suppose that you're also going to tell me that Julie and Garrett were never kidnapped and the bomb never went off? And that Andrew never fell down the stairs and smashed his head and never went to the hospital?"

"What on Earth are you talking about? I am starting to think you're delusional."

Alex, now experiencing pure mundane pleasure for the first time in three days, lies down fully, stretches, smiles, and says, "I'm not believing any of this. I really am dreaming right now. Lord, how can I thank you? Please don't let me wake up from this dream. Please."

Sonja now is confused herself. Alex thinks he's dreaming and that everything he's telling her really happened, at least in his mind. But the doctor told her that he couldn't have dreamed anything because he had no brain waves for three days. She's sure Alex was dreaming and had a nightmare, but she's most uncomfortable because she doesn't understand, and he's so adamant about what he's saying.

Alex then explains, "Sonja, it was so real. Real as can be. Our house exploded in fire, and I died and went to hell and heaven and then was going back to hell again. While I was going back and forth, I could see you and everything that happened here. It was real. It really was. The vision I had of you all was real time. You've got to believe me. I know for sure everything I said really happened.

"It turned into a reality of horror, and I couldn't take it anymore, especially being sent back to hell. So, I asked God if I could go into a dream because I couldn't die again since I already did. Apparently, He had mercy on me and now He's letting me dream this."

"Alex, you never died. You have been hooked up to life support this whole time and you have been alive this entire time. You probably simply dreamed all of that."

Alex insists what he experienced was absolutely real and now he is dreaming. "I don't want to wake up from this dream because if I did, I'd be going straight back to hell."

"Well, if that's the case and if you think you are dreaming now, then tell me if *this* is a dream?"

She then practically climbs on top of him and gives him an extended kiss that lasts a good half minute.

Alex closes his eyes and then opens them again and looks at Sonja. He gives her the loving smile that she so desperately wanted to see and says, "I am so confused. But it was so real. I can explain to you exactly everything that happened to me. I saw everything that happened to you and our family here while I was away. It was so realistic. I know it was real and it actually happened. It really did.

"I know exactly what happened to you when I was there. I know exactly what happened to Julie and Garret and the kids. I know what happened to Andrew and Alana and their kids. Everything really did happen. It was so real. I could see it plain as day. I want to explain everything to you. I can tell you everything in complete detail. I could see just about everything on Earth and what you were all doing. You must believe me."

Alex then looks over and sees the white blanket folded up and the white Bible sitting on top of it sitting on a table. Sonja sees him eyeing it and says, "We were told to bring those here. They wanted to test them for allergens or anything that may have caused your coma and why you had no brain activity, since they were on your chest when you took your nap."

"They what? What did they do to them?"

"Don't worry, they're fine. You can take them back home when they release you."

"Did they find anything?"

"No. They have absolutely no idea. It's a mystery to everybody."

"So, you're telling me that there was no explosion, no fire, no kidnapping, no terrorists, no bombs, Andrew never hurt his head, and that Andrew never died, right?"

Sonja then hangs her head down and mutters, "Well, not exactly."

"What do you mean?"

"Well, although most of what you said you saw didn't happen, some of it did. There's a global crisis involving Islamic terrorists who have threatened to blow up America and unleash a highly deadly and contagious disease. They've invaded the US and claim they've planted nuclear and other bombs across the country. They say they will explode at midnight in three days from tomorrow. They say one has been or will be placed at a special location that is so unique that it alone could render the entire country uninhabitable for years."

Alex gets all big-eyed and says to Sonja, "Go on."

"There's also a lot of news that this all just might be the beginning of the Apocalypse and the end of the world. Every major news source is reporting that there's no way to stop it and that it's definitely going to happen. Our world's going to end in three days." She starts to cry.

Alex then grasps her hand and says, "Well, I do remember some of that from before I took my nap, and I could see some of that when I was awake between hell and heaven. I'm aware of the bomb crisis and the biological weapon threats. I sure wish that wasn't true. How can you say that everything else that I said didn't happen but this is still going on?"

Alex sits back and contemplates everything.

Alex then thinks of the Arab and Officer Musty and asks about them.

"We haven't seen either the old white van or the Arab since before you took your nap."

"Good. At least we don't need to worry about him anymore. I'm glad he's gone. What about Officer Musty?"

"Well, as a matter of fact, we haven't seen him either. I think that Officer Musty may have irritated the Arab with his increased patrols and maybe drove him away."

"That is such good news! I guess then that we never had our dinner or the fireworks display that night?"

"No, we didn't. We took you to the hospital and never did have our dinner. But the neighbors still had the fireworks display even though we weren't there. We were here at the hospital with you instead.

"Alex, there's something else I want to tell you, but if you could see everything, you should already know this."

"What? Sonja, I meant to say that I could see just about everything that happened here, but not everything. There are some things that I could see and some things that I couldn't see."

"I want to let you know that Andrew is a believer now."

Alex perks up in bed and stares at Sonja, waiting for her to continue.

Sonja proceeds to tell Alex about Ammen and that Andrew believes that he's for real. She tells Alex that Andrew is following Ammen and appears to be obsessed with him.

"You mean that he's actually worshipping him?"

"I think so. I think he's anxious to talk to you about him. He thinks that you will be so proud of him. He thinks Ammen is the Second Coming and was meant to be because of the story in the book of Revelation. He actually read a little about this the other day. It was a big surprise to me.

"In fact, after the life support system was shut down, you woke up within seconds after Andrew said a short prayer to Ammen. He said, 'May Ammen always be with you,' and then you woke up. So he may be thinking that it was his prayer to Ammen that made you wake up. If he was not convinced before, he probably is now."

Alex looks dazed, closes his eyes again, and is quiet for a little awhile. He's thinking about so many things. He then opens them. "Sonja, can you bring me a glass of water? I could really use that now."

After another minute of silence, Alex says, "I think I'm ready to leave and go home now, but I'm afraid to. I might wake up. I cannot wake up from this dream." Then very emotionally, he cries, "I really don't want to go back to hell. You would not believe just how absolutely terrifying it is!"

"So you remember going to hell and heaven?"

"I remember going to both places, and I remember just how terrifying hell was, but I don't remember anything specific about heaven. I only remember it is an absolute paradise, but I don't remember anything else about it. But I was definitely there!"

Sonja looks at Alex as if she is agreeing with him in order to comfort him. "Okay. Let me go talk with the doctor, and I'll be right back."

Sonja leaves the room and finds his doctor just now returning to the nurses' station after making his rounds. She gives him an update on how Alex is doing.

He scratches his head and says, "Boy, I just don't know what to tell you. So, Alex is telling you that he went to hell and heaven and that he could see just about everything that was happening here when he was out like a light, but they never happened, huh? Is he really insistent about all of this? Sonja, he could not have dreamed any of that. I told you that he didn't have any brave waves whatsoever for three days. None. There's no way he dreamed any of that."

He scratches his head again and repeats himself, "I just don't know what to say. There's no explanation for it. Clinically, there's no way he could have dreamed any of that. I told you he didn't have any brain waves whatsoever. He was totally brain-dead.

"I think it's best that he rests here through the evening and that we continue to monitor him. He needs to go to sleep here so we can make sure he wakes up and the same thing doesn't happen again before we can release him. We'll continue the monitors for tonight. Perhaps we can release him tomorrow morning but not now. He should try to eat something now. I'll have a nurse discuss with him some light things on the menu, and he can choose whatever he wants. I'll also have the nurse remove his catheter."

In the meantime, after Sonja leaves the room, Alex sits up again and dangles his feet on the side of the bed. He looks out the window and gazes outside over the parking lot. His head is spinning with all sorts of thoughts, and he's desperately trying to reconcile everything. "What's going on?" he asks himself.

In looking out over the parking lot from his window, he notices that the parking lot is pretty much full of cars except for the last several rows in the back. There on the very last row, sitting all by itself in the parking lot under a tree, is the old white van.

Alex knows that it's the Arab. It's unmistakable. He wonders why the Arab was gone for the last three days but now is back after he's awakened, or after he entered his dream, whichever the case may be.

Chapter 52

Sonja returns to the room with a pitcher of water and a large cup. The nurse follows a few minutes later and discusses with Alex what he can eat. She tells Alex that if he can keep the food down and if he has a bowel movement, they will probably release him in the morning. That's assuming that his vital signs are still okay and he wakes up from being asleep overnight.

He reluctantly agrees. But actually, he's somewhat relieved that he can stay another night. Although he's very anxious to go home, he's still apprehensive that any radical changes to his routine just might trigger him to wake up from what he perceives to be a dream. He doesn't want that at any cost.

Alex tries to sits up again and turns around to reach the TV remote and briefly gets tangled up in his IV tubing and catheter. He asks the nurse if she can remove his catheter, and she removes it. Sonja helps him get comfortable, grabs the remote, and gives it to him. He turns up the volume.

Although the TV has been on, Sonja had turned the volume down and he had not paid much attention to it. But now he wants to find out what's going on in the world. He's very anxious to learn everything that he can about the status of the world crisis even though he's already somewhat aware of it.

Alex channel-surfs for a few minutes and finally settles on a major news network channel. He times it just right as there is a national emergency broadcast signal signaling a major development in the crisis.

The news reporter comes on to say that to declare the following broadcast to be extremely bleak would be the understatement of all time. The broadcast is a summary status of the current conditions based on announcements from the terrorists, from governmental intelligence sources, and from media reporting services.

This is exactly what Alex wants to hear. It's a complete up to date summary and status of all events as they currently stand. This will bring him up to date on everything.

The news broadcast reports the following facts:

"The terrorists are commonly known as ISA or the Islamic State of America and consist of a very well-organized and well-funded Jihadist group, which has secretly been planning their plot to destroy America ever since 9/11. The leader of the terrorists group responsible appears to be Muhannad Eblis Qadir, also known as Muhammad. He represents ISIS, affiliated with ISA, however he has ties to several extremist groups. He advances Jihadism to the worst degree and has even been referred to as the new caliph. It's thought that he operates out of a remote region of Syria or Iran, but this is not certain. It's evident that he oversees ISA, which operates out of the United States.

"They originally claimed to have strategically planted twenty bombs across the United States however government intelligence believes it's likely more like thirty to forty bombs. They claim to have planted these in major metropolitan areas across the United States at strategic locations. Some are known to be bona fide nuclear devices, but it is not known how many. Some nonnuclear bombs are suspected to have been planted or will be planted at major electrical energy distribution facilities, water supply systems, and other critical infrastructure.

"They claim that one bomb in particular in a secret location can destroy the entire country, if not the entire globe, making it uninhabitable as a result of its unique and strategic location.

"The terrorists have set timers so that all will explode at the same time at midnight three days from tomorrow. The reason why they're setting them to explode all at the same time so that they will have enough time to coordinate everything and achieve the highest glory and praise to Allah.

"It's believed that the nuclear bombs include some of unprecedented magnitude as well as some dirty bombs. It's believed that some may potentially be nuclear bombs larger than any nuclear bomb ever known to be developed. There are also many nonnuclear bombs as well strategically placed at crucial infrastructure locations.

"Previously one had been located in Washington DC. It was scheduled to have been detonated by now; however, the terrorists have reset the timer remotely to postpone its blast to be the same time as all of the other bombs.

"The bomb has a timer that can't be accessed. The bomb and timer are encased in an impenetrable glass case that is secured to the floor by bolts that can't be detached or tampered with. The bomb has sensors both inside and outside the case. There are sensors running along the bolts. Any contact with the case or bomb will set it off automatically. The bomb is 100 percent tamperproof. There is no way anyone can stop the bomb from exploding and it cannot be removed. The timer can be remotely accessed only by the terrorists with access codes only known to them.

"It's is believed that a terrorist leader enters a code only known to him periodically and that if this code is not entered timely on a regular basis, the bomb will automatically be detonated. Therefore even if the terrorist was captured or killed, the bomb will still explode.

"Authorities in Washington DC have studied the bomb for several days now and cannot figure out what to do. They are afraid to get very close to it because of the sensors all around it.

"Today, additional similar bombs with timers and sensors have been located in New York, Chicago, Dallas Fort Worth, and Los Angeles. It has been confirmed that at least one of these is a nuclear device. The authorities don't understand where and how the terrorists were able to acquire the materials to build the bombs; however, they've confirmed that the bombs are real and have real timers and remote detonation devices attached. They are fairly sure the sensors are active; however, there is no way to find out without setting off the bomb. There is no way to get close to the bombs because of the sensors, and there is no way they can be defused or moved.

"It's apparent that the terrorists have been working on this project ever since 9/11. At least one person has been arrested and interrogated in connection with the crisis. This person has provided some information regarding the development of the bombs. He has contacts at various nuclear research centers in the United States and abroad, has ties to the Russian government, and he's verified much of the information. The information is credible. This investigation is still in progress.

"In addition, the terrorists claim they have clinically produced a highly contagious and deadly disease that they plan to spread across America. ISA has sent samples to the CDC so that America will believe what the terrorists have claimed about it. The CDC has received the samples and is currently testing them to determine what it is. There was some initial speculation that it might be a mutated form of Ebola or perhaps the primary pneumonic plague. Testing is currently under way; however, the terrorists have insisted that it's both airborne and waterborne. It might very well be some other highly contagious and deadly disease not yet identified.

"There are additional investigations in progress and some of these focus on accusations and some evidence that the executive branch of the government previously had some involvement in the plot. This is a highly contested and obviously a fragile subject matter and will be addressed in a separate report.

"The terrorists have also hacked into and invaded the cyber space of America and have the ability to disrupt or take control over various telecommunications and the electric grid. They have already carried out some anti-cyber activities and have broadcast their own programs on some channels both through satellite and cable. There have already been some isolated instances of this in some major cities. They've infiltrated and hacked into various websites on the Internet in a major way.

"The crisis now has escalated to a possible global calamity. Russia, China, parts of Western Europe, and other countries with nuclear capabilities now are firmly entrenched in the matter. This is a very complicated set of affairs involving economics, power, and politics. However, each of these countries has issues with the others, and it's speculated that any nuclear bomb explosion anywhere could possibly result in an immediate global thermal nuclear war.

"All countries are on edge and each has warned of a first strike. It's feared that any launch of a nuclear weapon by anybody could result in every country immediately launching its own arsenal within seconds. This could result in worldwide destruction within minutes.

"Obviously, the Middle East countries and the terrorists have not been party to the NPT and have no reason to negotiate whatsoever. ISA is operating without a national sovereignty. ISA has been adamant that there will be no negotiation and that all bombs will explode no matter what. There is absolutely nothing that can be done to prevent it. It is their intention to destroy the United States and the Western world.

"The terrorists have warned that any country who supports the United States will suffer the same wrath that is being imposed on them. To date, the United Kingdom has announced formal support and it is believed that France and perhaps other countries may also. It is noted, however, that there are some extreme populations of Muslims in isolated communities in various European countries that complicate matters. Both England and France have nuclear capability.

"But regardless if any country launches or detonates a nuclear device anywhere, those planted in the United States are designed to explode. They will still be detonated even after the United States or another country strikes first. No matter what happens, the nuclear bombs and the other bombs in the United States will explode at midnight in three days. The US government has strongly hinted that if ISA does not back down or as soon as it detonates just one nuclear device, it may launch its nuclear arsenal against specified targets that it believes is responsible. This would inevitably result in a global nuclear catastrophe.

"Muhammad has stated that he will announce the locations of additional bombs by this evening. This announcement is expected shortly.

"In the meantime, there is sheer chaos everywhere. People in every major city are trying to evacuate the cities and metropolitan areas and this is resulting in massive traffic jams, looting, and utter panic in the streets. Crime has escalated to a level never seen before anywhere.

"Local police and other authorities in many cities have abandoned their duties to be with their families and to evacuate themselves, leaving no security force in place in many areas.

"People are attempting to flock to rural and remote areas such as the mountains to escape. When the masses of people reach these areas, there's no place for them to go. There's no food, no lodging, no facilities, and no water. In addition, they're running out of gas and many are stranded.

"Rural folk live there for a reason and are taking up arms to protect themselves. They don't want hundreds of thousands or even millions of people from the urban areas storming their land. There have been reports of numerous shootings and lootings.

"Others are attempting to escape to safer countries such as those in South America, Australia, Canada and other places if they can find a way to get there. These countries are denying entry and want no part of the conflict. However, they're nevertheless finding themselves thrust into it anyway against their will.

"However, most commercial airports and other modes of mass transportation have been shut down and are no longer operating in the United States and in many places in Western Europe.

"On the economic front, the US economy has come to a halt and is upon complete financial collapse. The economy of other countries is not far behind. The dollar has been significantly devalued, numerous commercial enterprises are no longer accepting cash or credit cards, and the stock markets have lost well over 30 percent of their value. The exchanges have been closed to prevent further decline. The price of gold and silver is skyrocketing, and the worldwide currency standard is in a state of flux. Many businesses have closed and are boarded up. Practically all gas stations have closed everywhere.

"It appears that it's been the intention of the terrorists to create total and utter chaos and panic in America and Western Europe prior to detonating the bombs and releasing the disease. They've certainly succeeded in doing this. There is absolute pandemonium everywhere, in every major city, and in many lesser cities throughout the United States.

"In this regard, many believe this is the beginning of the Apocalypse foretold in the book of Revelation. There is much dispute whether the current events match the prophecies, and there is much confusion in the world regarding this. However, the news of the possible end of the world is enough to influence many that this is the case. This includes prominent theologians, scientists, government officials, and other authorities. It is the hot topic in all corners of the world.

"As a result, some people have emerged claiming to be the Second Coming of Christ or some other savior in an effort to gain a personal following and glory. Most of these are fanatics and are nothing more than imposters, charlatans, and frauds.

"However, one person from the Middle East has appeared to be credible enough to have gained an enormous following that is thought to exceed well over a hundred million people and climbing rapidly. His name is Evedothlid Ammenofi. He goes by Ammen.

"He is almost always accompanied by a woman, thought perhaps to be his mother. He claims that he is of the sacred blood and will be accompanied by two other angels to see him through the glory but he claims that he has returned as the last angel of the father. He claims that those who follow him will have everlasting life and those who do not believe he is who he says he is will suffer for eternity.

"It is unknown who the woman is and if she is one of the other angels to whom Ammen refers. It is unknown whether Ammen is the return of Jesus Christ. Although some believe he is not, an astounding and significantly increasing number of people do. An astonishing number of people believe he is for real, including many from the clergy of various Christian denominations.

"Authorities do not know much about him and know nothing about the woman. He and his followers have provided videos and other literature about him. He claims to be the Second Coming. Many people including some prominent members of the cloth believe it is possible he could be the Second Coming of Jesus Christ. He has agreed to a live interview tomorrow. Because of the immense following he has, many people all over the world are taking him seriously. It is believed that the live interview with him scheduled for tomorrow will set a record for the number of viewers watching any televised programming ever."

Alex's eyes and ears have been deeply focused on the TV during the entire broadcast. He takes several deep breaths. Sonja comes over and kisses him and starts sobbing, "My Alex, the world is going to come to an end. It really is. Why? Why? Why?"

Alex squeezes her hand back and a tear runs down his cheek as well. At the opportune time, Alex's meal arrives.

After a few minutes of commercials, the broadcast resumes. "We now have received a list from ISA of some of the additional cities where the bombs have been placed. The list includes some specific locations and some unspecified locations within a hundred square miles of a target area. The list is extensive and covers every corner of the United States and includes all of the cities with the largest metropolitan areas in America.

"But one bomb listed is said to be a nuclear device and is located at an undisclosed prominent national park or historic landmark that the terrorists claim by itself could obliterate more than two thirds of the country, making it uninhabitable, and perhaps the entire world, but nobody knows anything more about this at this time. It's anybody's guess where this might be."

Alex exclaims "What's with this super bomb at a national park or historical landmark? What's with that? How can it be possible that one bomb alone could render the entire world uninhabitable simply as result of where it's located? Where would this place be? How can the uniqueness of one location impact the entire globe? Just how can it?

"And the others, well, is this some sort of joke? That is everywhere that was originally expected anyway. No real news here. And what's with this 'within one hundred square miles'? The terrorists are simply playing with us and mocking us. I guess if anyone has evacuated fifty to a hundred miles away, now they will need to go another one hundred miles to get further away. The way the bombs are dispersed, there'll hardly be any safe place left."

Although it was anticipated that his city would be on the list, confirmation of it now just intensifies his and Sonja's perception of the magnitude of the crisis. It hits home hard.

Just as the newscast ends, another nurse comes in the room and tells Alex and Sonja that they need to move Alex to another room. His room is needed for another patient, and Alex no longer needs life support. So they're going to move him to a regular patient room downstairs. The nurse then comments that a nurse's aide named John will be here soon and will help move Alex and his belongings to the new room.

Sonja excuses herself from the room and goes out to the nurse's station to discuss something and then returns after a few minutes. "Where am I going?" asks Alex.

Sonja responds, "Room 316. I want to make sure that you wake up this time. Remember I told you the last time you took a nap, you didn't wake up and that's how you got here. In your new room there's a larger window and there'll be more light. There's even a cross on the wall in that room. I know you'll wake up for sure there after you go to sleep tonight. I won't have to worry about it. She smiles at Alex and blows him a kiss.

But Alex says, "What do you mean wake up there? You don't understand. I don't want to wake up anywhere. I want to continue dreaming where I am now. If I wake up, I'll be going back to hell!"

About a half hour later, nurse assistant John arrives and helps Alex and Sonja get settled in room 316. Alex turns on the TV, and they resume watching it.

After more of the same on TV, Sonja starts to get tired. "Alex, I think I'll stay the night with you again if that's okay. I don't want to go home without you."

"That's fine and I'd like that very much. But I don't plan to sleep. I think I'll stay awake all night."

Alex is afraid that if he goes to sleep, he'll wake up back in the other reality world of hell. Something comes over Sonja and she's able to comfort him. "I'll be here with you."

A different nurse then comes in to take his vitals and refreshes his water. She offers a muffin to both Alex and Sonja that she accepts but Alex does not. She then takes out a vial from her pocket and injects the contents into his IV, turns around quickly, and turns off the lights on her way out.

Alex says to Sonja. "That's strange. Doesn't a new nurse or one on a change of shift usually introduce herself? She didn't seem too friendly, did she? She didn't say a word and didn't even smile or anything."

It's dark now, and Alex looks out the window. He's on the same side of the hospital and can still see the parking lot. It's been a long time since he last looked out there. Most cars have left for the day. However, under the parking lot lights, he can see that the old white van is still parked in the back. It hasn't moved.

"Sonja, do you know the old white van is back again? I saw it earlier in the parking lot in the back row, and it's still there now."

"Really? Are you sure it's the same white van with the Arab?"

"I'm pretty sure it is."

"Well, there's no way I'm going home with that van out there. That settles it. I'm definitely staying here with you tonight."

Sonja shifts the couch in the room into a bed, just like she's done the previous nights. She then pulls out her smartphone and starts making phone calls to let everyone know that Alex is doing just fine, although she also tells them he thinks he's still dreaming and insists that what he experienced the last three days was real. She first calls Julie and Garrett and then Alana and Andrew.

Sonja tries to sleep on the couch, but Alex continues to watch TV. He has found several channels of interest. He looks at his Bible sitting on top of the blanket and reaches for it to read some verses which he often does before going to bed. However, he can't open it. For some reason, it's still locked as if the pages are all stuck together.

Sonja, half-awake, observes this and says, "Alex, if I knew you were going to wake up, I would have brought your Bible from home.

But if you remember, it's so old it's coming apart. I'd be afraid to take it anywhere. I wouldn't want any pages to fall out."

"That's okay. I still want to get a new one sometime. I would really like one with a white cover, just like this one, but every time I hold this Bible and think of getting a new one, for some strange reason, I get this very feeling that I shouldn't and that I should wait. I wish I knew why I keep getting this strange feeling."

So instead of struggling with trying to open the Bible any more, Alex decides to learn more about Ammen and continues to watch TV instead.

He finds a channel that is showing a repeat of an earlier video of Muhammad. He then finds a repeat of an earlier video of Ammen and watches this for a few minutes.

Alex is astounded to find that there is a striking resemblance between Ammen and Jesus Christ based on the usual depiction of Jesus found everywhere in paintings and pictures. It's as if they are one and the same. He certainly looks like he could be Jesus, or perhaps he could be related to Him. He even teaches like Jesus did. He finds the appearance of the woman at his side in the video very comforting. He suspects she may be his mother or maybe his mother angel.

Alex then thinks of Andrew and what Sonja had told him. Even though Alex isn't convinced yet that Ammen is for real, for some reason Alex finds himself proud that Andrew has taken an interest in him. At least he's finally making an effort to find some religion, he thinks, regardless whether Ammen is for real or not. But for some unknown reason, he's drawn to Ammen and the woman in the video as well. They appear very familiar to him, as if he saw them in a vision somewhere, but he doesn't know where. Something tells him just maybe he just might be for real.

Alex then remembers the nurse put something in his IV, but he forgot to ask her what it was. He feels funny and is somewhat apprehensive about this and wonders what it is. Before long, Alex finds himself wanting to go to asleep. He is tired and can hardly fight staying awake any longer, not even with the TV still on. What's making him suddenly so tired? He struggles to try to stay awake.

Sonja suddenly opens her eyes and sees that Alex appears to be sleeping. Suddenly, she's apprehensive and becomes scared that Alex perhaps just may not wake up again. She thinks, "Just maybe he was right. Did he really truly experience what he said he did? Did he really go to hell and heaven? He said he did. He was so insistent that everything he said was real. And the doctor said there's no way he could have been dreaming because he was brain-dead. So, what then really happened?"

She decides to check on Alex but she can't move. She tries to say something to him but she can't talk. She's extremely tired. She prays and then falls sound asleep. The last thoughts she has before entering her own dream world is what happens when Alex goes to asleep and what if Alex doesn't wake up again? She wonders, "Will he wake up or not?"

Chapter 53

It's relaxing to simply just lie in bed where I can feel the freshness of the sheets, smell the air, and listen to voices and other sounds around me. I have control of my body again, and I no longer need to deal with all the uncertainties of the unknown, and experience the reality of the void. My eyes are closed, but I'm half awake and half asleep. I can hear the TV, but it's only background noise now.

I'm tired, but I'm afraid to go to sleep. I really don't want to reenter the nightmarish reality of hell. If I wake up from being here, I think there's a good possibility that I'll go back there.

There's so much for me to think about now. I find myself thinking of a myriad of things. My mind is spinning from all the thoughts I have. I know my experiences in hell and heaven were real. I know what I saw happen on Earth while I was traveling between hell and heaven really happened. But my being here in the hospital room is a reality also. But Sonja tells me that none of what I saw happen on Earth really happened except for the crisis involving the terrorists and Ammen.

I think of my family and want to see them. I think of Andrew. I look forward to talking with him about Ammen. It's so ironic that for over thirty years I've tried to raise him to be a Christian and I failed, and now he's probably going to try to convert me into believing in Ammen. Oh, how times have changed. How the tables have turned. Is Ammen for real or not? Is he really the Second Coming, perhaps with a different name?

I'm coming to terms with the very real crisis and the realization of what now looks like an inevitable end of time. I'll need to make a decision myself on whether to follow Ammen or not. And I know my family will be heavily influenced by my decision.

I think about my own faith and what I've believed in for over sixty years. I then think of my experience in hell and my visit to heaven. I don't want to abandon my belief in Jesus Christ. Not after sixty years. But it's tempting because of my experience in hell and feeling that I was abandoned the last time I was in the void. But I'll try my best to continue it.

But what if Ammen is for real? What would be the consequences if one did not follow him instead? Is he really the Second Coming of Jesus? Is this really the beginning of the end of the world? Can I worship both? I would think I can if they are one and the same. I need to find out. But what If I can't? What if I'm required to believe Ammen is the return of Jesus to be saved and I simply can't have faith in Jesus of the past anymore without also believing he has now returned?

The longer I dream about being in the hospital room the more my memories of being in hell and heaven start to fade away. But I remember my trip to the mirror and my life being evaluated. I remember going to hell and remembering just how awfully frightening and horrific it was. I remember then going to heaven and remember that it was more than a paradise. But I cannot remember anything else about heaven. The details are no longer a memory and pretty much have vanished. But I know I was there. I just cannot remember any details, but I wish I could.

The more I try to think about my travel to hell and heaven the more that journey starts to fade away into obscurity, and the more real my current experience in the hospital room becomes. But at the same time for some unknown reason, I find myself missing the experience in the void and my visits to hell and heaven. I wish I knew why. For some bizarre reason that I don't understand, going back to the unknown and hell beckons me like an open invitation. But at the same time I don't want to go back.

I'm starting to forget that experience and relate more to the experience of being back on Earth. I find myself confused as to which is real and which is not. I wonder if it's possible that one is a dream and one is not, but now I'm not sure which is which. I was confident at first, but now I'm not so sure. The more I think of these things, the more tired I become.

Now I'm very tired and although I'm trying hard to stay awake in the reverie of being back on Earth, I finally succumb to my weariness and exhaustion. I no longer hear the TV in the background. I no longer can feel the sheets or myself in bed. I lose contact with being in the hospital room and no longer sense I'm there. I've fallen asleep and I've awakened again in the void.

The void is exactly as I left it, but my emotions now are different. When I left and immediately prior to opening my eyes in the hospital room I was so scared I was pleading with God to save me from the nightmare reality of having being sent back to hell. Now I'm no longer terrified although I'm somewhat apprehensive. For some reason I feel a sense of confidence.

Again, I can see the lights of hell and heaven. The light of hell is much larger and getting larger as I float towards it. I know that I'm headed in that direction and again I have no control over my body. But the travel there, although previously was accelerating, now is taking longer, and I find myself floating slower and slower.

I decide to think back to what's happening on Earth and again I can see my family and know exactly what they're doing. I can see Sonja in the hospital room. She's looking at me, but for some reason she can't move or talk with me. I wonder why. I feel sorry for her. I try to look at myself in the hospital room, but for some reason, I can't see myself there. I can see everyone else but not me.

I then remember the spirit who was with me before, and I look up to see if it's still there. It's gone. I'm all alone again. I don't know where it went and I don't know if it will return. Again I ask myself, why does it continue to leave me? Where does it go? Why?

After drifting for quite a long time, I start to wish I was back on Earth. I'm so lonely, and I miss Sonja, especially being able to see her looking at me back in the hospital room. She's so worried about me.

I can see her lying there just looking at me. She is truly an angel. She has been an angel to me for all of these years.

There is something very special about her as her mystique has captured me from the day I met her and was enhanced the day we got married. That mystique has always been there and now it has intensified greatly. It grows every day. I think about her and get a feeling that God put her on Earth for a special purpose. I am so happy that she's my wife and I want to be with her.

Even though this time I'm not terrified like I was the first time, nevertheless I again pray to God that I may re-enter my life on Earth again. I want to go back regardless whether it be a dream or in real life. "Please, just send me back there. I want to be with Sonja."

I continue to float in the void of nothingness. No sense of time. No sights. No sounds. Not anything. Even though I'm lonely and think I know where I'm going, for some strange reason I find the solitude comforting. Everything is deathly quiet and still.

But suddenly, I realize the gates of hell now are much closer, and now I find myself floating toward it an increasingly faster pace. I start to become afraid again, and the terror overrides the initial confidence I had when I reentered the void. I'm almost at the gates of hell and can see Cerberus. Quickly, I realize what is really happening to me, and when I see it, I become immediately terrified. I could not be any more horrified.

Within seconds I will be passing Cerberus and entering the cavern. This all came up on me so fast. I wonder what chamber, level, and room I will go to this time. What's going to happen? Will I be here forever in eternity this time? The spirit is no longer with me. And now, I'm absolutely terrified again.

I enter the cavern and am immediately hurled towards a room of torture and torment. I again wonder what sort of room this will be and what kind of horrendous pain I'll encounter. And just as I enter the room a bright light sweeps over me, and I'm suddenly frightened even more by a most terrifying noise that interrupts the solitude.

Chapter 54

Alex is startled out of his slumber by the clanging of the water glass, pitcher and other things on the tray beside his bed. The morning nurse has taken over from the nightshift nurse and has entered the room. She's straightening the items on the tray, refreshing the water in the pitcher, and making all sorts of noise. She has also turned on the overhead light which has Alex squinting to see as he opens his eyes.

It's her intention to wake up Alex by making the noise and turning on the light. Seeing that she's accomplished this, in a most cheerful and bubbly voice she says, "Good morning, Alex. Time to rise and shine." She proceeds to introduce herself, takes Alex's vitals, and goes through her morning routine.

"What a rude but at the same time most pleasant awakening" Alex thinks as he tries to gather his thoughts. He then realizes that the night nurse may have given him something to help him sleep; but that was okay, because whatever it was, it worked for him.

In the meantime, Sonja has awakened and can move freely now. "Good morning. Alex, did you sleep well?"

By now, Alex has fully awakened. He sits there in deep contemplation. He can't believe that he's back in the hospital room. It's almost as if he actually willed himself to be there. He thinks long and hard, "Did I just reenter my dream of being in the hospital room, or did I simply wake up to a new reality? Or am I dreaming everything and none of what's happening is real?"

Then he suddenly realizes for the first time in four days that he needs to go to the bathroom. He no longer has the catheter, so now he's on his own. After a good night's sleep, it's time to go. As a result, that prompts him to think just maybe he's in real time now and being in the hospital room is not a dream.

He acknowledges Sonja, blows her a kiss, and then tells the nurse. The nurse says, "Okay, I can help you some," as she goes to the other side of the bed to wheel the IV pole over. As she does, she gives Alex the breakfast menu and tells him he can order whatever he would like.

By now, Alex wants to go home and figures he can risk it. Because he made it through the night and still woke up here, he assumes he can go home and wake up when he goes to sleep there. If he can go to sleep and wake up in the hospital, then he should be okay now to go home without fear of going back to hell against his will.

But he remembers that one of the conditions for him to be released is that he needs to have a bowel movement. So, without even looking at the menu, he tells the nurse that he wants the greasiest bunch of fried eggs, bacon, and sausage that they have, along with a muffin coated in extra butter and biscuits and gravy if they have it. He also would like to have an extra-large glass of prune juice.

The nurse laughs and tells Alex, "I know why you want all that, but I can give you a little something to help the process along if you want."

Alex says, "That's okay, but I'll try this first."

Alex swings his legs around to get into a sitting position and lets his legs dangle inches off the floor. The bathroom is only a few feet away, and he should be able to make it. He tells the nurse he's ready.

But as soon as he puts his feet on the floor and tries to stand up, he feels excruciating pain in his leg, in his toes, and in his feet. He abruptly lifts them. He tries again, more slowly this time; and again as soon as they touch the floor, they still hurt, but not as much.

The nurse doesn't know why he hurts so much. "What's wrong?"

Alex has a pretty good idea why they hurt, but he's not about to mention it. The nurse removes his socks and lifts up his patient gown and examines his legs, feet, and his toes.

She has him turn his legs in various directions and inspects the soles of his feet and his toes closely. "Alex, your legs look good, your feet look good, and although I have seen better tootsies, they look fine to me too. I have no clue why they hurt so much. Maybe it's from being in bed for three days."

With her help and a wheelchair, Alex makes his way to the bathroom. A few minutes later after relieving himself, brushing his teeth, and freshening up a little, he motions for the nurse to help him get back into bed. As he does, he comments, "It feels so good to be back on Earth again." Pointing to the bathroom Alex says "That's something I didn't have to do in hell or heaven. Nobody there has to worry about those sorts of things."

The nurse looks at him totally perplexed. "What did you say?" she asks him. In the meantime, in a most supporting and loving look on her face Sonja merely smiles. It's as if she had her own dream and knows what's going on now with Alex.

Alex, waiting for his breakfast, looks outside the window and turns on the TV. Outside it now is a little past daybreak and the sun is poking through the clouds just over the horizon. What an amazing sunrise! Alex comments, "This may be the most beautiful sunrise that I've ever seen."

But as he looks out the window, there still in the back row of the parking lot sits the old white van. Alex strains to see if anyone and especially the Arab is in it, but he can't see that far. "So strange," he thinks. He begins to think perhaps it's merely a coincidence. Maybe it's just another white van and not the one that's been stalking him. Perhaps he's just getting paranoid for no reason. Before, he was so sure about it. Now he's trying to talk himself out of believing it. He'd like to get a view of the side of the van if he could. He can barely see the side of the van, but is sure looks the van that's been following him.

The TV comes on, and it's the morning newscast with a status of developments overnight. The news begins, and it's not good. It's not good at all.

Chapter 55

The news starts off with an update on the bomb crisis. Since the last report and during the night, more bombs were found in Miami, Houston, Atlanta, and San Francisco. One of these was confirmed to be a nuclear device, but that location has not been revealed. In addition, massive explosive devices were found attached to the understructure of the George Washington Bridge in New York and the Ambassador Bridge in Detroit.

These are in addition to the bombs found in Washington DC, New York, Dallas Fort Worth, and Los Angeles to date. Therefore in total, about ten of the thirty to forty bombs have been accounted for so far and at least three of these have been confirmed to be bona fide nuclear devices.

In each case of the nuclear and other bombs the facts are identical. All are wired with sensors and timers and the nuclear devices are in impenetrable glass cases and cannot be touched or they will explode. Many are affixed to foundations with large bolts that can't be removed and that are also wired with sensors. Some are in parked semi-tractor trailers or other trucks and wired with sensors so that the trailers or trucks cannot be moved without the bomb being detonated.

Every single one is tamper proof. Each of the bombs has a timer that is counting down from midnight three days from now in a common time zone. Nearly every bomb is located at a critical infrastructure site. The discovery of these bombs enhances the credibility of ISA and that there are probably numerous other bombs planted elsewhere in America as well. And there is more speculation that additional nuclear devices may have been planted. They simply haven't been found yet.

In the meantime, global tension has escalated considerably. The president and vice president of the United States have apparently gone into hiding and have not been heard from for some time. They are presumed to be in underground bunkers somewhere. Other top-ranking government officials have also disappeared.

Late last night, on behalf of the president, an ultimatum was issued to Muhammad that if he doesn't deactivate the bombs within twenty-four hours the United States will launch part of its nuclear arsenal into the heart of the ISIS-controlled areas of the Middle East. It has also accused Russia as well as Iran, North Korea, and Pakistan in aiding ISA and has hinted it will also launch missiles there if ISA does not back down.

But upon hearing this, Muhammad issued an announcement that the Islam world will live in the kingdom of Allah if their homeland is destroyed and that if the United States wants to do that, that is okay. Muhammad then went on to say the United States government is being hypocritical because such nuclear strikes will kill numerous innocent lives which it preaches it wants to protect. He will not deactivate the bombs in America under any circumstances. He doesn't care what the United States wants to do. The bombs in the United States will still be detonated regardless of what it does.

Muhammad then threatened to advance the timers on the bombs in the United States because America was bold enough to issue the ultimatum. It's obvious that Muhammad doesn't speak for all of the Middle Eastern countries, and he's only speaking on behalf of the extremists who belong to ISA. But, he then retracted his statement and said he'll activate all bombs immediately if there is any further hint of any kind of retaliation by the United States or any other country.

In the meantime, Russia and several other countries have again warned that they will not hesitate to launch their missiles within seconds if any launch of a nuclear warhead threatens their country, allies, or economic partners. The geopolitical circumstances and foreign policies of all countries with nuclear capability are very complicated and the foreign relations are very fragile.

Then when a country like North Korea or Pakistan, which may also have nuclear capability is introduced into the mix, it becomes quite tenuous and even more volatile. The geo-political circumstances and foreign relations of all of the countries is a complicated mess. No targets were specifically identified.

It's currently speculated that no country wants to initiate a global thermal nuclear war and that a lot of the talk is purely rhetoric without any real intentions. But the certain detonation of the bombs in the United States would probably trigger immediate retaliation, which will result in a global catastrophe. The stress level is at its maximum. The entire world now is at the highest alert level.

A second person has been apprehended as a suspect who was believed to be instrumental in the program to plant the bombs in the United States. He's an ISA operative and has confirmed certain CIA intelligence regarding the bombs and their locations, however has refused to discuss other related matters. He was a United States citizen and knows high-ranking people who have worked in the nuclear research programs for many years.

He is an Islamic extremist and Jihadist. But what is most important is that he also has significant ties to the Russian government. He also is known to have ties to the governments of Iran, North Korea, and Pakistan. It now is evident that Russia has secretly worked with ISA in developing and implementing their bomb program for well over a decade. And now it is becoming more likely that North Korea and perhaps Pakistan may have also supplied the nuclear bombs or materials.

In Miami, several vans with what appeared to be terrorists were seen leaving the scene where one of the bombs was planted, however they escaped. Authorities are looking for them but have not yet been able to find them.

Alex stretches and makes a comment that Muhammad is playing with the United States as if it's his toy. "What can anybody do?" Perhaps the only thing anybody can do is pray. For one thing, the finding of these additional bombs proves that ISA is not kidding and means business. It *is* going to happen."

Alex's breakfast arrives, and it's exactly what he ordered. He gobbles it down in no time and makes a comment how delicious it is. He then comments that he didn't get to eat at all in hell or heaven, which again draws a perplexed look from a nurse's aide who entered the room. After a short break, the news continues.

The self-proclaimed savior of the world, a man named Ammen, who now has amassed a following of well over a hundred million people worldwide, has agreed to a live interview. This will be broadcast this afternoon, scheduled to be at 3:00 PM. A major and well-known national network news reporter is in route on a jet to a secret location in the Middle East to interview him. Speculation is that the news reporter plans to grill him with tough questions to determine if he is truly the Second Coming and savior.

Ammen has declared that he will make a very important announcement during the interview that will address the survival of mankind and that people will need to make the decision of their lifetime by tonight in order to survive. Undoubtedly, just about everybody in the United States and probably the rest of the world will be watching him with great interest.

No one in the history of time in the entire world has amassed a following of anywhere near the size of what he has accomplished in such a short time. Not even Jesus Christ wherein it took years to amass the following that Ammen has done in a matter of a few days. Could he actually be the return of Christ?

Alex watches the news with a focus that puts him into a trance. In the meantime, Sonja has eaten some breakfast and now is on the phone giving the family an update on how Alex is doing.

After a few calls, Sonja perks up and looks at Alex. "Alex, Andrew wants to host a BBQ this afternoon. He and Julie want to celebrate your recovery. They want to make up for the fact that we didn't have the BBQ on the Fourth because we came here instead. Also, I think he wants to show off his new big wide-screen TV that he bought last week. He wants everybody to come over and watch the live interview with Ammen at his house. He wanted his new TV to be a surprise."

"Well, that would be nice assuming that they release me today and if I'm able to get around. I wonder how Andrew could afford the TV. I didn't think he and Alana had that kind of money. Also, I was wondering if he ever got his propane tank refilled. I remember him saying last week that he ran out. It would be just like him to forget. If he forgot, he's not going to find any place open today to get it. If he doesn't have a propane tank, then he'll not be able to BBQ."

"Actually, Alana mentioned that on the phone with me. She said that Andrew knew of a place close by where he can get a new propane tank and that he's going there later this morning to get it."

"Well, I wonder where that could be. I seriously doubt if he can find anyplace open that sells it. No place is open and he wouldn't be able to buy it anyway. I hope he's not going anywhere where he shouldn't be going."

A little while later, with the assistance of a wheelchair, Alex is in the bathroom doing what he hoped to do so that he can be released. He is surprised that his pain has subsided considerably, and he can now stand up and walk without much help. He's excited that he will be released to go home. But he thinks of the old white van in the parking lot and becomes apprehensive about it. "What does the Arab want with me? Is he out to get me or something I have for some reason?"

Chapter 56

Alex is anxious to be released from the hospital. He's no longer concerned about waking up from his dream. In fact, by now he's telling himself that he's no longer dreaming and instead has been returned to Earth. He wants to accept that the present is reality and not a dream. But he still firmly believes that he indeed visited hell and heaven, although now he can no longer remember any details of either place. But deep down inside, he still has the unsettling feeling that he's still dreaming and wonders, is it perhaps subconscious?

He can remember going into the void, the mirror, the evaluation of his life, that hell was the most awful gruesome, painful, and frightening experience ever. He can remember that heaven was the most wonderful experience that anyone could ever have. But he cannot remember any details or specifics of either.

A little while later, the nurse comes back in and tells him if his pain in his legs and feet has subsided and if he can walk, he can be released. Within a short time, he proves he can stand up and walks a few steps and hides the fact that he still has some pain. He can handle it as it seems to be improving considerably. The nurse tells him they will release him midmorning. She then lets him know that she'll get the paperwork ready. She comes over and removes his IV. He can go ahead and get dressed.

Sonja packs up some things that she brought, including the blanket and Bible. She helps Alex get dressed. Alex can stand up by himself and is surprised that the pain is not as bad as before. "Perhaps whatever it was, it's healing now," Sonja says.

A half hour later, the nurse comes in with the paperwork and Alex is on his way out, being pushed in the wheelchair by the nurse's aide. Sonja walks behind and has an armful of things to carry.

They pass down a hall and then another hall to go to the designated elevators. They pass by the telemetry unit, the radiology unit, and the pediatric unit. As they pass by the pediatric unit, there are people coming in and out of a large conference room with young children.

Sonja comments to Alex that the hospital is having several conferences and sessions today for parents and children with autism. She learned of the sessions while walking down the hall the day before. As they pass by the unit and conference room, this prompts Sonja to remark that one of the doctors thought Lizzy might have a rare condition that may have something to do with dyslexia and that may be the cause of why she doesn't talk much yet. She goes on to say that she wonders if there are sessions like this that may be helpful for children with speech problems at her age.

Alex acknowledges her and says it would be up to Julie and Garrett, but he agrees and she can surely mention it to them if she likes. After they get on and off of the elevator they head toward the outside door down the final hallway.

A woman and a child about six years of age approach from the opposite end of the hall. The woman fumbles with her purse for some reason and just as they pass each other she accidentally drops a pen in front of Alex's wheelchair from her purse.

Everybody stops. Alex looks back at Sonja and sees her struggling trying to carry everything. He asks her to give some things to him so he can carry them out to the car in his lap in the wheelchair. She reaches for the bag with the blanket and Bible, pulls them out, and puts them in Alex's lap while taking a bouquet of orange blossoms that was in his room that he was holding. "There, this is not so heavy now. Thanks," she says.

Sonja puts the Bible on top of the blanket on Alex's lap. Now he can more easily hold everything in his lap and Sonja has a lighter load to carry. Alex then reaches down to pick up the pen for the woman. It's right there in front of him.

At that time, he finds himself face-to-face with the child. He's practically eye to eye at the child's level. For a few seconds, the child is completely stoic. He has a totally expressionless look on his face as he stares at Alex.

The child then looks up at Sonja, who smiles at him. As he's intently gazing at Sonja, he leans over and slowly puts his hand on Alex's forehead. The expression on his face doesn't change. He's as rigid as can be.

The woman suddenly says, "I'm sorry, mister. Joey, don't do that. Joey, Joey. Mister, I'm so sorry. He shouldn't be approaching strangers like this, but he doesn't know any better. He doesn't listen to me, and he doesn't know how to obey. He can't talk. He's never done anything like this before. I'm so surprised. I am really sorry. I'm so sorry. Joey, please leave the gentleman alone."

Sonja then leans over and puts the bouquet of flowers on top of the Bible and smiles at Alex. She then smiles again at the child. Alex then smiles at the child and says hi. The child then disengages his trance with Sonja, takes Alex's hand, and puts it on his forehead. With both of their arms extended on each other's foreheads, the little boy says hi back and smiles back at Sonja. Sonja mouths something that cannot be heard, and at the same time Alex gives the pen to the little boy and tells him, "Why don't you give this to your mommy and give her a big hug and tell her you love her."

The boy smiles at Alex then looks back at Sonja with an even larger smile, says "Thank you" to her, runs over, and throws his arms around his mother's knees and does as Alex asked him. At that point, the woman suddenly breaks down in tears and nearly faints. "What did you do?" She looks at Sonja in amazement. The woman is almost hysterical with joy. Her eyes are fixed on Sonja's. "How did you do that?" she asks her. She is so happy, she cries with excitement.

The nurse's aide resumes pushing Alex in the wheelchair with Sonja trailing behind. The aid briefly turns her head back and looks at Sonja. "What was that all about? How did you do that?" she asks Sonja.

Sonja simply smiles at her.

Alex is in deep thought with his head bowed as if he's in a spell. He has a look about him as if he has no idea of what just happened and he doesn't say anything. Sonja looks at the nurse as she adjusts the bags she's carrying and simply continues to smile at her. The aide looks at Sonja with a blank look as if she's a ghost.

A few minutes later, they're at the outside door and Sonja leaves to get the car. Sonja soon returns with the car and Alex is assisted from the wheelchair into the passenger's side. They both thank the aide for her help and Sonja drives away. The aide stands there like a statue staring at Sonja and is dumbfounded.

As they exit the parking lot Alex looks at Sonja. "I was wondering, can you take the long way home and drive through some country roads? I would really like to enjoy the beauty of the surrounding countryside and see some nature before entering our subdivision. It will only take about fifteen extra minutes or so."

"Okay. That sounds like a good idea. I would like that as well. It'll be good for you after what you've been through the last three days."

Sonja drives several miles out of the way. She turns off onto a country road, passes by an old farmhouse, a farm pond and a small lake, a field of corn, another farmhouse, some hills, and then a closed gas station. A creek runs along the side of the road. Alex is in a happy place, and he goes into deep thought.

I'm enjoying the drive through the countryside gazing at the flowers, the trees, the lake, the birds and butterflies fluttering about, and the overall beautiful scenery. I'm somewhat mesmerized as we drive through the countryside. I realize I'm enjoying raw nature. I then think, God made all of this and he created this all for us. That, however, prompts me to think suddenly of my experience in hell and how scared I would get if I go back there.

But then something comes over me. I have it all backwards. I shouldn't be scared to go to hell. That's not how this is supposed to work. Instead what's much more important is that I want to go to heaven and do what's needed to get there. I want to be part of God and give back to Him what he has given to me. That desire should trump being scared of going to hell. I should praise my God and not be afraid.

I find myself hypnotized by thinking intensely about all of this when a couple of bumps in the road suddenly bring me out of my trance and back to reality.

I watch the trees along the side of the road transition to bushes and we soon cross a bridge over the creek that now runs along the other side of the road. We drive by an industrial warehouse complex surrounded by a high barbed wire fence with a gate as we come out of the country and enter a more urban setting. Sonja comments about a critter that she sees scurrying along the fence line and into the bushes by the creek.

I observe the industrial warehouse complex and all of the junk in the yard including empty skids, pallets, 55 gallon drums and stacks of propane tanks and suddenly have a déjà vu experience. "Sonja, I don't know why I get this funny feeling. I've been aware of this here but it's like I saw it in a vision or something. Well, I guess it's nothing."

Shortly after we pass the entrance, Andrew comes up from behind us at a high rate of speed and pulls into the driveway to the gate to the complex. But I don't see him and neither does Sonja.

We drive a few more miles, and as we finally turn into our subdivision, Sonja looks into her rearview mirror, and then looks briefly at me. "Uh oh…oh no!"

Chapter 57

Alex and Sonja pull into their driveway, raise their garage door, drive into the garage, and quickly shut it. Sonja gives Alex some crutches that the nurse had loaned to her and assists him inside. He's feeling much better now and has minimal pain. He accepts the help to get around but probably doesn't need it anymore.

As soon as they get inside, they both peek outside the windows through the blinds. Sure enough the old white van has followed them home and again is parked up the street.

"I thought he was gone," says Alex.

"Me too," comments Sonja.

Sonja puts things away and helps Alex get comfortable. She brings him his slippers and helps him prop himself up on some pillows as he situates himself on the couch. It's close to lunchtime and Sonja suggests that she prepare a light lunch saying, "We'll be eating BBQ in a few hours at Andrew's house, if you still feel up to going. If we still go, we shouldn't eat too much for lunch."

Alex is anxious to go. "Absolutely, I feel much better and wouldn't miss it. I can't wait to see everybody. I can get by with a light lunch."

"I would hope so considering what you had for breakfast."

Alex turns on the news on the TV. It's been several hours since he got the last update. As already proven a lot can happen in only just a few hours.

The news is pretty much the same as it was before except that additional non-nuclear bombs have been found affixed to a series of bridges over the Mississippi river. Authorities have declined to reveal the bridges and highways but have announced that they are all major bridges in several states that are vital in linking the east and the west. Just like the others, all the bombs are tamperproof. As a result, all bridges across the Mississippi River have been closed.

The news then goes on to discuss the fiscal and political fallout including the fact that all stock market exchanges have been closed and the investment and banking industries have been turned upside down because of all of the developments.

The news then provides a brief update on the scandal involving why CIA intelligence and other government agencies were not aware of the plot or if they did why they didn't do anything about it.

The news eventually gets to Ammen. The time for the live interview has been set for 3:00 PM. It will be broadcast on every network news station.

As soon as Alex gets comfortable, the phone rings. The phone is right there on the table beside him, and he answers it. It's the woman who has been calling him and hanging up or being disconnected. She has a very soft voice that is shaking and quivering, again as if she is scared to say something or perhaps is contemplating whether to say anything. She sounds like an older woman, perhaps about his age or older.

She says ever so slowly in a deliberate manner with a distinct accent, "Alex, is that you?"

"Yes."

"It's very important that you need to know something. Maybe you've seen me."

"Can I ask who this is?"

Some further quivering and wavering is sensed in her voice.

"Who is this? I'm really sorry. Do I know you?"

"I need to tell you…it's very important that you need to know that…in a couple of hours from now…"

There is a click on the other end, and the phone goes dead. Alex wonders whether the woman hung up without finishing or whether they got disconnected or if something else happened. "Wow!"

He had turned on the speaker for the last part of the conversation so that Sonja could hear it as well.

"What do you make of this? Sonja, do you have any idea who that was?"

"Well, you certainly have some mysteries in your life. Why you suddenly went brain-dead, how you woke up from it, the Arab in the van, the woman on the phone, your dreaming about things that didn't happen, whether Ammen is for real…"

Alex interrupts her and cuts her off before she can list a bunch of other things. "Yeah, I know. We both do. I just can't figure all this out. I wonder if this is all connected somehow."

"Well, if it is, I'd say that's quite the puzzle to solve. Sounds like you have some sort of puzzle of life to figure out."

Then the phone rings again, and it's Alana. She wants to talk with Sonja about the BBQ. Sonja takes the phone into the kitchen and Alex sits back to relax in the living room. She tells Sonja that actually Julie and Garrett are bringing all of the food and that Andrew has volunteered to cook the meat on their grill. Sonja tells Alana that she wishes they could have used the meat from the Fourth that she had but she had to throw it all out. But Alana has some disturbing news.

"Sonja, Andrew left about two hours ago to get some propane for the BBQ pit and hasn't returned yet. He should have been home a long time ago. I'm really worried."

"Alana, there are no places where he's going to be able to buy a new propane tank or get his filled up. And he can't go far because of all of the traffic issues and closed bridges."

"I guess I should confide in you. I thought I told you earlier; Andrew knows of a place close by where he can get a new propane tank. However, he says it's a secret. But he should have been home way before now. Hours ago. He knows that the live interview with Ammen is scheduled for this afternoon, and he said he wanted to be finished doing the BBQ before it starts. He is so much looking forward to it and wants the entire family to watch it at his house with him. I wanted to ask you, per chance, did Andrew come by your house?"

"No. We just got home, but I'll let you know if we see or hear from him. Did you try to call him on his cell phone?"

"Yes, I have been trying for the last hour, but he doesn't answer it. I don't even know why we spent the money for it. He never uses it. I'm really getting worried. Where could he be considering the circumstances out there? He's been gone now for almost two solid hours if not more. I think something is terribly wrong."

Alana then has two more bits of disturbing information. "Sonja, I also have some other things to tell you."

"What is it dear?"

Alana quietly whispers into the phone, "I think somebody broke into our house."

"What?"

Alana whispers again, "When we returned home from the hospital, the dead bolt on our back door was unlocked. The other lock was secured, but not the dead bolt. I know it was locked because I personally checked it before we left. Also, I had just vacuumed the carpet before we left, and I could swear I saw footprints on it."

"Was anything stolen? Are you missing anything?"

"No, I've checked everything. Nothing is gone at all. How strange. I don't want to tell Andrew because he'll get all shaken up about it. Why would somebody just come in our house and then leave without taking anything? This gives me the creeps. Do you think it may be the Arab out to get us or that perhaps the Arab was looking for something?"

Sonja has no answer. "I don't know what to say. Do you think you should call the police?"

But then Alana drops a bombshell. "Sonja, I was debating whether to tell you this, but I have some more disturbing news. I need to talk with somebody about this, but I don't know who."

"And what is that, dear? You can tell me. You know you can always talk with me about anything."

"Well, I accidently found a copy of the Koran that Andrew had hidden in one of his dresser drawers. He doesn't know I found it."

"What? You're kidding me, right?"

"No. I also found buried in the history of Google searches on our computer several references to the Sharia and other Islamic stuff. I have been so distraught over this, I've been a basket case. I don't know whether to confront him, or tell someone, or not tell anybody. I don't know what to think or what to do."

"Well, maybe he's just curious. Maybe it doesn't mean anything at all. After all, he's following Ammen now."

"Or maybe he's being recruited. You don't think he's connected to the terrorists do you? You know there's been talk all over the news for months about them recruiting people like him who aren't Christian. But why wouldn't he have said something to me if he's only curious or merely interested? Why is he hiding this? I wonder if maybe this has something to do with his being away for extended periods of time when he leaves to go on errands. I can't help but think about the Arab following Alex around. You don't think the Arab has anything to do with Andrew being interested in Islam do you?"

"I doubt it, but you are sure raising some interesting questions."

"Sonja, I never did mention this to you, but not too long ago, when Andrew left the house to go shopping and brought home the two enormous garden wagons, I noticed that the Arab in the old white van appeared out of nowhere and followed him from our house. Andrew said he followed him all the way to the store. When he returned home, the Arab followed him home and then left. I was so angry with Andrew for spending the money to buy both wagons I demanded to know what got into him to prompt him to buy them. I remember him sarcastically telling me with a laugh that the Arab told him to do it. What kind of answer was that? You know how Andrew is always kidding about stuff, but what do you make of that?"

"Wow, I don't know what to say. You're telling me that Andrew said the Arab told him to buy the wagons? I thought the Arab was only following Alex around. I didn't know he was also following Andrew as well. You don't think Andrew and the Arab actually met each other do you? I simply can't imagine that happened."

"Well, I think Andrew was just kidding when he said that, as an excuse, but I get a funny feeling thinking about it as if they both really did meet. When I pressed Andrew about it, he got even more sarcastic and said the Arab came to him in a dream and told him he must buy them. Sonja, I assume he's kidding me, but truly I don't know what to think about all of this. I don't see anything good about the Arab at all. He gives me the creeps. Please don't tell Alex about any of this. He'd go off the deep end if he ever found out."

"Okay. I agree. I suppose the only thing we can do is pray for him and watch him closely. For now, let's act like we don't know anything and see if anything develops. After all, keep in mind that Andrew's obsessed with Ammen. Or at least he seems to be anyway. How can he be interested in Islam but follow Ammen at the same time? Unless perhaps it's a ploy for us to think he is when he's really converting to be a Jihadist and he doesn't want us to know it."

"Well, I don't think he's really interested in Islam. I really do think he is obsessed with Ammen."

"I sure hope so."

"Me too. I know. At least that's a little comforting. Perhaps I should thank God for Ammen and that Andrew wants to follow him. I just can't believe that Andrew would have any thoughts of being recruited into Jihadism or whatever it's called. It's just hard not to think about all of this though, especially when he's been gone for about two hours and with the Arab hanging around. I wonder where he is. What's he doing? Why has he been gone for so long? I think something's terribly wrong."

Chapter 58

Sonja tells Alana that she'll discuss the BBQ and the fact that Andrew is missing with Alex, but not mention anything else they discussed, and call her back. She tells Alana that perhaps they can come early. She wants Alex to rest for a bit since they just got home and they both need to get somewhat organized. Perhaps they can come on over in the next hour or so.

In the meantime, while Sonja is on the phone and after lying down for a bit, Alex gets up and hobbles into their bedroom and then his office across the hallway. After a while, Sonja comes in to check up on him. He's sitting at his desk with their computer on.

"What are you doing, Alex?"

"Well, for some reason, I decided to check our finances, and I think I want to give half of what we own in our investments and retirement accounts to charity."

Sonja simply looks at Alex and doesn't say anything at first. She then spots several boxes on the floor across the hall in their bedroom. "And what are these for?"

"I've decided to go through all my clothes and I think I want to give half to Goodwill and other charities as well. A lot of them I hardly wear anymore anyway."

Sonja bluntly but with a smirk on her face asks, "What's gotten into you?"

"Sonja, we have to do this. But more importantly, I want us to do it regardless that we need to do it. I know that we can't afford to do it, but there are others out there who have nothing. Besides, it looks like in three days it's not going to matter anyway, right?"

Sonja meditates for a few seconds. "So is that why you suddenly want to do this? What prompted you to feel this way?"

"Actually, I don't know. Something just came over me."

"Well, I want to let you know that I was actually thinking about this as well. And I don't know why I thought about it too. I'm just so surprised that you actually started this when I happened to think about it at the same time. Are you able to read my mind?"

"I don't know what made me think to do this. So, you're telling me you prompted me to do this by using some sort of mental telepathy?"

"Not deliberately. I decided to wait to see if you might bring it up first. I support what you want to do fully. I'll tell you what. When we return home, I'll help you. We'll have all day tomorrow and plenty of time to work on it then as well. Right?"

She then thinks for a few seconds and says, "Or perhaps I should say maybe we won't?"

"What? Why is that? Do you know something I don't?"

Sonja doesn't answer, and Alex lets the topic go.

Alex agrees to wait and returns to the bedroom to change clothes to prepare to leave to go to Andrew's house. About a half hour later Alex and Sonja are headed out to their garage. Alex is feeling much better now and can walk on his own. The pain in his leg, feet, and toes is nearly gone. It's almost healed. He wonders how this could have healed so quickly. He wants to drive, but Sonja won't let him. But he's capable of driving if he needs to. He quickly goes back into the house, grabs his keys anyway, and puts them in his pocket.

It's now about one in the afternoon. Alex gets in the car with little assistance and begins thinking of the bombs. He knows that beginning at midnight tonight will be the countdown of three days before they're detonated.

He wonders what type of announcement Ammen will have. He remembers that Ammen mentioned midnight tonight as being very important. Alex knows that midnight will be a very important time and wonders if everybody will be required to profess their belief and faith in him by then. He remembers that Ammen said everyone must make the most important decision in their lifetime then and wonders if he must declare whether he believes Ammen is the return of Jesus Christ by that time. He presumes that he'll eventually find out. Jumbled thoughts go through the back of his mind. He senses there is a lot more going on that he doesn't know about, and he's confused.

He contemplates why Ammen came on the scene. If he is for real, then that doesn't conform to the prophecies told in the book of Revelation. If he is really the return of Christ it would be too early for that to happen. And that cannot be. But on the other hand, as a result of the probability the world will be destroyed, Ammen cannot automatically be ruled out either. That may not be wise to do so. Perhaps to entirely ignore him just might be the worst decision one could make. The prophecies of the Bible and especially in Revelation can be so difficult to understand. How does one know?

In short time they arrive at Andrew and Alana's house. Matthew and Daniel are waiting for them with smiles on their faces. As soon as they pull into the driveway they come running out to the car to greet them. Then Alana comes out and greets them as well. Alex receives the expected well-wishes. Alana gives him a hug. " It's so good to have you back home." As she welcomes him, they all head inside.

Sonja asks, "Any word from Andrew yet?"

Just as Alana is about to answer, Andrew pulls up in the driveway. He gets out of his car and hurriedly carries a new propane tank around back to the BBQ pit. A few minutes later, he comes in through the back door. As he greets everybody and welcomes Alex back home, the tension in the room goes up a few notches when everyone realizes that Alana is staring at him intently. "Where on Earth have you been?" she asks firmly.

"I found out there's an Ammen rally today downtown and decided to go check it out. There were so many people there was an unbelievable traffic jam and I couldn't get home as fast as I wanted. They were handing out free T-shirts with Ammen's picture and name on it, and I stood in line for the longest time, but they ran out.

They're supposed to get more. After the interview this afternoon, I plan to go back to get one. Does anybody else want one too?"

He then notices a questionable look on Alex's face. "Have you heard about Ammen? They're going to have a live interview with him this afternoon and he's supposed to have something very important to say regarding midnight tonight. What do you think?"

Alex smiles at Andrew and calmly says, "Yes I've heard about him and I've seen him on TV. I know that he has an enormous and growing following, but I've not decided yet whether to put my faith in him or not. I need to make sure I don't make any premature decisions."

Alex so much wants to tell Andrew just how proud he is of him committing to something albeit Ammen, but he has trouble finding the right words to say anything. It's obvious that Andrew is proud of his commitment and he is looking for encouragement.

As Andrew looks at Alex and waits for him to continue and say something to support him, Alex then finally says "You know, after following and worshipping Jesus Christ for over sixty years, it's so difficult to merely abandon Him and follow someone else if that's what I'm supposed to do. I question whether Ammen is the Second Coming because I'm not sure he's one and the same as Jesus. And I'm not sure if what's happening is supposed to happen anyway. Something tells me it's not the right time for Him to return and that he may be someone else. I'm not sure whether everything adds up or not."

Andrew is really dejected after hearing Alex say this and it shows. Andrew has a look on his face as if he's about to burst into tears.

But after a brief pause, Alex, wanting to appease Andrew, continues, "But, it's hard to argue when well over a hundred million people think he's the real thing. Perhaps he is. There's something inviting and welcoming about him. But the jury's still out with me and I need to think and pray about this some more before making up my mind. I need to mull over additional information that I don't have. Maybe this live interview this afternoon will help me decide."

That was encouraging enough to satisfy Andrew. Andrew points to his newly acquired big flat screen and says, "Well, there's where we'll see it all. That's where the action will be." He winks at Alex, and Alex nods in return.

Alex then remarks, "Well, it looks like we better get it right. Depending on whether one follows and worships Ammen as the return of Christ may determine where we will spend eternity in our afterlife. It's going to be either one place or the other. One place you really really, really don't want to go, believe me. Assuming that our world is going to end in three days or less, it'll be the most important decision of one's life. So, we better get it right."

Alana is suddenly taken back by Alex's comment. She realizes that both Alex and Andrew are taking this very seriously even though they may not necessarily agree at this time. Up until now, she had not really thought about it in this context or considered how very real this all is. Sonja on the other hand has a look about her as if she already knows.

Alana surrenders any thought about chastising Andrew about being late and returns to the kitchen to be by herself for a minute to contemplate things.

Andrew goes back outside to start the BBQ of pork steaks, chicken, and hot dogs for the kids that Garrett had brought over earlier. Alex sits down in their living room where it's much cooler and turns on Andrew's new TV.

The news is on, as now it's nearly a twenty-four-hour nonstop news update event of the terrorists' activities and Ammen. After a little while Alex learns that three more bombs have been found since the morning. One was found in Tulsa and one was found in Seattle. However, the third one has been confirmed as a bona fide nuclear device that has the potential of destroying at least two-thirds of the United States within days of detonation and potentially destroying most of the world within weeks simply as a result of the unique place where it is located.

That device was found to be imbedded in Yellowstone National Park at a strategic location of the dormant but subterranean active super volcano. Considering its strategic placement, it is feared that detonation of that device could trigger eruption of the super volcano, which experts predict could result in a worldwide calamity including a layer of ash possibly up to least several feet thick that could spread up to one thousand miles away, leaving two-thirds of the country completely uninhabitable, in addition to creating a volcanic winter that could extend globally for years.

There is also some speculation such an eruption could possibly trigger powerful earthquakes as well. The fault lines gaining the most interest include the Cascadia Subduction Zone, the San Andreas, the Hayward, and New Madrid faults. Although it may be unlikely such an eruption could trigger such an earthquake in these areas, the incredible additional devastation caused by a quake that might result from the detonation of any nearby nuclear device nevertheless also has drawn considerable concern, especially considering the population along these fault lines.

Although experts are not all in agreement as to the likelihood of the eruption or extent of the damage, they are all in agreement that there is a real possibility that the detonation could result in an eruption and that it could have the potential to be catastrophic across the country and entire globe. A volcanic winter could render much of the world if not eventually the entire Earth uninhabitable for a very long time.

All have timers set for midnight three days from tonight and all are 100 percent tamperproof. The device located at the site of the super volcano also has sensors that make it impossible to move it or defuse it. There is fear that an Earth tremor or quake may trigger it even before the scheduled detonation time.

Alex comments, "How in the world could these terrorists have built or acquired all of these bombs and placed them in all of these places without getting caught? I'll bet Russia had something to do with this. I wonder if some other countries such as North Korea or Pakistan or maybe even Iran were also involved in supplying the nukes."

The news then continues but is pretty much the same as what Alex has heard previously. But then almost as if in response to Alex, the news reporter says, "The terrorists have been plotting this ever since 9/11 and had plenty of time to coordinate things without the United States government knowing anything about it. But it's still an unbelievable mystery why government intelligence didn't uncover the plot or why the government didn't mention anything about it until now if it knew anything."

The news reporter then discusses the failures of our past presidency and government and for them to let this happen. He then warns the viewers that there is speculation that this is not the end of it. There is a rumor going around that the terrorists have plotted even more. In addition, there are reports that some similar bombs have been found in London, and that England is accusing Russia of being involved in the matter as well. In response, Russia has warned the Western World that it won't hesitate to launch its nuclear weapons in a preemptive strike if it is threatened. Russia insists that it was not involved and is pointing its fingers at North Korea and Pakistan as the suppliers of the nuclear devices.

Chapter 59

A car pulls up and it's Garrett, Julie, and their kids. Lizzy and Mikey run into the house with smiles on their faces and Julie and Garrett lag behind carrying Emily, her diaper bag, and a bunch of bags of food. Alex receives more well-wishes and more hugs. Alex now is experiencing reality again and he knows it. How enjoyable it is to be with his family. "This is real," he says to himself. "No doubt about it." Julie, Garrett, and Alex settle into the living room and get comfortable.

As he's thinking to himself, Julie asks, "Dad, Mom said that you think that you're not awake and that you're dreaming all of this. What's going on? Can you explain this to us?"

Alex takes a few deep breaths. "Well, I remember going before a big mirror that evaluated my life and then I went to hell, and after a while was sent to heaven. Then I was ushered back into a void of nothingness and was on my way back to hell. It turned out to be a real-life nightmare, and I couldn't take it anymore. So, I asked God to let me go into a dream to escape the reality of horror I was going through. While I was traveling back and forth in the void I could see almost everything happening back on Earth. But then after asking God to let me go into a dream, the next thing I knew I woke up in the hospital. Sonja told me that I was merely in a coma and then pronounced brain dead for three days after I never woke up from my nap on the Fourth. She said I merely dreamed all of that."

"Really?"

"You have to believe me. It was all very real. I could see visions of what was going on back home on Earth. But this is all very real to me too. But now I've pretty much resigned to the fact that I'm awake and not dreaming. But for some reason I can't explain, I'm not absolutely sure about this. But seeing you all, I suppose not. You all are definitely reality to me. But I really did go to hell and heaven. That is an absolute certainty."

"Wow. Really? Well, then what was hell and heaven like? Did you meet God?" she asks him point-blank.

"I can no longer remember all the details of both hell and heaven, but I can remember that hell is the most awful gruesome and painful place that is more frightening than anyone can imagine, and that heaven is a paradise that is beyond anyone's imagination. I don't remember any specifics and I don't remember meeting God, but I assume I did."

"Wow! Mom also said you dreamed that your house exploded and our kids were trapped inside, that we were abducted in a kidnapping, that a nuclear bomb exploded just a few miles from here, that the terrorists were looking for you, and a bunch of other stuff. What's with all of that?"

"At the time, that was all very real. Something tells me that all of that really happened too. I know you think I'm crazy, but it was as real as can be. But that is all past, and I suppose was merely a dream. I'm so glad to be here with you now."

"Well, I certainly hope so. You don't know how much we missed you."

Sonja looks at Alex perplexed because she remembers that the doctor told her there is no way Alex could have dreamed anything. He had no brain waves of any type the entire time he was in the hospital. She's beginning to think that Alex was telling the truth about what he saw and experienced, but she wonders just how can that be? She doesn't say anything. Convinced by the doctor's comment, she wonders just how Alex could have actually experienced what he said when she and the rest of the family didn't. Just how did that happen?

The topic then turns toward the pending cataclysm and Ammen. Julie asks, "Dad, do you think the world is really going to come to an end in three days?"

"I don't know for sure, but I'd say from everything I know and feel, I think it is all but a certainty that the bombs will be detonated, and the disease will be spread. I'm not sure if this will be the end of the world, but it could very well be the beginning of the end. The Islamic terrorists will not give in. They're 100 percent determined. I don't see how anything or anybody can stop it."

"Wow, what do we do?"

"Pray."

"Do you think maybe God can stop it?"

"If he can, just how would he do it? The bombs are real and will be detonated. The disease will be spread. Everything is certain and is happening right before our eyes. But maybe we should have faith."

"Well, maybe this will really be the end of the world and perhaps that's the reason why Ammen came on the scene. Maybe God really did send Jesus back to Earth as Ammen and if people believe in His return, they will at least be saved in their afterlife after the world is destroyed. Do you think that's possible?"

"I don't know. But, it sure is beginning to look like that might be a possibility."

By now, everybody's in the room except for most of the kids who are playing out back. Andrew has finished the BBQ and brought the meat in for Alana to place in the oven to keep it warm. He joins the discussion and soon afterwards Alana and Sonja come in from the kitchen. It's now almost 3:00 PM and the live interview with Ammen is about to begin.

"I wonder what's so important about midnight tonight," comments Garrett.

Andrew asks the same question, referring to the remark that Ammen made earlier about it determining everybody's fate.

Alex responds, "I don't know for sure, but I'll bet everyone will be required to profess their faith in Ammen being the return of Jesus by midnight or be left out. We'll see."

As all eyes focus on the TV as the interview is about to begin; however, the news program is abruptly pre-empted by a video broadcast from Muhammad. It's obvious that his insurgent terrorist group has hijacked the news broadcast and has interrupted the program.

"I can't believe this!" says Andrew angrily.

Garrett comments, "I've heard this has been going on in various places throughout America and now it is happening here in our city."

Alana adds, "Well, I hope the electricity doesn't go off. I've heard that the terrorists are taking control of the electrical grid in parts of the country and that there have been outages here and there."

Andrew is very upset about the fact that Muhammad now is broadcasting a video about himself and what ISA is doing in place of the live interview with Ammen. Most of what Muhammad is saying is pretty much what he has said before. He's mocking the United States and playing with it as if the country was a toy.

Andrew looks at his watch and stares at Muhammad on the TV screen and shouts out, "We're missing the damn interview with Ammen, you son of a bitch!"

Everyone in the room is equally visibly upset. Everyone knows the critical importance of watching the interview and Andrew becomes irate that they're missing it.

Andrew gets up, grabs the remote, and tries other channels. They're all either showing the same video of Muhammad, or for some reason, the screen is nothing but static.

He looks at his watch again and screams, "We're missing it, damn it!"

Garrett comments, "Perhaps the entire cable communications system has been hijacked and not just a few stations or channels where we live. I wonder if we miss it, whether we can catch a repeat later or through the Internet."

"By then, if and when it's available, it may be too late. We need to see it now!"

While waiting for something different to happen on the TV, Julie asks Alana, "Did you ever find out anything more about somebody breaking into your house?"

Everybody looks at her. This is the first that anybody has heard about this except for Sonja and Julie.

Alana is reluctant to say anything, but concedes. "No, while we were at the hospital, it appears that somebody broke into our house through the back door, but that it didn't look like anything was taken. I'm pretty sure about it because the door was unlocked and I saw the footprints in the carpet. I vacuumed it right before we left."

"Well, that doesn't make any sense. Why would somebody break into the house and not take anything?" asks Garrett.

Andrew angrily states, "I didn't know anything about this. Why didn't you tell me?"

"Well, you weren't here, remember?"

"Well, I'll bet I know who it was. I wonder if it was that Arab who's been following Alex around lately. *If* he didn't take anything, maybe he planted a bomb in our house instead." He sort of chuckles under his breath, as if it was a really good joke.

"That's not funny," remarks Alana.

Garrett then states, "I forgot to tell you. That old white van with the Arab drove down the street just behind us after we parked here and he parked just up the street." He peeks out the window and says, "It's still there. It's parked just two houses down on the other side of the street. Also, it looks like we have a bad thunderstorm approaching. The clouds are as black as I've ever seen them and the wind is really kicking up. The kids are still outside. I'll go out and get them."

Then no sooner than Garrett says this suddenly it gets dark as the menacing clouds gather overhead and a lightning strike lights up the room, followed by a clap of thunder that rocks the house. The electricity goes out. The TV turns off by itself, the hum of the air conditioner wanes and stops, the lights go out, and everything becomes deathly quiet. Then another bolt of lightning again suddenly lights up the darkening room and another clash of thunder is heard that is so deafening it sounds like the house was hit. As the kids come in the house, they scream.

Chapter 60

After everybody jumps and a few more screams are heard it gets quiet again. Then the rain can be heard slamming against the windows. Some lightning can be seen off in the distance and a few more rumbles of thunder are heard. After a few minutes, things settle down somewhat but the electricity is still off. Andrew continues his ranting and raving about missing the live interview with Ammen.

Sonja then calls out from the kitchen, "Since the electricity is off and the food is ready, we should eat now before it gets cold."

Everybody agrees, and after saying grace, soon nearly all are crowded in the kitchen loading their plates buffet style.

In the meantime, Alex is resting in the living room when Daniel and Matthew come up to him and climb up in his lap. Both are sobbing. "What's wrong?" asks Alex, thinking that the storm scared them.

Daniel says, "We were playing a game in the backyard and some of the neighborhood kids were playing with us and I came in last. I was the last one." Then Matthew says, "And I was the second to last one. Yeah, we didn't win." Both obviously are very upset. Matthew says, "I think one of the other kids cheated."

Alex then proceeds to tell both of them, "It's okay to be the last one. And it's okay to be the second to last one. You didn't lose. It's because if nobody's the last one, then nobody would win. So, being the last one is very important.

"And if somebody was not the second to last one, then nobody would be the last one, so that makes the second to last one just as important. So everybody is just as important and that means everybody wins. Right?"

"But the other kid cheated," says Daniel.

"Well, if somebody cheated and came in first because he cheated, then that means that he really didn't win either, even though he thinks he did. That means that because he cheated and you didn't, then both of you really won and he actually lost, right?"

Although it's questionable whether Daniel and Matthew understood all this, their eyes are beaming with glee and their sadness turns instantly to joy. They both immediately give Alex a big hug and say, "Thanks, Grandpa."

At this time, Sonja walks back in the room and overhears all of this. She smiles, looks at Alex, and asks, "God helped you say all that, right?"

"I really didn't know what to say. I thought it was you telling me what to say. Maybe I was subconsciously reading your mind…again."

Although Alex is somewhat confused as to just what happened, nevertheless he finds it comforting. Sonja then helps Alex get up so that he can fill his plate and eat as well.

At that time, Andrew who returned to the room continues to mutter something about Ammen being the last angel and that he wants the TV to come back on so that he can watch the interview before it's too late.

Shortly after everybody finishes their dinner, the electricity comes back on. It now is going on 4:00 PM and everybody assumes that they missed the interview with Ammen. Andrew runs over and powers up the TV, and after a few minutes, the same channel appears. As soon as the screen brightens and the sound comes back on, the commentator is seen making the following statement:

"Again, we apologize for the technical difficulties. Coordinating this broadcast from this barren place on such short notice to around the world has been a very challenging exercise considering the circumstances. We also apologize for the delay in bringing you this broadcast. We now resume the interview which is in progress."

Sitting on a wooden chair by a tree next to a burned down church is Ammen. Although it's dark, desolate mountains can be seen in the background. He seems to be in his thirties. There's a remarkable resemblance between him and the pictures and other depictions of Jesus Christ of which everybody is familiar. Beside him on another wooden chair sits an older woman, perhaps in her sixties. She has somewhat of a wrinkled face and looks forlorn and despondent. Both chairs look horribly uncomfortable.

Ammen is dressed in a gray tunic and the woman is dressed in a dark wrap with a scarf of a similar color. The woman has her hands folded and as always is holding a small bouquet of white flowers. As in the other videos, she lays the flowers down in her lap when Ammen begins to speak. The interviewer is out of sight, but presumably sits opposite of them next to the cameras and lighting.

INTERVIEWER: So, as we were discussing, in summary, is the world going to come to an end? Is this the Apocalypse foretold in Revelation? There is much dispute regarding this and whether the prophecies are all being met. It appears to many that they are not. Can you clarify what is happening?

AMMEN: There is extreme peril and unrest that will affect all mankind. In exactly eighty hours from now, there will be a light of the worst kind, then darkness, and then a great light of salvation for those who know the way. For those who do not, there will be only darkness, agony, and suffering.

INTERVIEWER: But are all the events that are happening consistent with what has been written in the Book of Revelation? It appears to many that they are not.

AMMEN: What has been written is the Word of God. But, do you really understand what has been written? You must trust what is written. There are also many who believe that they are consistent.

INTERVIEWER: You speak of those who will know the way. So, how will they know the way? Who will these people be?

AMMEN: The people who will have faith in me will know the way.

INTERVIEWER: And what do you mean by "the way"? What will happen to them?

AMMEN: Through faith in me they will be rewarded through the glory and will enter a place where they will be with me and my creator everlasting.

INTERVIEWER: Can you elaborate what you mean by faith in you?

AMMEN: The people must believe in me and trust in me that I am who I say I am. I will rise and return after midnight in three days to bring glory to the people who have faith in me. My return to the people was foretold. You must believe.

INTERVIEWER: What do you mean by return again?

AMMEN: The Scriptures foretold of my return and I have. I will again return in three days to save those who will have faith in me before I leave.

INTERVIEWER: What do you mean by rise and return after midnight? Where will you be before then?

AMMEN: In approximately eight hours I will retire to a place where you will not find me. In places like perhaps Qaraqosh or Mosul more Christians will be persecuted by the reign of the insurgents, just as your brothers and sisters, and your mothers and fathers were. I too was persecuted, but now am in flesh. My death is in the blaze of glory. At midnight in three days I will return and will take those who believe in me with me. It is within the order of my creator.

INTERVIEWER: So, those who will have faith that you will save the souls as you say will be rewarded?

AMMEN: No. You must declare your faith before I leave. Not after I return in three days.

INTERVIEWER: You mean by tonight?

AMMEN: Yes.

INTERVIEWER: Why?

AMMEN: Because if one waits it will be too late. One can then not have faith. After I leave tonight, you and the people will not see or hear from me again until I return. If you wait and do not declare your faith now before I leave, you will surely perish.

INTERVIEWER: But it is said the great peril will take place in three days. Why can't the people wait three days before declaring their belief and faith in you?

AMMEN: Because I will return in three days, likewise you must declare three days before I return. When I return, your world will become dark. To find the light you must also decide three days before.

INTERVIEWER: But that's three days before when the bombs are supposed to be detonated."

AMMEN: Yes. That is when I will take those who know the way with me. Those who follow me may perish on Earth but their souls will live in the light. They will be with me and my creator and be rewarded with everlasting life.

INTERVIEWER: But, if you are the return of Jesus, are you going to be put to death again? Where you not already put to death many years ago? How can you die again?

AMMEN: I will not. My death becomes life. I will never die. It is because I have returned in flesh and it is the will that you be given another opportunity to believe. A second chance for all is a gift from my father.

INTERVIEWER: So, how do people know to trust you? How do they know you are who you say you are?

AMMEN: Through faith. Without faith, you cannot live the light. There would be no riches or treasures, but much pain and agony. Without faith, people will surely die and will not be with me or my creator. If you believe in my return, then you will return with me to the light.

INTERVIEWER: You talk about your creator. Who is your creator?

AMMEN: My creator is my father. Through me, one will live through him and be with him. My creator is within me and I am within him. As it has been said before, that time has come again.

INTERVIEWER: People want to know if you are really the Second Coming of Jesus. Are you one and the same person as Jesus?

AMMEN: I am the last angel. The angel of the father and in the father. Your Jesus was that angel of the past. I am likewise of the present. My return was foretold. You must believe in me returning as the last angel of the father and in the father to be before you.

INTERVIEWER: Jesus performed miracles which motivated people to believe in him. Have you performed any miracles to help people want to believe in you?

AMMEN: Why do you need to see me perform miracles? Haven't they already been done? The only miracle you should be concerned about is the miracle to take place three days from now if you believe in me, just as you may have believed in your same Jesus in the past.

INTERVIEWER: The people are still trying to reconcile your presence today with that of Jesus.

AMMEN: It is because of the present peril that I am here. Not the past. It is up to you to have faith in me now. If you do not think I am who I say I am and if you are more interested in the past, then you will surely perish. Belief in only the past will not be sufficient now and will not reward you in the future. You must instead believe in me now as well. I am one and the same, so you must believe in me now, as you may have believed in the past.

INTERVIEWER: You refer to Jesus and speak of him in the third person as if he is another person and is not one and the same as you. Why?

AMMEN: That I have not said. Jesus has been your savior through the ages. But because of the current peril before you, you must believe that I have returned for you now. That is why I am here.

INTERVIEWER: And why is that? Isn't the belief in the resurrection of Jesus in the past just as, if not more important to Christians today? What has changed? Why are things different now?

AMMEN: In view of the current peril, your belief in the resurrection and what happened in the past must now be met with your belief in me now. If you believed in the past, you must also believe in me now. As the last angel of the father to come before you, only belief in me can save you now. How can you be saved by only believing in the past when I give you the opportunity to again believe in me now? Isn't it the same faith that will reward you now as it has in the past? May I ask you why you think faith is different now than it was before?

INTERVIEWER: What do you mean by "last angel"?

AMMEN: The test given by the father will be passed and I will then become the last angel before you before eternity. There will be two other angels with me. The blood runs the same in these angels and in me. That blood is sacred. It is by the order of the creator that I become the last angel to you.

INTERVIEWER: And who will these other two angels be? Can you tell us whether one will be a woman or a female angel? Is one maybe your mother?

AMMEN: Those ordained in the order by the father will be the angels with me.

INTERVIEWER: So, you are not going to come right out and say that one may be a woman, right? Then may I assume that one may be a woman? I ask this because I wonder if it's possible that the person who sits beside you may be one of these angels who will be with you. Is she the angel of your mother by chance? That would mean that you share the same sacred blood and she could be one of the angels you speak about. Am I truly looking at you as Christ and your mother as an angel?

AMMEN: The second to last angel will be on my right side when I enter and will be my sentinel. The third to last angel will be on my left side and will also be my sentinel. Both of these angels have been with me and will be with me.

INTERVIEWER: May I ask who the woman is who sits beside you? She currently sits on your right side.

AMMEN: She represents the spirit of those who will follow me and is the mother angel for those who will have faith. She is indeed an angel to me. She will also be an angel to you, if you know the way.

INTERVIEWER: You have said that you and the other two angels are from a sacred blood line of the people at the time of Jesus from over two thousand years ago. Are you saying you are of the same blood of Jesus and are Jesus himself? Are you actually the Second Coming of Jesus himself, one and the same?

AMMEN: You will see no other angel after me. My blood line goes back over two thousand years ago and it is the same now as it was then. The angels who will be with me are of the same blood. They are of the same spirit and within my sacrifice will bring the spirit in the name of glory to be given to you. It is a sacred blood. You may have believed in Jesus in the past. To enter you must likewise believe in me again today.

INTERVIEWER: Are you possibly referring to one or more of Jesus' brothers, or perhaps I should say your brothers, (actually stepbrothers) as the other angel or angels who will be with you? Your brother, as your mother would be of the same blood. I suppose that blood would be sacred. Are your mother and one of Jesus's or your brothers the other two angels to whom you refer? That appears to be the only logical explanation of the sacred bloodline. Is that the case? Is that what you are implying?"

AMMEN: The angels who will be with me have always been with me. They have been of the sacred lineage. You must believe in them too. They, along with certain others, were chosen to spread the word, and as you remember them, you must believe in me.

INTERVIEWER: You tell people that your name is Ammen. In the first coming the name of the Savior was different. He was referred to as Jesus or Emmanuel, the Messiah, among other names. If you are one and the same, why is your name different today and not the same as it was before?

AMMEN: Hallowed be the name of the father. But why are you concerned about my name? The name was given to me by my creator, my father. My name today refers to the last angel of the father which is the way to the light amidst the peril before you. But it is not my name that will bring you glory. You cannot be saved by a name. Do not be deceived by my name. Is it more important to you to trust my name or is it more important to have faith in and trust me? You must have faith in me, not in my name.

INTERVIEWER: What will happen to those who do not know you? In other words, what will happen to those who are not even aware that you have returned as the savior?

AMMEN: Their final destiny will be the same as those who never knew Jesus of the past. You are blessed to know who I am. You are blessed to have this new opportunity now before you.

INTERVIEWER: One last question: Is it possible that one may be saved by you by simply believing in Jesus Christ since theoretically you are one in the same as you appear to indicate, or are people required to believe in you regardless of whether they believe in Jesus of the past? You have not come right out and definitively said you and Jesus are the same, or that you are Jesus Christ and I'm sorry to keep asking this. However, everybody wants to know. In other words, if you are indeed one and the same, then why can't we just simply worship and have faith in Jesus?

AMMEN: Your Jesus was then. He was of the past. But I am also now. Do you wish to follow the past or do you wish to follow the present? Are you not concerned with the peril that is happening now? Look at what will happen in three days. What is more important? Is it the past or the present? The sacrifice has already been made. However, the peril before you now cannot be met with only belief and faith in the past. Unless you believe in the return of your savior now and believe in me as I sit here before you, you will surely perish and will not be rewarded.

INTERVIEWER: And that is why you say you have returned?

AMMEN: That is why I am here for you. That is why you are given a new opportunity now. This new opportunity is a gift to you from my father. If you do not follow the opportunity given to you now before I leave tonight, you will surely die and will not be with me and my creator. It is up to you to decide whether I am who I say I am. It is up to you to decide whether you wish to have faith in me.

INTERVIEWER: And, regardless that we may also believe in Jesus in the past, you say that we must also irrevocably commit our faith in you now as well to be saved by tonight?

AMMEN: If you want to live in the light after three days, you must decide and declare your faith that I have returned for you, by eight hours from now. Belief in the past will not be enough. Otherwise, you will surely die and will live in the agony and darkness forever. You will never be with me or my father. You are now granted a new opportunity to believe again. You should not deny this new opportunity that is granted to you. It is a gift to you from my father.

INTERVIEWER: The viewers and I want to thank you so much for your time. I apologize for asking such difficult questions, but the viewers and your followers will be comforted to have heard your answers. Again we thank you very much for this wonderful opportunity to hear you.

AMMEN: Thank you for the opportunity. Likewise, you have been given the gift of a new opportunity as well. Are you going to accept it or deny it? It is my intention and that of my father to bring everlasting life to those who believe in me and accept this new opportunity given to escape the peril that cometh.

The interview concludes and the channel resumes its normal newscast. The commentator then reports that the news network attempted to organize a round table discussion of theologians and other experts to analyze the interview and to reconcile the current events with the prophecies of Revelation. However, because of some logistical issues and the delay, it's unclear whether that can be accomplished. "Stay tuned," the commentator remarks.

"So, what did you think?" asks Andrew encouragingly as he gets up and turns down the volume.

Everybody just sits there speechless. There is complete silence in the room for a good thirty seconds.

Then Alana breaks the silence by saying, "You mean that we need to declare by tonight at midnight whether to believe in and worship Ammen as the return of Jesus or not believe in him and continue to only have faith in Jesus Christ of the past? And if we get it wrong, we could go to hell in three days when the world ends?"

"And be there forever?" asks Julie.

"Or if you get it right and follow Ammen, you will have riches and treasures and will go to heaven," says Andrew excitedly.

"So, I presume that you believe that Ammen is for real?" asks Alana.

"You bet. He sure looks like the way to go for me," says Andrew.

"What do you think, Dad?" asks Julie.

Alex sits back and takes several deep breaths. He is contemplating a symbol that looks like a backward comma that he thinks he saw stitched on the shoulder of Ammen's robe, and he is startled by Julie talking to him. He briefly wonders if anybody else saw it, or if only he could see it. Then he takes several more deep breaths and then speaks in a very calculated and deliberate manner. Every word he says is taken in with an intense focus by everybody.

"I really do not know. There's something about him that is welcoming, refreshing, and inviting. It's as if he enters your soul when you look at him and listen to him. The interviewer sure did ask the right questions and some very tough questions. I'm surprised and glad he asked such tough questions, but you know what?"

"What?" asks everybody.

"When you think about it, Ammen really never did answer any question directly. It was like he was talking in riddles and a lot of what he said can be interpreted different ways. And I question whether the events including Ammen coming on the scene at this time all match what is supposed to happen per the book of Revelation. I don't think they're the same. He answered every question with an indirect response. Nothing was direct or absolute. Something tells me that things don't add up.

Take for example his answers to the questions about the prophecies or comparing him to Jesus. He didn't really answer them. He never once said that he is actually Jesus or was of the exact same blood of Jesus although he led you to believe that. I have worshipped Jesus Christ for over sixty years and I don't know if I'm willing to risk jeopardizing my afterlife with Ammen, hoping they are one in the same. If they really are one in the same, then I don't understand why we must differentiate between them."

"But he explained that. He said regarding the prophecies you must trust what is written even though you may not understand it and you should be concerned about what is happening now, not what happened in the past. He said his return is a gift of a new opportunity. He said you must also believe in him returning now, regardless of your belief in him as Jesus of the past. Isn't that reasonable?" asks Alana.

"I agree," states Julie. "Ammen explained why it's so important to have faith in him no matter whether you believe in Jesus of the past or not or what you believe the prophecies to be. It's a new opportunity. A second chance he said."

"And he has a following now of almost two hundred million they say," comments Andrew. "And he looks just like Jesus too. What if he really is Jesus who has returned as the Second Coming? Do you know what will happen to you after you die if you decide not to accept him now, regardless if you still believe in the Jesus story from the past? Just what if you are wrong? Just what if he is really for real?"

"I know," remarks Alex. "I know. If there are that many people in such a short time that believe in him, then perhaps something can be said for that. There is something about him and the woman with him that looks familiar to me, as if I've seen them in a vision or something, but I just can't recall it. I am tempted to believe in him too. I know I've seen them before somewhere, but I don't know where. It's as if they very well could be the last two angels, as he indicated."

"You know, Jesus also talked in parables and didn't always speak directly with clear answers either all of the time," says Julie. "He talks in ways just the same as the Bible said Jesus did. That suggests perhaps Ammen is for real. Maybe there's a reason why he couldn't simply say he was Jesus. Maybe our faith in him wouldn't count if he just came right out and said he was Jesus and maybe that's why he couldn't be clear about it. He implied if he did, then we wouldn't be able to have faith. But, Dad, I understand where you're coming from. I'm not sure either, but I can see why Andrew wants to believe in him. Nearly everything about him suggests he is really Jesus."

"It sure is tempting and I'm sort of inclined to agree with Andrew," adds Alana.

"But how Ammen answered the questions was different," says Alex. "What does everybody else think?"

"But we explained all of that, just as Ammen did. There's an explanation why he answered the questions the way he did," says Julie and Alana together. "Ammen could be for real."

Nobody else says anything and everybody is looking at Andrew and Alex for the answer.

"Well, let me give it some serious thought. I'll also address it with serious prayer and ask for divine guidance. I hope to make a decision soon this evening. But, I suggest you also pray for divine guidance as well. You should not rely on either Andrew or me. You should make your own decision."

Andrew then looks at everybody. "Well, I'm going to leave and go downtown to the Ammen rally to see if they have any more Ammen T-shirts. Does anybody else want to go with me or want one?" he asks.

Nobody responds and he then leaves and says he'll be back soon.

Sonja who has always been the most religious, the most quiet, the most reserved, retaining her great wisdom for the opportune time, and being like an angel herself, comments, "All of these years, we have tried to get Andrew to believe in Jesus Christ. We have taken him to Sunday school. We have preached God's word. We have done everything, and he has refused to have faith. He never did believe in Jesus. For all of these years Alex has done everything he could to get him to be a Christian without success. Maybe Alex's father could have converted him if he was still alive, but we could not.

Now, after all of these years, it is Andrew who in a matter of only a few days is confident about his savior, and now it is Andrew who is trying to convert us to Ammen. It's just the other way around now. Oh, how the tables have been turned. Is this the way it's supposed to turn out?"

Chapter 61

By now it has stopped raining. Sonja, Alana, and Julie disperse to clean up after dinner and go back outside to watch the kids. Garrett also goes outside. Everybody is in deep thought, however it seems that all eyes and ears are on Alex and Andrew. Whatever they decide will likely influence their decision.

Alex remains in the living room and sits there in deep contemplation. He is lost in thought. He prays for guidance but is not successful in getting an answer.

On one hand he doesn't want to risk abandoning his devotion to Jesus Christ of over sixty years to worship Ammen and then later finds out he's not for real. But on the other hand there is something about Ammen that appeals to him. Ammen's talk of the tests being passed in a blaze of glory and being before Satan, being accompanied by two other angels, about an order, being of a sacred blood line, being persecuted, and being the last angel sounds so familiar. It's as if he's having a déjà vu experience but he has no idea why this all sounds so familiar. Where has he heard this before?

And where did he see the vision of Ammen and the woman before? They look so familiar to him, he is certain he saw them in a vision, as if they're real, but he doesn't remember where or when he saw them. He wonders if it was while he visited heaven, but he doesn't know because he can't remember the details of his experience there.

When Alex thinks of Ammen and everything he said; he feels him entering his soul like a spirit. Now he knows why he has almost two hundred million followers and why Andrew is obsessed with him. Alex is finding himself wanting to believe in him also. He doesn't want to be left out and the only one who resists.

Alex is torn between staying the course with Jesus Christ or following Ammen. Why does everything Ammen said sound so familiar to him? Where did he see the vision of him and the woman? He senses it but can't identify where he's heard it before or where he's seen them. He must make a decision and announce his faith in only a few hours.

Sonja then calls out to Alex from the kitchen and wakes him up from his deep thought. "Alex, I just remembered, we forgot to bring the ice cream. I had promised Alana I would bring some to surprise the kids. You know how much they like ice cream cones and they never get them here. I just bought some at the store the other day and we should have plenty. Do you feel like driving back home and getting it? It shouldn't take that long, but you don't have to if you don't want to. How's your leg? Are you up to it?"

Alex thinks for a minute and decides that's a good idea. He can do it. That will give him some time to be alone by himself so that he can have some uninterrupted time for thought and prayer in isolation at home for a few minutes. Maybe that's what he needs to make the right decision.

"Okay, I'd be happy to go."

"Alex, can you also bring back two of the full bouquets of orange blossoms too? You'll find the cones with the ice cream in the freezer and the bouquets on the kitchen counter."

Alex doesn't know why she wants the bouquets but has an unusual feeling that she knows something that he doesn't. He doesn't ask her but acknowledges her and gets up to leave.

Alex tells Julie, Alana, and Garrett that he's going back home and will return shortly. As he goes outside he notices that the old white van has left, but in its place is a patrol car. It's Officer Musty. "Wow," says Alex to himself. "I was not expecting this at all."

Officer Musty sees Alex approach his car and he starts up the patrol car and pulls alongside of Alex.

"Good evening, Officer," says Alex.

"Officer Musty here at your service, it's so good to see you again. I heard about your mishap. I hope you're feeling better now. I didn't think you would make it. Actually, I'm surprised to see you. I'm so glad to see you."

Alex responds kindly, "We were wondering where you've been. Sonja and the family haven't seen you since before I was in the hospital. They missed you."

"Well, I have been out of town so to speak on some other business, but that has brought me back here now."

"Do you know what the status is with the Arab and the old white van? I'm told it was also gone for the last several days, but also recently showed up again."

"Yes, I understand that he's been out of town also. As a matter of fact, he and I have run into each other a few times, not physically of course," Officer Musty chuckles a little.

"I don't think he'll give you any more trouble since I'm back. He knows I'm here. I think that's why he left just a little a while ago when I drove down the street. He probably saw me. What are you all doing this evening? Will you and your family and Andrew be together later?"

"Yes, I need to go home for a few minutes and then will be right back. My family will probably stay together for a while here this evening." Alex is tempted to bring up the topic of the terrorist crisis and Ammen but waits for Officer Musty to bring it up first. But Officer Musty also avoids the subject. Alex assumes it's too sensitive of a subject for a civilian and a police officer to discuss.

Officer Musty then says with a friendly smile, "Well, I hope you and your family have an enjoyable evening together tonight. I'll be around to keep an eye on things. You'll probably see me around here now that I'm back in town. If the Arab returns, don't you worry. You shouldn't even have to think about him at all. I'm here. I'll watch over you and your family."

Alex thanks Officer Musty for his protection and services, wishes him well, and then says he has to go.

As he turns away, Alex notices what appears to be a backward comma stitched across the shoulder of Officer Musty's uniform.

Alex thinks, "Did I just imagine that, or did I really see it?" In the back of his mind, he remembers seeing the same symbol on Ammen's tunic. He also thinks he remembers seeing the same symbol elsewhere before as well, but he's not sure.

Anyway, for some strange reason, it's comforting to him to know that both a police officer and the possible savior who are both looking out for his best interest both sport the same symbol on their clothes.

Alex then waves good-bye to Officer Musty and then leaves to go home. Officer Musty returns to his patrol car.

Chapter 62

Several minutes later Alex arrives at his house. The first thing he does is to get the ice cream and cones. He opens the freezer in the garage and finds about a half-dozen cartons.

He then laughs and asks himself why Sonja bought so many cartons when she last went to the store. He thinks of how smart she is, knowing to stock-up considering the circumstances. She truly is an angel. She's always on top of things. It's as if she has a divine knowledge of everything and knows what's going to happen. He thinks if the world is going to end in three days, at least they can enjoy a lot of ice cream in the meantime. She certainly knows how to look out for him and she's always there for him.

He separates the cartons that he will take, puts them along with the cones in a bag, puts the bag back in the freezer, and goes into the house. He goes into the kitchen and grabs the orange blossoms that Sonja wanted and puts them in a bag and places it by the freezer so that he won't forget them.

He then goes into his office and turns on the news on a small TV in the corner and sits back in his office chair to think. Now that he's alone, he's able to concentrate more.

The news broadcast is reporting that another bomb has been located. This one was found in Orlando, but the location is not disclosed in part because of the hidden location. Alex immediately thinks perhaps it was probably placed at one of the theme parks. Like the others, this bomb has a timer to go off in three days and is also tamperproof.

Alex gets sick to his stomach realizing that the terrorists would put a bomb in such a place. They have no regard or respect whatsoever to not only human life, but to children as well. The news goes on to say that the authorities have not figured out any way at all how to deactivate or remove any of the bombs found to date in any city. The news also reports that there is some speculation that a few more of the bombs discovered appear to be nuclear devices than what was previously reported.

They've been studying these for days now and cannot figure out what to do. It appears that everything that Muhammad has said is true. It appears that every bomb in every city will detonate at midnight three days from now and that there is no way to prevent it. Even Ammen hinted that the world will end in three days. Alex presumes that Ammen may be correct.

Alex then turns down the volume, reclines back some more in his office chair, closes his eyes, and goes into a deep prayer asking God for guidance. "Please show me the way. Please give me a sign which way is right. Should I continue to worship only Jesus Christ or should I now worship Ammen as the return of Jesus? Are they one in the same? Any sign. Anything. Please, provide me with guidance. Please give me a sign. In the name of Jesus Christ, please help me."

He then opens his eyes and begins to think. For some reason, he thinks of his father and what he used to tell him when he was a little boy. "Think outside of the box," he remembers. He recalls his father telling him that one day he will be confronted with the puzzle of life and that he will need to be able to put together all of the pieces to figure it out. He remembers his father talking about an Apocalypse. Whether what's happening is really the Apocalypse doesn't matter. This *has* to be what his father talked about. He suddenly realizes that this *is* the puzzle of life that his father spoke about so much when he was a little boy. How did he know this would happen?

Now he thinks he understands why his father said he will always be with him. His father somehow knew that these events would come someday. He wanted Alex to remember what he said back when he was a child about the need to figure out puzzles and to think outside of the box. "He is helping and guiding me now by me remembering this," Alex thinks.

He then starts thinking of all sorts of things and soon his mind is running rampant with thoughts. In fact, his mind is recalling visions and thoughts faster than he can separately think about them all. While he's thinking of myriads of ideas that now are speeding through his mind, he looks out the window. Unfortunately, he sees the old white van parked across the street, and temporarily comes back to reality.

He cannot believe it. "What? I don't need to worry about this now. Why is the Arab here again? Is he out to get me for some reason? What does he want from me? Where's Officer Musty when I need him?" He thinks that the reason why Officer Musty remained back at Andrew's house was to protect his family. But now Alex wishes he was here at his house instead.

Alex says to himself, "I can't worry about the Arab now. He hasn't done anything to me or to my family so far, so I must assume I'm safe." He closes the blinds to the window and resumes his thought process. Within a minute the thoughts and visions are racing through his head again. "I need to concentrate," he says to himself.

Suddenly, he senses a spirit coming over him. Alex is optimistic that he will be provided a sign and begins to remember some of his experience in hell and heaven. Although he forgot about the details of his experience there and cannot remember anything on his own, the spirit is helping him remember some, but not all of what he learned there.

He thinks about the mirror and the evaluation of his life, seeing his life in reverse going backward.

He remembers the massive formula, the equation that measures all of the good and bad in his life, his level of faith, and all of the symbols in the equation. He thinks of the backwards number six again, the sideways 8, the sign of the trinity, and the other symbols in the immense formula. He remembers the wheel of balance.

And with the help of the spirit now he remembers the Council Room of God. He remembers some, but not all of the details. He remembers seeing the backward number 6 on the vacant chairs.

He remembers that there was going to be an ordination process of sorts that was required of the last angel and the second to last angel.

He remembers that there will be not one but two angels to be sent by God who will help the last angel who will be needed to save the souls from Satan.

He remembers that all three angels will be of a same sacred bloodline.

He also remembers some other things told about the last angel and the ordination process.

Alex then realizes that this is almost exactly everything that Ammen said! Is Ammen right?

Is perhaps Ammen the last angel and the Second Coming to save those who will follow him? Did God send him? Why else would Ammen say the same things that Alex heard in the Council Room when he was in heaven? How else would he know? Therefore, perhaps Ammen is the last angel!

Then Alex remembers the vision he had in the viewing room to the Council Room in heaven of the two souls who he thought may be the last two angels. They appear to be Ammen and the woman who is always by his side. And, then he remembers thinking of who the last two angels would be after his studying the pattern on how the angels sat around the tables. Again, they appear to be consistent with Ammen and the woman. Are Ammen and the woman with him the last two angels? They sure appear to be. Surely his earlier visions cannot be wrong.

But then he starts to question everything. "Was I dreaming? Or am I still dreaming? Which life was or is real? Did I really go to hell and heaven? Did I really experience the Council Room? Or did I merely dream that and all of this is a figment of my imagination?" For some strange reason, Alex gets the feeling again that everything he experienced was a dream. Now he's confused again.

He looks up at the TV and there is another repeat video of Muhammad. He casually looks at the screen and spots something. He suddenly perks up, reaches for the remote, and quickly freezes the screen. There stitched on his tunic on his left shoulder is a small backward comma. That is so strange, Alex thinks. He remembers where he's seen these before.

He first saw the symbol on Ammen. Then he saw it on Officer Musty. Now he sees it on Muhammad. That makes three backward commas.

He wonders if this is a sign. By now, his mind is racing with thoughts as he is trying to figure out the puzzle. But the more he thinks, the more the puzzle appears to be getting more complicated rather than easier.

Then he realizes that the symbol may not be a backwards comma, but instead may be the number six. It looks like it a little bit. Maybe it is, but maybe it isn't. Where these only visible to him, or were they real? Did anybody else see them? If the symbol is supposed to represent the number six, that would make three sixes, "666." But if that's the case, why would that make any sense? That can't be.

But he then thinks maybe he has everything backwards. He thinks maybe the backward commas have a meaning if thought of the other way around. If he were to look at it this way, they would not be all sixes but instead would all look like backwards sixes. That's one of the symbols he saw on the high back chairs in the Council Room. And there are three of them. And there are supposed to be three angels. A lot of other things appear to be backwards to him. So, maybe he's supposed to think of these commas backward to understand what it means. Maybe that's the sign.

He then thinks of a lot of things and asks himself why so many things appear to be backward. He thinks of his evaluation in the mirror going backward, seeing his life in reverse, the backward number 6, the backwards commas, looking backward to his father when he was a child. He then thinks of many other things that appear to be the other way around in one way or another. Should he be thinking backward to Jesus instead of forward to the present and

Ammen? Is that the sign that he needs? He then thinks maybe he has everything backward.

But then he acknowledges to himself that he's overstimulated and is thinking of all sorts of things that don't make sense. Of course none of this is as profound as Ammen and the woman that is with him being identical to the vision of the last two angels he saw in heaven and what Ammen said is nearly identical to what he heard in God's Council Room.

So, what sign means something and what doesn't? Everything is so confusing. Alex begins to think he's over analyzing things and perhaps may even be seeing things that aren't there. He's thinking of the absurd and he's thinking of the pure nonsense, but nevertheless he's brainstorming. He is trying his best to think outside of the box. He's thinking of anything that he can to try to identify a sign. "This is nonsense," he mutters to himself. "What is the sign? Please, dear God, please let me know the sign."

When he thinks of his father again, he decides to retrieve the treasures that were left to him after he died. Maybe these will give him the inspiration that he needs. Maybe he can find a sign that he can rely on by looking at these. "If I can't find any other sign that's really meaningful, then it appears I must rely on the sign given to me that Ammen and the woman are the last two angels as they appeared to me when I was in heaven. That must be it if I can't find anything else that makes sense."

After several minutes he's on his way back to his office carrying the blanket, the Bible, and his old shirt he wore when he sat on his father's lap. Alex misses his father and wishes he was there. He wants to reminisce. He wants his biological father to help him now. But Alex tells himself that he can't. Even though his father told him he would always be there to guide him, he's long gone.

On his way back he stops briefly in the bathroom and looks in the mirror. He gets a very strange sensation. He remembers his evaluation in the mirror before he went to hell.

After a minute or so, he returns to his office and sits down. He rests the folded blanket on his lap, puts the Bible on top, and looks at it. He admires it but remembers that it won't open and again wishes he had one just like it, with a white cover. Again when he tries to open it he gets the strange feeling that he should not get a new one and that he should wait, but he doesn't understand why. Then he rests the folded shirt on top of the Bible. He closes his eyes and again prays for guidance. All he wants is a simple sign. All he needs to know is whether to worship only Jesus Christ or Ammen as the return of Jesus. He opens his eyes and looks at his watch. He only has several hours to make a decision.

Alex then looks down at the shirt and unfolds it to admire it. It is old, somewhat ragged, and dusty. He looks at it and practically jumps out of his seat.

The symbols and letters on the middle line that were previously faded in the fabric now are materializing. It's not bold and clear, but he can start to see them. After a minute or so, he can see them fully. He still can't read them since they all look like hieroglyphics to him. Although he can't read what it says, he now can clearly see the symbols and letters. He is shocked. "What is happening?"

He feels great optimism and a sense of wonderment. He is absolutely flabbergasted. He is astonished at what he sees. What does this mean? How could this have happened? He wishes he could read and understand it but he can't. The symbols and lettering makes no sense. But at least now they can be seen on the shirt. Is this the sign? But if it is, what does it mean?

He then starts thinking about other things. For example, why does the number three keep coming up? What is the significance of all of the threes he sees in a lot of things? He remembers all of the things that require three of something, or has the number three or that relates to the number three for one reason or another. He looks at the three lines on the shirt. He has experienced the number three many times lately. Maybe this is a sign?

He then thinks of many other things, many of which he had thought of the wrong way. He is looking for a sign. Any sign. As he's thinking he looks at the TV. It's playing a repeat video of Ammen's interview. He and the woman look exactly like the vision of the last two angels he had when he visited heaven. He thinks that Ammen must be the last angel and she is the second to last angel, just as he indicated. Alex looks at the woman and suddenly realizes that when Ammen starts speaking, she lays the bouquet of white flowers upside down in her lap. He recognizes that the flowers are orange blossoms. He stares at her intently.

He stares at the upside down white flowers and gets a very funny feeling about her. Then, he remembers what his father told him when he was a little boy during his sessions. He recalls him saying "If you ever see her hold the bouquet of orange blossoms upside down, then you should be very concerned. You should remember this always, for the rest of your life." Alex then remembers what his father said what the upside down bouquet of white flowers would mean. It's as if he knew this would happen! Is this what he was referring to?

He looks back at the TV and focuses on the woman sitting beside Ammen. He then looks at the bouquet she is holding upside down on her lap again. The flowers are definitely orange blossoms. He looks up at her face again and becomes transfixed by it. He looks at her eyes. She appears to be looking right at him! Alex nearly goes into shock. He cannot believe it. With a burst of insight, now he knows who she is! Tears roll down Alex's cheek, and he's shaking with emotion.

He stares even more intently at the woman sitting beside Ammen. That brings on more tears. He wipes away the tears streaming from his eyes; however, his mind now is in full focus. "How can this be? This certainly cannot be the mother coincidence of all time. It's been so long!" Did his father really know this would happen? Alex cries out, "She's conveying a message to me! To me! And to think, it's probably been about sixty years since I last saw her!"

Now he knows, his father told her that someday she would need to do this. This was her puzzle of life to figure out and do! He has his puzzle of life to figure out and this is hers. How did he know this would all happen someday? And now he knows the solution to her puzzle.

Why else would his father have told him about the flowers when he was a little boy and to remember for the rest of his life to always make sure she held them right side up? "How could I have missed this? It was right before my eyes and I didn't see it. I can't believe this is happening; it's so hard to believe."

He then thinks of the woman who has been calling him with important information about her and him but who apparently hangs up or they get disconnected. Now he knows who she is also! Alex starts to shake with emotion. He can't take his eyes off the woman sitting by Ammen. This brings on more tears. It's as if the woman and Alex are looking right at each other through the TV. He continues to weep in wonder with what's happening. He can't take his eyes off of her. "It's been so long!"

He thinks of the three backward commas again and tries to analyze the meaning both ways again. He then realizes that there are three of them, regardless whether the symbol is a six or a backward six or whatever it is. There's that number three again. Maybe the number three is more important than the fact that the symbol might or might not be a six. But is there really any need to think about commas and sixes and threes and other things anymore when he has received this sign? The upside-down bouquet held by her is all what he needs to know. That *must* be the sign he must rely on!

Again he is stunned to think of what all of this might mean and what he now has learned. "How come I didn't realize this before?" he thinks. Then Alex feels the spirit come over him again. It has been there all along. It's helping him remember and understand everything. He could not remember anything about his visit to heaven and the Council Room on his own, but the spirit now is helping him remember. Everything is starting to click. Everything is starting to make sense. He just needs to figure out a few remaining pieces of the puzzle.

He becomes obsessed with the woman and thinking about the upside down bouquet and what it means. He has figured out a lot of what he needs to know, at least for now! Finally, he knows at least what's most important to make the decision.

He thinks again about Ammen saying all of the same things that he heard in God's Council Room. Can this be pure coincidence? How would Ammen know this? And the visions Alex had of the last two angels when he was in heaven are nearly identical to Ammen and the woman who is always with him. And they're the same as who he thought the last two angels would be when he studied the pattern of where the angels sat in the Council Room. There's only one reason why it appears that Ammen and the woman are the last two angels.

And he remembers Ammen's answers in the interview were not direct. They were not clear-cut. His answers required interpretation. But, that is how Jesus often taught. A lot of His teachings were not clear and were indirect also. Even his parables required some thought to understand. Ammen appears to be the return of Jesus in every respect. Alex thinks "How clever! How ingenious! My father told me I need to think outside of the box, and that's the only way I could have seen through this. And to think, I was nearly on the verge of being fooled otherwise!"

Although Alex has received several signs, there is one that is the most important on which he can rely. That is the upside down bouquet of orange blossoms. Now, Alex knows one answer to the puzzle. It is the most important piece of the puzzle. He knows whether or not to accept Ammen and who he must worship! And, he knows for sure the right answer and who it is.

He gets a strong feeling that there is more that he will learn. There are more pieces of the puzzle that will need to be figured out, but there is no time for that now. He will worry about that later. But for now, he has solved the most important piece.

He will still need to revisit all of these thoughts again later because the remaining pieces of the puzzle are also critically important, but for now, he knows the answer to the most important question of all. Is it Jesus Christ or is it Ammen? He knows without a shadow of a doubt whether or not Ammen is actually the return of Jesus. He now knows with absolute certainty whether he is actually one and the same as Jesus Christ. And, he must tell everybody back at Andrew's house.

Alex quickly looks at his watch and notes that he is rapidly running out of time. Midnight is only several hours away. He turns off the TV, and takes one last peek outside of his window. He sees that the white van is still parked up the street. He looks at the blanket and remembers that it is a precious and perhaps priceless heirloom.

If it really goes back over one thousand years, it must be invaluable. But he remembers that his father told him that it was very special and must stay in the family forever. Why is it so special? And why is the Bible that was wrapped with it also so special? They always seemed mystical to him. He again admires the Bible and wonders why it's so mysterious.

Alex remembers again that his father said something about them being so special. He wonders for an instant if perhaps that the Arab knows that he has this blanket and wants to steal it. Maybe that's why the Arab has been following him around. Nah, how would he know that he has this?

But maybe he does. Alex then remembers that Andrew had asked some questions about the blanket not too long ago, since he knew that Alex had it and that Andrew would inherit it someday. Andrew wanted to know if it had any monetary value. This upset Alex because that is not what he wanted to hear from Andrew. The blanket was to stay in the family for future generations forever, not to be sold for money. Alex wonders if perhaps Andrew had done some research on it or if he mentioned it to anybody. Maybe that's how the Arab found out about it. Alex hopes not. But you never know.

Then he remembers that Alana said that somebody broke into her house but didn't take anything. "Hmmmm," he thinks. So, just in case and to be on the safe side, he grabs the blanket, the Bible, and the shirt to take with him. Better safe with him than here in his house when he's away.

He turns off the light and the TV and rushes through the house. His leg, foot, and toes still hurt a little, but he can make it. In doing so, he, stuffs the old small shirt in his pocket, carries the blanket and Bible, and then heads out to the garage to get the bag with the cartons of ice cream and cones, and grabs the bag with the flowers. Within seconds, he lays the items in the car on the passenger seat, closes the garage door, and speeds up the street to return to Andrew's house. "I need to get back there as fast as I can," he thinks to himself. "Everybody is going to want to know what I have decided."

In the rearview mirror, he sees the old white van start up. It's now following him.

"Now what? Not again. What does he want with me?" Alex eyes the blanket and the Bible on the passenger seat. "I need to guard these with my life," he thinks. But the van drops back and is following him from a distance. "As long as he stays way back there, I guess it's okay." But the van continues to follow him back to Andrew's house. As the van continues to follow him Alex gets a gut wrenching feeling that something horrible is about to happen.

Chapter 63

Alex is driving back to Andrew's house and despite being followed and some trepidation as if something bad is going to happen, he also feels good. He has the cartons of ice cream and cones which will be a surprise for the kids. They would not be expecting that at Andrew's house. He has his treasures as well as the bouquets with him. And, most importantly, he has the answer to whether or not Ammen is for real and is the return of Jesus Christ.

As he's driving along, he notices that the clouds are getting darker ahead of him. A few raindrops fall, and then he sees some lightning hit about half mile away followed by a clash of thunder. "Great, another thunderstorm," Alex says to himself.

Soon the winds pick up and a torrential rainstorm buffets his car. As he approaches the intersection to take the short way to Andrew's house, he suddenly feels his car rocked and tossed to the side of the road. He initially thinks it's a gust of wind, but then it happens again. This time, he nearly loses control and almost drives off of the road. He suddenly realizes that another car has sideswiped him.

He cannot see the other car because it has gotten considerably darker and it's raining cats and dogs. Then the car hits him again on the side, causing him to swerve at the fork in the road. He slows down and looks around, but doesn't see another car. He continues to drive for a few seconds and realizes that now he's on the road that is the longer way to Andrew's house. It's still raining heavily. He can

440

hardly see anything through the windshield. Fortunately, there's no other traffic.

The only thing that Alex can think of is that the car that hit him is the old white van with the Arab. He wishes that he could see it but he can't. It's raining so hard and because of the dark clouds, he can barely see anything.

The road is the country road that passes several farmhouses, a pond, the closed gas station, the creek, and the entrance to the industrial warehouse complex. "Okay," he thinks. "I don't know what is happening, I don't see the other car, but I know my way on this road. It may take me a bit longer, but I'll just continue to drive."

A few minutes later, the rain picks up again, and again he is hit, this time very hard. This time he nearly loses control and comes within a foot of rolling down the embankment, a drop-off of about eighty feet. Alex regains control of his car, slows down some more, and continues to drive, looking for the other car. He still can't see it. He wonders again if perhaps it's the Arab who was following him who hit him.

As he's looking off to the passenger side and behind him, he's suddenly hit again on the driver's side which causes him to lose control and roll his car which goes off the road and lands upright against a tree. Although his car had rolled over once, it miraculously ends upright and is still running. It's resting against a large tree next to a ditch.

He can't believe that his airbag didn't deploy. He figures that perhaps somehow when his car rolled over and then hit the tree; it didn't hit the tree hard enough. "How strange," he thinks. "I would have thought for sure I'd have an air bag in my face right now."

Alex looks around and still doesn't see another car and begins to wonder if he's dreaming all of this. He's okay except for a bruise from hitting the steering wheel. Even though his car is all banged up, since his engine is still going, he decides to continue to try to drive. He's able to put the car in reverse and get back on the road. There's dirt, leaves, and other debris all over his car and a lot on his windows that obstructs his vision. Fortunately, his windshield wiper still works, but he can't see out of any of the other windows. When he turns on the rear wiper, it smears it and makes it worse.

His car drives all right, but is a little misaligned. After driving a bit, he eventually sees smoke coming from the cracks in the hood and realizes that his engine is on fire. Then he can see the flames. That must have happened when he rolled over he surmises.

As he decides to pull off on the side of the road, the rain picks up again and now is coming at him in torrents sideways. The wind is pounding his car as well. He can hardly see a thing again. Another lightning bolt hits about a quarter mile away lighting up the countryside and is immediately followed by another thunderclap that rocks the car. That startles him and at the same time he's again hit from behind which causes him to veer off the road and head straight towards the entrance of the warehouse complex. Within the rain, smoke can be seen coming from underneath the hood and makes it harder to see.

"Who is this? Who is doing this to me? Is he drunk or what?" He tries to slow down and stop, but instead for some unknown reason, his accelerator is stuck and he's going faster. Actually, he's going much faster. The car hitting him from behind now is on his rear bumper, and is pushing him through the entrance gate. Alex quickly thinks, "Why is this gate open? We drive by here often and it's never open. Who would leave the gate open? Why can't I see the vehicle that's doing this to me?" His rear window is caked in mud, which the rain has smeared to the extent he can't see a thing.

At that time, the rain abruptly stops and the sun peeks out from behind a cloud. The passing storm was short lived and everything here is dry. But, he still can't see in his side mirrors and can barely see through the windshield. He can't see anything out of any of the other windows.

He's now going nearly fifty miles per hour and can't stop the acceleration. He doesn't know why he has no control over it. Alex realizes that he's headed straight for the propane tanks. The fairly long driveway is now turning into a wider paved lot and the tanks are rapidly coming into view directly in front of him.

By now there are flames coming from his hood and he can't see because of the smoke. He then tries to steer his car away from the propane tanks, however he has no control of his steering either. He continues to apply his brakes and slams on the emergency brake. Neither works. He tries to turn the key to shut down the engine and the key is stuck and won't budge. He puts the car in neutral, but it is still traveling at an accelerated speed. As a last resort, he decides to open the door and jump out.

Going about 50 mph he knows that would be near suicide, but hitting the propane tanks would be certain death. He grabs the blanket and tries to open the door, but it's jammed. Because the car had rolled over, the side of the car is bashed in and the door won't open.

His accelerator doesn't work and is stuck. Both of his brakes don't work. His steering doesn't work. His key is stuck. And his door won't open. Nothing works at all. He has totally lost all control of his car and he's at the mercy of the car pushing him ahead from behind. The driver is acting like a maniac. Alex can't see who it is not only because of the mud smeared on the windows, but the smoke now is entering the inside of his car as well. He's being pushed straight toward the propane tanks with his engine on fire.

It's now obvious that the driver behind him is trying to kill him. Is it the Arab? Alex looks back but can't see anything. The smoke from the engine is blowing behind the car as well. Now the front of his car is nearly engulfed in flames and he has absolutely no control of it whatsoever.

He's within only a few feet of crashing into the propane tanks and is going so fast that there is no way that he can avoid them now. When he hits them, it will surely result in a massive explosion and he will instantly die in an inferno of fire. The tanks come into view through the smoke right in front of him and he's only a second away from hitting them.

Chapter 64

Back at Andrew's and Alana's house, Andrew has returned from the Ammen rally and is sporting a brand spanking new Ammen T-shirt. He is so proud of it. He's showing it off to everybody. He wanted a red or black one for some reason but had to settle for a white one. He got one of the last ones they had.

Imprinted on the front is a color photo of Ammen's face across the chest. There are three broken lines that run horizontally across the shirt underneath his photo. Ammen's full name in bright red letters are on the first two rows. It reads EVEDOTHLID AMMENOFI. ON THE BACK SIDE ARE THE LETTERS IBI AMMEN in black.

The rest of the family is back in the living room discussing Ammen and the crisis. They have also learned of the new bomb found in Orlando.

Andrew resumes explaining his support for Ammen. Everyone except for Sonja seems to be on the fence but appear to be leaning towards agreeing with Andrew. They're waiting for Alex to return because they want to hear what he has to say, now that he has had time to think and pray about it. Garrett comments that he would not be surprised if a debate between Andrew and Alex may be in the works when Alex returns. Andrew states that he expects Alex to side with him and to follow Ammen. Alana and Julie indicate they sort of expect Alex to decide to worship Ammen as well. Garrett then somewhat reluctantly agrees.

It appears that Sonja is going to side with Alex no matter what his decision is, however that's expected anyway. Sonja is a woman of a divine nature and most everyone thinks that she already knows how both she and Alex will decide. But she won't tell anybody. She could probably accurately predict a number between one and a million that Alex would pick ahead of time. It's as if she can read his mind and he can read hers. She is just like that. Sometimes people get the feeling that somehow she can predict the future, but will never tell anyone. Sometimes, people refer to her as an angel because of her angelic like qualities. But nobody is willing to ask her what she thinks.

The couple do everything together, usually, but not always go everywhere together, and are hardly ever seen disagreeing with each other. They support each other on everything. They are both considered true elements of wisdom. Everybody in the family knows it and they desperately want to know what Alex will say when he returns. He will officially speak for both of them.

So, everybody else except for Andrew is pretty much relying on Alex's advice. Not that they can't make up their own decisions. Alex did clearly tell each of them to separately pray and think for themselves before he left, but it's easier for them to listen to him first. Alex is nearly always right about everything even though they don't want to admit it. They value his insight but don't want to let on to it.

In the meantime, Andrew is asking everyone how they like his new T-shirt; however, he's not getting much of a response. He then teasingly asks the kids what they think knowing that they're too young to understand. He's clearly looking for a positive response from anyone. Both Matthew and Daniel say they like it and Mikey shows some interest but with some hesitation. But Lizzy is a totally different story.

When Andrew shows Lizzy, she looks at it, studies it for a few seconds and then turns her head away and starts crying. "What's the matter?" asks Julie. Lizzy runs over and buries her head in her mom's lap.

Alana says, "I wonder what made her cry?"

"Well you can't ask her because she won't talk," Andrew sarcastically comments. "She can't talk, remember? She has that stupid illness. And we all know that she can't read yet."

Obviously, he's distraught that even a child who doesn't know any better doesn't like his shirt. He desperately wants attention and support for the Ammen shirt he acquired, but he's not getting it. Now that a child who doesn't even know any better openly doesn't like it, he's beside himself.

Alana stares down Andrew and resolutely says, "Andrew, that is enough. How dare you make comments like that! You need to apologize!"

"Maybe she doesn't like the picture of his face on the shirt. Does she know who he is?"

Julie can hear Lizzy sobbing in her lap. Lizzy then whispers something softly to her mom and points at the shirt. Julie looks at her dumbfounded, doesn't know what to think, and then comforts her.

Chapter 65

Suddenly, the house is rocked by an explosion. The house shakes violently and the explosion echoes throughout the entire neighborhood. Garrett jumps up and runs outside and returns to tell them that there was an explosion southwest just a few miles from the house. Everybody runs outside to look. They can see flames on the horizon and black billowing smoke rising into the air.

They watch this for a while and then return into the house. Julie comments, "Where's Alex? Shouldn't he have been home a long time ago?" Everybody agrees, except for Sonja who comments that Alex probably got sidetracked at home.

A little while later, the TV programming is pre-empted by a local news alert. The local news anchor comes on the screen and reports the following:

"We have a rapidly developing local news event of significant interest. We have reports that a massive explosion has occurred at an industrial warehouse complex located southwest of town. Initial reports are sketchy, but it appears that at least one car and probably two cars have driven into a concentration of propane tanks causing the explosion.

"However, there are also unofficial reports that at least one eyewitness claims two cars were consumed in flames and that a third car may have also been involved and drove off. Initial reports are that it's believed none of the vehicle's occupants could have survived the blast.

"Firefighters and the police are at the scene and we have a team of reporters headed there now. We will bring you an update with live coverage as soon as they arrive and when we have additional details to report."

The family sits around and waits for Alex and the news update. They all know this warehouse complex well. They pass by it often in route from one house to another and to and from the stores where they shop. Andrew knows about it more than anybody for obvious reasons that nobody is willing to discuss.

After about a half hour, they start to get very nervous. Julie finally mentions what everybody has been thinking but was afraid to bring up. "I wonder if the explosion has anything to do with why Alex is so late."

Then the local news comes back on with an update on the explosion. The news team is on site at the scene with live coverage and a reporter starts the broadcast with a live video of the crash site.

"We just arrived here at the industrial warehouse complex where a massive explosion has occurred within the last hour. Reports are still somewhat sketchy, but it appears that two vehicles drove into a storage area containing dozens of fully loaded industrial and commercial propane tanks. It is said that someone may have seen a third vehicle leaving the crash site, but this has not yet been confirmed.

"The explosion was heard ten miles away and the smoke was seen for over ten miles as it drifted into the atmosphere. We will try to get an interview with someone from the police or fire department but until then, here is what we know.

"The firefighters were on the scene within minutes and have been able to put the fire out. Over here we can see the burned vehicles involved in the crash. Initial reports are that the occupants of both of these vehicles are presumed to have been burned instantly in the explosion and did not survive.

"Authorities are combing the site for bodies, however have not been able to find any remains yet. It's feared that they may have been burned beyond recognition. When they are found, names will not be released until their identities are confirmed and the next of kin has been notified."

The camera which was focused on the crash site, then swings over and zooms in on the two scorched vehicles. One is an older model van that is burned beyond recognition. The other is a late model SUV that is also burned to a crisp except for the rear end of the vehicle which is only partially charred.

Almost simultaneously, Julie and Alana let out an ear-piercing scream. The one car, the SUV, looks like Alex's car. In addition, the license plate which Alex had personalized "FSHMAN" can be seen lying on the ground next to it. Everybody knows it.

There is immediate hysteria in the household and everybody is shaken to the core over what they just heard and saw. For the next half hour, everyone is in a state of shock. Julie and Alana are crying and asking "Why, what happened?"

They all assume that Alex died in the explosion. What was Alex doing driving in the warehouse complex? Why was he there? Why did he drive into the propane tanks?

In addition, now they won't know what Alex has decided about Ammen and Jesus. The midnight hour still lurks ahead and is fast approaching. Alana, Julie, and to some extent Garrett was relying on what Alex had decided and now they won't know. Now it looks like each will be on their own without his advice.

Sonja is sitting outside on the porch by herself in prayer. It's as if she knows exactly what's going on.

Garrett is on the phone trying to get additional detailed information and confirmation, but he has no success. Everybody is shaken up and emotions run rampant.

Chapter 66

At the crash site, a police officer is questioning someone.

"I can remember being headed straight into the propane tanks with the front of my car in flames going about fifty miles per hour. I was previously sideswiped and nearly ran off the road by an unidentified vehicle. I do believe that for some unknown reason, the driver wanted me to have an accident or was trying to kill me. I think it was an older white van, but I don't know for sure.

"The car crashed into me several times and then pushed me from behind through the open gate and directly towards the propane tanks. I had lost control of my steering and had no brakes. My accelerator was stuck. I couldn't turn my engine off and my emergency brake wouldn't work either. My door was jammed. I was totally at God's mercy.

"But just as I was about to be pushed by him from behind one final time into the propane tanks, a third vehicle came out of nowhere and hit me broadside and knocked my car to the side allowing me to miss the propane tanks by inches. My car then hit the wall of the building behind these Dumpsters. Then the vehicle right behind me followed and crashed into the propane tanks setting off the explosion.

"I cannot believe I survived this. These bruises from hitting the steering wheel and the deployed air bag seem to be my only injury. The airbag probably helped saved my life. The driver of the car that knocked my car to the side right before I was going to hit the propane tanks definitely saved my life.

"The Dumpsters protected me just enough from the explosion. The vehicle that was bumping me and pushing me from behind then drove straight into the tanks causing the explosion after I was knocked to the side. I never saw that happen, but that's what I figure.

"In fact, whoever was driving that third vehicle stopped for a minute and helped me out by opening the door from the outside. I couldn't open it from the inside at all. That person actually pulled me out. My car was on fire. I could hardly see a thing. There were flames and smoke everywhere. It all happened so fast.

"But as soon as I was able to get out and get away and take refuge behind the Dumpsters when everything exploded, that driver got back in his or her car and drove away. I couldn't thank him or her. I don't even know what he or she looked like. I was so dazed and confused. There was a lot of smoke. Whoever it was also removed my things I had on the passenger seat next to me and gave them to me.

"What's left of my car is not from the explosion, although it looks like it. It's from a fire that started in my engine after the second car crashed into me and after my car rolled over.

"It looks like the car that had earlier crashed into me and that pushed me into the propane tanks then drove into the tanks causing the explosion. That's the other car that's burned to a crisp."

The police officer tells Alex that other eyewitnesses have verified his story almost exactly. They claim that there was at least one other vehicle involved. The one that crashed into Alex and drove him into the warehouse was an older model white van, being the other vehicle completely burned up.

One eyewitness indicated that there was a third vehicle and that driver apparently saved Alex's life by knocking him to the side right before he was about to hit the propane tanks. She said that everything happened so fast and there was so much smoke, it was difficult for her to see from her vantage point. She was fairly far away. She knows for sure that there was a third vehicle, but is having trouble remembering any specifics. But she thinks she can recall some things, but isn't sure.

She said that she believed that both vehicles were very similar in appearance. She thinks that both vehicles had one occupant being the driver. And she thinks but is not sure that the driver who briefly stopped and got out of the car to help Alex may have been wearing a uniform of some sort. This is because she remembers seeing such a person walking away from the crash site a minute or two after the explosion and then disappearing in the smoke. Then the third car drove off. The third vehicle drove off through the smoke and she was not able to get a good look at it. There was just simply too much smoke from the explosion and fire.

Then the police officer reports to Alex something very strange. The authorities have combed the burned van and the entire crash site. They have looked in the burned vehicle and sifted through all of the rubble and ashes and have not been able to find any bodies or any human remains anywhere. But they're still looking.

The police officer wants to know what Alex thinks about this or if he's willing to speculate what happened. He wants to know if Alex is aware of anybody who had any issues with him or who may want to kill him for any reason, or if he has anything that they may want.

Alex comments, "I have no idea. The only person who may be somewhat suspicious is somebody who appears to be an Arab who's been following me around lately. But I want to be clear. I don't know who he is and he hasn't caused any trouble, or at least so far anyway to date."

"Do you know what type of vehicle he drove?"

"It was an older white van. I don't remember the make or model."

"Bingo," says the police officer. "We're still looking for the other vehicle. We would certainly like to find out who saved your life. But right now, we're more interested in finding whoever it was who tried to kill you. We know that driver was definitely driving an older white van for sure. From what you're telling us it appears to be this Arab person you described."

The police officer then continues to talk with Alex for several additional minutes and completes some additional paperwork. Then, he offers to drive Alex to Andrew's house. Alex grabs his things and graciously accepts the ride. As they leave, Alex scans the area to see if one of the policemen there is Officer Musty, but he doesn't see him anywhere. While looking for him Alex wonders who the person is who saved his life and drove off, and wishes he knew who it was.

Chapter 67

The police officer drops Alex off at Andrew's and Alana's house. Alex walks up to the front door, and as he does, he starts to drop everything he's carrying. He stops and sets everything down on the sidewalk. The blanket was already unfolding, so instead of folding it back up he throws it over his shoulders and wraps it around his neck. Now it's hanging down in front of him. He'll refold it when he gets into the house. Now he can more easily carry the bag of cones and cartons of ice cream that is probably at least half melted by now, the Bible, and the bouquets.

Alex opens the front door and sees everybody in the living room facing the other way intently watching the TV. They're watching the news about the propane tank explosion and are looking at the video of his scorched car. They're all sobbing and crying. It's somewhat dark in the entryway as Alex enters into the shadow.

They don't see Alex and don't hear him come in. He silently walks in right behind them and stands behind the sofa where the adults are sitting. He's still in a shadow. They're all facing the other way looking at the TV. They still don't see him or hear him.

Suddenly, Matthew and Daniel let out a bloodcurdling scream that makes everybody jump out of their seats. The kids have spotted Alex. Everybody turns around and sees Alex and they think they see a ghost.

They don't recognize him with the white blanket draped over his entire body. He actually looks like a ghost coming out of the shadow in the dark behind the sofa. It all happens so suddenly and with everybody already at the peak of emotion, hysterical screams of fright go on for a good ten seconds or so.

Then without saying a word, Alex removes the blanket, refolds it, and lays it down along with the bag of cartons of ice cream and cones, the Bible, and bouquets on the credenza. As he does this everybody finally recognizes him. But, that produces gasps and trepidation as everybody can't believe it's him. Now they're sure they're seeing a ghost. They surely had thought he died in the explosion.

After a few seconds they come to their senses and their fright turns into joys of excitement and happiness when he greets them. Alex is welcomed with hugs and kisses from everybody. Sonja is the last one to greet him, allowing everybody else to go first. She approaches him as if she knew all along that he would return.

After Alex spends some time explaining what happened and the women dipping the half melted ice cream for the kids, everyone goes outside to be with the kids in the back yard, except for Alex and Andrew.

Andrew, beaming with pride asks Alex, "What do you think of my new Ammen T-shirt? I got one of the last ones. Isn't it great! Can I assume you reached a decision? You know, he's the only way to go, right?"

"Andrew, I know you're sure that Ammen is for real. But I think it's best for me to tell everybody at the same time what I've decided."

Andrew then addresses the qualities of Ammen and borders getting angry with Alex for not readily supporting him.

"Andrew, what does everybody else think? Have you talked with them? Have they said anything?"

"They're all waiting to hear your decision. But I think they're all leaning towards Ammen."

"What about Julie?"

"She wants to hear you first, but I think she believes in Ammen."

"What about Alana?"

"She's undecided, but I think she's inclined to agree with me too. I think she also believes in Ammen."

"What about your mother?

"You probably already know what she thinks. She's probably known all along. She can do no wrong. As far as I know, she could be the third angel who Ammen talks about."

"Really?" comments Alex. Alex is not going to challenge Andrew's sarcasm and refrains from saying anything else about Sonja.

"What about Garrett?"

Andrew then even more sarcastically comments, "Garrett is the angel of the family, he has never done anything wrong, everything he does is right, he's always the hero, and that as far as I know, Garrett could be the other angel that Ammen is talking about if Sonja isn't."

Andrew's animosity toward Garrett is finally officially displayed.

"Really?" retorts Alex again. Alex is not about to further instigate anything and says nothing more regarding Garrett.

Andrew's hostility has grown even more. He desperately wants attention and wants somebody to officially agree with him and believe in Ammen along with him. Although Julie, Alana, and Garrett are leaning toward following Ammen and only need Alex to confirm what they think, Andrew wants more of a commitment from somebody and he can't wait to get it.

"Andrew, it's ironic that for over thirty years you have rejected your mother and my attempts to raise you to be a Christian, and now it's you who is trying to convert us. Let me ask you a hypothetical question.

"Let's assume Ammen is for real and I would agree to follow him. Now let's suppose just for hypothetical purposes that you were to die soon, say within the next day or so, or let's say in the next few hours. Do you think that you would have enough time before you die to undo over thirty years of a bad life and to fulfill God's purpose? For over thirty years you have not only failed to repent your sins and not had anything that even resembles faith, but you have actually rejected Jesus Christ. Would you be able to reverse this in such limited time? What would it take to please God in such short a time?"

"It doesn't matter. Ammen will save me. Hasn't anything that Ammen said mean anything to you? Remember that Ammen talked about being with other angels, that his blood was sacred, that the test would be passed, that Ammen was going to be the last angel, and that he was going to fulfill the order, whatever that is. Hundreds of millions of people believe in him. He's got to be for real!"

Alex mulls over this for a few seconds. All of what Ammen said does have a spiritual ring to it. It all sounds familiar and Alex now knows where he has heard this before. He again remembers what was earlier relayed to him about what he experienced in the Council Room. What Ammen said is nearly identical to what he heard there. He's tempted again to let Andrew know about this, but he doesn't.

But Alex is not going to reveal his decision until the rest of the family joins him and he again tells Andrew this. Andrew shuffles about and is getting very upset because he wants Alex to tell him and not wait. Andrew wants immediate support from Alex and he's not getting it.

"Dad, if you don't think Ammen is for real, you are dead wrong! You're as wrong as one plus one equals three."

"But, Andrew, one plus one can equal three."

"What. How can that be?"

"Because when you add A and B together you get a third item, A and B combined. That has a different property than A and B separately. Therefore, when you add one item and another item together, the result is a third item, not two items. But all three of the items are the same even though they are different.

"That's ridiculous."

"No it's not. The idea is plausible when the paradigm assumes a different set of standards not normally thought about in the conventional way of thinking."

"You're talking nonsense."

Sensing the tension developing between them, Alex then decides to break the mounting stress between the two of them.

"No, I'm not, how about if I show you a simple example? Do you want to see how one plus one can equal three? I'll show you."

Andrew, surprised by his remark, says "Some hocus-pocus? Okay, I guess. Show me."

Alex then proceeds to tell Andrew a riddle. In doing so, he grabs a piece of paper and pencil lying on the coffee table and gives them to Andrew.

"Andrew, anybody can do this. It's very easy. Try it yourself. Think of any number between 20 and 99."

Andrew asks Alex, "You're going to have me add or subtract some numbers and then predict the result, right? I know how you're going to do this. You're going to ask me to subtract the same number I started with somewhere along the line so no matter what number I picked, you will know what the final answer is. That's not magic."

"Andrew, I am going to predict your number but no, I'm not going to ask you to subtract your number; not even a combination of numbers that add up to that. I will not tell you to do that. I will not know what your number is. Depending on what number you start with, you will be adding and subtracting different numbers of which I will have no knowledge."

"Well, then it's impossible that you can do this then."

"Well, let's just see. The number you chose should be a two-digit number, right? Let's call that result A. Then add those two digits together. Let's call that result B. Then subtract that result B from A. Let's call that result C. That result should be another two-digit number. Then add those two digits together. Let's call that result D. Let's say D stands for the devil.

"Now add that result D and the number 666. Let's call that result E. E stands for evil. Now add to that result the number 3 which represents the trinity. Let's call that result F. The letter F represents 'faith.' If you did the math correctly, you should have faith in me that I can predict the number you arrive at no matter which number you started with."

"No way."

"Way, Andrew. Try it. You keep the number to yourself or hidden on your paper and I will tell you what it is in about five minutes."

Andrew then takes the piece of paper and as Alex repeats the steps, he silently thinks of a number and then adds and subtracts exactly as instructed. He folds the paper and holds it in his hand so that Alex can't see it.

Then Lizzy comes in through the door and jumps up on Alex's lap. She buries her face in Alex's shirt as she tries not to look at Andrew.

"What's this all about?"

"She doesn't like my shirt, but I have no idea why," says Andrew.

Then Lizzy feels a lump in Alex's pocket. "What's this?"

She reaches down and puts her little hand in Alex's pocket and pulls out the shirt that Alex brought with him before he left his house. She again points to it and again asks, "What's this?"

Alex encourages her to unfold it, which she does. Alex then explains to her that he wore that shirt when he was a child about her age. Lizzy looks at him and then looks at the shirt. It's old, somewhat ragged, and still a little dusty. She can relate to it because it's just about her size.

Andrew looks at it and then looks at Alex. "What are the three lines for?"

"I don't know. What do the three lines on your shirt mean? I see that they're broken lines on your shirt whereas the lines on my old shirt are straight. I also don't know what the symbols and letters on my shirt mean."

"What symbols? What letters?"

Alex then looks at the shirt and clearly sees the symbols and letters on the middle line. But Andrew doesn't see them. To Andrew, he can only see the three lines. He can't see the symbols and letters on the middle line, but Alex can.

"You mean to tell me that you don't see anything written on the lines?"

Andrew snobbishly states "No! There's nothing there. There are just three blank lines."

Alex then asks Lizzy. "Do you see the symbols and letters on the shirt?"

Lizzy looks at it and studies the shirt for a few seconds. She holds the shirt up to her chest as if she's wearing it and studies it by looking down on it. Then she nods yes. She then says yes and smiles from ear to ear. She then jumps up and gives Alex a big hug. She is all smiles and is beaming with joy.

Alex asks her in somewhat of a mocking voice not expecting any answer, "But you can't read them, can you? Do you know what it says?"

Lizzy looks down on the shirt again and nods yes, climbs up farther in Alex's lap, leans over glowing with happiness, and whispers something in his ear very softly.

Alex is absolutely flabbergasted. He is shocked and stunned. So she can read the symbols and letters, but he cannot, and Andrew can't even see them. Also, he's stunned that she even put several words together in a sentence as well. This is the first time she has said anything like this to anybody. Usually, she speaks only one or two words from a very limited vocabulary.

But what surprises Alex the most is what she whispered in his ear. Does she really see any symbols or letters on the shirt? Really? If so, does she really know what they say and mean? The symbols and letters are nothing but hieroglyphics to him. How does she know? How can she read them and understand them? What she whispered in his ear is a complete shock to him.

Alex wonders whether she really can read it, and speculates that perhaps she's merely making it up. He doesn't know for sure but he gets a strange feeling maybe she knows something. He sure wishes he could understand what the symbols and letters mean, but so far he hasn't been able to do so.

Lizzy then carefully folds up the shirt, gives it back to Alex, looks at him and puts her finger over her mouth and says "Shhh. Secret." It will be a secret just between her grandpa and her.

Alex sits there absolutely bewildered. He sees the symbols and letters but has no idea what they say or mean. But Lizzy knows. He goes into deep thought.

Lizzy sits there beaming with happiness. She claims she can read them, but can she really? She sits in Alex's lap with a huge smile from ear to ear.

Andrew sits there dismayed. He claims he sees nothing and he's totally disgusted. He's furious that Lizzy likes Alex's shirt but not his. Especially considering that Alex's shirt is small, ragged, old, and dusty and his shirt is new, bright, and is much larger.

Alex then asks Andrew if he has his number ready. Andrew perks up and says, "You bet," thinking there's no way Alex will be able to predict his number. The odds are way against him. He thinks that the probability is something like only 1 in 80 that he can predict his number.

Alex says, "Andrew, there are two more steps. If you followed the instructions correctly, you should have a three-digit number, right? Now add those three digits together. Now you should have a two-digit number. Let's call that result G. G stands for God. Now, the last step is to add those digits together. Let's call that result H. You got it? Do you have your number?"

After doing some more adding, and hiding his paper so Alex doesn't see it, he says, "Done, I got a number. There's no way in hell that you'll know my number."

"Andrew, on the sixth day, God finished his work, on the seventh day He rested, and on the eighth day He admired his creation some more and wondered if He would ever need to change anything again."

"What? What do you mean by that?"

"Andrew, there are two elements in which you must have faith but they are essentially one. One is God and the other one is Jesus Christ. You can consider God the Father and Jesus His Son. When you add the Father and His Son together you get the answer."

Andrew blurts out, "*If* you add one and one together, you get two. Ha, you didn't guess my number."

"No. You're being premature. I haven't told you the answer yet. When you add the Father and the Son together the answer is not two. Andrew, your number is three."

Andrew opens his piece of paper and is dumbfounded. He is entirely perplexed. "How did you do that? How in the hell did you do that?"

"Andrew, you should know better than to be cussing like that, especially when there're children around. Let's use the word heaven instead. Your last result was H, correct? Well, I suppose that you can consider that the letter H may represent either heaven or hell. But, the answer is that it represents heaven in this particular case."

"And why is that?" asks Andrew.

"Heaven. Do you know why it represents heaven? It's because the answer to the question is the number three. Do you know what the number three means? Believing in the trinity will get you into heaven, not hell. The Father, Son, and Holy Ghost equal three in my book. And that result is made possible by God and Jesus Christ. If it weren't for both of them, you wouldn't have all three. One plus one does equal three. Now, how's that all for some hocus-pocus?"

Andrew just sits there like a deer caught in headlights. He's absolutely speechless. He thinks, "Is my dad some sort of magician or what? Just how did he do that? I could have picked any number from 20 to 99. Just how did he do this? Does he have the capability of reading my mind? Also, how can one plus one equal three?" But in this instance, it did.

Alex then explains to Andrew when he was a little boy, his father always told him and his sister puzzles and riddles like this, but that back then, he was too young to understand. But he tells Andrew that he's old enough to understand. Alex comments that he wishes now that he would have paid more attention to his father back then, but that Andrew has the advantage that Alex is still around to explain these things to him because he's older and can understand these things.

Andrew finally says, "Well, I suppose you're telling me you plan to tell everybody you will still follow only Jesus and not Ammen right? I thought you said you were going to wait and reveal your decision to everybody at the same time."

Alex looks straight into Andrew's eyes. "I never said I was not going to follow Ammen. I still value your opinion and insight. Have you given any thought that perhaps I'm giving you a final opportunity for rebuttal and I may need you to help further solidify my support and agreement with you if that is what I plan to do? Maybe I need you to explain to me how what I said is wrong. You really don't know what my decision is at this point, do you? I listen to you, but I need to know if you are really listening to me and if you think what I'm saying makes sense. And if not, why not? I'm willing to fully and seriously evaluate everything. Are you? You will find out my decision when I tell everyone at the same time."

After this comment, Andrew is somewhat relieved and wonders if perhaps Alex just might agree with him after all and wonders what his decision will be that he'll tell everybody. He can't wait to find out.

Chapter 68

The sun is starting to set and it's starting to get dark now. Everybody comes back into the house. Alana is the last one in because she's picking up toys and wheeling the wagon that the children were playing with from the backyard around the side and back into the garage. This is one of two giant wagons that Andrew bought about a week ago. It's a large garden wagon and is big enough that several children can fit in and play in it.

Alana was upset that Andrew spent the money to buy them but Andrew wanted them not only for their garden but for his children to play with. It's larger than anything that his neighbors have. It has a long handle, is light weight but very sturdy, and rolls very easily.

Although she finds it useful to carry the toys she's picking up, she mutters something about how irresponsible Andrew was in buying these. They didn't even need one much less two of them. And, she' still upset that Andrew jokingly told her that the Arab told him to buy them. After she rolls the wagon in the back of the garage, she briefly looks for the other wagon but can't find it. It's identical to the one she brought into the garage. Eventually, she finally enters the house through the garage door.

The family gathers around in the living room. The TV is still on and the news is reporting that two additional bombs have been found. One was discovered in San Diego at a port facility and the other was found in the Boston area. One is a bona fide nuclear bomb

463

of enormous magnitude and is similar to the others found to date. Both are 100 percent tamperproof, just like all of the others.

Julie looks at Alex as she sits down. "Well, we all know where Andrew stands. We want to know what you think, Dad."

Alana then looks at Andrew and comments, "You know, your parents have done everything they could to raise you to be a Christian, but without success, and now you are trying to convert them into believing in Ammen. How ironic. I'm so interested to see if you're going to succeed. What a change in course this would be."

Garrett then walks over and turns down the volume on the TV as Alex prepares to speak.

After everybody gets settled in and comfortable, Alex stands up and looks at everybody for a few seconds before speaking. He starts off by asking everyone if they have prayed for guidance and if they have given the question any serious thought. The entire family hangs their heads down and avoids eye contact with Alex, except for Sonja.

Nobody says anything. It's obvious that except for Sonja, nobody has given the issue much thought and that probably nobody prayed. While Alex was away, Julie, Alana, Garrett, and Andrew speculated that Alex may declare his faith in Ammen, but Garrett indicated that he would not be surprised if a debate between Alex and Andrew ensues first. They want to hear what Alex has to say and for all practical purposes will likely rely on his decision. They expect him to declare his faith in Ammen and can't wait to see Andrew's happiness.

Garrett comments, "Well, it looks like there are four possible scenarios. One, Ammen is for real, and if you declare your belief in him, you go to heaven. Two, Ammen is for real and if you do not declare your belief in him, you go to hell. Three, Ammen is not for real, and if you declare your belief in him, you go to hell because you are following him instead of Jesus. Four, Ammen is not for real and if you do not declare your belief in him and continue to follow Jesus, you may go to heaven."

Alex looks at everybody and states, "You are absolutely correct." He then starts off by asking them a point-blank question. "Do you think that your life on Earth is long or short?"

Everybody unanimously states, "Long." It's a long time, a very long time. Unless you die prematurely, there's an enormous amount of things one can do in many years of a lifetime. There are immeasurable experiences that can be had in the many years of one's life. Life on Earth is long because it is a very long time from birth to death.

Alex then delivers a philosophical discourse that's like a mini sermon. In doing so, he practically hypnotizes everybody. He preaches:

"Let's assume that your lifetime on Earth is equal to a single grain of sand. But that single grain of sand is more important than anything. It is absolutely critical and decisive in what happens after you die.

"Now, count all of the grains of sand on all of the beaches and deserts in the entire world. The result is immeasurable. Then multiply this number times the number of rain drops that has ever fallen from the sky since the beginning of time. Then multiply that result times the number of snowflakes that have fallen since the beginning of time.

"Then multiply that result times the number of all living plants on Earth counting every leaf, flower, and blade of grass separately. Then multiply that result times the number of all living creatures that have roamed the Earth since the beginning of time again counting each and every insect, bird, animal, and human separately.

"Then multiply that result times the number of all of the fish and other creatures that have lived in all of the seas, lakes and rivers since the beginning of time. The result is an exponential multi-googolplexian number of an absolutely unimaginable magnitude.

"Let's say this final result represents eternity. But eternity is actually longer than this. Life continues to multiply into new life and more raindrops and snowflakes will fall. But compared to this, only one single grain of sand represents your lifetime on Earth. So, let's compare your lifetime on Earth which is nothing more than a single grain of sand compared to eternity in this perspective. Now, let's reconsider the original question. Is your time on Earth long or short? It's quite short, isn't it?

"So, let's measure the time you will spend on Earth compared to the time that you will spend in either heaven or hell. How you live that very short time on Earth will determine where you will spend your entire afterlife forever. That's why your time on Earth is so critical, even though it's so short. Every single second on Earth counts. Do you realize the enormity of this test? Is it worth it to neglect how you live any second on Earth when it may determine where you spend eternity in your afterlife?

"Is it worth the risk to ignore this? Does eternity mean anything to you? Have you ever really thought about it in this context? Or has it only been an afterthought or a superficial concept without you actually thinking about it and feeling what it will really be like? You will not have a chance for a redo. You need to look at eternity in a way as to how it will really affect you.

"The reason I mention all of this is because you must look at it in this perspective to understand why it is so important to make absolutely sure you are making the right decision about your faith. You cannot be nonchalant about it or rely on somebody else. You must address it with all your heart and soul. You need to be absolutely sure about your decision. Where you spend your entire afterlife depends on it.

"The decision you make and the measure of how strong and sincere your faith is and how much you repent your sins will be the most important decision that you will ever make. It absolutely must be made with your heart and soul. It cannot be superficial. It will be your own decision to make, not mine, not Andrew's, not anybody else's. You cannot rely on anybody else to make that decision for you. You must make the decision yourself.

"*If* you only see with your eyes and only hear with your ears and only feel with your skin you will surely die. Your life and your world may not be as you think it is. You must close your eyes and close your ears, and then see, listen to, and feel God with your heart and soul. Only then, when you open your eyes and ears you will truly understand and be able to seek and know the truth, and you will live.

"Your future depends on your past. You must look backwards. Your life is a moving target. The longer you live on Earth, the more the past becomes and less your future on Earth will be. The time left will get shorter and shorter. That's how time works. There is no paradox here.

"You must look at yourself. But, you cannot see yourself without looking in a mirror. You must look in that mirror to see your life, going backwards. What makes that up will go into a mammoth equation and the wheel of balance. And, how you live in the future, which time may be shorter than you think, will also be figured in the wheel of balance. That is a behemoth scale that only God understands. You do not want the scale to tip the wrong way.

"What is in your everlasting future will depend a lot on your past. But it will also depend on your remaining life as well. Is a change of course in order for you? When are you going to make it? Or are you going to wait too long and will it then be too late? Are you waiting to die or are you going to die waiting? You cannot depend on getting a "get out of jail free" card at the last minute. It will be your decision.

"But you have been given a trump card that will help you balance the scale the right way. But that trump card is actually required no matter where the pendulum stops on the scale. When are you going to play it? Or are you going to wait too long and waste it? The sooner you play it the better.

"That trump card is very simple. It's merely the repentance of your sins and having faith in and loving Jesus Christ. All you need to do is repent your sins to God and accept Jesus as your savior. You must love Him with all your heart and soul and you must ask for forgiveness and forgive others. Simply, you need to develop a personal relationship with Him. What is the cost of getting this priceless trump card? The price you must pay for it is absolutely nothing. It is God's gift to you. Have you ever really thanked God for this gift he has given to you? You must be sincere in doing so.

"You must look backward and have faith in what Jesus has already done for you, not what is proclaimed what will be done for you now. What is happening now on Earth is not the Apocalypse. The four horses have yet to appear. The bowl judgments have not occurred. We have not heard the trumpets. In fact, the seals have not all been broken. There has not been the tribulation period. And there will not be any rapture at this time either. Maybe some time, but not now.

"Ammen asked why we should expect him to perform miracles to motivate us to believe in him considering that Jesus already did that. Likewise, I ask why we should be required to believe in what Ammen said he will do when Jesus already did what he did for us. The Gospel is God's word. Where in the Bible does it say that Jesus will return before the prescribed time per Revelation or that we must ignore what he already did for us? Where does it say we will be required to believe again in his return a second time before the prescribed events occur? Where does the Bible say that Jesus will return as Ammen and where does it state what he said he will do? I'm not aware that the Bible states any of this.

"Regardless whether the Beast, the Antichrist may or may not already be at work, Jesus Christ has not yet returned. It is too early for that and that day is yet to come. God is not ready for that yet. What has been prophesized in Revelation has not actually occurred yet.

"There is only one Jesus Christ. When He returns, then He is still Jesus. In that case, you are still worshipping Jesus. He is not anybody else. He cannot be anyone else. Jesus is Jesus and nobody else can be Jesus. There can only be one God and no other Gods will come before him. When Jesus returns, he will return per the Word of God, not to require us to pass an entirely new test again that has not been prophesized. It's that simple. That *is* the answer.

"Ammen is not Jesus. Ammen is not the Second Coming. Ammen is not any savior. Perhaps Ammen may be viewed as the Anti-Christ. In fact, he is the demon of the devil. Ammen is the false Christ. He is operating in disguise and he is deceptive in incredible ways that you cannot understand. He is an imposter and should be condemned. Satan is deceiving you into thinking that Ammen is the Second Coming, but he is not.

"I hereby profess my faith in only Jesus Christ, and I denounce Ammen as a charlatan and a fraud."

Alex then looks at everybody one by one, ending with prolonged look at Andrew, and sits down. He rests his case. Now, it's up to everyone else. Who's next?

Everybody is aghast at what they just heard. Everyone sits perfectly still and nobody says anything. They cannot believe what Alex just preached. They are silent and no one moves a muscle. Everybody is in a complete trance. They are astounded to hear Alex be so resolute. They sort of expected something like this, but this was pretty heavy and hit them all hard. In less than two minutes, Alex has accomplished what Andrew has tried to do over several days. Everyone is afraid to say anything.

Everybody was looking forward to what Alex was going to say. They sort of anticipated that he would side with Andrew and accept Ammen, but they were not expecting this at all. It was not only a huge surprise to them, but nearly overwhelmed them as well. Everyone is absolutely speechless.

After Alex sits down he looks at Andrew again and says, "Andrew, I am truly sorry."

Andrew looks back at Alex and remarks, "That was all meant for me, wasn't it?"

Chapter 69

Everybody has been truly shaken by Alex's sermon and now is contemplating what he just said. They all realize what Alex has attempted to instill in them, however it's so difficult for anybody to focus on the matter as much as Alex has. Some of the kids start to whine and the women take advantage of that to go into the kitchen to attend to them. Garrett follows them. Alex and Andrew are left alone in the living room again.

Andrew breaks the silence and asks Alex some questions. "So, if you're saying what is happening now on Earth is not the Apocalypse, does that mean the bombs will not go off and the world really won't be destroyed? How can the world come to an end without it being the Armageddon you hear about from the Bible? If it's not yet the time for the world to end, then how can it?"

"Andrew, I'm surprised you would know this. But no, the bombs are still supposed to be detonated. Perhaps it could be the beginning of the end."

"But I don't understand. How can that happen but not be what your Bible says?"

"My Bible? It's also your Bible if you would let it be. That's why you need to believe in Jesus and forget all about Ammen. There *is* an answer to all of this. If you really want to learn more and find out if and when it can happen, you could."

"How? When?"

"When you finish reading the book."

"What book?"

"The book I tried to give to you several times, but you rejected it. In fact, maybe I should also read it more than I do. Sometimes it's not easy to understand and it's also so easy to forget what it says sometimes. But for now what's most important is to simply put your faith and trust in Jesus."

"But how can this all be possible?"

"Andrew, you need to trust and have faith in Jesus."

"Dad, you're dead wrong. I know you are. How can nearly two hundred million people be mistaken? You know, Ammen has an enormous following. Ammen proclaims that he will live. Why can't you understand that?" If you don't follow Ammen, that means you will probably go to hell. I don't want you to go to hell. I don't want to go there either. How can you not believe in Ammen when about two hundred million others do? How do you know he's not real?"

"I would rather trust what I believe in my heart and soul and look backwards and follow what Jesus has done for me and not follow two hundred million other people now who only think they trust in what Ammen said he would do in the future. Where does the Gospel reference that Jesus would return as Ammen now before the prescribed time? Where does the Gospel say that we would be required to do what he said? Many more people have believed in Jesus in the past than who now follow Ammen. In the history of time Jesus actually had billions more followers than Ammen.

"Even though Ammen may have two hundred million worshippers now, this is miniscule compared to those who have followed Jesus. How can you not understand that? I do believe that the two hundred million people who want to follow Ammen are being influenced by the devil. Perhaps they are possessed. Ammen is deceptive in ways you would not understand. He is incredibly cunning, shrewd, and he has found a way to enter their souls. He almost fooled me in ways only I now can understand, and he has deceived every one of them."

"So, what made you think Ammen is not for real?"

"When I saw the flowers. They were all pointing down and not up."

"What? What is that supposed to mean?"

"You wouldn't understand. But I can see how those who believe in Ammen are fooled. They are fooled because the devil has entered their souls."

Now Andrew starts to gets angry. "And that includes me, right? So you are telling me that I am possessed by Satan?"

"Maybe. It depends. He has certainly deceptively influenced you.

"Ammen says that he will do something now to save me, so I want to believe in him. Jesus was over two thousand years ago. He's out of date. He is passé. Ammen is now. Ammen even said we must believe in him now, not the Jesus of the past. Ammen will serve me just fine."

Alex responds softly but firmly, "Why are you concerned about how you should be served? You should instead be concerned about what you can do to serve in the name of Christ. You have it backwards."

"So, what is Jesus doing to save you right now? It has not been scientifically proven that the Jesus story was for real, and that if he were for real, he would be doing something about this crisis right now."

"It has not been proven that the Jesus story is impossible either. So what makes you think that God is not doing something about the crisis right now in the name of Jesus? Maybe he is. Maybe it's up to us to believe and have faith. You're a doubting Thomas. What exactly has Ammen done to save you? Jesus has already done this for you. What makes you think that Ammen is the savior or one and the same as Jesus? He never really said he is. And I say he's not. One needs to have real faith. One needs to have faith in Jesus. That's been inherent in history for over two thousand years.

"Now, it's up for us to decide and save ourselves. That is over two thousand years of unbridled commitment. It does not have to be proven. If it were scientifically and unequivocally proven, then there would no longer be any need to have faith. And one needs to have faith in Jesus. That's your ticket to heaven."

"I don't want to die. And I'm scared to go to hell. I want to follow Ammen because he says I'll live and be with him."

"And where do you think that will be? Did he tell you it will be with God in heaven? Or did he say it will be with his creator? His creator is the devil. Now, do you still want to be with him? You should want to be part of God in heaven and give back to Him what he has given to you. If you simply repent the sins and wrongs of your life and believe in, love, and follow Jesus, ask for forgiveness and forgive others you would not need to worry about hell. It really is that simple. If you build your life around Him, He will come. Trust me."

Given thought to the fact that Andrew's given and first name is Thomas under which he was baptized, Alex remembers verses 24-29 of chapter 20 of the book of John and asks Andrew, "So, I suppose you need absolute proof, right? What would it take?"

Andrew clearly does not like what Alex said. Andrew is not getting any support at all and to boot, for all practical purposes Alex is calling Ammen the Antichrist and hints that Satan has entered Andrew and he might even be possessed. Now Andrew is getting angrier by the minute and is resenting everything that comes from Alex's mouth. He emphatically states, "Ammen says he will live and we will too!"

Alex asks, "Where? Someplace where you do not want to be? Jesus has already done that and He is still alive today. He is here."

"Well, if I don't follow Ammen, things will go really bad for me. I can't handle bad things that happen. The world is going to be destroyed. Everybody says it will. Explain to me just what can happen to make the bombs and disease to go away so I don't have to worry about it anymore. It's impossible for them to simply go away. How can that happen? I need Ammen to save me."

"Why are you concerned about what will happen to you? Do you not care what will happen to everybody else? Andrew, yes, our Earth is going to be destroyed. It *is* going to happen. That is a certainty. But, bad things that happen are a function of actions, however not all things that appear bad may actually turn out to be bad. It's like reading a book or watching a movie where there are a lot of events that appear will turn out bad. The reader might want to give up and stop reading the book or stop watching the movie because he or she doesn't want to keep reading or watching bad things. But often it has a happy ending. It takes time. You need to have faith.

If you have faith and keep at it, maybe things will turn out good in the end. But if you don't, maybe they won't. But what's more important than the ending of your life and the beginning of a new one is what you do, your actions to get you there. That's because they affect how it ends and how it will begin again. Seeing that you've made it this far, then congratulations, there's still a chance that things may turn out good for you in the end. In other words, if you at least try to have faith in Jesus and give Him a chance, perhaps your life will have a happy ending and more importantly a happy new beginning. But it won't if you follow Ammen. In that instance alone, it will have a very bad ending and no new beginning. Trust me."

By now, Andrew is almost furious. He will simply not give in. He has too much pride, and he's obsessed. He refuses to let his father try to convince him. He takes his shirt off, opens up a drawer in the credenza and takes out a black magic marker and writes in large bold letters, LIVE, below Ammen's name on his T-shirt on the third broken line and practically rubs it in Alex's face. "See this? He and we will live. LIVE!" He then proudly puts his shirt back on. The word LIVE appears in bold black below Ammen's full name on the third line on the shirt.

Andrew states emphatically, "Ammen said he will live and we will too. See, it says LIVE. You sound like you said your father did when you told me about him doing that hocus-pocus stuff when you were a little kid. You're talking in riddles and not making any sense."

Alex, again wanting to break the tension, then asks Andrew, "You want to see some more hocus-pocus? How about something that involves the shirt you're wearing right now? "How about if I told you that I can have you look at your shirt in such a way that it will tell you a hidden message and that you will see something entirely different than what you see right now?"

That stops Andrew dead in his tracks. He was not expecting such a comment and for Alex to change channels in the heart of the debate. Feeling that a little more magic will ease the tension again, Andrew says, "Sure, why not."

Andrew is thinking that there's no way Alex can change the image or Ammen's name on his shirt unless he has some sort of magical or divine power. "There's no way he will be able to do this. I know what I see. No way can he change this," Andrew thinks.

Alex then asks Andrew another hypothetical question "You say you are willing to take the chance that Ammen is for real and will save you, but you really don't know, right? Let's say there may be some risk with that because deep down I don't think you are certain. Would you be willing to burn and suffer in an inferno of fire for a time in order for you to spend eternity in heaven, if this would be absolutely guaranteed unconditionally by accepting Jesus Christ? Or would you risk it all by gambling on Ammen? In that case, you may be right and you may be wrong. You really don't know, do you? What if you're wrong? There will not be any chance for a redo. You would go straight to hell without any chance of going to heaven."

"What?" asks Andrew defiantly. "I want to see your hocus-pocus with my shirt. I want to see you change what I see on the shirt I'm wearing."

"Okay then. I'll show you. Follow and listen to me closely." Alex then points to Ammen's full name on the shirt and then points to the word that Andrew wrote on it with the black magic marker.

"EVEDOTHLID AMMENOFI—LIVE."

"Andrew, Ammen is trying to deceive you. The letters in his name are actually scrambled. They're all mixed up. They're all mixed up because Ammen is trying to confuse you. You need to unscramble the letters to fully understand who he is. If you un-mix the letters and put them in the right order, then you will fully understand. Let's rearrange the letters in his name so that they read, LIVEDEHTFO NOMEDAMI instead. If you look at his name the right way, you will see a secret message." Alex then takes an 8 1/2 by 11 piece of paper out of the drawer of the credenza, places it horizontally, and writes in big black bold capital letters LIVEDEHTFO NOMEDAMI using the same marker that Andrew used. He then cuts the paper so it will fit over the name on his shirt above the word LIVE that Andrew wrote on it. He holds it up for Andrew to see.

Andrew looks at it and says, "Those letters mean nothing. I don't see any message. No message at all."

Alex comments, "That is because you are not looking at them the right way. You are still looking at things backwards. In order for you to understand things better and your life better you need to look at yourself in the mirror. I suggest you look at yourself in the mirror and when you do, hold this piece of paper up and cover the name EVEDOTHLID AMMENOFI on your shirt. That way you'll be reading his name and the word you wrote on the shirt in the mirror the right way after the letters are put in the right order. You will then be reading the letters after they're unscrambled. It will give you a message. One that you won't expect, but will need to know, and that you should seriously consider.

Andrew says confidently, "Well, if I look at the letters in the mirror, they will say LIVEDEHTFO NOMEDAMI. That is Ammen's full name even after I unscramble the letters as you've rearranged them. And the word I wrote on it will simply say LIVE. I don't need to read them in a mirror. I can see them perfectly fine right now."

Alex then looks directly at Andrew and softly says, "No they will not. They will absolutely not say that! They will tell you something else. They will tell you a very important message, a very specific message about Ammen. You really need to know this.

"Just get up and go look at the letters in a mirror. Go ahead. It won't hurt to do this. Cover his name on your shirt with the letters I wrote on this piece of paper and read them instead in the mirror when you look at yourself. Also, look at the word LIVE you wrote in the mirror. You may need to stare at the letters for a bit and you may need to reverse some of the letters so they face the other way, but eventually you'll see the message. Then after you look at the letters in the mirror, let me know what you see and what the message says, okay?

"Anybody can do this. Anybody who does this and sees these letters in a mirror will see the same message. They're the exact same letters but merely rearranged. Go ahead and do it! After you stare at the letters for a bit, you will eventually see the message."

Andrew is suspicious, and he's entirely unaware of what Alex is trying to do. He's reluctant to get up and see the letters in a mirror. He has no idea what Alex is up to. He then meticulously accounts for each letter in Ammen's full name to make sure that Alex has accounted for exactly the same letters. He wants to make sure about this, and after doing this, he's confident that Alex hasn't inserted any additional letters or omitted any letters. He agrees they are the same exact letters, but merely rearranged in a different order.

Andrew is hesitant, but he's curious and wants to see Alex attempt some more magic that he doesn't believe he can do. He finally gets up and walks into the bathroom and holds the piece of paper over Ammen's full name on his shirt and looks at them in the mirror. He focuses on Ammen's full name, as rearranged by Alex, LIVEDEHTFO NOMEDAMI in capital letters as well as the word LIVE that Andrew wrote on his shirt. He stares into the mirror and focuses on the letters to turn some of them around so they face the other way to understand the message.

In the meantime, Alex quietly gets up and peeks around the corner and notices that as Andrew stands in front of the mirror, a beam of light from the last rays of the setting sun coming through the window is creating a spectrum of brilliant colors through the prism on a glass vase on the window sill. The radiance and vividness of the colors are unlike anything he's ever seen.

He can feel the colors singing melodies that enhance the moment, but he knows that Andrew cannot hear them. But the beam from the last rays of sunlight bouncing off the prism casts a reflection of two bright red glows exactly where Ammen's eyes are on the shirt in the mirror.

"Wow!" Alex says to himself. "That was an added effect I didn't expect."

Alex then quickly rushes back and jumps back into his chair in the living room before Andrew returns.

Andrew continues to stare in the mirror for some time and is appalled at what he sees. He is utterly shocked and starts shaking. Alex is correct. When read in the mirror, Andrew reads a message that he was not expecting at all. In fact, it's the very last thing that Andrew expected or wanted to see.

About a half minute later, Andrew returns to the living room and looks as white as a ghost. He is shaking, trembling, and is absolutely petrified at what he just saw and what he just read.

Alex then says, "Now how's that for some more hocus-pocus? But there is no magic here. It is real. Actually, you can arrange the exact same letters to say the same thing without looking in a mirror as well. No matter how you look at it, either way, when you unscramble the letters, the message is there. And it's genuine and absolute."

Andrew looks like a deer caught in headlights. He had been wearing that shirt all afternoon and evening and he was so proud of it. Millions of others are also wearing similar shirts throughout the world. Only if they knew, but they don't.

But will this be enough to convince him? Andrew has been persistent and simply doesn't want to give in.

Chapter 70

Andrew looks at Alex and appears exhausted. Alex's number riddle, mini sermon, the debate, and now all of the hocus-pocus that Alex performed has pretty much drained all the energy out of him. Andrew is at a loss for words anyway. He doesn't know what to say. It was as if by looking in the mirror and contemplating everything that Alex said, a demon was identified within. Alex wonders what Andrew is thinking about.

Andrew is so fatigued by everything he mutters he's tired and wants to lie down to rest for a bit. Alex suspects that Andrew needs time to contemplate things. The sun has set, and now it's starting to get darker. Andrew proceeds to lie down on the couch in the living room. Soon, he's asleep. Alex would like to take Andrew's shirt off but for now lets him be. He thinks, "It's good that he's taking a nap now even though bedtime is only several hours away. He needs some time to think things over."

Everybody else is either still in the kitchen, downstairs, upstairs, or back outside, except for Sonja. Sonja had slipped into the opposite corner of the living room and observed the entire event. She also saw Andrew go into the bathroom and look in the mirror.

Alex continues to sit in the corner chair in the living room. He and Sonja see each other, and she smiles and winks at him. Alex smiles back and nods. One can sense an immense amount of love flying back and forth between the two of them, almost as if they know what each are thinking and as if they are one. It's as if Sonja, like Alex, knows something that the rest of the family doesn't know.

Alex looks at his watch and then closes his eyes to relax. He says a short prayer. Suddenly, he realizes that a spirit is above him once again and is relaying some information to him. More pieces of the puzzle have come into place and a few more are about to be inserted into their proper spots.

Alex feels the presence of God, and God speaks to him. Alex is told that up in heaven the second to last angel has been found and that the extraordinary portion of the ordination process of the second to last angel now is in the completion stage. He also is provided a vision of his recent experience in the Council Room, and he sees the two remaining seats where the last two special angels will sit. He sees that one seat has a spirit materializing in it. He cannot see who it is. He wonders if it's the woman that he envisioned earlier. The other seat is still vacant.

Alex is then reminded that the last angel must still be found and that the ordination process must start within the next two hours or so because in about three hours it will be midnight. He is reminded that the ordination process of the last angel will take three days to fully complete. Therefore, the process of finding and beginning the ordination process of the last angel must begin immediately within the next two hours or so. He then remembers that Ammen said he will leave by midnight. "Wow," he thinks. "How clever Ammen was in deceiving me and everybody else."

Alex is then told of the special prayer told to him by the angel and he's advised that he is indeed the chosen one asked to pray that the last angel can be found in time and that the ordination process will be successful. Alex is stunned. "Is this really true? God selected me to be the chosen one to say the special prayer required? I can't believe it. Why me?"

But as shocked as he is, he feels a sense of honor and commitment and is more than happy to oblige. Alex then remembers what the angel told him when he was in heaven. But he is *not* told that he must pray three times.

He's informed that now is the prescribed time to pray. Timing is becoming critical. Because of his prayer, God's plan can be successful if the ordination process is successful. Alex understands that this is a solicitation from God for him to join others recruited by Him to help pray that God's plan will be a success. But Alex's prayer will be the special prayer required by the order.

He then thanks God for the opportunity and prays with all his heart and soul that the last angel can be found and that the process will be successful, just as he was asked to do.

Alex has learned that half of the order for the change in course now is being finalized. The other half needs to begin very soon and will depend on finding and ordaining the last angel. It will take a lot of prayer to make this happen and he is more than happy to fulfill his responsibility.

Alex would like to know more. He would like to know who the last two angels are and how God is finding them and what is going on in the process. He remembers that they both must come from the same bloodline and that it must be a sacred bloodline. He again wonders what makes the bloodline sacred. He recalls what he surmised previously that one would be an older woman and the other would be a middle-aged man, both from the Middle East, but that is about it. But who they are is not made known to him.

However, he doesn't need to know. All that is needed from him is the special prayer that he was asked to provide. Alex understands that's his role in God's plan. He recalls that his visit to heaven was because the spirit who accompanied him needed to attend the meeting, and as a result he was called to be the chosen one to pray the special prayer. He understands that his special prayer is his assigned role in God's plan to defeat Satan.

"God simply wants me to help in providing that prayer and that's why God has come to me now. The bombs will automatically be detonated and the deadly disease will be spread at midnight three days from midnight tonight. Therefore, time is of the essence." Alex then decides to repeat the special prayer a second time, and does so again with all his heart and soul.

The presence of God increases. Alex then learns more of the puzzle. After about ten minutes deep in prayer and meditation and listening to the messages from God, Alex finally opens his eyes. He looks over at Sonja, and she too is just now opening her eyes from her own prayer. He wonders if she actually enters his prayers and knows what he's praying.

After a few minutes, Alex reflects about the day and the evening. On one hand he questions how this can all be possible and whether God's plan is authentic. He doesn't recall anything in the Gospel that addresses any of this. But on the other hand, he's drawn in and finds himself accepting what's happening as if it must be the only option.

He continues to think, "Despite what I told Andrew, perhaps I should just accept what is happening just in case it's true. Even though Ammen is an impostor and Jesus has not yet returned to Earth, perhaps God's plan is still for real. Now that I think about it, God's plan that I learned in the Council Room never really did say anything about the last angel being the return of Jesus to Earth at this time.

"Ammen cannot be the last angel because that would be entirely unreasonable considering the specific tests the last angel must pass. And, Jesus has already performed his sacrifice for us. But maybe the last two angels are still needed for God's plan to work. So, even though it doesn't make any sense that this can all be for real, maybe everything else about the plan is still true anyway. Perhaps I should simply accept it to be on the safe side."

Then he has a fleeting thought and remembers the documentary that he saw on TV the night before he took his nap when everything began to change in his life. He remembers what he saw in part 1 and remembers that part 2 is scheduled to air tonight. But after thinking to himself for a few seconds, Alex knows that he cannot watch part 2 and that he'll miss it. He needs to attend to something else that is necessary and much more important because it's a required piece of the puzzle. He's disappointed because he was so much looking forward to watching it.

He gets up and peeks outside through the window. Just as he expects, Officer Musty is sitting in a patrol car just up the street. Alex then walks over to the credenza, stuffs his shirt back into his pocket, and picks up the white handwoven blanket and his Bible.

Alex walks over to Andrew, unfolds and then refolds the blanket in three layers' thick into a triangular shape, and then lays it on Andrew's chest with one corner facing his head and the other corners facing sideways and then rests the Bible on top of the blanket. Anyone seeing this will think this is Alex's way of getting in the last word. Andrew will see it when he wakes up from his nap.

Then Alex remembers the orange blossoms he brought earlier, which he put on a table in the corner of the room. He retrieves them and gives them to Sonja. But Sonja was actually just approaching Alex to ask for them. "I wondered why she wanted these," he mutters to himself, but he thinks he knows. Sonja then walks over to Andrew and places one of the bouquets on top of the Bible. She takes the other bouquet, splits it into two bouquets, and carries them with her.

Alex then goes outside the front door, and as soon as he does, Officer Musty gets out of his patrol car and approaches him. Alex and Officer Musty exchange pleasantries and briefly comment on the weather.

Alex then notices that Officer Musty is driving a new patrol car and asks him about it. Officer Musty remarks, "Yeah, there was a little accident a little while ago and I had to get a new one. I can't drive my old one anymore. You wouldn't even recognize it anyway. But I'm okay and didn't get hurt. There's nothing like a brand-new patrol car, right? I actually just got it earlier this evening."

"Well, I'm certainly glad to hear you're okay."

Officer Musty then comments about how active Alex's family is and that there is always somebody outside, others inside, somebody going or coming and so on. "Is your entire family going to be together in the house this evening, or will you be going home soon?"

Before Alex can answer, Officer Musty gets a call and excuses himself and walks back to his car to take the call. He's gone for nearly five minutes. During that time Alex is waiting and on a whim decides to look up the meaning of Officer Musty's full name on his smart phone.

He Googles the names *Asad Namirha Mustafa* and visits several websites that provide the meanings of names. After a few minutes and visiting several sites regarding names in Hebrew, Arabic, Islam, and others offering different interpretations, he can't find anything meaningful. But on a whim, he decides to look up *Asad* and *Namirha* backward. This would be *Dasa* and *Ahriman*. He is surprised and nearly shocked to learn what he finds out. All along, something in the back of his mind told him, but he never paid attention to it. But what a huge surprise this is. He wonders, "Does this name really mean anything, or is this merely a coincidence?" However, he learns another piece of the puzzle that he was given.

But this piece of the puzzle is hard to swallow, and in fact what Alex anticipates may happen and what he needs to do now borders being almost impossible for him. But things now are clicking, and he knows what needs to be done. The puzzle is almost completed. He almost has it all figured out.

Officer Musty returns and resumes his conversation with Alex. Alex tells him, "I'm going back to the house now and the entire family will be in the house together for a family prayer for the next ten minutes or so. After that, I cannot guarantee where any of the family members will be. They may disperse again and be outside, inside, or wherever. Some may even return to their homes. It was so good to see you again."

"Excellent! It is so good to hear that you will continue to spend time with your family this evening. I am so glad you are finally able to be all together for once."

Alex and Officer Musty exchange final greetings, and Alex again thanks him for watching over him and his family. They say good-night to each other, and Alex returns to the house. Officer Musty returns to his patrol car.

Alex opens the front door, and with it starting to get dark, everyone including the children is inside. The children are somewhat dispersed in different parts of the house; however, Julie, Alana, Garrett, and Sonja are all back in the living room.

Alex immediately goes over to Andrew and tries to wake him up. He snores and doesn't wake. Alex tries again. Then Alex starts shaking Andrew, trying to keep the blanket, Bible and bouquet balanced on top of Andrew. Andrew makes some cynical remark under his breath and refuses to be awakened.

Alex now is getting frantic. He then leans over and picks up Andrew, throwing him over his shoulder—not easy to do, but was manageable since Andrew was already lying down. In doing so, he grabs the Bible and bouquet in one hand, and holds the dragging blanket up in the other. Andrew, thrown over Alex's shoulder suddenly wakes up and is kicking and screaming "What in the hell are you doing? What are you doing? Put me down! Why are you doing this? What's gotten into you? Put me down!"

Alex then quickly walks over to the back door as fast as he can and finds that Sonja is already there opening it. Alex immediately steps through the open door, steps out onto the patio and lays Andrew down on the ground in the backyard. Andrew is still yelling and screaming and cannot believe what Alex is doing.

Within seconds, Garrett, Julie, Alana, and Sonja all follow Alex outside. Julie, Alana, and to some extent Garrett are also screaming at Alex, "What are you doing? What are you doing? Why did you pick him up and take him outside? What on Earth has gotten into you?"

Only about five seconds go by and then the house is shaken by an explosion inside the house followed by one exterior wall collapsing and massive flames shooting out some of the windows. The explosion knocks everyone to the ground. Windows can be heard shattering and broken glass is flying out into the yard.

Debris including some on fire is falling everywhere around them. Julie, Alana, and Garrett are beside themselves. They are dazed and confused. Alana yells at Alex, "Did you know this was going to happen? What's going on? How did you know this was going to happen?

Because of the suddenness and surprise of the explosion, it takes them a minute or two to gather themselves and stand up. Part of the roof can be heard starting to fall on one side of the house; and Alana, Julie, and Andrew get up and run around to the front yard.

Garrett lags behind because he's been hurt by falling debris landing on his leg. He stumbles and half crawls up the incline. Alex also lags behind and also stumbles because he hurt his back carrying Andrew, and he's trying to carry the blanket, Bible, and bouquet.

Eventually, all make it to the front of the house. There is debris in flames all over the yard and some in the street. Some debris from the explosion landed on car hoods and tops. Everybody makes their way across the street and up a house or two to get away from the smoke that by now is billowing out some of the windows and the open side of the house.

Alex looks up to see if Officer Musty is still there and now finds his patrol car parked up the street about a half dozen houses away. Apparently, for some reason, he moved farther up the street. "Is he going to do something, or is he just going to simply sit there and watch?" Alex is pretty sure he knows what's going on now.

Almost simultaneously, Alana, Julie, and Andrew scream out, "Where are the kids?" Andrew cries out "My God, they're still in the house!"

Andrew no sooner cries out when Matthew and Daniel can be seen in an upstairs bedroom window above the garage, crying hysterically, "Daddy, Mommy, Daddy, Mommy!" Smoke can be seen blowing in front of the window from the other side of the house. The fire has engulfed one side of the house and is spreading rapidly to the side where Matthew and Daniel are. It's evident that within minutes the bedroom will also be engulfed in flames. There is no sign of any of the other kids.

Garrett is on the ground groaning, but is on his cell phone calling 911. He sees Officer Musty's patrol car up the street and listens for sirens. The firehouse is not that far away.

Again, Daniel and Matthew can be seen through the smoke crying out the window for Daddy and Mommy. "Help us, help us, help us! Daddy, Daddy, Daddy!"

Everybody is totally struck by emotion and panic. Andrew is crying looking up at the window at his kids who will shortly be consumed by the flames. He looks at Garrett and Alex. Both of them are sitting on the ground nursing their injuries. It's obvious that they can't do anything. As a result of their injuries, they can barely even stand up.

Andrew runs over to Alex in total panic mode and screams, "What can we do? We can't wait for the fire department. It'll be too late!"

Alex and Andrew then lock eyes for several seconds. Alex tells Andrew that if his kids are going to be saved from the fire, he'll need to go in after them himself. There's nobody else who can go in and save them. Andrew shouts, "That would be pure suicide! If I do, I'll die for sure!" Alex continues to stare at Andrew, and Andrew thinks he's seeing right through him.

The kids can again be heard screaming, "Daddy, Daddy, Daddy, please help us!" With that, part of the roof caves in on the other side of the house and more flames can be seen.

With their eyes locked, Alex tries to enter and pierce the soul of Andrew and tells him that if he goes in the house after the kids, he must take Jesus with him. To have faith in Him is the only way. Nobody else can help him. He can do it. Both he and Garrett are hurt and they can't help. Do or die. Andrew looks back at Alex and is crying and shaking his head slowly from side to side. In the midst of his weeping he softly says, "No, no, no, you're wrong, I know you're wrong," as he continues to shake his head sideways.

"Daddy, Daddy, Daddy!" Then one of the upstairs bedroom window frames breaks loose, a flame erupts from one of the windows above the garage, and the kids can no longer be seen or heard.

Chapter 71

Andrew sees this, and as his kids disappear from the window, he disengages his trance with Alex; and without even thinking about anything except his kids, he runs straight through the smoke and enters the house through the garage. Fortunately, the garage door was left open, and he simply runs inside the garage and enters the house through the door in the back corner. The garage is the only entrance that is not yet on fire. He's not protected by anything. There is nothing to protect or help him except for perhaps Ammen or Jesus who he may or may not have taken with him. Alana and Julie are screaming. Garrett is on the ground squirming and moaning as it appears that he's in excruciating pain.

A minute goes by and the firestorm continues to rage. Then along the hillside on the other side of the house some movement can be seen in the smoke. After a few seconds, struggling to get up the hill is Lizzy, who is trying her best to pull one of the large garden wagons in the smoke. Julie runs over, temporarily disappears in the blowing smoke, and meets her. "Lizzy! Lizzy! How did you get out? Where are the other kids?"

Lizzy points inside the wagon and there squeezed together are Mikey and Emily. Julie is absolutely hysterical. She helps wheel the wagon up the hill and across the street where everybody is standing or sitting on the ground. Mikey and Emily are lifted out. Julie desperately is asking Lizzy how they got out and where are the other kids, but all Lizzy can do is point to the house. She says, "Fire, fire, inside, inside."

"Did Andrew help you get out?"

"No," Lizzy again points to the house and struggles to say "Matthew, Daniel, Hannah, inside". She can't say anything else.

They have no clue how she got out and how she was able to get Emily and Mikey. What a miracle they are still alive. But where are the other children? And what about Andrew?

Now it has been several minutes and still there is no sign of Andrew or the other kids. Finally, sirens can be heard and the fire department is on its way.

Within a minute or so, the fire department pulls up, and as they do, the entire roof caves in on one side of the house and a ball of fire explodes into the air. One entire side of the house now is totally engulfed in flames and the front exterior wall collapses. The garage side of the house is still intact but some flames and smoke can be seen from some of the windows above it and some from the garage door area.

The firefighters are running around and immediately prepare their equipment. There is so much smoke that it is difficult to see the house. Everyone is forced to move farther away.

Alana is hysterical, sensing that her entire family has perished in the flames. The reality is starting to set in. Everyone knows it, but nobody says anything. They are still holding out hope, but with every passing second, the hope fades and the reality that they didn't make it sets in more.

Alana runs over to one of the firefighters who just arrived and screams at him, "My husband and my kids are still in the house!"

The firefighter calmly says, "Nothing we can do about that, madam, not until we get the fire under control. There's an inferno in there. Nobody would survive in there now, nobody. Sorry."

With that, the entire remaining front exterior wall collapses and there's nothing left of the entire house except for the garage and the area behind it. The house is a long ranch house that has a bedroom above the garage. Behind the garage are the steps to the upstairs where Daniel and Matthew were last seen in the bedroom directly above the garage. At this point, the fire has engulfed the entire house except for the area immediately behind the garage and above it. Alana knows this and still holds out some flickering hope. But from the outside, it appears the entire house is ablaze.

However, within seconds, the fire spreads to the bedroom above the garage as flames are now shooting from both windows. The garage catches fire as a wall of flames appears through the billowing smoke from one end of the garage opening to the other, blocking any escape. This was the last and only way in or out of the house. And now it's gone

Alana falls to the ground and cries hysterically and uncontrollably. Sonja is trying to comfort her and tries repeatedly to tell her that everything will be okay, but obviously, that doesn't help. Alana knows that her family is gone. She knows that they are gone forever.

Julie is attending to Garrett on the ground as he's still in excruciating pain.

Sonja is attending to Alex, who is also hurting, but has finally been able to stand up and is leaning against a tree where they've been sitting. Alex is looking up the street to see if he can see Officer Musty and is wondering where he is.

He then spots the old white van parked just up the street on the other side of the fire trucks, and he spots Officer Musty parked just a house or two away from the van. "Why isn't Officer Musty down here? Why is he just sitting in his patrol car?" But Alex knows.

"And why is the Arab back again?" Alex asks himself. "How strange this is. Wasn't the van burned to a crisp just a few hours ago?" He squints to look at the van in the distance because it looks different, but he doesn't know why.

Alex decides to pray and closes his eyes for a few seconds. As soon as he does, he senses that God is with him and is talking to him again. All of the remaining pieces of the puzzle now are made known to him except for one last piece. Now he knows just about everything. He thanks God and prays to God to help Andrew and then he opens his eyes.

Alex looks at his watch and finds that it now is after 10:00 PM. While standing there waiting, he's looking at the old white van and Officer Musty's patrol car parked so close to each other. He remembers earlier in the evening Googling the meaning of Officer

Musty's name and finding out how surprised he was to discover that it was not what he expected.

On a whim, he decides to Google the name of the Arab. He might as well since there's nothing else he can do except watch the house burn. He still has his smartphone in his pocket and pulls it out but has difficulty getting a good signal. But in addition, he cannot remember the full name of the Arab that Officer Musty told him. That was days ago. He tries to remember a name on the side of the van but can't.

In the meantime, additional emergency vehicles are arriving on the scene including more fire trucks, police cars, and some other vehicles presumed to be the media. There are flashing lights and sirens everywhere.

Amidst all of the commotion, Alex spots several men in suits running among the houses up the street, but it appears that they're trying to hide from something. Alex is the only one who sees them. He finds this odd, but then redirects his attention to the burning house. He prays for Andrew and the kids again.

Suddenly, the garage explodes and a giant fireball shoots out of the double wide garage door opening followed by a smaller explosion. "Must be the gas tank used for the lawn mower or the mower stored there," he thinks.

Simultaneously, when the garage is demolished by these explosions, the entire roof of the garage caves in resulting in more fireballs and all of the walls and roof collapse. Debris is flying everywhere. In the blast, two small bicycles fly out into the air and land on the front yard, tumbling along before coming to a rest. The weed eater and a wheelbarrow are blasted into the air and come crashing down on the driveway. The large garden wagon covered in flaming debris can be seen rolling down the driveway out of the garage and stops in the middle of the street. Other lawn equipment and toys from the garage tumble out onto the front yard in flames.

More fireballs come shooting out of the garage, and there's so much smoke that everybody can hardly see anything anywhere near the house now. Flaming debris continues to fly from the blast, even several seconds later. The entire house is an inferno of fire and is completely demolished. Even the garage is fully engulfed in fire now which previously was the only way into or out of the house. There is nothing left.

Alex who was leaning against a tree a house or two away, hobbles up to the front yard. He's immediately restrained by the police as he's not allowed to get any closer to the inferno. However, he talks to the police, and they let him proceed. The police let him go because by now there's a sizable crowd assembling up the street and they need to go up there to control them.

In the meantime, Alana, who by now has resigned herself to the fact that Andrew and her children have perished, looks up and sees the wagon roll and come to a rest in the street.

She then cries out, "What's my comforter doing all rolled up on top of the wagon?" Her comforter was on one of the beds upstairs but now is covered in flaming debris on top of the wagon. How did it get there?"

Julie remarks, "I don't know. I saw the wagon roll out through the wall of flames just seconds before the garage exploded."

As she's looking at this totally perplexed, she sees Alex hobble over to the wagon. As soon as Alex approaches the wagon, he puts his hands in the air and the flames on the comforter subside somewhat. Alex screams over to the firefighters to come quickly. One of the firefighters runs over and puts out the remaining flames and helps Alex remove the smoking comforter. It's rolled up and lying on the wagon.

It takes both of them to remove the comforter. It's difficult because the comforter is waterlogged and very heavy. It's been saturated with water sprayed on it by the firefighter to put out the fire and seems to weigh a ton. In addition, it's charred and still smoldering, and the blowing smoke makes it hard for them to see. When they roll the comforter off the wagon, there underneath it are Matthew, Daniel, and Hannah all tucked together like sardines. Each of them is crying hysterically, but each is alive and well. There is no sign of Andrew anywhere.

Chapter 72

Alex and the firefighter roll the wagon up the street to where Alana is sitting on the ground and show her what they found. Hysterical, uncontrollable cries of sadness and grief immediately turn into hysterical uncontrollable cries of joy. Julie and Sonja are quick to come over and help get the kids out. Within seconds, all three kids are swarming all over Alana, trying to hug her.

"Where's Daddy?" she cries out to them.

Matthew points to the house and starts crying even louder. Alana looks at the house and becomes even more hysterical. She watches her house collapse in flames and wonders how Andrew got the kids in the wagon and rolled it out through the flames. She can't believe he remained inside to die for them.

Daniel on the other hand points to the smoldering comforter. Alex limps over to the smoking comforter and this time sees two burned shoes barely sticking out one of the rolled up ends. With the help of the fire fighter he slowly unrolls it. Inside is Andrew.

How did he get in there? Alex assumes after he put the kids in the wagon, he rolled himself up in the comforter that he got from the bedroom, somehow got it and himself on top of the wagon to cover the kids and rolled the wagon by pushing it with his feet through the wall of flames out of the garage and down the driveway just before the garage exploded.

Alex can instantly see that Andrew is in really bad shape. He's not wearing his shirt and is upper body is badly burned. His pants are burned and his hair is singed. His arms and legs are also badly burned. He's unconscious and motionless. Alana sees what's happening, asks Sonja to watch her kids, and runs over to him. Julie follows right behind her.

She sees Andrew and gasps. "Andrew! What happened? Andrew? Andrew?" She sees that he's barely alive if at all. After what seems like eternity, Andrew then slowly forces one eye open and mutters, "We did it!" He then gasps to take in what appears to be his last breath, closes his eye, and again is unresponsive.

Julie asks, "Who is 'we'? Who's he talking about?"

Alana responds "I wonder if he means Ammen? Maybe he took Ammen with him and prayed to him to help him."

"Are you sure? How do you know he didn't take Jesus with him? Where's his shirt?"

Both look at Alex as if they want him to comment. But all Alex can do is gaze at Andrew's apparent lifeless body and say a silent prayer. Alex has what appears to be a baffled look on his face. Alex cannot believe it. Julie and Alana have no idea what Alex is thinking. They wonder, "Was Alex wrong and was Andrew right after all?"

Alana looks at Alex and says to Julie, "I'll bet he took Ammen with him. I'd bet that he prayed to Ammen and asked him to help him. He made it and saved the kids!"

A firefighter who is a medic comes over and attends to Andrew. He tells Alex, Alana, and Julie to move back to give him some room. The firefighter calls out to the other crew members for some help with the medical equipment as he's trying to keep Andrew alive. With that, another fireball shoots out from the house and lands a short distance away, forcing Alana and Julie to move away. Alex follows.

Within seconds, the firefighter is yelling for help. He's calling for somebody to call for an ambulance right away. Andrew is in such bad shape he fears that he's not going to make it. The firefighter then screams out, "If we don't get an ambulance here right now we're going to lose him!" Andrew is, for all practical purposes, on his deathbed.

Another firefighter tells him the ambulance district dispatch was notified when they got the call for the fire, and at least one should have been here by now. He tells him he doesn't understand why it's late and that he'll call again to have several sent.

Alex and Alana return to the tree where the rest of the family is located, and Alana goes into an uncontrollable panic. Sonja again tries to comfort her, but without success. Alex sits down to rest and then looks up the street.

Alex sees Officer Musty get out of his car and start walking down the street toward them. At the same time, he again spots the old white van parked at a distance behind him. This time he can see it a little better. Alex is surprised. It appears to be the same van the Arab has been driving, but the front side of the van is badly damaged. Apparently it hit something and was in an accident. Again, he had thought that the old white van had been burned in the propane tanks explosion. He thinks, "Maybe there's more than one white van. What's going on? I wish it wasn't so dark up the street and I could see the side of it."

He then observes the Arab getting out of his van up the street behind Officer Musty. They are fairly far away and are walking down the side of the street. The Arab follows Officer Musty, but it appears he's deliberately staying in the shadows behind him and doesn't want to be seen. Alex is perplexed.

This is the first time Alex has actually seen the Arab outside of his van, and he immediately gets very nervous. What's he up to? He suspects that Officer Musty doesn't know that the Arab is following him from behind. It's dark at the end of the street. He fears the worst is about to happen.

Alex then remembers the Arab's full name. It's *Misa Hajiba Ihcalam*. Alex quickly pulls his smartphone from his pocket and finds that he has a signal. He immediately Googles the Arab's full name. He finds out that *Misa* and *Hajiba* have feminine references, and on a whim he decides to look up the Arab's name backward. This would be *Asim Abijah Malachi*. Within a few minutes or so, he has visited several websites that provide the meanings of male names in Arabic, Islam, Hebrew and a few others. He finds these names on several websites and he's shocked to learn what the meaning of his name is. Alex is totally stunned. "This can't be possible. Is this really true?

Or is this perhaps another coincidence? Why didn't I look up these names before?" he asks himself. He can't believe what he's found out. He wonders if the meaning of his name is real or if he's being led astray again. He thinks, "This all just can't be. Everything that's happening is so surreal."

A brief prayer is answered to verify what he's thinking and his knowledge of the answer to the last piece of the puzzle is confirmed. At the end of this prayer, he decides to pray a third time that the ordination process of the last angel will be successful and may be completed in time as per the will of God. In this special prayer, he again prays with all his heart and soul.

Alex opens his eyes and realizes that now he knows the very last piece of the puzzle. At the same time, he feels a rush throughout his body. As he watches both Officer Musty and the Arab approach from behind him, he knows exactly what's going to happen. He also knows what he needs to do. The puzzle is complete, and now he knows everything.

Alex looks back up the street and now finds that Officer Musty has returned to his patrol car and is driving it down the street closer to where the family is located. In the meantime, the Arab has disappeared in the darkness somewhere between the houses or amongst all of the emergency vehicles. He has no idea where the men in suits ran. He presumes they are close by somewhere hidden for some reason.

Officer Musty parks his patrol car as close as he can and gets out and approaches Alex. Officer Musty greets Alex and asks him if everything is okay. Before Alex can respond, Officer Musty says, "I thought you and Andrew were in the house. How did you get out so quickly?"

Suddenly, the Arab comes out of nowhere and is seen standing only a short distance away in the shadows. He's dressed in a wrap of clothing of some sort, like a robe, and is wearing a turban wrapped to cover his face and head. His sudden presence and being so close to them scares the bejeebers out of Julie, Alana, Garrett, and all the children who are all together. He's like a ghost who suddenly materialized out of thin air. And he's only a few feet away. They become terrified, and they all start screaming.

Officer Musty sees the Arab, draws his weapon, wheels around, and shoots several bullets at him. The Arab drops down to the ground and lies there still in the shadows. Everybody jumps in a panic, but they're relieved that Officer Musty has appeared to have taken care of the Arab. Now they don't need to worry about him anymore.

But then Officer Musty completely surprises everybody and does something entirely unexpected. He walks over to the firefighter who is attending Andrew and shoots him at point-blank range with several more bullets. Everybody is shocked and perplexed! What's he doing? Doesn't he know the firefighter is a medic who is trying to save Andrew? Or does he think the firefighter knows the Arab perhaps? Is the medic another terrorist?

Alex hobbles over and approaches Officer Musty. Officer Musty then waves his gun in the air and tells Alex not to come any closer. "It's a dangerous situation," Officer Musty yells out. Officer Musty then appears to aim his gun in Andrew's direction and then pulls it away and waves his gun in the air again. "Stay back," he shouts.

Everybody is in a state of panic. What's going on? Is there someone else behind Andrew? Who is Officer Musty aiming at? What's he going to do? He's not going to shoot Andrew, is he?

In the meantime, the Arab gets up off the ground, reappears in the light, and approaches Andrew. Officer Musty, only a few feet away, sees him out of the corner of his eye and swings around to shoot him again.

Officer Musty is only a few feet away from the Arab and aims at him at point-blank range. He pulls the trigger, but instead of gunfire, several clicks are heard. It appears that he's run out of ammunition.

Chapter 73

Officer Musty runs back to his patrol car, apparently to reload. With all the commotion, everybody now is in a state of total panic. The police now are far away trying to control a growing crowd of onlookers and traffic wanting to enter the street at the top of the hill. It's questionable whether they're even aware of what's happening because of the noise from the sirens and the attention given to fire. In the meantime, Alex staggers to get back to his family as fast as he can.

Everybody is looking at Officer Musty running toward his patrol car, and every eye follows him the entire way. Meanwhile Alex sees the Arab trying to pick Andrew up. Julie turns around and also sees the Arab picking Andrew up and screams again. She yells out, "The Arab's trying to kidnap Andrew! How did he survive? He was shot multiple times! Why is he taking Andrew? What does he want with him?"

Within only a matter of seconds, Officer Musty immediately reappears from his patrol car running with two guns, one in each hand. He again approaches the Arab who has Andrew in his arms, and aims both guns at him. But he then raises both guns and fires several warning shots straight up into the air and hollers, "Everybody stay back and do what I say!"

As he's firing into the air, the Arab lays Andrew back down on the ground and stands between Andrew and Officer Musty. Officer Musty then shoots the Arab several times at point-blank range again, but the Arab doesn't fall. Then Officer Musty walks up to him, shoves his gun in the Arab's chest, and shoots several more times. But again, the Arab is still standing and doesn't fall to the ground. The Arab continues to stand between Officer Musty and Andrew. The Arab pushes Officer Musty away.

Officer Musty abandons the Arab and Andrew and runs over to Alex and the family. Officer Musty is extremely upset that things are not going his way. What does he want? What on Earth is he doing? Officer Musty looks at the white blanket lying on the ground. Alex had laid the blanket and Bible by the tree between Sonja and him earlier. Everyone can see him eyeing the blanket. Does Officer Musty want the blanket?

There is pandemonium, and nobody has a clue as to what he's going to do next. Has Officer Musty gone mad? Why now is he running toward them? Everybody is terrified. The entire family stands up and prepares to run.

He aims both guns in the direction of the family, and as he approaches he zeroes in specifically in the direction of Alex and Sonja. It looks like he's aiming at them. Or perhaps he's aiming at something or somebody behind them. Everybody looks behind them thinking that he's aiming at somebody else who is going to attack them from behind in the shadows. But if so, who? Instantly, two men in suits run out from the shadows of the house across the street and fire at Officer Musty.

They keep firing at him as they run through the shadows across the front yard. The men in suits hit Officer Musty multiple times, riddling him with bullets, but he doesn't fall. Officer Musty turns around and fires at them as they duck behind a patrol car.

Garrett, Julie, and Alana all wonder, "Where is the shooting coming from and who is Officer Musty shooting at?"

Then Officer Musty turns around and again aims his guns in the general direction of the family as he walks toward them. Everybody is screaming and looking around. Who is he going to shoot at now? What's going on? He has gone mad! Why didn't he fall when he was shot? He was shot in the chest multiple times. Is there somebody else behind them he's going to shoot at? Surely he is not going to shoot at the family, is he?

He then yells out something that nobody understands, and a grimace can be seen on his face as he's about to pull the trigger again. This time he is aiming directly at Alex!

But just as officer Musty is about to pull the trigger, Alex reaches down and grabs his Bible that he brought with him and points it at Officer Musty and he also says something nobody understands. Officer Musty freezes in place like a statue, and he and Alex stare at each other. Alex limps over to him, holds the Bible over his head, says something else that nobody understands, and with that, Officer Musty slowly collapses to the ground, dropping both guns.

At that point, additional men in suits arrive out of nowhere. They swarm and jump all over Officer Musty, pull his arms behind his back, and handcuff him. Several more men in suits appear and drag him away to an SUV parked nearby. Who are these men in suits and where did they come from? What's going on?

Finally, everything seems to have settled down except for the action of the firefighters still trying to put out the fire and the emergency vehicles everywhere.

Everybody breathes a sigh of relief but is confused as to what just happened. Why was Officer Musty acting like he did? Why did the men in suits jump out of nowhere and start shooting at Officer Musty? Why didn't he fall and die after being shot numerous times? Why did the men in suits handcuff him and take him away? Who are these men in suits? It all happened so fast.

One of the men in suits then comes over to Alana, Julie, and Garrett and identifies himself as an FBI agent. Soon several more agents join him.

Garrett, still sitting on the ground in pain, immediately asks them what's going on. Simultaneously, Julie asks if they know the status of where the ambulances are. "In addition to Andrew, Garrett and Alex need medical attention. Where are the ambulances?"

One of the agents informs her that the police or fire department should have called the ambulance dispatch, and he expects that at least one should be on its way.

Then everybody asks again what happened. They all want an explanation as to what's going on.

One agent explains they've been recently investigating and tracking Officer Musty undercover and tells them that he is not really a police officer at all. The FBI agent explains to everybody that the FBI and CIA have been tracking Officer Musty and others in a worldwide investigation and that he's been identified as a disciple of ISA and has ties to ISIS. He's an Islamic extremist and professes and advances Jihadism.

At that point, another FBI agent arrives and states that the FBI found three detonation trigger devices in Officer Musty's patrol car. "All of these devices are used to detonate explosives remotely and one was used just a little while ago. It's undetermined why the other two were not activated and it appears that they may have malfunctioned."

Officer Musty has been caught red-handed trying to blow up Andrew's house and everybody in it.

The agent continues to explain, "It appears that he was trying to kill somebody in the house or was after something in the house, or possibly wanted to destroy something in the house."

"You're kidding, right? But why?" asks Alana.

"We don't know. Was there anybody in the house who had any issues with him, or were there any items of value in the house that perhaps he may have been after or anything he wanted destroyed?"

They all indicate no, either not being aware of the background of the white handwoven blanket or perhaps they forgot about it.

Garrett, Julie, and Alana are surprised and can't believe it. Never did they ever think that Officer Musty would be a terrorist. "You're kidding us, right?"

"No, ma'am. The officer is an Islamic extremist and just blew up your house. And now he just tried to kill Alex."

Alana then screams, "Where's Andrew?" Everybody looks over, and only the body of the firefighter medic is seen on the ground. Andrew has disappeared. In only the short time that they were preoccupied with Officer Musty and the FBI agents coming on the scene, Andrew has vanished. Additionally, the Arab is nowhere to be found either. Andrew certainly could not have walked away by himself. He was on his deathbed.

Everybody thinks of the obvious. While they all feared for their lives watching Officer Musty, the Arab must have picked up Andrew again and is kidnapping him.

One of the agents then motions to some of the other agents and they immediately set out to look for the Arab and Andrew. They start looking between the houses and in between all of the emergency vehicles. Alana is beside herself. "Why didn't I keep an eye on Andrew?" she cries.

While they search for Andrew and the Arab, another FBI agent tells them that CIA intelligence has revealed that Officer Musty also has ties to Muhannad Eblis Qadir and other ISA terrorists. In fact, their surveillance revealed that he was on a satellite phone with them briefly just before the explosion.

But more importantly and as the biggest surprise of all, he states that Muhammad is a half-blood relative of Ammen, who is part of the same terrorist group. Their surveillance indicated he had also talked with the officer just prior to the explosion on a satellite phone.

"What?" everyone exclaims. "You're kidding, right? Ammen is a terrorist? No way!"

"Nope, I'm not kidding. They're actually believed to be stepbrothers. The names which people refer to them are not their real names. There are additional relatives who are other leaders of affiliated terrorist groups and the group of which Officer Musty was a member. These are thought to include additional brothers and cousins. They're all Islamic extremists. They are all either part of ISA or are working with them.

"We've obtained extremely credible evidence from CIA and other intelligence sources that proves Ammen and Muhammad, as well as others, have conspired together to promote the agenda of the Islamic terrorist extremists. They're all Jihadists. CIA intelligence has revealed that they're all working in coordination with each other, as well as with others. They also believe that Officer Musty and Ammen are demonic and have powers granted by Satan."

"Really?" Garrett asks. "Now just how would you know that? Just who is this Muhammad? Is he the new caliph?"

The agent says, "Not sure about that, but everything else is true. We know that for sure. Some think he's the 'beast.'"

"Who is Ammen?" responds Garrett. "How can he be a terrorist? That's impossible! We don't believe you!"

"Are you sure he's also a terrorist?" asks Julie. "He can't be!"

"Are you sure he's a demon? That's hard to believe!" asks Alana. "I don't believe it at all. He preaches he'll save everyone, he can't be a terrorist and a demon!"

The agent continues, "It's true. Ammen is an impostor, and some say he actually just might be the Antichrist. Our operatives tell us that Muhammad and others have conspired to turn the world into total chaos and panic so that everyone will follow and worship Ammen. Ammen is really a demon doing the work of the devil. That has been their agenda all along. Officer Musty's role is unclear, however CIA intelligence believes that he was apparently out to kill somebody in the family, presumably Alex, Sonja, or Andrew, or maybe all of them or was interested in something they had, or possibly both."

"This is so difficult to believe. Are you sure? Why?" asks Alana.

The agent responds, "We are absolutely positive about Ammen being an impostor and a demon. We're not sure exactly what Officer Musty's role was. We're told that the more people who follow and worship Ammen, then the more power Satan would have and can use that over God. This is the reason why the terrorists have planted the bombs and why they have created total chaos in America. This is why Ammen came on the scene. It was an effort to get as many people as possible to abandon Jesus Christ and worship Ammen instead."

Julie responds, "You mean everybody who follows Ammen is actually worshipping the devil?"

"Ammen tried to deceive everyone in believing that he was the return of Jesus. It was all part of a master plan. Our sources tell us that Satan himself initiated all of this by working with the extremists. They had a common agenda to persecute the Christians."

"And just how would you know all of this?" Garrett inquires. "That's impossible. It's impossible that you would know this!"

"We have our sources. But it's true. Trust us," the agent says. "It is absolutely true."

"So you're telling us that the Islamic extremists are all possessed by the devil and this is all part of a master plan to abolish the Christian faith, or as much of it as they can?" asks Garrett.

"Well, I don't know if they're all possessed by the devil, but Satan certainly is working within them. But I'm referring to only the Jihadists, the radical ones, not all of Islam. Actually, the Jihadists' agenda is to convert those of all religions to the radical extremist views of Islam, not just Christians. Or they wish to otherwise abolish them. But it sounds like you're suggesting that it might be possible that the extremists, the Jihadists so to speak, are all possessed by Satan?" responds the agent.

"Well, I suppose that hasn't been proven to be impossible. I wouldn't be surprised," Julie remarks. "They both do have the same objective to at least go after the Christians when you think about it. They do have the same agenda, so maybe after all they are possessed by the devil. At any rate, the devil has certainly had something to do in influencing them."

Garrett then asks the agents, "Well, if this is all true, do you or the CIA happen to know who the woman is who is always sitting by Ammen in the videos and in the interview with Ammen?"

One of the agents explains, "As a matter of fact, we do know a little about her. We needed to investigate her when we investigated Ammen and the other terrorists. One of the agent operatives in the Middle East was able to secretly talk with her just very recently. She's not related to Ammen, and she has nothing to do with him. She lived near him, befriended him, and actually told him that it would make him look better if he had her always sit with him and he thought it was a good idea and agreed with her.

"But actually, she deceived Ammen, but he didn't know it. She had an ulterior motive and was trying to convey a secret message by placing the bouquet of white flowers upside down in her lap when Ammen spoke. She especially wanted Alex to see her in the video doing this. She said Alex would see the secret message and know what it meant."

"Alex? Why Alex? He would know what?" asks Garrett.

"When she held the bouquet upside down and the flowers pointed down and not up, it could only mean one thing. Ammen wasn't aware that she did this."

"Why would she do that? What message? Why convey the message to Alex? Does she know him? Why would he understand the message? Who is she?"

The agent continues, "She said that Alex would understand. She and Alex grew up together when they were young children, but they haven't seen each other for almost sixty years. She said something about a puzzle of life that their father told her and Alex when she was a little girl and that she figured out it was her destiny that she needed to do this. She said Alex would know all about this and could explain everything. Alex knows her and he can provide further information about her.

"Also, if it were not for this woman, we may never have linked Ammen and Muhammad with Officer Musty. It was because of her that we ended up doing an undercover investigation of Officer Musty who we discovered was a member of the same terrorist group and was trying to befriend Alex. She desperately wants to meet Alex, and we can try to arrange for that in the next few days, before the end of time comes."

Julie asks, "Who is the Arab? What do you know about him?"

"We can't say. But we know that he has been seen a lot lately in the vicinity of the officer."

"You mean Officer Musty? Do the Arab and Officer Musty know each other? Is the Arab also a terrorist?"

"Can't say right now. Who you refer to as the Arab is somewhat mysterious. We don't know anything about him yet. But I suppose anything's possible."

The agent then tells them that all the facts about the conspiracy between Muhammad and Ammen and the other terrorists can be proven and that he would have hoped that the details and further evidence would be released on the news. Everybody would then be told the truth. However, he doesn't think that can happen for several reasons.

The agent advises that within the last hour the terrorists have hacked into and taken complete control of all communication systems. Even if there was an available medium to broadcast on, it would take several days to sort things out considering the protocols they need to deal with to release it to the news. It won't happen in time. It will be too late. Nobody will know.

"However, knowing this does not resolve everything. Not by a long shot. The global crisis involving the bombs and spread of the deadly disease has not gone away. That big problem is still with us. All the bombs including the nuclear devices are still set to explode and the United States will be completely obliterated if the volcano erupts when the device planted at Yellowstone is set off. And the government has vowed that as soon as one nuclear device goes off, it will unleash its nuclear arsenal and send it to Russia and the Middle East. That will result in a domino effect and a worldwide thermal nuclear catastrophe. The entire world will be annihilated. That is an absolute certainty."

The agent then continues, "They have not been able to capture Muhannad Eblis Qadir or any members of ISA and none of the nuclear and other bombs can be deactivated or moved. The bombs are all 100 percent tamperproof. And they are all still scheduled to explode in almost exactly seventy-two hours from now. There's no stopping it. It *will* happen.

"CIA and other intelligence now report that there are more than forty massive bombs across the United States that will all explode in three days. They are mostly at critical infrastructures. Some of them and perhaps many of them are nuclear bombs but it is not known how many. Also, within the last few hours additional bombs have been found in Western Europe. But the major concern is the nuclear device that could possibly trigger the eruption of the super-volcano. That would render most of the country if not the entire world uninhabitable for years.

"And the deadly disease will be released. The CDC has completed their tests and has confirmed that the disease which the terrorists have threatened to unleash is a new strain of bacteria and is the deadliest and most highly contagious disease ever known to mankind. They have labeled it as EDAC 666. It is both airborne and waterborne and thrives and multiplies in any environment. Any contact with the air or water in which it is present would result in a certain and most horrific death within twenty-four hours.

"The government cannot believe the extent of the bombs and the strategic places where they have been planted by the terrorists. It's unfathomable that the terrorists were able to acquire the materials and knowledge, and to build the bombs and place the bombs. And it's equally incomprehensible that United States intelligence was not aware of the plot before now or did not make it public if they knew about it. I suppose that's partially our fault. However, the CIA and other agencies were more responsible than we were for obtaining any intel on that. This ISA group here is unbelievably sophisticated. A hell of a lot more so than anybody would have thought. We only learned about them very recently.

"But the terrorists have had over well over a decade to plan this and put it into place. That's a long time and anything is possible. It's also evident that Russia, Iran, North Korea, and Pakistan all were involved one way or another in assisting ISA in the plot through funding and manufacturing of the bombs or in supplying and smuggling them in the country. Because these countries were involved and the terrorists have also targeted Western Europe and other parts of the world, that helped escalate the crisis to that of global status.

"The United States government has vowed and told Russia that because it has assisted ISA in the nuclear bomb plot, it will unleash its arsenal of nuclear warheads against it if and as soon as only one nuclear device is detonated in the US. The United States government has told Russia that the only way it will not do this is for Russia to convince ISA not to detonate any of the nuclear bombs in the United States. If Russia cannot convince them, then this would be in retaliation of Russia helping ISA in their plot.

"However, the Russian government has been adamant that it cannot persuade ISA from not doing this, and if the United States sends any nuclear bombs towards Russia, it will simultaneously send its arsenal of nuclear bombs to the United States. Other countries would inevitably get involved. Therefore, the standoff will result in an Armageddon and global nuclear destruction. This is a certainty.

"Every nation with a nuclear arsenal practically has their fingers on the button. When multiple nuclear bombs are detonated to this extent, the resulting aftermath and fallout alone will result in years of darkness and will destroy life just about everywhere around the globe. However, in advance of that, when the disease is spread, it could wipe out nearly the remaining population in this country alone in a matter of only a few months or less. And an eruption of the super volcano could spell disaster all by itself!"

"But think of all the people who are worshipping Ammen. They won't know the truth. The entire globe is in total panic and hundreds of millions if not billions are relying on him to save them. And, because they will have abandoned Jesus and instead will be worshipping Ammen prior to their death and won't know he's a demon and not their savior, they will actually be worshipping the devil and will likely all be doomed forever? Is that right?" Julie asks.

"I suppose so," says the agent. "Armageddon is still for real they say. Nobody can stop it. It *will* happen."

As soon as the agent says this, another agent runs up and in a frantic and excited voice exclaims that Officer Musty has escaped.

"What?" shout two other agents.

"We had him in handcuffs and locked to the back seat of the vehicle. All of the doors were locked from the outside and he couldn't have opened them or the windows from inside anyway. But when they went to check on him just a few minutes later he was gone!"

Another agent comments, "It's like he's a ghost or a bad spirit or something. I've never seen anybody survive multiple gunshots into the chest like he did. And, how did he get away? His hands were handcuffed behind him and locked to the seat and he couldn't have gotten out even if he freed himself. He must be a demon or something."

"I told you he was," says another agent.

Several other FBI agents are then seen frantically coordinating a search for Officer Musty and any other terrorists who may be in the area. Most of the agents then disperse and head back to their SUVs parked up the street. One agent remains with the family.

The agent then comments that there may be more terrorists in the vicinity in addition to Officer Musty. The family is still at risk. There still may be somebody they want to eliminate or perhaps something they want here. He says that the terrorists have a clever way of deceiving people in making them think they are somebody other than who they are. "You just cannot trust anybody these days," he firmly states. "A terrorist can be anybody."

His remarks prompt Alana and Julie to think that the Arab may also be part of the same terrorist group. But if this is the case, then why did Officer Musty shoot him? Was he trying to deceive everybody into thinking the Arab is his enemy, when perhaps he might also be a terrorist? Perhaps the Arab is another demon working with Officer Musty? After all, maybe that's why he also couldn't be killed. They think that must be the case—that the Arab is also a demon and is actually working with Officer Musty, and together, they deceived everyone!

Perhaps Officer Musty and the Arab have been working together all along and simply tried to deceive everyone by making it look like they were enemies. Maybe it was a plan to distract the family so that the Arab could capture Andrew. If that's the case, they both may have Andrew and are getting away with him. Who else may be a terrorist involved in all this? Who else might be another demon? But most importantly, what does he want with Andrew?

In the meantime, the agents still search for Andrew, the Arab, Officer Musty, and anyone else suspected of being a terrorist. But there are no signs of any of them anywhere.

Chapter 74

The information told to them by the FBI agents was absolutely staggering and had everyone so spellbound and captivated that they suddenly realize that both Alex and Sonja are also both missing. They were both there just minutes ago but now have vanished. Nobody saw them leave.

Then Julie remembers the handwoven white blanket and remembers Andrew telling her once that it was destined to be an invaluable inheritance of his, perhaps trying to rub it in that he will inherit it and not her. She's aware that it is supposed to have a Middle Eastern history and go back over one thousand years and may be mystical in some sense. She wonders if perhaps the Arab is trying to steal it and if that has anything to do with what's going on. Is that why he wants Andrew or is why he was approaching Alex? Or is it for some other reason?

She looks over where Alex and Sonja were previously guarding the blanket with their lives by the tree and discovers that it is also missing! It appears the Arab or perhaps Officer Musty also stole the blanket!

They call all the children to account for them. All are accounted for except for Lizzy. Lizzy is also gone! When asked where Lizzy went, both Daniel and Matthew say that she just suddenly ran away into the darkness up the street. They have no idea where she went. None of them saw Alex or Sonja leave either. And where is the white blanket and the Bible?

Andrew, Alex, Sonja, Lizzy, and the Arab are all gone as if they disappeared in thin air. How is it that nobody noticed any of them leaving? They could not have gone anywhere far with all of the emergency equipment and lights flashing around. But they did. It appears they just disappeared.

The last FBI agent on the scene looks at his watch and mutters that it will be midnight before you know it, and he needs to leave to catch up with the other agents but will return shortly. He then tells them that they will all need to make themselves available for some additional questions. "It won't take long," he says. "I want you all to stay put and not move until we can secure the area and find Officer Musty, the Arab, and the missing family members. I'll be right back."

Again, Julie, Alana, and Garrett are still panic-stricken. Their emotions have been on an enormously traumatic roller coaster for some time now, but this time it's the worst. Each has a really bad feeling about the outcome of this.

Julie, Garrett, and Alana are all huddled together, reliving all the events and desperately trying to figure everything out. What all just happened? It all happened so fast. Where are Alex, Andrew, Sonja, Lizzy, and the Arab? Where is the white blanket and Bible?

Garrett is still moaning and holding his leg. The children are all sitting in front of them on the ground.

Alana, still in hysterics, yells out, "This is like a nightmare! I can't believe this is really happening! Somebody tell me that I'm only imagining all of this! I want to see Andrew!"

Julie suddenly shouts out, "Where's the ambulance? We need a lot of ambulances. I can't believe they're still not here yet! Garrett needs medical attention. Andrew is dying somewhere. Alex, wherever he is, also needs medical help. Where are they? Didn't anybody call an ambulance? Where is it?"

Daniel hears the desperation in Julie's voice. "I saw an ambulance."

Alana quickly asks him, "Where?"

Daniel then points up the street. "Just a few minutes ago."

It's dark up the street and it's difficult to see because of the haze, the smoke, and the glare from the flashing lights of the emergency vehicles.

Then Matthew argues with Daniel. "That wasn't an ambulance."

Daniel says, "Yes, it was. I saw it."

Matthew comes back, "No, it wasn't. It was a white van."

"It was an ambulance."

"No, it was a white van."

"It was an ambulance. I know what it looked like."

"No. It was a white van, and I know what I saw too. The front of it was all smashed in. How can a van turn into an ambulance? It's not like one of your transformer toys. It's too big. It was a white van."

Daniel then gets angry with Matthew and emphatically states, "Matthew, you're wrong. There was a white van parked there earlier, but then it was an ambulance. I don't know if the van left and the ambulance came or if they changed places or if it turned into an ambulance or what, but I saw it. It was definitely an ambulance."

Everybody looks up the street but can't see anything because of the smoke, haze, and glare from the lights.

Alana, not sure exactly what they saw, then asks, "Did you see anybody go up the street?"

Daniel then says, "Yes."

Alana asks him desperately, "Who? What did you see?"

"I saw somebody just a few minutes ago. He was wearing a robe and a strange looking hat and was carrying somebody. I think the man in the robe was the man in the shadows who the policeman shot. I think he was carrying Daddy. Is he going to try to help him?"

Alana now is absolutely frantic. She knows exactly who Daniel is referring to. It's the Arab. Everybody now believes for sure that the Arab has kidnapped Andrew. Why? What does he want with him? Andrew may even be dead.

Chapter 75

Alana gets up and starts running up the street towards the ambulance or white van or whatever it is. She's screaming for the police and FBI to come help. She's yelling that the Arab is kidnapping Andrew, but all the FBI and police now are far away attending to the growing crowd and other matters. They can't hear her. It's still a scene of utter pandemonium, which is enhanced by the haze, smoke, flashing lights of the emergency vehicles, and an intermittent siren heard every once in a while. The entire scene is surreal.

As she's running up the street and negotiating her way through all the parked emergency vehicles, she sees a white ambulance leaving the scene and driving away. She stands there absolutely panic-stricken. She can't see which way it went as it drove into the darkness far up the street. The police had blocked off the intersecting streets on both sides but this was around the corners and out of sight. For some reason the ambulance didn't have its lights on. But she saw an eerie glow disappear into the night.

She assumes regardless of what has transpired that maybe the ambulance took Andrew to the hospital. Maybe Daniel was wrong. That wouldn't surprise her. But assuming it went to the hospital, which one? Is it going to the north hospital or the south hospital? Depending on which way the ambulance turned would determine to which hospital it went. She's thinking of Andrew and desperately wants to go to the hospital to see him. She wants to know if he's still alive. She wants to be with him. He's the only thing that she can think about.

As she stands there looking up the street, suddenly she sees a lone small figure walking down the street out of the darkness from where the ambulance was parked.

It's Lizzy.

"Lizzy, where have you been? Are you okay?" cries Alana.

Lizzy sees Alana and runs to her. As they walk back down the street together, Lizzy sees the rest of the family and runs to them. Alana follows her to where Julie is sitting on the ground next to Garrett and the children. Lizzy flies into Julie's arms and is all smiles.

Julie is ecstatic that Lizzy has returned, but after all this turmoil and what's transpired, how can she be so happy? Doesn't she know she wasn't supposed to run away like that? Doesn't she have a clue as to what just happened? How they wish she could talk and explain things to them.

They want to ask her so many questions. She's the only one who saw the ambulance up close and knows where it went. She also appears to be the last one to have seen Andrew and perhaps Alex. Maybe she's the only one who knows anything about Andrew, but they assume they will never know. She can't say more than a word or two at a time.

Alana looks at Lizzy and in desperation asks her which way did the ambulance go.

Nobody expects Lizzy to say anything.

Lizzy then climbs out of Julie's lap, stands up, gets all big-eyed, and with a happy face, she looks at Alana. She then says as clear as day, "The ambulance went that way," and points up the street.

Everybody is amazed, and for several seconds, they're speechless. This is the first time in her life that any of them ever heard her say more than one or two words at a time or has strung more than one or two words together.

Alana then asks her again, "Which way did the ambulance turn at the top of the street?" Alana desperately hopes that Andrew was taken to a hospital regardless that the Arab may have taken him.

She wants to know whether to go to the south hospital or the north hospital.

Lizzy clearly states, "The ambulance didn't turn either way. It went straight."

Julie then asks Lizzy, "Why is it that you can suddenly talk? How is it that you can talk now?" Julie is overjoyed. She is beside herself and is absolutely awestruck.

Lizzy says "Grandpa."

Julie looks at her. "What do you mean?"

"Grandpa put his hand on my forehead."

"What? Where did Grandpa do this? When did he do this? Did you see him?"

"Yes. I just saw him. I know everything."

"What do you mean you know everything?"

"Everything. Grandpa put his hand on my forehead, and I know everything you need to know."

Then Julie and Alana, both in hysterics and in a frenzy and with emotions boiling over, they fire a series of questions at Lizzy.

"Where did the ambulance go? It had to turn either left or right. That's a T-intersection. If it went straight, it would have fallen off the cliff. Which way did it go? I need to know which hospital to go to."

"It went straight."

"What do you mean it went straight? It couldn't have. It had to turn either left or right."

"It went straight. It didn't turn either way."

"That's impossible. Was Andrew in the ambulance?"

"You mean Uncle Andrew? Yes, he was. Is it okay if I just call him Andrew?"

"Well, he is your uncle, but now that you're just starting to talk, it's okay to call him Andrew if you want. Who was driving the ambulance?"

"The Arab."

"The Arab?"

"Yes. The Arab."

"Was anybody with him?"

"Yes."

"Who?"

"Grandpa."

"Grandpa? You're kidding me, right?"

"No. The Arab was driving, and Grandpa was in the ambulance too. So was Andrew."

"Oh no! Did the Arab kidnap both of them?"

"They were all in the ambulance."

"Did the Arab also take Alex's white blanket? Did you see it?"

"Yes, it was in the ambulance. The Arab was wearing a white robe. Like a bathrobe. It was all shiny white."

"What?"

"Grandpa was wearing a white robe too."

"He was?"

"His robe was exactly like the Arab's."

"Alex was also wearing a white robe?"

"Their robes were the same. Grandpa's was also shiny white. The Arab was driving, and Grandpa was in the back of the ambulance trying to help Andrew."

"He was?"

"The Arab's robe had three lines on it. There were letters on the first line. They were like it was his name or something. The next two lines were blank."

"On who?"

"The Arab."

"Go on."

"Grandpa's robe had three lines on it too."

"It did?"

"The same letters were on the second line on his robe.

"And?"

"The letters were exactly the same on both the Arab's and Grandpa's robes."

"Letters? What letters?"

"They were also the same letters on the shirt that Grandpa showed me back in the house he said he used to wear when he was about my age."

"What did the letters say?"

"You have to look at the letters a special way to be able to read them. Grandpa put on a similar white robe on Andrew. His robe had three lines on it too."

"It did? Where did they get these robes? Did Andrew's robe have any letters on it?"

"Yes."

"And what were those letters?"

"There were two blank lines at the top and then some letters on the third line."

"What did they say?"

"I don't know.

"What do you mean you don't know."

"I couldn't read the letters because they weren't clear. The letters blended in with Andrew's robe and were faded. But I saw the letters on the Arab's robe and on Grandpa's robe. They were the same."

"What did the letters on their robes say? What were the letters? Tell me what the letters were. Tell me!"

"LEGNASDOGMAI. But these are the letters when you look at them upside down. That is the only way you can know what they are. But you also need to read them a special way."

"How did you know to look at them upside down?"

"When I held Grandpa's shirt against my chest as if I was wearing it and looked down on it."

"So, what do they mean?"

"I can't tell you."

"Why?"

"It's a secret. Only I know how to read the letters. Only I know what it says and means."

"Why? What were the letters again?"

"LEGNASDOGMAI. If you look at them upside down the letters are LEGNASDOGMAI."

"Why can only you read them and know what they say and we can't? What is the special way to read them?"

"I know how to read them, but you don't. You don't know how to read them but I do."

"Why?"

"You need to look at them in a mirror to know what it means. I don't need a mirror, but you do."

"A mirror?"

"Yes, a mirror. You can read the letters in a mirror and know what they say, but I can read them without a mirror. LEGNASDOGMAI. When you look at the letters in the mirror, you may need to turn some of them around so they face the other way, but when you do, you can read it. I don't need to do that though."

"Why?"

"Because I don't. Grandpa was covering Andrew with his white blanket and a book."

"Alex's white blanket? What book, his Bible? The one with the white cover?"

"Grandpa was careful to fold the blanket a certain way and then covered Andrew with it. He then put the book on top of the blanket. These are the ones that he keeps as his treasures. Grandpa and the Arab were all dressed in white, their eyes shown like lights."

"What do you mean?"

"Their eyes were all glassy and had lights in them."

"Both of them?"

"They were really cool."

"What does that mean?"

"I can't tell you."

"Why?"

"It's a secret."

"A secret? So you know but won't tell us? How do you know?"

"Because I do. You need to look at the letters in a mirror."

"What?"

"A mirror. If you look at the letters in a mirror, then you will know."

"Did you ask him where they're taking Andrew or when we could see him?"

"Yes."

"Where? Which hospital are they taking him to?"

"They're not going to a hospital."

"Why not?"

"Grandpa said they had to prepare Andrew and take him on a trip."

"On a trip? What trip? Where?"

"First they need to stop at the mirror and wheel of balance."

"The mirror and wheel of balance? What is that? Why are they going on a trip?"

"So Andrew can pay the price."

"Pay the price? For what? What price? What in God's name are you talking about?"

"Grandpa said that they need to take Andrew someplace to pay the price."

"Where?"

"It's a secret."

"Where? Tell me! Tell me!"

"He said after they stop at the mirror and wheel of balance, then Andrew will need to go to the chamber."

"Where?"

"The chamber."

"To a chamber? Where is this chamber?"

"He said it's a place where you don't want to go. He said nobody wants to go there ever. He said that it's a really bad place. I think it's supposed to be really scary and they hurt you a lot there."

"Who do you mean by 'they'? If it's a bad place, why does Andrew need to go to this chamber?"

"Grandpa said because Andrew needs to pay the price."

"I don't understand."

"He said that Andrew will be able to survive it though."

"What do you mean? How would he survive it?"

"Because Grandpa will be there with him and help him. He will help Andrew know what to say and what to do. But Grandpa will be invisible and Andrew won't know he's there. The Arab will also be there, but he will also be invisible and Andrew won't know he's there either."

"Invisible? You're not making any sense at all. So, just how will Grandpa know what to tell him?"

"Because he's already been there."

"Grandpa's already been to this chamber? When did Grandpa go to the chamber?"

"I can't tell you. It's a secret."

"Well, tell me anyway!"

"He was there just a few days ago."

"He was? That's impossible. He was in the hospital and declared brain-dead then!"

"But he was."

"So, how does Grandpa know what to tell him to say"

"He said when he was there the Arab was there with him and helped him. The Arab helped Grandpa know what to say and that's how he knows. But he said the Arab was invisible. He couldn't see him. Grandpa didn't know he was there. The Arab was like a good spirit, an angel who was with Grandpa then but Grandpa didn't realize it at the time."

"Really? So the Arab was like a good spirit, an angel who helped him, and that's why he was invisible and Grandpa didn't know it?"

"Yep. He also said that Andrew might need to go to more than one chamber. His experience may be a lot worse than what Grandpa experienced there. Maybe a lot worse."

"Andrew may need to go to more than one chamber? How many chambers are there? What happens in these chambers?"

"The chambers are awful. They're terrifying and you get hurt there a lot. You get really scared there too. If you go there, you will suffer in pain that's a lot worse than the worst pain you can ever imagine. But he said the Arab and he will both be there to help him because others will be trying to get him."

"Others will try to get him? What others? What on Earth are you talking about?"

"The others. Did you know that Officer Musty is one of the others? They're already trying to get him now. They tried to get Grandpa earlier. They're from the chambers. But Grandpa and the Arab will help him. They will protect him. Just like the Arab helped and protected Grandpa. Andrew will be really scared in the chamber but he'll be okay because Grandpa and the Arab will help him there too. But Andrew won't know they're there and won't be able to talk with them. There'll be invisible."

"What do you mean he won't be able to see them or talk with them? That doesn't make any sense."

"I just told you. He said that the Arab and he will be helping Andrew but he won't know it. Just like when the Arab was there to help Grandpa when he was there, but he didn't know it either. The Arab has helped and protected Grandpa a lot during his life but Grandpa never knew it."

"What are you talking about? The Arab helped Grandpa? What is this chamber? Why would he or anybody go there?"

"He said Andrew needs to go there to pay the price. He said other people may have to go there too sometime. Even all of us might have to someday. Maybe even you, even though you don't want to."

"What? Even us? You said that nobody wants to go there ever. How do we make sure we don't go to the chamber?"

"He said whether you go there will all depend."

"Depend? Depend on what?"

"He said you need to take a good look at yourself in a mirror. He said whether you go there is up to you. It will be your choice, but you won't know while you're alive. Then God decides."

"What are you talking about? You're not making any sense."

"He also said that you need to play the trump card. If you play the trump card right, maybe you won't go there. He said that is most important for everybody."

"A trump card? What are you talking about? None of this makes any sense."

"He said that when you play your trump card, you should not just flip the card on the table."

"What on Earth are you talking about?"

"He said that when you play the trump card you should slam the card down on the table like you really mean it. He said that you need to play it with all of your heart and soul. You can't just play it casually without really thinking about it. When you play it right, you'll be born again."

"What?"

"He said depending on how hard you play it will determine whether you have to go to the chamber. You can't be nonchalant about it. It's your choice. Mommy, what does nonchalant mean?"

"Did Andrew play the trump card? Will he play it?"

"He said that you should play the trump card when you're still alive and the sooner the better."

"What do you mean by trump card?"

"Grandpa already told you earlier in the house what the trump card is. Remember? The trump card is the absolute most important thing there is and can ever be He said that after Andrew goes to the chamber, then he'll be able to go to the Council Room."

"To where?"

"The Council Room. That's a really good place. Hardly anybody gets to go there. You have to be very special to be able to go there."

"What is that? Where is that?"

"He said they all sit around two big tables there."

"They? Who are they? Who are you talking about?"

"That's where the angels and special angels sit. The angels sit around an oval table. The special angels sit around the round table. They're connected. He said that Andrew needs to fill a very important seat there. It will be the very last seat. It will be at the head of the round table."

"What seat? What are you talking about? Where is this seat? Why is it the last one?"

"I can't tell you. But Grandpa and the Arab know. Grandpa said that the Arab, Andrew, and he will all sit next to each other. They will sit at the head of the round table but where the others sit is random. The others don't sit in any order."

"What are you are talking about? I don't understand any of this. How can there be a head of a round table? Where is this place? Where is this seat where Andrew will sit?"

"I told you. It's the last seat in the Council Room. Grandpa gets to sit in the second to last seat. The Arab gets to sit in the third to last seat. He's already been there."

"What do you mean he's already been there?"

"The Arab already got to sit in his seat in the Council room. He's been there for a long time. He's been there for many years. In fact, he was there when Grandpa was there."

"What? For many years? How can that be? You just said he was in the ambulance."

"I told you already. You need to read the letters in a mirror."

"Tell me more."

"Grandpa said it was Andrew's destiny."

"You said that the Arab was driving the ambulance. Who is the Arab? Do you know who he is?"

"Yes."

"Who is he?"

"It's a secret."

"A secret?"

"Yes."

"Who is he? Tell me! Tell me! Tell me!"

"He and Grandpa know each other. Grandpa knows him very well. They haven't seen each other for a long time. The last time Grandpa saw him was when he was a little boy. Do you know the Arab saved some kids from a house fire when Alex was a little boy? Grandpa didn't know that happened until now. Nobody told him then."

"You're kidding me, right?"

"That was a long time ago. Grandpa didn't know who the Arab was until just a little while ago. They were both so happy to see each other again. Mommy, I've never seen two people so happy to see each other and to be together. Now I know who he is too."

"So who is he?"

"He said if you look up the Arab's full name and you will know who he is."

"What do you mean look up his name?"

"When you do, you'll find out what it means and know why he's been following Grandpa everywhere. But you have to look up his name a special way."

"What? How so?"

"You have to look up his name backwards."

523

"And why's that? How did you know this?"

"Because I found out that's how I can read. Grandpa told me. Remember you once said I might have something like dyslexia? But I found out I actually have something more like strephosymbolia."

"What? Now just how would you know such a big word?"

"Grandpa told me. The Arab was so happy to see me. I was really happy to see him too. The Arab wanted to meet the rest of his family too, but he and Grandpa were in a hurry to take Andrew."

"I don't believe this! Did he say anything else? Did you ask him anything else?"

"I asked Grandpa if Andrew was going to die or if he was going to be saved. Mommy, it looked like Andrew was going to die. I was really scared when I saw him before Grandpa put on his white robe."

"What did he say?"

"He didn't say that Andrew was going to be saved or not. Instead, Grandpa said that everybody will be saved. He said that everybody will have another chance."

"Everybody? Another chance? Another chance for what?"

"It's a secret."

"A secret? What on Earth are you talking about? Why is it a secret?"

"He said that the order will be completed because the Arab, Grandpa, and Andrew are all from the same blood line and because they will all have passed their tests."

"What order? Same blood line? Why is that important? Tests? You're not making any sense whatsoever. What are you talking about?"

"I told you. The Arab will sit in the third to last seat. Grandpa gets to sit in the second to last seat, and Andrew will get to sit in the last seat. The last seat is the most important. That's what's needed."

"Needed? Needed for what?"

"To complete the order. It's a very special order. They all need to sit in these seats. They get to sit in these seats because they share the same blood line. It's a very special blood line. That is required to sit in these seats. But, they also have to pass a really hard test first. The test is in parts. You wouldn't believe how hard the test is."

"What test?"

"The tests are so hard, they're almost impossible to pass, but Andrew will be able to do it. Just like Grandpa and the Arab did. The Arab passed the test a long time ago. Grandpa passed the first part of his test on the Fourth of July three days ago and then passed the second part of his test over the last three days. He completed the last part of his test today."

"What test did he pass on the Fourth of July? How could Grandpa have passed any test over the past three days? I told you he was declared brain-dead in the hospital that entire time!"

"But he did. Andrew still needs to pass the test though. But he will. They're taking Andrew away. They're going on a trip so that Andrew can pay the price. Then, after he passes the second part of his test in the chambers, then he'll be able to go to the Council Room."

"I thought the Arab was kidnapping Andrew and Alex and was stealing the blanket. Where did the ambulance go? Which way did it turn?"

"It didn't. It went straight up."

"What do you mean up?"

"It went straight up into the sky."

"You mean that you didn't see which way it went, right?"

"No. It disappeared."

"What do you mean by that? That's impossible."

"The ambulance just disappeared when it went up straight into the sky. I think maybe it's because of the other person in the back of the ambulance."

"Somebody else was in the ambulance too? Who? You're kidding me, right?"

"No, there was another person who went in the back of the ambulance right before the back doors closed. I think it was a woman."

"What woman?"

"The woman was carrying some white flowers. I saw her put the flowers on top of the book that Grandpa put on top of the blanket on top of Andrew. Grandpa covered Andrew with the blanket and then put a book on top of it. Remember? Then right after she put the flowers on the book, the back doors of the ambulance closed and it went straight and then disappeared into the sky."

"Who put the flowers on the book?"

"I can't tell you."

"Why?"

"I couldn't see the person. I only saw its shadow, it was like a ghost. Right afterwards, the ambulance left and went straight and then disappeared in the sky. But I think I know who it was."

"You know who it was?"

"I think so, but it's my secret."

"Another secret?"

"The flowers were really shiny. They glowed like a really bright light. There were all sorts of colors coming from the flowers. And there was some really nice music too. It was beautiful. I never heard music like that. Can you buy me the CD with that music?"

"I thought you said the flowers were white."

"The flowers were white but then turned into colors. They lit up the whole inside of the ambulance. It was like a glow. I have never seen colors like that before. I've never seen anything so beautiful. My coloring book, crayons, and markers don't even have these colors. I want to get some colors like that. Can you get them for me?"

"When can we see Andrew?"

"Grandpa said we would see him when he wakes up."

"What do you mean when he wakes up?"

"He said we could see him when he wakes up from his nap."

"What do you mean?"

"From his nap. He took a nap this afternoon. Remember? It was when Grandpa put the blanket and book on his chest and after Grandma put the flowers on top of the book after Andrew laid himself down on the couch in the house. It was after Andrew and Grandpa were arguing with each other."

"What on Earth are you talking about? That's impossible. Alex woke him up and carried him outside. The house then caught on fire. You just said he was in the ambulance. So, how can he still be taking a nap in the house when he's in the ambulance?"

"But that's what Grandpa said. You need to believe him. He said you can see him when he wakes up from his nap."

"That doesn't make any sense. The house just burned down. Andrew can't still be taking a nap in there. You said he's in the ambulance."

"But Grandpa said you can see him when he wakes up from his nap. Grandpa is right. You've got to believe him."

"That's impossible. Did you ask him where we can see him?"

"Yes."

"Where?"

"He said to look for the white blanket and the Bible."

"What are you talking about? Didn't you say that the blanket and the Bible were also in the ambulance? Then, how can that be possible? They can't be both in the ambulance and in the house at the same time. The house just burned down."

"But that's what Grandpa said. He said you will need to look for the white blanket and Bible. Andrew will be on the couch where he took his nap. The blanket and Bible will be there too. That's where Grandpa put them. You need to believe Grandpa. Grandpa's telling the truth. Andrew will wake up from his nap and you will find him, the white blanket, and Bible there."

"Child, you're driving me crazy! Are you saying we can see him after we find the ambulance and he wakes up then? I want to see him now."

"No. I said you can see him when he wakes up from his nap he took this afternoon in the house."

"You're not making any sense at all. Grandpa sure said a lot to you. He didn't say anything about the bombs, did he? I'm sure he didn't talk about the nuclear bombs. Or did he?"

"Yes, he did."

"He said something about the nuclear bombs?"

"Yes."

"What did he say?"

"Grandpa said there won't be any bombs."

"No bombs? This is nonsense. How's that possible?"

"They won't disappear, but they'll all be gone."

"They won't disappear, but they'll be gone? How's that possible? What about the terrorists and the deadly diseases? Did he say anything about that?"

"He said there won't be any terrorists and there won't be any deadly diseases spread by them either. You won't have to worry about any of that anymore. No bombs. No disease. No terrorists. Even Ammen will be gone. They can't go away but they'll all be gone."

"How's that possible?"

"He said because the order will be fulfilled and there'll be a change in course."

"What does that mean? All of the terrorists, the bombs, and the diseases will simply vanish? That's impossible. How can they vanish but not go away?"

"He said that it's God's will. He said now God can make it happen because the last two seats are being filled. He'll be able to do that because Andrew will sit in the last seat after he pays the price. The last three seats must be from the same blood line. It's a very special blood line. That's where the Arab, Grandpa, and Andrew will sit. That's where the special angels sit in the Council Room after they pass their tests."

"So, your saying that the Arab, Grandpa, and Andrew are the last three special angels and because of them God will make the bombs, terrorists, and disease go away? Tell me more about these tests."

"The Arab and Grandpa had to pass the tests and now Andrew will too. All of their tests are the same. Otherwise, the terrorists, bombs, and the diseases would still be with us. But, they won't because the Arab and Grandpa passed the test and so will Andrew. Andrew's in the process of passing his test now. He just passed the first part of the test tonight. Do you know who he took with him when he went in the house to save Daniel, Matthew, and Hannah?"

"No, I don't know. Who did Andrew take with him…Ammen? Did he pray to Ammen to help him?"

"No. He didn't take Ammen. Andrew got it right."

"You mean he took Jesus with him? Andrew really took Jesus? Andrew prayed to Jesus?"

"He also asked Jesus to forgive him for the bad life he's lived. He was so sorry for everything he ever did."

"He did? You're kidding, right?"

"The test is in parts. Andrew just passed the first part of the test, but he still has to go the chamber. Grandpa said what Andrew finally did was most incredible. He said it was a most remarkable and extraordinary act of faith. Grandpa is so proud of him. You wouldn't believe how happy Grandpa is because of Andrew's decision. Grandpa and the Arab also had to pass the same test. When Andrew passes all parts of the test, then God can exercise His power."

"Power? Power to do what? Do you mean to make the bombs, disease, and terrorists just go away? Even if it's God's will, just exactly how will He make that happen? I want to know how He can do this. I know God works in mysterious ways, but I want to know exactly just how He can make them be gone, especially if they don't go away!"

"Grandpa also said that he doesn't need to watch Part Two of the documentary that he missed because he already knows the answer."

"What documentary? What answer?"

"He said part 2 would explain it, but he knows the answer is indubitable. Grandpa knows the answer for sure. So, he doesn't need to watch it because he already knows. But only he, the Arab, and Andrew will know. And I think Grandma will know too. He said the rest of us won't."

"Grandpa knows what answer, the answer to what? You're using some awful big words. Do you know what that means? What on Earth are you talking about?"

"In fact, Grandpa said we'll all be there."

"What do you mean? We'll all be 'where'? Where are we going? Child, you're talking utter nonsense."

"Grandpa said it's not been proven to be impossible."

"What?"

"Grandpa said there won't be any bombs, disease, and terrorists, but they won't disappear. They can't."

"What do you mean they can't? They're either gone or they're not. You're contradicting yourself."

"No, I'm not. They can't go away, but they will all be gone."

"What in the world are you talking about? You're not making any sense at all. How can they not go away but be gone?"

"They will. I just told you how. Grandpa said he also knows why the blanket and Holy Bible with the white cover are so special. He said his father told him they were special when he was a little boy, but he didn't know why then. It was when Grandpa's father also told him he would always be with him in his life and guide him, even after his father died. But Grandpa didn't believe it then either. But now he knows. His father guided and protected him during his whole life. All the way up through tonight. His father was right."

"He was right about what?"

"He's always been with him and protected him, even after he died when Grandpa was a little boy, just like he said he would."

"Are you saying the Arab is Grandpa's father? That's ridiculous. You said the Arab is in the ambulance. How can he be in the ambulance and be Grandpa's father if he died when Grandpa was a little boy?"

"I told you. You need to look at the letters in a mirror. Grandpa also told me all about the blanket. Now I know all about it and why it's so extra special."

"What do you mean you know all about it? What's so extra special about it? Grandpa said the blanket was first owned by a distant relative and is over one thousand years old. Isn't that why it's so special?"

"It's more special than that. In fact, it's more than two thousand years old. Do you know that Grandpa is a descendant of that distant relative? That distant relative was the original father to dozens of generations of offspring all the way to Grandpa. He was like a great-great-grandfather to many generations who passed the blanket down and kept it in the family."

"No. I knew the blanket was first owned by a distant relative of Grandpa, but I didn't know Grandpa and he were of the same blood. Who was he? Who was this distant relative of which Grandpa has the same bloodline?"

"That distant relative actually grew up with Jesus and played with him when Jesus was a little boy. He was a little younger than Jesus though. When he grew up he eventually became a very important person back then along with others who knew Jesus. He and his friends eventually told a lot of people all about Jesus all over the world."

"Do you know his name? Did Grandpa tell you?"

"His name was James."

"Really? Is that so? But you wouldn't know who made the blanket for him, do you? Did Grandpa tell you that?"

"Yes. His mother, Mary."

"You're kidding me, right? You mean to tell me that Mary wove the blanket for James, and that Grandpa is a descendant of him? I thought that was debatable whether Mary had any other children other than Jesus. I can't believe this! If all this is really true, do you know what that means? Do you know what that makes Grandpa?"

"Yes, and also the Arab, and Andrew too. That's why the bloodline I told you about is so special. It's a sacred bloodline. It was required by the order."

"And that bloodline would then also include Julie, Mikey, Emily, Matthew, Daniel, and Hannah?"

"And me!"

"I can't believe this! Is this really true?"

"And that's why it was so important for all of the children to be saved from the fires."

"Fires?"

"Yes. Because we were all saved, now the bloodline can continue to be carried forward in the future."

"This is so hard to believe. And you learned all of this from Grandpa? I want to see Andrew. When can we see him?"

"Grandpa said you can see him in three days."

"Why three days?"

"He said that it takes the course of three days to make it work. That's when Andrew will wake up from his nap. That's when everybody will wake up."

"Lizzy, up until about a half hour ago you couldn't talk at all. Now you're talking in circles and uttering complete and ridiculous nonsense. You're not making any sense whatsoever. We don't understand. This all just can't be."

"It's all true. Grandpa's telling the honest truth. And I know he is."

Then Julie asks everybody, "Where is Mom? Has anybody seen Grandma?"

Garrett, still moaning from his injury and in total awe of what all Lizzy just said over the last several minutes, responds "Last I saw Sonja, she was sitting right there," as he points to the base of a tree just several feet away from him. Everybody looks over to where Garrett is pointing.

Sonja had been sitting on the right side of the tree and Alex had been either sitting or leaning against the tree on the left side. Between them on the ground was where Alex had laid the white blanket and the Bible that he took from the house when he carried Andrew out. It was as if Alex and Sonja had been guarding the blanket and Bible between them with their lives.

But in that spot, the blanket and Bible are no longer there. And Sonja is not there either. Instead, where these were, now sits a bouquet of orange blossoms in their place, leaning against the tree. The flower petals are all pointing upward.

Just as everybody looks at the spot, the bouquet of orange blossoms is suddenly illuminated. The blossoms are the purest white color unlike any white ever seen and radiates in absolute brilliance with a light and color of its own that steadily increase in brightness. It is a magnificent sight in the darkness of night.

The light coming from the blossoms is so brilliant that it's almost blinding. The brilliance is pulsating like a heartbeat and progressively grows stronger.

Within seconds, it intensifies so much that it suddenly explodes into an unimaginable and almost blinding spectrum of colors the likes of which nobody has ever experienced or can even fathom is possible. The colors expand and absorb into the entire area where everybody is standing and sitting. It's so stunning that everybody is completely speechless and totally mesmerized.

A most glorious melody can be softly heard being emitted from the colors. A chorus of a thousand languages can be heard singing in perfect synchronization and harmony all blended into one. It is a most fantastic, pleasant, and wonderful feeling. The splendor is so breathtaking and overwhelming that everyone is in a complete and total trance. Everyone is transfixed, is in a state of bewilderment, and is so spellbound they cannot even think. They cannot think of anything. Then suddenly time seems to stand still.

Their minds are frozen in time. So are their bodies. Everyone is completely motionless. Nothing moves. Nothing moves at all. Nobody can see anything. Nobody can hear anything. Nobody can feel anything. Nobody can think or perceive anything. Nobody can say anything. It is as if they're all in a hypnotic state of transition. The experience seems unbelievably surreal.

Chapter 76

In three days, the world will be entirely destroyed. As it turns out, only a handful of the bombs discovered in the United States planted by ISA were active nuclear devices and that were actually detonated. Although in the end it was unrealistic that ISA could have planted as many active nuclear devices that it claimed it did, it was not inconceivable at all for ISA to have planted several of them. It is believed that these nuclear devices were acquired from North Korea or perhaps Pakistan by ISA members, was coordinated in Iran, and smuggled into the United States.

However, the most significant nuclear device was the one strategically imbedded at the site of the dormant super-volcano at Yellowstone. Detonation of that device would trigger the eruption of the super volcano resulting in massive volumes of ash spread into the stratosphere for a long time and the country and other parts of the globe suffocating in a "volcanic winter". Vast lands will become uninhabitable for years.

Within seconds after ISA detonated only one, the United States government made good on its promise of retaliation and immediately launched multitudes of its nuclear bombs against Russia because it believed it was involved in the plot and its failure to convince ISA to stand down. In addition, it also launched its arsenal against several sites in the Middle East and a few other places. After all, it had absolutely nothing to lose. If the United States would be destroyed by them, then so will the other countries who were responsible. This resulted in Russia countering with an immediate launch of many more multitudes of nuclear bombs and this started the domino effect.

Many made it through air defense systems and with the looming spread of the airborne and waterborne deadly disease as well, the United States for all practical purposes was entirely decimated and every corner of the country was destroyed and rendered uninhabitable; numerous populous locations of Russia were likewise obliterated; and other countries, mostly in Western Europe and in the Middle East were also destroyed. The eventual years of darkness from the aftermath of the eruption of the super volcano and radioactive fallout from the nuclear bombs as well as the deadly disease, and the wrath unleashed by other countries with their nuclear capabilities finally resulted in total global annihilation.

Prior to that, Satan deluded the souls of the Earth into believing Ammen was the return of Jesus when he instead was an instrument of the devil. However, Satan's plot of deception and destruction has been overcome. As a result of Alex's persistent and inexorable faith and especially Andrew's act of incredible and extraordinary faith, the change in course has been successful. Almighty God was the Creator, and after all, He is still the Creator. What the world perceives and perhaps also speculates about what God has created, what constitutes the only and entire universe of which they are aware, and their awareness of the sole dimension in which they live represent only a single grain of sand compared to what is not manifest before it.

The total destruction of the Earth does not mean the end to the world. And all who were duped by Ammen will survive. But how can this all be possible?

After three days of going into a state of suspended animation following the illumination of the bouquet of orange blossoms everyone will wake up in their beds from a sound sleep, except for Andrew. He will not be in his bed. They will find Andrew lying on the couch in the living room with the white blanket folded over his chest and the bouquet resting on the blanket. His head will be propped up on a pillow, and he'll be reading the Bible, the one with the white cover. And yes, the Bible somehow miraculously opened up as soon as he touched it. He will have woken up from his nap that he took after his argument with Alex. The page he is reading is that which contains verse 16 of chapter 3 of the book of John.

They will all be in another world. But more importantly, so will their souls. Their souls will have another chance.

Most everything about their lives will be absolutely identical as it's been all along, as if nothing else happened. However, some things will be different. It will be a quite tranquil world with not much to worry about.

When they all wake up there won't be any terrorists, or bombs, or deadly disease in their new world. They won't know that these ever even existed. They will not be able to remember them or anything that had to do with them because they are in a different world now.

The terrorists, bombs, and disease will not be gone but will be left behind in the old world, a world that was obliterated by the terrorists and which now will destroy them. But the souls of those who were deceived will no longer be of that world, but will now be of the new world. They now will be given a new life and another chance. In this new world, a world which is otherwise identical to the old world, the terrorists, the bombs, and the disease never even happened.

Chapter 77

"Alex! Alex! Wake up! Wake up! Alex!"

"Huh? What happened?" he mutters as he slowly opens his eyes, sits up, and removes the bouquet, Bible, and blanket from his chest.

"Julie, Andrew, and their families will be here in about thirty minutes or so. You need to wake up! You need to get ready!"

Alex suddenly finds himself awakening from his nap as he's being shaken and tossed about by Sonja. He has been sound asleep during the course of about three hours after taking his nap prior to everyone coming over for the Fourth of July BBQ and fireworks.

"What happened?" Alex again asks.

"I don't know. Shortly after you closed your eyes, you started talking in your sleep."

"Sonja, you would not believe the incredible dream I just had. It was the most vivid and craziest dream I have ever had in my life! It was so strange. And it was in astounding detail and was so real!"

"I know."

"You do?"

"Yes, I was mesmerized by what you started to say in your sleep and I went into a trance and also fell asleep. You're not going to believe this, but I think I may have dreamed the same thing that you did. I suddenly woke up in this chair by you just seconds ago and realized what time it is. What did you dream?"

"You know how some dreams can be really bizarre? I've never had a dream like this. There was so much going on. In fact, I think I may have actually had a dream within my dream. But maybe not. I'm not really sure. I can remember parts of the dream but not all of it."

"What parts do you remember about it? Tell me."

"I remember lying down to take a nap and first having visions of when I was a little boy, my father, and my sister. But I don't know if those were real memories or not. Maybe they weren't real. I'm not really sure. But then things got even stranger. There were explosions and our house caught on fire and Julie's kids were trapped inside. I died after I came out of the fire and somebody, apparently in an ambulance, took me away but nobody could find my body. I went to hell and then to heaven but God eventually returned me to Earth and required me to do something that was important to the world but I didn't know what it was I was supposed to do. I thought I woke up in a hospital but really never did and everything that happened after that was still part of the same dream.

"Julie and Garrett and their kids were abducted by Islamic terrorists and a nuclear bomb went off. The terrorists were looking for me or my body, but nobody knew why or where I was.

"There were other terrorists who claimed they would blow up America with other nuclear bombs they planted in the US, and the whole world panicked. Satan deceived everybody by sending a demon to Earth named Ammen claiming he was the return of Jesus to save them. A network station interviewed this Ammen and hundreds of millions of people believed in him, but you and I didn't. We were about the only ones who didn't accept him. Andrew and I got into a big argument. I tried to convince him to believe in only Jesus but he would not have any part of it and he tried to convince me to follow Ammen instead. I tried to convince him that Ammen was a demon and to trust in Jesus but he refused to listen.

"Then Andrew's house exploded and caught on fire and his kids were trapped inside and Andrew finally went in to try to save them. But when Andrew entered into the flames in his house to save his kids he knew he was going to die in the process and he decided to finally believe in Jesus and asked Him to help him, and he worshiped Him and asked Him for forgiveness.

"Then our Earth was completely destroyed as a result of what the terrorists did. But, when Andrew suddenly understood and actually felt what Jesus did to save him, he found faith in Jesus and was born again. As a result, he became the last angel and God saved everyone after they fell asleep by transferring all of the deceived souls to another Earth in a parallel universe that He created that was identical to the old one, but without the terrorists and bombs. I think my father and I also had something to do with this, but I'm not sure.

"There was really a lot more going on than that, but that was basically the gist of things. I'm already forgetting everything else about it. It was an incredible dream. It was the strangest and weirdest dream I've ever had. I can't believe how detailed it was! A lot of the things that happened in the dream were entirely unrealistic. At one point I thought I woke up from my dream when I was in the hospital, but really didn't. Everything after that was still part of the same dream."

"Yes, I must say, that was quite a hallucination you had there. But what's so strange is that I pretty much had the same dream you did! Why is that? It was like a movie or a storybook the entire time I was dreaming it!"

"That's exactly how I experienced it! The dream was just like a motion picture or a story of some sort, just as you said! It was so strange; it was out of this world."

"And you're right. It did seem so real at the time! But was there really a dream within a dream? I don't think you ever woke up until now. I also don't remember a lot of it but I remember the same parts you described. I wish I could remember all of it, but I can't."

"Me too. There was so much going on, including a lot of stuff that was so unusual it was entirely impractical. A lot of it was entirely not credible. There's a lot I can't remember either. But it sure seemed real at the time."

"Why was it that we both dreamed the same thing? How strange this is! And Andrew finally believed in Jesus and became the last angel, and as a result God saved everyone? How strange is that? But I dreamed that too. How can that be? You don't think any of that really happened or could happen, do you?"

"Well, I think perhaps a little of it could happen. And it's not been proven that some of it is impossible to happen. But for the most part, a lot and perhaps most of it absolutely could not have happened and can't happen. It was all merely a dream. But, you know how some dreams can be unrealistic but be symbolic and actually have a meaning about them? Maybe the dream was an interesting way to get our attention and intended to deliver a message."

"Like what?"

"Perhaps it intended to deliver several messages. For example, there is only one Jesus Christ and we must follow and have faith in Him to fulfill God's purpose. One must love and believe in Him from the heart. One must develop a personal relationship with Him. Talk with Him. *That* is the ticket to heaven.

"Also, God has such immense power, the power of creation among other things that is so unfathomable, it is incomprehensible to us. However, when Jesus returns and the world ends, it can only be as the Gospel said it would and the events must conform to it on God's terms. There is only one way that will happen, and that is the way the Bible says it will. It cannot happen any other way."

"So, exactly when does the Bible say it will happen?"

"Nobody knows. It could be any time, but it must conform to the prophecies whenever it happens, even if you don't understand them all. Same goes for when your or my time will end. One just doesn't know when that will happen either. That's why we must trust and put our faith in Jesus now and not wait. But, another message is that the Holy Bible is the Word of God, it cannot be altered, and to distrust it is to distrust God. But, if something is not in violation of the Word as written, to remember that it may not necessarily be proven to be impossible. And, to remind us of the power of prayer.

"Also, how can Andrew or anybody else for that matter do what Jesus did for us? God would not expect that. Perhaps Andrew becoming the last angel merely represented one's true understanding of and belief in Jesus's sacrifice for us and becoming born again. In other words, only Jesus can save us. Nobody else can."

"Well, that sounds reasonable. But I still don't understand why we both dreamed all of this. What or who caused us to dream this? I sure wish Andrew would have also received these messages. I wonder whether there was an ulterior motive for the dream. Do you think that's possible?"

"Maybe. Don't really know. But, although the dream may have intended to deliver these and other messages to us, most of the events themselves in the dream simply cannot happen. For one thing, the dream violated the Scriptures in many of these respects and that can't happen in real life.

"Per the book of Revelation 22:18-19 absolutely nobody is allowed to alter the prophecies of Revelation. If they did, they would be doomed forever. One cannot add to or subtract from what is written. I certainly do not intend to do that. What is written in Revelation is what it is. And that's that. We must follow and believe in the Word of God as stated. We cannot change it or even suggest that God can change the events that have been prophesized. I only dreamed this. And I don't know why. I'm certainly not suggesting it."

"But isn't God supposed to create a new Earth and a new heaven as written at the end of Revelation?"

"Yes, but that's different. That would conform to the events of the prophecies as written. The Words of the Bible won't allow for it or for anybody to even suggest that it can happen any other way. If it did, that would change Biblical history and defy what has been written. That cannot happen. Revelation 22:18-19 is quite clear about this. Also, the Bible doesn't say anything about a lot of what happened in the dream. A lot of what happened in the dream is simply not realistic at all."

"But what if Satan violated the prophecies by instigating his wrath prior to when the prophecies said the world will end? What if that isn't god's will? Is it possible that could happen? What would God do then?"

"That's a good question, but I doubt if that can happen. From what I understand what is written is what it is and what will happen will be on God's terms, not Satan's. That's why the dream can't make any sense. It simply cannot happen."

"So, what parts of the dream do you think could be possible then?"

"I don't remember all of it, but if anything could be possible it would need to be something that does not violate what's stated in the Gospel. For example, perhaps it's conceivable that the terrorists could actually acquire or build nuclear weapons and eventually use them. Maybe it was possible that God created our Earth and universe based on another one in another realm that's billions of years old and that's how it came to be, but the way I understand it, the history told in the Gospel and events prophesized in the book of Revelation and elsewhere in the Scriptures cannot be changed going forward. But in this regard, I don't think the Gospel says the end of the world would not be preceded by the actions of the Islamic terrorists, so maybe this could happen."

"So, regarding what the terrorists say they'll do, I suppose we'll eventually find out how everything will actually all shake out. Maybe things will actually turn out differently than what we dreamed about. Hopefully in real life our world won't be being destroyed after all at this time."

"I sure hope it won't. All I know is that everything we just experienced was merely a dream. The return of Jesus and the end of the world cannot happen before the time prescribed in the Scriptures, even though we don't really know when that will be. However, if the Islamic Jihadist terrorists actually do acquire nuclear weapons and really do detonate them, I suppose it could very well begin events that could result in the end of the world. If that were to happen, then it could be for real, but it then must conform to the prophecies as written."

"Do you really think the terrorists are able to build or acquire a nuclear bomb?"

"Well, it's not been proven to be impossible."

"So, you're saying that if the terrorists do acquire and use nuclear weapons, then it may be the beginning of events consistent with the prescribed end of time per the Scriptures?"

"Perhaps. Although it may not be the end itself, it could be the beginning of the end. I suppose it's possible. Just look what's happening in the Mideast and all of the millions of refugees who have fled to other parts of the world. There's a lot going on in our world that begs one to think about these things.

"But everything needs to be done now to stop them from acquiring a nuclear weapon. Everything. Whatever it takes. They simply cannot have any nuclear weapons. Period. Imagine just how stupid one would be to trust them. Especially after they chant 'Death to America!' The terrorists can't be trusted at all. That's absolutely for sure. Why give them anything or try to even bargain with them? If the Islamic Jihadists or any irresponsible country were to get a nuclear weapon and use it, well then yes, I think it appears quite possible it could happen. Either our generation or perhaps the next one then may find out, right?"

"Satan must be behind what the terrorists are doing. Why else would they be so intent on killing us and others? Do you think God would ever forgive the terrorists for killing everybody or would He punish them and send them to hell?"

"The way I understand it, believe it or not, He actually could forgive them but only if they sincerely repent for what they've done with all of their heart and soul, sincerely ask for forgiveness, and truly believe in Jesus. Otherwise if they don't, then they'd spend eternity in the Lake of Fire."

"What if they do that but aren't that sincere about it? They can't just go through the motions, right?"

"God will know if they truly mean it, just like everybody else. They need to do this through very deep prayer to God. If they actually do this and become born again so to speak, I understand He would save them too."

"So, they can be saved and go to heaven too if they do this, but won't if they don't. Well, that seems simple enough. I just can't believe what they continue to do. Why are they so insistent in killing everyone merely because we don't have the same beliefs they do?"

"There's only one true God and He would never approve of that. Don't they realize this? The Commandment, 'Thou shall not kill,' is the Word of God and it also applies to those of the Islamic faith, including the Jihadists. Anyone including the terrorists who defies this commandment when it's not justified by God Himself actually denies the Word of God, and thus rejects God as well. And if they defy this commandment and kill anybody, they will be doomed for eternity. It's all that simple."

"Why don't they understand this?"

"Satan *must* be behind what they are doing. And they don't even know it. But, God has given them the means to escape from their sin, just like He has with everyone else. All they have to do is to really want to do it. He will help them if they sincerely repent and truly believe in Jesus Christ as their savior. It simply starts with deep prayer through Jesus Christ.

"You know, it is interesting that the Jihadists' answer is violence and to kill people, but the Christian answer is to love and pray for them. Remember, Jesus said to love your enemies. You would think that by mere reason alone, they would adopt the Christian answer simply by applying common sense. Imagine then if one Jihadist did this and then converted another, and so on. I wonder what would happen if every single Christian would actually pray for them."

"It would be interesting to find out. But considering what the terrorists are doing, do you think just maybe we're watching our destiny materialize right before our eyes? Is what the Jihadists are doing really the beginning of events leading to the end of our world?"

"Don't know. Maybe. You know, even though our world is strong and resilient, it's also at the same time most vulnerable. But most people don't acknowledge this. Imagine the very real possibility of a nuclear weapon or some other event that could make part or our entire world uninhabitable. For example, just imagine what would happen if our country alone didn't have electricity for an extended period of time. Everything depends on it, absolutely everything. All it would take is one single event. It is very possible."

"Like what?"

"All it would take to eliminate electricity everywhere would simply be an EMP, either manmade, from an EMP weapon, or perhaps a big solar flare. It would be that simple. All across our country there would be no air conditioning, probably no heat, and no light. People would not be able to access their money and it would be worthless. There would be no communication. There would be no refrigeration. Eventually food would become scare or not attainable. Maybe there would not be any potable water. There would not be any sanitation. There would be no gas or fuel, and vehicles would not work. Travel and transportation would be near impossible. Hospitals, banks, stores and other establishments could not operate and would shut down. Hosts of serious, deadly, and extremely contagious disease and sickness would abound without any treatment, and on and on and on.

"We'd all have to live like the people did hundreds and hundreds of years ago before the age of electricity. But it would be so much harder for us in this day and age, more difficult than anyone can imagine.

"The probability of that happening, perhaps simply from an EMP is a lot higher than one might imagine. An EMP weapon has already been developed by several countries. All it would take is just one. People just don't think about these things. They don't realize just how vulnerable our life on Earth really is. It would be a lot easier for that to happen than people think. And this wouldn't be for only a few hours or a day or a week or so. It could be for months or years. Nearly everybody if not everybody would certainly die if that were to happen.

"All it would take is for some lunatic who has the ability to launch it to simply 'press the button'. And, it would not even have to be a world power. Maybe even a terrorist country who might have the capability or perhaps a country like North Korea could do this."

"I don't want to even think what would happen if a nuclear weapon was ever obtained and used by them or if we completely lost electricity in this day and age. We just can't allow any terrorist organization or country to have one. You're absolutely right. They can't be trusted at all, especially when they chant 'Death to America.' And you're correct, we're more vulnerable than we think."

"But I suppose it could happen sooner than you think though. It is really possible. It can really happen."

"I sure hope what's happening now isn't the beginning of that and I sure hope that doesn't happen, at least in the near future or in our life time."

"Me too. Well, time will tell. But, I'm sure glad we have Jesus though, right? If it does happen, at least we will be saved by Jesus if we believe in Him."

"Amen to that! Only if Andrew would understand just how important Jesus is. He died for Andrew's sins so he could be saved just as He did for everybody else and Andrew refuses to accept that. I just don't understand why he refuses to believe in Him and understand the importance of His sacrifice for us."

"But you know, in one respect it's a shame that the dream wasn't real. Now that I think about it, I like how the dream ended. I sort of wish it all really happened because that would mean that Andrew finally found faith in Jesus."

"That would have been such a nice birthday present for you."

"Yes, it would have been the greatest birthday present ever. But now that we woke up and came back to reality, that's wishful thinking, right? I suppose we'll forget about it in due time just like any other dream. And now that we're awake in real time again, I guess we need to accept the fact that Andrew still refuses to believe. You know how much it breaks my heart that he won't even try to accept Jesus as his savior. Sonja, we've tried to convince him for over thirty years."

"Yes, I know. Me too, dear. It breaks my heart also."

"You know, looking at and holding this old blanket I remember several things about my father. He was such a mysterious man, but in a good way. I remember when I was a little boy he would always tell me to think outside the box. He told me that he would always be with me and guide me during my entire life. But how could he do that after he died?

"But, what I remember was most profound about my father, is when I was a little boy, it was said he had an uncanny ability to convert the most hardcore atheists or agnostics to Christianity. I sure wish he was here now so he could convert Andrew or at the least he could have taught me his special ability so I could convert him. If my father was here now, I'd bet he could convince Andrew to believe in Jesus."

"Alex, in order for that to happen, your father would need to return to Earth as an angel. You're reminiscing aren't you?"

"Yes, I suppose so, but you know, when I unwrapped the blanket and folded it and put it over my chest right before I took my nap, somehow I felt my father's presence. In fact, I still do. You don't think that had anything to do with what we just experienced in this dream, do you? Why did we both dream the same thing? It was like we were all in the same dream. What do you make of all of this? Was there a special motive for this? You don't think my father had anything to do with this dream we had, do you?"

"I have no idea. Like I said, if your father had anything to do with this dream we had, he must be here in the form as an angel."

"You're not suggesting that, are you?"

"I don't know if he had anything to do with this, but how would I know? I agree the experience was so strange. My memory of that dream is already starting to fade away, and I can't remember much of it anymore."

"Same here. My memory of the dream is also going away. Soon it will be completely forgotten. But, for now, I need to freshen up and get ready before everybody comes over for dinner and the fireworks. How's the food coming along?"

Sonja suddenly remembers she was working with her orange blossoms and preparing the food for dinner before being mesmerized by Alex talking in his sleep. She gets up to go into the kitchen to check on things. Although nearly three hours has elapsed, she's surprised to see nothing is burned and everything is just fine, as if no time had passed at all.

As Alex goes into their bedroom to change clothes and freshen up before everybody arrives, the telephone rings and Sonja answers it in the kitchen.

"Hi Sonja, it's me, Alana. Listen, we'll be a little late coming over. Andrew took about a three-hour nap after lunch today and just woke up. He started acting somewhat strange and said he needs to run a quick errand. So, we'll be a little late."

"What do you mean?"

"When he woke up, he kept muttering something, but I really didn't understand what he was saying. He was very excited and wouldn't stop talking to himself. He then said he needed to go somewhere."

"Where did he go?"

"The bookstore."

"The bookstore? Why?"

"When I asked him why, he told me that an Arab told him to go."

"An Arab?"

"Yes. I thought he was kidding me at first. You know how he's always kidding about stuff like that. But, Sonja, you know what?"

"No, what dear?"

"He was as serious as he can be. And for some really strange reason, I get the feeling that I believe him. I don't think he was joking this time. I don't know why I feel this way."

"But isn't the bookstore closed today?"

"That's what I asked him. But he told me that the Arab told him it would be open."

"So, an Arab told him to go to the bookstore and that it would be open today? Really? Now, just how did that happen? They didn't actually meet each other, did they? That's hard to believe. I suppose this Arab also told him to get a book, right? I'd sure like to know who this Arab is. Who is this Arab anyway? Do you have any idea who he is?"

"I don't know. Now that I think about it, I remember that he also told me that this Arab told him to buy the two huge garden wagons several days ago. I thought he was kidding when he told me about that too, but now, I'm not so sure."

"Okay, so the Arab told him to do this and we have no idea who he is, right? What book did Andrew want to get?"

"He said he wants to get two books and wants to give one to Alex for his birthday today when we come over. He's going to use the money Alex gave him for his birthday several days ago."

"Really? So, did the Arab convince Andrew to do that too? Andrew hasn't acknowledged his father's birthday in many years, in fact not since he was a child. Why all of a sudden now?"

"Don't know. He said it was very special. I think it's because of a dream he said he had this afternoon. He was all smiles and had a happy face."

"What did he say his dream was about?"

"I'm not sure. He said I wouldn't believe what he experienced in his dream during the course of three hours while he took his nap. He told me it was like a movie and it was like he was in a different world; it was very involved; and the entire family was in the dream. He also said for the most part it was impractical and was unrealistic, but nevertheless it delivered a message, in fact several messages."

"Like what?"

"He said to understand you need to think outside the box. I don't know what he meant by that. You would need to ask him."

"You're kidding? This is so hard to believe! And this is all because of this dream he had when he took a nap this afternoon and this Arab? So, I suppose this Arab is responsible for all of this. I sure wish I knew who this Arab is. What book is Andrew getting him? Do you know?"

"I'll tell you, but don't tell Alex. Andrew wants it to be a surprise. He said he wants to get him a very special book that has a white cover. He wants to replace the one Alex has with a new one because he knows his is getting old and coming apart."

"Really! You're kidding me again, right? You said he's going to get two books. What is the other book he plans to get?"

"The same, identical book he's getting Alex. He wants to get two of the exact same book."

"Really? Who's he getting the other book for?"

"Himself."

"Himself? Are you kidding me?"

"No. He said he can't wait to read it. He wants to read it from cover to cover."

"I'm absolutely beside myself. What on Earth got into him all of a sudden?"

"He then said the messages to him in the dream were profound. He said he learned that if you pray and sincerely believe in Jesus and ask Him to show you the way, He will then come for you."

"Andrew really said that? I can't believe this! We've been trying to tell him that for over thirty years, but he would never listen to us! But now he learned all of this from this dream he had? I wonder what caused him to dream this. Just who delivered these messages to him? Let me guess…he said the Arab told him that, right?"

"I asked him that too. When I asked him who he learned this from, he simply smiled at me, winked, and said, 'An angel.'"

The End

Postscript

According to the Scriptures, God created the heavens and the Earth and all that is in it including man. This is clear and indisputable. Furthermore, pursuant to the common interpretation of Genesis and the genealogy found in the Old Testament, if the words are taken literally in their ordinary meaning, God's creation occurred only a little over six thousand years ago.

However, scientific evidence strongly supports that Earth and our universe has existed for billions of years of evolution, not from being suddenly created only about six thousand years ago as written in the Gospel.

Can the words of the Gospel be wrong? Do we dare to challenge and not believe in the Word of God as written in the Scriptures on the basis that billions of years of evolution has been all but scientifically proven whereas creation only about six thousand years ago has not?

How can the Gospel be correct considering a preponderance of scientific evidence supports that life resulted from billions of years of evolution and not sudden creation only about six thousand years ago?

Do we dare believe that the Word of God written in the Scriptures is not true? But, how can it be true considering that life resulting from billions of years of evolution is supported by overwhelming scientific evidence?

So, which is right?

Maybe they both are.

But, how can this be?

Some things you don't see are right before your eyes.

Some things you don't hear, but are there for you to listen.

Some things you don't feel, but are there for you to sense them.

Some things you don't think you perceive, but you are aware of and don't know it.

And, some things you may think are totally unrealistic, but they have not been proven to be impossible.

You simply just need to think outside of the box.

myAbwJ

About the Author

C. J. Rysen, author of *In the Course of Three Hours*, was born, raised, and lives in the Midwest of the United States. As more and more Christians and others have been persecuted around the world at the hand of Islamic extremists, the Jihadists, C. J. pondered what would happen if the terrorists were to acquire and use nuclear weapons. Is it possible this could actually lead to the end of time? In what way can the end of time not happen? But more importantly, when it does, on what terms must it happen?

After contemplating possibilities, he was inspired to write the book after receiving several visions and felt compelled to share these thoughts and messages. However, rather than simply spell them out, he has delivered these in an inimitable way through a Christian-themed story involving mysteries, suspense, imagination, and some abstract reasoning that offers the opportunity for it to be interactive with the reader. By doing so, he has infused even more going on behind the scenes. Some readers may pick up on it. Many may not.

However, the messages delivered will only become clear at the end of the story when the events of the story are met head on by the truth. His book will prompt one to think and contemplate many elements of the story. Although what will eventually happen in our lives remains to be seen, it is important to be aware of the very real possibilities, and that there is much that has not been proven to be impossible.

CPSIA information can be obtained
at www.ICGtesting.com
Printed in the USA
BVOW09s1228120717

489161BV00002B/135/P

9 781635 251487